Praise for John Lawton

RIPTIDE

'The sense of London during the Blitz is strong and the story, with its mix of real history and believable invention, is fast-paced, twisting and tense . . . These elements combine to produce a novel that is sheer entertainment' *Observer*

'This is a splendidly plotted yarn and Lawton revels in its twists, neatly interweaving drama, pathos and comedy . . . Frederick Troy is a character of real depth and subtlety' *Independent*

'*Riptide* is one of the most entertaining thrillers I have read in years: jam-packed with incident and rich in human colouring . . . the characterisation is inspired' *Sunday Telegraph*

'Jokey, chilling and occasionally lyrical, this novel defies categorisation . . . the book's scope . . . is almost Dickensian'
Mail on Sunday

SWEET SUNDAY

'This literate novel has all the plot and tension of a thriller, and marvellously evokes an era when America tore itself to pieces over Vietnam' *Sunday Times*

'Now and then one comes across a new author whose writing sets the pulse racing and the jaded responses tingling . . . I entreat you, dear reader, to search out John Lawton and cherish him to your bosom, for he is truly an original' *Irish Times*

BLACK OUT

'A fizzy, fast-moving tale of spying in high places, *Black Out* offers the authentic whiff of wartime London' *Sunday Times*

'Wonderfully captures the atmosphere of wartime London . . . original and entertaining'
Robert Harris, author of *Fatherland*

John Lawton is an angry, degenerating misanthrope who lives in a remote hilltop village in Derbyshire. He is not entirely sure why. It rains a lot. He likes T. C. Boyle, Chuck Palahniuk and Cormac McCarthy – and considers the seminal text of our time to be *Myron* by Gore Vidal. He is keen on the cultivation of the onion and obscure varieties of potato (e.g. Aura, Edzell Blue). He hates Tories, teachers and travel (who wouldn't?), but loves to visit Arizona, Florence . . . New York . . .

By John Lawton

1963
Black Out
Old Flames
A Little White Death
Riptide
Sweet Sunday
Blue Rondo

Troy novels in chronological order

Second Violin
Riptide
Black Out
Old Flames
Blue Rondo
A Little White Death

RIPTIDE

John Lawton

PHOENIX

A PHOENIX PAPERBACK

First published in Great Britain in 2002
by Weidenfeld & Nicolson
This paperback edition published in 2001
by Orion,
an imprint of Orion Books Ltd,
Orion House, 5 Upper St Martin's Lane,
London WC2H 9EA

An Hachette Livre UK company

Reissued 2008

1 3 5 7 9 10 8 6 4 2

A CIP catalogue record for this book
is available from the British Library.

ISBN 978-0-7528-4789-4

Printed in Great Britain by Clays Ltd,
St Ives plc

The Orion Publishing Group's policy is to use papers that
are natural, renewable and recyclable products and
made from wood grown in sustainable forests. The logging
and manufacturing processes are expected to conform to
the environmental regulations of the country of origin.

www.orionbooks.co.uk

for
SHEENA McDONALD
– back from the edge –

Acknowledgements

Cosima Dannoritzer, Iris Schewe (of the *Stadtmuseum*, Berlin) and **Alfred Gottwaldt** (of the *Deutsches Technik-museum*, Berlin) who steered me around pre-war Berlin. **Gordon Chaplin** who let me retreat to his Manhattan loft to write my novel, while he retreated to Florida and wrote his. **Antony Harwood,** my agent, once described in the *Grauniad* as a 'leather-jacketed rock'n'roller with the soul of an aesthete'. He has long since given up the leather jacket. The rock'n'roll persists. **John Bell,** who knows really odd things about the London Under-ground.

STILTON

§ 1
Berlin April 17th 1941

It was an irrational moment. A surrender of logic to the perilous joy of common nonsense. When the train stopped between stations on the S-Bahn, Stahl felt exposed, fearful for his life in a way that made no sense. High on the creaking metal latticework, the train tortured the tracks and juddered to a halt. Then the lights went out and Stahl knew that there was an air raid on. Yet again the RAF had got through to a city that the Führer had told them would never see a British plane or hear the crash of a British bomb. Berlin the impregnable, some of whose citizens now trembled and wept in the darkness, packed into a swaying train, high above the streets.

It was irrational. He was no more at risk here than on the ground. It just seemed that way – as though to be stuck on the elevated tracks like a bird on the wire made him into . . . a sitting duck. He recalled a phrase of his father's from the last war, one every old Austrian soldier used occasionally – every old British soldier too, he was certain – 'If it's got your name on it . . .' which meant that death was inevitable, and urged a grinning stoicism on those about to die.

The raid distracted him. He had been pretending to read a newspaper. He always did when he waited for the word. Tonight he had been oddly confident that there would be word. So confident, he became worried that he would miss her. More than once he had carried the pretence into practice, and had been caught engrossed in some nonsense in the *Völkischer Beobachter* and all but oblivious when she had brushed past him and muttered a single sentence.

The train moved off, the lights still out, sparks visible on the tracks below – hardly enough to make them the moving target his fellow-Berliners thought they were. At *Warschauer Straße* station passengers shoved and kicked till the doors banged open, a human tide surging for ground level and the shelters. The moment had passed, he was happier now in the open air and, as ever, curious about the men who dropped death on the city night after night. He stepped onto the platform, gazing into the clear, night sky hoping for a glimpse of a Blenheim or a Halifax. This was a reprisal raid. Last night – and into the small hours of the morning – as the wireless had crowed all day, the Luftwaffe had blasted central London.

She brushed his shoulder. So quick, so quiet he could have missed her. A dark woman in a belted, brown macintosh, almost as tall as he. He could scarcely describe her face – he didn't think he'd ever seen her eyes.

'You are in the gravest danger. Go now. Go tonight.'

He heard his heart thump in his chest. He had expected this for so long that to hear the words uttered at last was like a body blow. The wind knocked from his lungs, his pulse doubled, a weakness in the knees that was so hackneyed a response he could scarcely believe it was happening to him.

'Go now,' she had said. 'Go tonight.'

'Leave Berlin,' it meant, 'leave Germany.' And with that phrase, twelve wretched years of his life were stitched and wrapped and over.

A uniformed corporal grabbed him by the arm with not so much as a 'Heil Hitler', and pulled him towards the staircase. His cap went flying, rolling onto the tracks, the little silver skull glinting back at him in the moonlight.

'It's a big one, sir. We have to take cover.'

Stahl knew the man. That meant he was getting sloppy. He should have known the man was there. An Abwehr clerk – a privileged pen-pusher, the sort who'd never see the front line except as punishment. Stahl could not recall his name – odd that, that he should have a hole in his memory, a memory so precise for words heard, so precise for words seen – but he let himself be manhandled, clerkhandled, into a shelter: a concrete blockhouse beneath the S-Bahn station, hastily thrown up in the winter of 1939. Throughout the false start of Czechoslovakia and the easy victories over Poland and France, the Führer had made swift provision for bomb-shelters, whilst reminding them all that they weren't going to be bombed. It was a brave man – in Stahl's experience, a drunken man – who pointed out the anomaly.

Stahl was surprised. He'd never been in a street shelter before. He'd half expected satanic darkness, piss in the corner, vomit on the floor. But it was clean and only faintly malodorous. It was warm, too – the combined heat of all those bodies and the pot-bellied French stove against the back wall, looted from the Maginot Line less than a year ago, into which an enthusiastic youth, with phosphorous buttons on his jacket, was stuffing the remains of a beer crate. He stripped off his raincoat and draped it over one arm. The concrete cell was dimly lit by a ring of bulkhead lights – light enough for people to see him for what he was.

A middle-aged man in rimless spectacles had both arms wrapped around a whimpering woman. He stared at Stahl, patted his wife gently on the back. She too turned to look at Stahl and, finding herself looking up at an SD Brigadeführer in full uniform, less hat – all black and silver and lightning – she stopped whimpering. Stahl stood shoulder to shoulder with the corporal, sharing a small room with fifty-odd strangers, and heard the murmurs of fear and reassurance dwindle almost to nothing as though he himself had silenced them. It wasn't him. It was the uniform. It possessed a power he had never thought he had. He wore it out of choice. His job permitted him civilian dress if he saw fit: Canaris wore plain clothes, Schellenberg wore them more often than not, but the dulled imaginations of the Geheime Staatspolizei – long since abbreviated to Gestapo – favoured a 'civilian uniform' of trilby hats and leather greatcoats. Stahl felt better in a real uniform. In a world where all identities were false it was a plain statement. The boldness of a bare-faced lie. It seemed to him far less sinister than the ubiquitous leather coat. Why the Berliners should be more scared of him in a shelter than on a train needed no thought – they were showing treasonable fear in the presence of a man whose power over them might well be life and death – and he stood between them and the door.

When the all-clear sounded, Stahl found himself in the street with the Abwehr corporal once more. This time the man saluted. The contrived formality of a barked 'Heil Hitler' – contrived, Stahl knew, since there was hardly a man in the Abwehr who didn't secretly despise Hitler, the Party and the SS. Stahl returned the salute, scarcely whispering the Heil Hitler. Perhaps he'd said it for the last time?

The man was right. It had been a heavy raid. They'd listened to the bombs explode, felt the earth shake, for well over an hour – wave after wave of bombers, so many he'd given up the focused monotony of counting. Now the air stank of cordite, and a haze of dust hung over the city in the moonlight.

He walked home through blitzed streets of dust and

4

debris, almost empty of traffic – cars were abandoned at the roadside, trams did not run, people scurried like ants in all directions, directionless. Stahl turned the corner into *Kopernikusstraße* ten minutes later. It was deserted, almost silent. His apartment block and the one next to it had collapsed like bellows, breathed their last and died. The main staircase clung precariously to the wall where the strength of the chimney-breast had resisted the blast. He could see the top floor as clearly as if someone had pulled away the front, like the hinged facade of a doll's house. He could see his own apartment, the floor hanging skewed, his bed with one leg resting on nothing, four floors of nothing, his mahogany wardrobe, one door open, almost tilting into the void, and his overcoat flapping on the back of the bedroom door.

There was no sign of rescue. In the distance he could hear sirens, but he'd had to climb over piles of rubble to get this far, and as far as he could see the other end of the street was no better. It would be an hour or more before anyone, any vehicle, got through.

He stepped into the remains of the concierge's sitting room. The old woman sat at her piano, her forehead resting on the upturned lid, symmetrically between the candlesticks, dead. There didn't seem to be a mark on her. What had killed her? Had her heart simply stopped at the sound of the bomb? Had she hit middle C and died? She sat in a ring of rubble but, it seemed, all of it had missed her, falling around her as though some invisible shield had guarded her body even as her spirit fled. He had liked the old woman. He had played this piano many times at her request. She had let him play simply for the pleasure of it, not caring what he played, but Stahl had seen tears in her eyes when he played Mozart. Mozart – Mozart had been the first snare. He had used Mozart to snare Heydrich. He had attracted his attention by appealing to the man's taste, by playing

Mozart and by playing upon the man's childhood memories. Heydrich had grown up with music – his father had taught music in Dresden – he played the violin well, not as well as Stahl played the piano, but well nonetheless. It was the weak link in a man not known to have weaknesses, and Stahl had used it to work his way into Heydrich's confidence. Not his affection. He had never seen affection for anyone in Heydrich. All the Nazis were mad – Heydrich no more nor less mad than Hitler or Himmler, but he was, Stahl thought, cleverer, more self-contained. Whatever lurked in Heydrich was well battened down. He threw no tantrums. He had his emotional outlet – music.

When, one day in 1934, after dozens of impromptu pootlings by Stahl, Heydrich had asked him if he knew a Mozart piece for violin and piano, the A major Mannheim Sonata, Stahl knew he had hooked him. They had played the piece at least fifty times over the year – many others besides, but Heydrich always came back to the Mannheim Sonatas as his starting point as though the duets, those sparse dialogues between the violin and the piano, held a significance for him that he would not utter and of which Stahl would not ask.

It was a pity. Stahl liked them. He'd never play any of them again now. They would be for ever associated with Heydrich in his mind and he had no wish to see a mental image of Obergruppenführer Reinhard Heydrich again. He would, almost daily, but he'd try not to.

In the back room Stahl found the body of Erwin Hölzel. At least he assumed it was Hölzel. There was a bloody fruit pulp where the face had been. The poor bugger had been blown through from the floor above.

Stahl looked up, past the jagged edges of floorboards, through Hölzel's apartment, through his own, into the night sky. Then it came to him. He could scarcely believe his luck. Perhaps there was a God after all?

He climbed carefully up the staircase, testing each tread with one foot before putting his whole weight on it. From the top floor he looked out across the street. There were half a dozen people milling about – but distractedly, unfocused, bewailing their lot and crying for the dead and missing. If he was quick he would not be seen. They were all looking down, not up.

He clung with one hand to the steel conduit that ran the electric cable to the light switch, and with his other hand reached into the wardrobe. He tried to grab a plain, black suit and missed by inches. He lowered his grip, clung as tightly as he could, braced one foot against the wall and thrust out with his right hand. It was too sharp a movement. The floor sagged, the wardrobe wobbled. His fingers locked onto the suit. He pulled it towards him to find the whole wardrobe tilting and the suit still attached by its hanger. He pulled again. The suit jerked free and the balance of the wardrobe shifted, tipping it into space to tumble four floors and splinter on the mound of rubble below.

Stahl found himself clinging to the conduit, the suit flapping like a flag in his hand, all his bodyweight poised over the void. He pushed with his feet, pulled with his fingers, and regained the wall. He grabbed his coat from the door and ran down the stairs, not caring if they tumbled behind him step by step like a house of cards.

It took a quarter of an hour or more to strip off Hölzel's clothes and dress the corpse in his own SD uniform. Roughly, the two men were the same size. Hölzel was ten years older, but that would only have shown clearly in the face, and he had no face. With a little luck it would be days before anyone figured out that it wasn't Stahl. He had no tattoos, no blood group written on the sole of his foot, no SS insignia on his arms. If they had any doubts when they found the body, they'd have to turn to dental records.

He could not leave his *Ausweis* – or his Party membership card. They'd be the clinchers, but he'd need them to get wherever he was going. But if a body of his size and age were to be found in the remains of his apartment building, wearing an SD uniform, who wouldn't draw the immediate, the wrong conclusion?

Stahl stepped into the street, buttoned his overcoat. He had no hat. He wished he had a hat. A hat was an identity. He had lost one when his cap rolled on to the S-Bahn track. The black suit, the black coat, another damn disguise, seemed incomplete without a hat. Two doors down was a channel that led back towards the *Frankfurter Allee*. It wasn't blocked, it was strewn with broken brick but it was passable. He picked his way along, clutching the rolled ball of Hölzel's bloody suit, dropped the suit down an open coal chute, cut across the side streets and emerged into the *Frankfurter Allee* just in time to see a fire engine roar past.

Some part of his mind, less clear than a voice, less formed or shaped than an idea, more resistible than an impulse, wanted to turn – to turn and look back. But he had promised himself when he had joined the *Nationalsozialistiche Deutsche Arbeiterpartei* in 1929 that he never would. To look back was more than an indulgence, more than a parting whim – it was to die of pain and grief and irredeemable heartbreak.

§ 2

It was going to be a blue day.

Alexei Troy had spent a morning looking back. It was heartbreak, heartbreak of the sweetest kind.

A cloud-puffed blue spring sky outside his window. Great bouncy billows of cumulo-nimbus. For the first time in weeks the skies over north London blissfully free

8

of aircraft. Not so much as a training flight – all those young men, boys, boys, boys, those Poles and Czechs, the odd Canadian, the odder American – clocking up the hours on Hurricanes and Spitfires before they got into a real dogfight. Only the barrage balloons, hawsers taut, tethered as though to some giant hand, broke the skyline.

And blue flowers in the window box that hung on the wall of his Hampstead home.

And a blue uniform clothing his elder son. Flying Officer Rodyon Alexeyevitch Troy, RAF. Interned, released, enlisted, trained and promoted all in less than three months. The insignia of rank barely tacked onto his sleeve. If the next promotion were as swift as the first he'd be a Flight Lieutenant by the end of the month. This had baffled Rod. He had tried to explain it to his father some time ago.

'I said the obvious thing. "Are you sure I'm ready for this?" Sort of expecting the genial "Of course, old chap" by way of answer – and they said "Ready? Of course you're not ready. Ready's got bugger all to do with it. You're thirty-three, man, you've held a pilot's licence for ten years. We need people who can fly, people who can command a bit of authority, people who might look as though they know what they're doing even if they don't. You couldn't grow a moustache, could you?"'

There were times when this seemed to Alexei Troy to be an apt summation of the precarious state of Great Britain a year or so after Dunkirk – a year in which the British had fought on alone. Finest hour stretched out to breaking point. All that stood between them and defeat was his son's moustache (which he had never grown) – symbolic of the colossal bluff the nation and its leaders seemed to be perpetrating on the world stage.

And blue-lined paper on the legal pad upon his desk. Alex had reached a natural hiatus in the writing of his

Sunday Post editorial. It was known to working hacks as a 'whip and top', spinning the same words over and over again – getting nowhere.

When I first came to these islands in the winter of 1910, I knew I had seen the last of my native Russia. [move this??] The prospect of England opened up to me when I watched M. Blériot take flight and I entered into an exchange of letters with Mr H. G. Wells on the subject of powered flight. [more about HG? will the old fart take umbrage?] ... Mr Wells invited me to visit him in England. I came. I stayed. My wife, our son, our two daughters and I ended our years a-wandering. [hiatus here. what?] Perhaps the luxury I have allowed myself of speculating upon the fate of that ~~tragic~~ unhappy [?] land has been the ~~whimsical~~ [nostalgic?] indulgence of an exile – or a necessity. In their fate lie [or lies?] all our fates. [Can I say all this again?] Two years ago, I warned my readers that the Nazi-Soviet pact was not the act on which to condemn a country making itself anew. I was all but deluged in mail, none of it complimentary. [Zinoviev letter?] Well, I am going to ~~badger~~ hector you again upon that same matter. Russia ...

And on that word the axis of his thought, the top so whipped, spun to no conclusion. Time to read. When in doubt about your own prose, read someone else's verse.

As ever he had a volume of poetry on his desk, next to the lamp. A blue-bound book. He riffled the pages to see if they fell open at a blue poem. He read a line of Lawrence.

Not every man has gentians in his house ...

The blue flowers in his window box were pansies. He could see them from where he sat. The first pansies of spring – a late spring, the first day of double summer-time. Long, light nights to come. A deep, velvety royal blue, not the sky blue of the Bavarian gentians Lawrence was describing. It had been years since old Troy had been in Bavaria. England had gentians. He had vague memories of a pinkish plant with a Saxon-sounding name like blushwort or bladderwort – English was full of worts – but the 'true' gentian would not grow in this climate. His country home in Hertfordshire was a high plateau, but high in English terms meant a couple of hundred feet. Bavarian gentians were subalpine. He was seventy-nine. He'd probably never see one again. If the war ended tomorrow, he'd probably never see one again.

Not every man has gentians in his house . . .

He read on. Few poets were so long a-dying, few poets had dealt in death so long as D. H. Lawrence.

'What are you working on, Dad?'

His son Rod had come into the study. Doubtless sent by his wife to tell him lunch was ready. Old Troy looked up at his elder son, tore a page from his blue pad and balled it. Tossed it onto the growing pile in his wicker wastebasket.

'The old, old story,' he replied, not meaning to be cryptic.

'Russia,' said Rod, not inflecting the word as a question.

'Russia,' Alex muttered.

'Tough going, is it?'

Alex looked at the pile. He had balled twenty sheets or more already.

'You could say that.'

'What about Russia?'

'I was thinking about when she would join us.'

'Join us?'

'Us. The war.'

Odd to be spelling out the condition in which they all lived, so simply, so bluntly, to a man in uniform. The war was total – the war was, without exaggeration, England. History compressed. All history brought to fruition in this moment – this meaning. The meaning of England.

'Sorry. I wasn't being dense. I meant, isn't it "if" rather than "when"? Can we be at all sure they will join us?'

'That's the problem, my boy. I'm sure. Hardly anyone else is.'

'I mean, one could pose the same question of the Americans, couldn't one?'

'Quite,' said the old man. 'When I get round to it.'

Rod opened his mouth to speak, but his mother Maria Mikhailovna appeared in the doorway and cut him short and soundless.

'*Vite! Vite!* Lunch has been upon the table these five minutes.'

Alex rose, gathered his dressing gown about him, rubbed with one hand at the two-day stubble of his beard. His wife would give him hell if he were late for a meal; she would not dream of commenting on his appearance.

As they followed her down the corridor, he turned to his son and asked, 'Will Freddie be joining us?'

Alex had two sons, Vienna-born Rodyon, and London-born Frederick. His 'English child', as he thought of him. Frederick was twenty-five, and had sloughed off his blue uniform, almost as Rod had donned his, when Scotland Yard had made him first a detective and then a sergeant.

'God knows,' Rod replied. 'Am I my little brother's keeper?'

§ 3

Stahl had been lucky. The morning after his departure from Berlin a Heavy Rescue lorry had hit the house next door and demolished the party wall. Twenty tons of rubble had buried the late Herr Hölzel, and it was only on the day after that that a team of diggers finally recovered the body. Sergeant Gunther Bruhns, stuck with the task of reporting back to Heydrich at SD HQ on the *Prinz Albrechtstraße*, had not been lucky. Herr Obergruppenführer had a headache.

'Read it to me,' he said when Bruhns stuck the report on his desk.

'Read it?'

'Aloud.' Heydrich put his fingertips against his high forehead and proceeded to knead the skin with both hands, eyes down, not looking at the man.

The sergeant harrumphed and began.

'Body found this morning in *Kopernikusstraße*. 9.53 a.m. Aryan male, approximately one metre nine, approximately seventy-seven kilos in weight. No recognisable physical features. Uniform of a Sicherheitsdienst Brigadeführer. Letters and notebook in inside jacket pocket are those of Brigadeführer Wolfgang Stahl. Body removed to city morgue. No time of death established, but the house had been all but destroyed by secondary blast on the night of the seventeenth. The local warden said the bomb hit a house on the other side of the street about 9 p.m. I checked the duty log. Brigadeführer Stahl did leave here at seven fifty-eight. It is perfectly possible that he had arrived home before the air raid.'

Heydrich had stopped kneading his skull and was staring at the back of his hands – long, long fingers outstretched.

'No recognisable features? What about the blood group tattoo?'

'Not everyone has them, sir.'

'They're compulsory.'

'I checked. He broke two appointments to have it done – didn't show up for either. He was booked in to have it done next week.'

'The face?'

'There is no face.'

'The hands.'

'The hands?'

'Bring me his hands.'

'Eh?'

'Bring me his hands! Go to the morgue and chop off his hands! I want to see his hands!'

Heydrich laid his own hands flat upon the desk, palms pressed, fingers fanned as wide as they would go. He called the sergeant back before he reached the door.

'Bruhns, has the Führer been told?'

'No, sir. Not yet.'

Not yet. Somebody would have to tell him. It was perfectly possible to keep secrets from the Führer. Often the only way to deliver what he wanted was not to tell him the bad news. If he but knew it, the Führer was a man habitually lied to by every member of his entourage from his cook to the Chief of the General Staff – but this was unconcealable. Word would spread. If Stahl had died in the raid, then he was, to date, the highest-ranking Nazi officer to die on the Home Front. There was propaganda to be made. If Stahl was dead, Hitler would notice his absence. One day soon he would ask. But if Stahl was not dead . . . if Stahl was not dead. Heydrich found it hard to believe in such a coincidence. Stahl denounced to him as an enemy agent only hours after he died in an air raid? The denunciation explained one thing – why Stahl had chosen to live in the East, in a petty bourgeois block off the *Frankfurter Allee*, when the Party had offered him his own villa in Dahlem – one of those taken from the Jews. It was not fitting for an SD Brigadeführer – Heydrich had told him to move when they'd promoted him – but it put distance between Stahl and the rest of the Party.

He spread his fingers that bit the more – it hurt.

Late in the afternoon Bruhns returned with a silver tray, draped delicately with a large linen napkin. He set it down on Heydrich's desk. Heydrich was staring out of the window. Bruhns whipped away the napkin. Whoever it was had done a neat job, a piece of surgery worthy of Baron Frankenstein. All the same Bruhns pulled a face behind Heydrich's back, wincing more at the gruesome notion of hands on a platter than at the sight itself. It inevitably put him in mind of John the Baptist – but the silver tray was all he could find to put them on. It was the tray he used for the Obergruppenführer's morning coffee. The pathologist had sent the hands over wrapped in brown paper like two bits of haddock fresh from the fishmonger's slab. Heydrich was a stickler for neatness – you didn't serve up anything to such a fastidious man on a bloody sheet of wrapping paper.

'Got 'em,' he said simply.

Heydrich turned. One glance at the hands and then straight into Bruhns' eyes.

'What are you waiting for?'

'Nothing sir.'

'Then get out.'

Heydrich waited for the door to close. The left hand was broken, the fingers splayed at unnatural angles, the flesh black and blue. He spread the right, free of rigor, as wide as it would go. Then he laid his own hand across it. Cold. Softer than one would imagine. Dead meat. Nothing more than dead meat. Like picking up a pig's trotter at the butcher's. His own spread by far the wider.

He knew his capacity at a keyboard – a slightly better than average span at an octave and two. This man scarcely touched an octave. It was a fat stubby hand. Heydrich had watched Stahl's hands glide across a keyboard countless times. His span was an octave and four. There was no piece in the repertory of the piano the man could not play for want of the span of a hand. These were not the hands of Wolfgang Stahl. Stahl was alive. Alive and with a forty-eight-hour start on him.

'Bruhns!'

Bruhns appeared at the door, blankly expressionless.

'Call the Chancellery. Get me an appointment with the Führer. And arrange a funeral for Brigadeführer Stahl.'

'Private, sir? Family and friends?'

'What family? Stahl had no family. No man, public. Large, lavish and public. We are burying a hero.'

§ 4

Ten days later Bruhns found himself flipping the lid on a couple of steins of wheat beer with his old pal Willi. He and Willi went back to the twenties together – to their schooldays. They'd hated their teachers then. Now they hated their officers and met every so often to drink beer – wheat beer was great for inducing that delicious, deliriously sodden feeling; a nice heavy, cloudy brew, heavier still since the Reich had seen fit to boost public morale by raising the alcohol level of beer to ten per cent – and to moan about their bosses. Willi was in the Abwehr, a corporal in Military Intelligence – it was something to write home about, but Bruhns' job was the more interesting. Not everybody got to work for a flash bastard like Heydrich. At best Willi got to pass Admiral Canaris in a corridor – he'd never even spoken to the man. And not everybody got the afternoon off to go to a top-notch Nazi funeral. All that goose stepping and dreary music, but it had to be better than working. Another thing he and Willi had in common, they'd both volunteered to avoid the draft. Get their pick of regiments. Bruhns had even joined the party for appearances' sake – the trouble he'd had learning the Horst Wessel song! Didn't make either of them into loyal Nazis – as far as Bruhns was concerned they were just two blokes trying to get by, occasionally get laid, and more often get rat-arsed. His old man had been a paid-up Commie, but he had no politics one way or the other. Nothing against the Jews – well not much, anyway – and for all he cared they could bring back the Kaiser – silly little prick with his wonky arm and daft hats. He should care.

'You get to see the body then, Gunther?'

Bruhns was puzzled, but too pissed to want to argue – daft question all the same.

'Nah. Mind, I saw his hands though.'

'His hands?'

'The boss had 'em cut off.'

'Cut off? Why?'

'Search me. One minute he's quizzing me about tattoos and things – wants to know if that body was Wolfie Stahl – next thing he's damn certain it is and rushes off to tell old 'Dolf.'

'Keep your voice down! Do you want us both to end up in a camp?'

'Wossitmatter? Nobody's listening.'

'Gunther – this is Germany. Everybody's listening. It isn't just walls have ears – the floor, the ceiling, the doorknob and the garden shed have ears.'

'Well if they're listening, let 'em 'ear this. If that body was Wolfie Stahl, then my name's Fatso Goering! Now it's your round. Get 'em in.'

§ 5

Calvin M. Cormack III sat in his Zurich office, breathed on his glasses, wiped them on his handkerchief and hooked the wire ends over his ears. The M in Calvin M. Cormack III was something Calvin M. Cormack III would have preferred to forget entirely. The M in Calvin M. Cormack Sr and in Calvin M. Cormack Jr (his grandfather and father respectively) stood for Michael. The M in Calvin M. Cormack III stood for Manassas, the battle of the Civil War in which his grandfather had lost an arm, almost eighty years ago. The old man – still going at ninety-seven – always called it 'the war' (pronounced 'wawer'), thereby ignoring the Spanish-American War, the World War and eighteen months of what the British were already calling World War II regardless of its global imprecision. He had served under General Jackson in Virginia, and had worn the arm, or rather the absence of an arm, more proudly than any medal. General Jackson had emerged from the battle with the nickname 'Stonewall'; 2nd Lieutenant Cormack had been less lucky: 'Catch' – as in 'One-handed Catch' – Cormack. A one-armed hero, but a hero all the same. Years later, nearer the turn of the century, when he had been elected Senator for Virginia, he had been cheered into the Senate like a returning warrior – and he played the part to the hilt in a white linen suit, a frock coat, the empty sleeve pinned to the side, his frame spare to the skeletal, a shock of white hair combed back from his forehead, looking like the caricature of a circuit judge in some long-forgotten Twain story. A Southerner from tip to toe.

'It's crap,' said Cal's father. 'He filled me up with all that rebel stuff when I was a boy. I love the old guy – and so should you – but take everything he says with a pinch of salt. All he wants to do is put back the clock. Can't be done. We're one nation. Don't ever forget it.'

'But why the name? Why Manassas?' Cal had protested at about age twelve.

'You're a Southerner. Don't ever forget it.'

It was years before this struck Cal as anything other than a paradox, and paradox was not a word he knew at the age of twelve. His father had served the Democrat party machine in Virginia, but he'd also served it in Pennsylvania and New York. It had been convenient to send Cal to school upstate New York. On the first day they had called the roll in full, and when they got to Cal the boys had sniggered at Manassas. The kid next to him had said, 'Manassas? What kind of a name is that?'

'Bull Run' Cal had whispered back. 'It means Bull Run, that's all. That's what it was called by the South.'

'Bull Run? Who in hell'd name a kid Bull Run?'

And so it had gone on. Five years or more. Manassas quickly became Molasses – he was stuck with it. 'Molasses, molasses, skinny kid in glasses!'

When Cal was fourteen his father won a congressional seat in his home state – and he'd done it by declaring his independence of the Senior Senator for Virginia – on everything from the Silver Standard to the Pershing Expeditionary Force. Calvin M. Cormack Jr was nobody's boy. No one, to his face, ever called him son of Catch, or dared to air the notion that he was riding the political high road clutching onto his father's frock coat. To his own son he said, 'I had to do it. I couldn't live that plantation-owner gimcrack. There's not a Cormack so much as plucked a boll, let alone jumped down, turned around and picked a bale. I appeased the old man with your name. Let him know I'd never betray the South – whatever else I did. Freed us to get on with being Americans the rest of the time.'

But then, by then, Cal had worked that out for

himself. He'd heard too many of the rows between his father and his grandfather. Ante-Bellum man versus All-American man. And he had little faith in either.

The letter on the top of his in-tray was an airmail from his father. He'd know that copperplate script anywhere: 'Capt. Calvin M. Cormack III, United States Consulate, Zurich', written with all the pride a man could put into his son's rank and address. He eased his glasses forward a fraction on his nose. Held the letter, not wanting to rip it open. Light as a feather. He could all too easily guess its contents. His father had been ranting at him for years now. Like father like son. It was enough to make you want to break the cycle. Fuck your life away and never marry – never, never, have children. If his grandfather flew the tattered flag of the Confederacy and talked sentimentally of the Rebels, his father flew the near-invisible flag of Isolationism and talked contemptuously of Europe. What was World War II to a beleaguered little island was 'a European skirmish' to Representative Calvin M. Cormack Jr of Virginia, Chairman of the all-powerful House Ways and Means Committee, and 'little or nothing to do with any right-thinking, God-fearing American'. Not that his father feared God. His father feared nothing, as far as Cal had ever been able to tell, and certainly not an entity in which he did not believe in the first place. At least they had that in common, all three generations of them. Not much, and not enough.

He'd read it later. He just wasn't in the mood right now. He dropped it in his in-tray and slipped a brown cardboard file out of the top drawer of his desk. In it was the decrypted message he'd received from Berlin a little over two weeks ago: 'TIN MAN DEAD'. A simple, too simple, conclusion to a complicated life. His assistant had filled the file with clippings – more than twenty snipped pieces from the German press. A hero's funeral. He looked at them every day. Not disbelieving. Wanting not to believe.

His office door opened. Cal was still staring at the clippings. He looked up slowly and found himself panning up from a pair of stiletto heels – albeit in army colours – the length of two short, shapely legs, across a non-regulation, over-tight, over-tailored skirt, an olive green blouse thrust out by big breasts, two corporal's stripes on the sleeve, to a pretty face, red lips, nut brown eyes, under the shortest haircut he'd ever seen on a woman. She was clutching a single sheet of paper to her bosom. He'd no idea who she was.

'Have we met?' he said simply.

'Sure, day before yesterday. Can I help it if you got a memory like a spaghetti strainer?'

'You're new?'

'Cypher clerk. Whole bunch of us got in Friday. I guess you were too busy to give us the twice-over. I settled for the once-over. Hurts to know how big an impression I made on you.'

Cal was dumbfounded – no corporal in the United States Army had ever talked to him this way – but he was a slave to his upbringing. He'd been taught to stand in the presence of a lady – even a New York loudmouth like this one – so he stood and offered her his hand.

'Calvin Cormack,' he said.

'Larissa Tosca,' she replied. 'But you can call me Lara. Now you wanna read what I got or you just wanna flirt with me? You could read it now and if it's nothing we could flirt some more, or we could flirt all morning and let the war go hang.'

'Er . . .'

'OK. This is what it says. It says "Tell RG everything. Yrs Gelbroaster".'

'"Tell RG everything – Gelbroaster"? That's all?'

'Yep.'

General Gelbroaster was the head of US Army Intelligence, London. There were plenty who thought him nuts, but in London his word was little short of law. Even when his word was as terse as this.

'I was curious about the R and the G. I checked it every goddam which way for mistakes but that's the way it comes out. RG. Every combination I tried I still get RG.'

'That's OK. I know who he means.'

'Fine. Look me up when you've finished.'

Corporal Tosca slapped the paper on Cal's desk and walked out. Buttocks sashaying in the tight skirt. Quite the shortest, rudest woman he had ever met. He wondered if Gelbroaster was now recruiting people as nutty as he was himself. They'd sent him some wackos over the last two years, but this one took the prize.

Cal called the British Consulate and asked for Lt. Col. Ruthven-Greene. He heard the mechanical, ratchet rattle of the switchboard and then an unsurprisingly hearty English voice.

'Calvin – dear boy. Just the chap I was thinking of. Tell me, do you think you could fit in a spot of lunch today? Here at the Consulate. A bit of a chat over beer and sandwiches, eh?'

§ 6

Cal knew Ruthven-Greene fairly well. He had met him on his last London trip in '39, and on a dozen other occasions when the man had shown up in Zurich.

Reggie was an affable man. Indeed, you might be fooled into thinking that affability was all there was to him. He cultivated the faintly raffish air of a man who knew where the good times were to be had, and all in all gave the impression of being a man who had just failed the audition for a Hollywood role that had gone to George Sanders instead. He was always in civilian clothes, and although Cal had heard members of the embassy staff address him as Colonel, it was pretty clear he was no regular kind of colonel. He was too young, at thirty-nine or forty, to have seen much of the last war – at best he'd've been a subaltern in the last weeks. It was possible he'd spent the long weekend between the wars on the reserve list, only to be called up at once when rain stopped play at Munich. It was possible he'd been promoted in the background. Much more possible, to the point of highly likely, was that Alistair Ruthven-Greene – known to his friends as Reggie – was a career spook. Nominally a serving soldier, but who'd not seen a parade ground in years, and wore his uniform only on occasions of state – whatever they were. The funerals of kings, Cal thought, and the British didn't lose kings on anything like a regular basis. Still, who was he to quibble? There were states in the Deep South where colonels were dashed out as honours faster than the Pope created counts.

Ruthven-Greene swept him into a large office – a partner's desk, a low table framed by a couple of deep-cushioned sofas, made his own office look at best perfunctory. And on the low table sat a plate of roast beef sandwiches, a pot of strong English mustard and two tall bottles of pale ale. Ruthven-Greene was being literal, he had said beer and sandwiches so beer and sandwiches it was. Cal had learnt that when the British served beer with beef they meant to talk turkey.

Ruthven-Greene flipped the top off a bottle and poured it into two half-pint tankards. Cal helped himself to a sandwich – minus the English mustard. What kind of a nation was it that could delight in so searing its taste buds?

'What was it you wanted to talk to me about, Reggie?'

'Codes, dear boy. Codes.'

Codes? They didn't share codes. We have ours and they have theirs. Never the twain . . .

Ruthven-Greene took a small leather-bound diary from his inside pocket. A sheet of white paper larger than the book itself was sticking out. He extracted it and handed it to Cal.

'I'm sure you're familiar with this,' he said.

Cal took one look at it and hoped he had not turned white – or worse, blushed red. The note was preceded by several lines of numerical gobbledegook, but in the centre of the page, in capital letters, it read 'TIN MAN DEAD'.

'You've broken our code?'

'Well. Yes and no.'

'What's the yes?'

'We broke it last year. Best part of twelve months ago, in fact. We regularly monitor all your embassy transmissions from the Cape to Cairo, from Timbuktu to Tokyo. Sorry. But there you are. We're not allies. Well, not yet at any rate.'

'And the no?'

'It isn't taken from any communiqué of yours. We got it from a German radio transmission. We've cracked your code. And I'm rather afraid the Germans have too.'

'Again?' Cal thought, but said nothing. It was only a year since MI5 had caught a cypher clerk at the US Embassy in London passing the code to the Germans. The British had tried him in camera – they weren't going to make the Americans look like fools – locked him up and thrown away the key, for the duration at least. It was beyond embarrassment. There was scarcely a word strong enough to describe it. As a result the Americans had tightened up their security, changed all the codes – which, it now seemed, the British had cracked immediately – and suffered an on/off, hot/cold relationship with

24

their M15 counterparts on the sharing of information. Sometimes it seemed they told you everything, at others as though they trusted you about as far as you could chuck a buffalo – and always they asked for more. Since the war began, and increasingly since Winston Churchill took over, the British had become a nation of Oliver Twists. There was nothing they wouldn't ask for, whilst guarding and rationing anything you might reasonably expect from them. It was, he thought, a bit like being importuned by a beggar in top hat and tails. And – worse yet – it was only four months since an American magazine had printed the design specifications of the next generation of British warplanes, for no better reason than that it had not occurred to the War Department in Washington that they might be secret. Cal could readily see why the British might be touchy on the matter of secrets – and it required but a short leap of imagination to realise that of course they'd spy on the Americans. Why wouldn't they? And if they spied upon the Germans as they in turn were spying upon the Americans to retrieve information third hand via two separate codes – well, scratch it if you can.

Ruthven-Greene indulged himself in one of his teeth-sucking, airy pauses. 'Now – about your man Stahl. They're onto this bloke, I should think that's pretty obvious by now. We must have him. Really we must. Sorry to insist and all that, but we really must.'

Cal was startled, not by the juxtaposition of the names – if they knew his codename why would they not know his real name? But two and two were not making four.

'Reggie – I think you've just crossed a wire. Stahl *is* the Tin Man. Stahl is dead. He's dead, goddammit. They buried him ten days ago. Full military honours. Hitler was there. Heydrich was there. Half the papers in Germany carried the story on their front pages!'

'No. That's just my point. He isn't dead.'

It was not in Cal's nature to seek confrontation – he did not enjoy confrontation – but it seemed inevitable that there would be one. Perhaps the best thing was to get it over with as soon as possible.

'Reggie – are you going to talk in riddles all afternoon?'

Ruthven-Greene dug around in his pockets as though searching for the last stick of gum or a book of matches. He handed Cal a typed sheet folded over several times. It was tight and grubby as though it had sat in his jacket pocket forgotten for days and could not possibly be of any importance. But, he knew, with the British that was often the way, the trivial stood on, perched upon with full blasting dignity, the world-shattering passed across as though it were an afterthought. Cal unwrapped the sheet of paper.

'It's a de-crypt of a message we received about a week after Stahl is supposed to have died. Very hush-hush,' Ruthven-Greene explained.

Cal read it – curiouser and curiouser.

'This guy says he saw Stahl alive *after* the air raid. I don't get it.'

'He's our man in Berlin. Well placed. Corporal in the Abwehr, as a matter of fact. If he says he saw Stahl alive after the air raid, then he did. You'll note that he confirms from a source in Heydrich's own office that Stahl didn't die on the seventeenth. No two ways about it. I gather your sources, like ours initially, reported him as having died in the raid.'

Cal let the paper fall. A web of loyalties and assumed alliances tearing themselves up and reforming in his mind even as he spoke.

'Yes,' he said softly.

'Then I think we've reached the same point. Two questions. Why would Heydrich go to all this trouble to convince the Boche he's dead?'

'Perhaps because he thinks he is dead?'

'Good Lord, no. Stahl was his deputy, well, one of his deputies, for seven years. I'd say he's the one man Stahl could not fool. Whoever they buried, and I rather think they needed a body for that, it wasn't Stahl; and, if there was a body, Heydrich would have torn it to pieces, and I do not mean that as a figure of speech, to be certain of his identity.'

Cal looked around the room, as though seeking reassurance in the solidity of the furniture.

'Two questions, you said. What's the other?'

'Much the same as the first really. Why would your Tin Man go to all this trouble to convince the Boche he's dead?'

'Reggie – I've been told to co-operate with you. Don't play games with me. You haven't come all the way to Zurich to have me tell you Stahl spied for us. You know that already or you wouldn't be here.'

'Quite. I saw General Gelbroaster the day I set off. He gave me the bare facts. Sort of wanted you to fill me in with the detail.'

'Sort of?'

'You know, first hand. You knew the blighter after all.'

'Is this room secure?'

'Secure?'

'I mean,' said Cal, 'can we talk?'

'My dear fellow, we are talking.'

Reggie tucked into a sandwich. Cal found his appetite had vanished. He'd dreaded this moment ever since he got Gelbroaster's 'Tell RG everything.'

'Stahl is Austrian. I've never been certain of his age but I'd think he was in his early thirties, say thirty-two or -three. He joined the Nazi Party in 1929, and a couple of months later he contacted the Polish Secret Service and offered to spy for them. You'll recall, the Poles looked like bigger players in Europe at that time than they've done at any time since. It wasn't such an odd move. They checked him out, and took the risk. They trained him. He's not the kind of man you'd ever want to go up against without a tommy-gun in your hand. Stahl then joined the SS – must have been one of the pioneers, certainly in the first five hundred – and then moved sideways into the SD. Early on he met Heydrich and at some point in the mid-thirties Heydrich took him up, became, I guess, his patron in the party. At which point the quality of Stahl's information became almost price-less. At least it would have been if there'd been the political will to evaluate it. He supplied the Poles with infrequent but accurate high-level information right up to the invasion of Poland.

'About a year before this some bright spark in Polish Intelligence foresaw the outcome pretty clearly and offered Stahl to the British. If you've been honestly briefed by your own people, Reggie, you'll know that your own side turned him down. There were plenty of people about that time, in the summer of thirty-eight, in any country you care to name, telling themselves the war was not going to happen. So the Poles offered him to us. We took Stahl. They flew me out about the time of the fall of Warsaw to run him from here. It's pretty much what I've done ever since.

'I met him half a dozen times, when he was part of some official delegation at our embassy in Berlin, the reciprocal visit in Zurich and at those dreadful *Bierabends* the Nazis used to organise for the foreign press and diplomats. I've heard him play duets with Heydrich, and I've seen him fend off questions from Ed Murrow and Bill Shirer, but I doubt I ever got more than fifteen minutes alone with him at any one time. Usually in the middle of Berlin. With Gestapo thugs all over the place.

I don't think I've ever felt so scared in my entire life. Everything else has come via couriers and codes. He rations what he tells us, and needless to say we ration what we pass on to you. We did nothing to draw attention to him as the source of our information. It worked well, until now. I don't know what's gone wrong. An air raid I could believe. Lousy luck, but believable. But if he's faked his own death and vanished . . .'

Cal had no idea how his sentence should end. Reggie finished it for him, half-eaten sandwich poised in the air, his voice not much above a whisper.

'. . . And all he knows has vanished with him . . . We must have him. Really we must.'

'I know. You already said that. What is it you think he knows?'

'Anything or everything, it really doesn't matter. That close to Heydrich for that long. Whatever he knows we must know too. I gather Heydrich is mad with frustration or grief – do these buggers feel grief? do they feel at all? – whatever, he has lost someone of immense value. That much is obvious. I rather think he's up to something very clever in faking that funeral. He'll have his men looking for Stahl. I pray to God we find him before they do.'

'Find him? I don't even know where to start looking.'

'England, dear boy.'

'England? Why England?'

'Where else can he go? If he were coming to you he'd be here by now. He's had more than a fortnight. He'd have been here in a couple of days, or so I should think. No, he's heading for England. I know it in my bones. He's heading for London. And so should we.'

'We?'

'You and me. You're to accompany me to England. Gelbroaster's orders. A spot of liaison.'

Ruthven-Greene said 'liaison' as though it were lunch. A pleasant way to pass a little time, rather than a diplomatic quagmire.

'I guess I don't have a lot of choice, do I?'

'No, you don't. If I'm right and your Tin Man shows up in London, we'll need you to identify him. Would you believe we don't have a single clear photograph of the man?'

Yes. Cal could easily believe that. He'd seen hundreds of shots of the Nazi hierarchy. He'd yet to see one in which Stahl had not managed to be in shadow or behind someone taller. Always the blur at the edge of the frame.

Ruthven-Greene put a copy of the *Deutsche Allgemeine Zeitung* on the table. Last week's big story. Stahl's funeral. The photograph of Stahl had been blown up, magnified many times, from a crowd shot – so coarse was the grain it could have been anyone. Stahl's own mother would not have known him. The *12-Uhr Blatt*, the *Beobachter* and the *Börsen Zeitung* had all carried the same picture – it was probably all they had.

'Is that all? Just identify the man? I was his control officer for two years.'

'Quite. I meant . . . help us find him . . . help us . . .'

Ruthven-Greene thrashed around for the right technical term.

'. . . Help us . . . de-brief the bugger. That's it. De-brief him.'

He smiled with satisfaction at having mastered the term. Cal half liked, half loathed this about the English – the dreadful affectation that they were all amateurs, that precise and specific was the sort of thing you paid someone else to be rather than bother with yourself. War as cricket – gentlemen and players. They had to be kidding.

Ruthven-Greene showed Cal out.

'You know, I'm still a bit puzzled,' he said.

He could not be half as puzzled as Cal felt.

'Tin Man. Don't you think it was a bit . . . well . . . obvious? For a codename, I mean. A bit close. Stahl, steel, tin? Geddit?'

'I didn't choose it, Reggie. Stahl did.'

'All the same he's damn lucky no one put two and two together.'

'Perhaps he was overfond of *The Wizard of Oz*?'

'Ah . . . perhaps so . . . if he only had a brain, eh?'

'That was the Scarecrow. The Tin Man wanted a heart. You didn't grow up reading Frank Baum, did you?'

'Never heard of him. But then I don't suppose you grew up reading E. Nesbit and *The Railway Children*, did you? Ah well. Toodle pip. See you in the morning.'

Ruthven-Greene went away whistling the Tin Man's song to himself. If he only had a heart. Blasé as ever. Toodle fucking pip.

It was only in the staff car going back to the embassy that Cal pondered the truth of what Ruthven-Greene had said so casually, 'We're not allies, at least not yet.' He had the feeling that he'd just given away his birthright. Ripped off the bloody bandage, thrown down the fife and drum. That in sharing with this not-yet-ally he had somehow diminished himself, wiped out his own *raison d'être*. There were times when he felt not that he was Stahl, exactly, but that without Stahl he was, not nothing, exactly – but something other, something lesser, not quite Calvin M. Cormack III. His identity was bound up in Stahl's identity. On the other hand he'd walked into the meeting with Stahl dead and come out with Stahl alive.

Then the other thing Reggie had let slip – did Reggie let anything slip? Wasn't every word planted to a measure and a stick? The British had cracked the German code. Not any routine traffic code, but the codes used by Intelligence and Counter-Intelligence, by the very people who'd broken the US Embassy Traffic code. The British had broken the codebreakers' own code. What, then, did they *not* know?

§ 7

The outer office was empty when Cal got back. There was usually a cypher clerk stuck out front, nominally his assistant – his secretary if they'd both but been civilians. Janis – Sgt Doyle – had reported sick two or three days ago, and he hadn't seen her since. But the desk was neat, no mail unopened, no memo pad full of urgent messages. Somebody was doing the job.

On his own desk, in his in-tray was the letter from his father. He tore it open. It was weeks old. The mail was taking longer as the war grew older.

Dear son,
    Well – it's done. The Lease and Lend is passed into law. It's a bum's charter – a licence for the English to come panhandling whenever they feel like it. I was not alone in this view, believe me, but such is democracy – or such is presidential arm-twisting. Not a day went by without one of us being summoned to the White House for an informal chat, and most of them came back shaking their heads and apologising. He sent for me last of all. All teeth and smiles. Told me he'd got the votes, didn't need mine – made that perfectly clear – so why didn't I roll with it and vote with the majority instead of looking like a 'stubborn maverick'? I told the sonovabitch that if so much as a plugged nickel of that money got through to Communists in Russia I'd see him impeached. . .

Cal skipped on – this kind of complaint usually went on aimlessly for paragraph after paragraph. Cal did not doubt the honesty of his father's conviction – he'd fought the bill tooth and nail – nor the honesty of his actions – if he said he'd told FDR he'd see him impeached, then he'd done it. It had simply ceased to interest him long ago. He found the chat, what really mattered, the family news.

> Your Grandfather's in a lot of pain from sciatica. I think he washes it away with bourbon ... Your Mother's worried about the house – we had a wet spring this year, the columns at the front are splitting open – cement and plaster over cast iron, would you believe, and the iron's well rusted ... Good God, is nothing what it seems?

Cal loved the house – a modest mansion (if there were such a thing) on a hilltop in Fairfax County, looking out across the Potomac to Maryland, dating from the time of Andrew Jackson. It had stood a hundred years. In American terms it was old – and if it was splitting open it would not be the only thing in his native land to burst like rotten fruit before this war was over. It seemed all too symbolic to Cal. He knew this was no worry to his father. It was only a matter of money and they'd money aplenty – but it was change, and his mother hated change. He'd left home, for good as it turned out, when they sent him to a military school prior to West Point. His mother kept his room just as it had been in 1925. His childhood in aspic.

A thump-thuddy-thump brought him back to the present world, the present continent. It was coming from his outer office. He pulled the door open and looked out. Corporal Tosca was bouncing a half-size basketball off the wall and occasionally dropping it into a half-size net tacked up above the President's photograph. She bounced with it, breasts rising as she stood on tiptoe and pitched. It was all but impossible to balance well. Her next throw went wild, the ball roared back over her head and Cal caught it neatly. She turned to him. Snatched the ball back.

'You can't play,' she said through a mouthful of gum. 'You're taller'n me.'

Most people were, Cal thought.

'Where's Janis?' he said.

'Who's Janis?'

'My regular woman.'

'You have a regular woman?'

'I mean . . . I meant . . . my regular assistant.'

'Oh. Her. She flew home. Pregnant. (pause.) Wasn't you, was it?'

'No, it wasn't!'

'Guess not. You don't look the type. Still, she's gone now. I'm your regular woman.'

'You are?'

'You bet.' She chewed vigorously and bounced the ball off the floor with the flat of her hand. She dribbled better than she threw. 'Tell you what, you can play if you take a handicap.'

'Handicap?'

'You have to stand on one leg.'

Cal was a lousy player, but even standing on one leg he beat her five times out of five. Every time he dropped the ball through the net she chewed furiously on her gum. At six out of six, he said, 'I have to go to England.'

'Lucky you.'

'I hesitate to say this, but if you're my clerk you'll be in charge of the office while I'm gone.'

'Okey-dokey. I'll dust your spook files and darn your spy's outfit, and knit little covers for your tommy guns.'

'Jesus Christ,' said Cal. 'Is nothing serious?'

Tosca stopped chewing, blew out a bubble of pink goo

to the size of a cue ball and then burst it with her teeth.
'Not much,' she said.

§ 8

It was a pity they could not run to a two-way mirror.
Stilton had never seen a two-way mirror. The FBI had
them in the flicks. A two-way mirror would really make
him feel like a spy rather than just a policeman. Not that
he was not utterly proud to be an officer of the
Metropolitan Police Special Branch – it just lacked a
whisper of romance, that dark hint of adventure.

He sat in the next room with the lights out. Watching
Thesiger and his quarry through the inch-open door.
Thesiger was talking to a Dutchman – Jeroen Smulders. It
was the third time he'd had him in since he was picked up in
a dinghy off the coast of Essex. He was Dutch – Stilton was
satisfied of that – and neither he nor Squadron Leader
Thesiger had been able to find a codebook among his
effects – a Dutch/English pocket dictionary, a Lutheran
bible, a collection of half a dozen worn, well-thumbed love
letters – but he was, beyond a shadow of a doubt, a German
spy. Thesiger had had the man checked out by the M.O.
'Just for your own sake – no communicable diseases, that
sort of thing.' And the M.O. had confirmed everything
Stilton had suggested. Smulders was nearer thirty than the
forty his papers claimed – his hair had been taken up at the
roots over the frontal lobes to age him – his sideburns
treated with peroxide – two teeth pulled recently – and
fifteen pounds of flab added by stuffing himself over a
matter of a few weeks to disguise a hard core of underlying
muscle. He could take it off as easily as he had put it on with
a dash of will-power. Smulders was young, fit and probably
trained.

'Trained what?' was the question Stilton had put to

himself. Your run-of-the-mill spy (was there such a thing?) didn't need to have the physique of a Spartan warrior. Your run-of-the-mill spy more than likely was a forty-two-year-old Dutch printer, hotfoot from Delft, telling you he was fleeing the enemy. The Germans had gone to a lot of trouble with this man. But too quickly, the new body, the new persona, sat atop the old too loosely.

Stilton saw the two men rise. Saw Thesiger shaking hands with Smulders, wishing him good luck. Smulders gathering up his papers, walking out into his new life, safe in Britain, an island haven in an occupied Europe.

Thesiger lit up a fag. Stilton took his hat and his macintosh off the back of the door and pulled it wide. Thesiger perched on a corner of his desk, the epitome of calm. He was not one of those officers for whom 'on duty' required a stiff upper lip and a ramrod backbone, any more than it seemed to require a regulation uniform. Thesiger was frequently to be found in corduroy trousers or a rough woollen pullover or with a tatty old cravat tucked around his neck – the blue battledress with its insignia of rank the only concession he made. Most of the time he was to be found with his feet up – and on cold days this winter he'd sat with his feet in the bottom drawer of his desk for warmth, until the day a Wren came in without knocking and he'd stood too sharply in the presence of a lady and shot through the bottom of the drawer.

'Have you got a few minutes?' he said.

'O' course. He gets a lift to the station. One of my blokes gets on the London train with him. Another picks him up at Fenchurch Street. Routine stuff. Doesn't need a Chief Inspector.'

Thesiger held out a packet of Craven A.

'No thanks, sir. I've given up. Strictly a pipe man from now on.'

'Given up?' Thesiger could not keep the astonishment out of his voice. People didn't give up cigarettes. They either smoked or they didn't. 'Ah well . . . tell me, Chief Inspector. Do I detect a sour note in your use of the word "routine"?'

'All I meant was that anyone could do it. I meant no offence.'

'And I took none. But it does seem to me that you think all this is a bit beneath you.'

'Not exactly. But it's hardly using me to the full, is it? When I was seconded to the unit I thought it was because I'd fluent German, because I knew Germans . . . and I've picked up more than a smattering of Polish and Czech in the last four years.'

'Anyone could do what you do?'

'Doesn't take what I know to tail a few blokes around London.'

'Then we must see if we can't make better use of your talents.'

It was the kind of remark Stilton had become used to from the toffs. Three years a serving Tommy and almost thirty as a copper had rubbed in the deferential nature of the Forces. Merit had little or nothing to do with it. You were born to lead or you weren't. And Stilton wasn't. It all came down to class. Age – he was fifteen or more years older than Thesiger – and experience – he'd been in the last war, when Thesiger was still a schoolboy – counted for little. It was the sort of thing that took a war to change. The first year of Walter Stilton's war had been routine. The second year, since Dunkirk, had been one of the best of his life – working for Thesiger as a 'spycatcher'. He and Thesiger got on very well. He'd rarely met a toff less strait-jacketed by his class. They understood one another very well. Thesiger could drop the upper crust habitual allusions and ellipses of speech to talk plainly when he had to. And still it left Stilton frustrated. Thesiger's generosity of spirit was sincere, as sincere as his material generosity (he was the sort of bloke who'd share his flask and sandwiches with you), but it was unlikely to be followed up by any action. He'd interrogate Jerry – Stilton and blokes like Stilton would traipse after them in the pouring rain noting their movements in little black notebooks.

Thesiger sat down again – stretched out his legs, heels resting on the edge of his desk, talked through a puff of smoke, the cigarette waggling in his lips as he did so.

'While we're on the subject, Walter, I wanted to ask you – what news of our Jerry in Derby?'

This was a man professing to be a Belgian refugee. Thesiger and Stilton had spotted him at once and decided to turn him loose. Let him find his place in Britain and then use him to feed back misinformation.

'He's snug as a bug in a rug at the Rolls Royce works. We've got him making up parts for what he thinks is a new fighter engine. It's about as likely to fly as a pig. Most of it's made up from the plans for my wife's sewing machine, blown up to twenty times the scale. At worst we might inadvertently give Krupps the idea for a two-ton Singer.'

Thesiger grinned. Class notwithstanding, Stilton liked the man. It was largely thanks to him that MI5 could boast that there was not a single German spy in Britain they did not know about.

'We can't afford to lose Smulders. Not for a day. He's not here to stay. He's not a sleeper. He's on something quite specific. If I knew what it was I'd not have turned him loose. As soon as we know you'll have to pull him in. There's a risk of course – if Jerry has some way of communicating with him, then the minute he goes active he'll try and vanish. We must be ready for that, really we must.'

'Do you mind if I stick in me two-penn'orth?'

'By all means.'

'He's a twitchy sort of a bloke. One of the nurses came up behind him a bit too quiet like during his medical, and he rounded on her faster than a ferret after a rabbit. He'd grabbed her by one arm before he checked himself. All smiles and apologies. She'd dropped her kidney dish. He helped the lass pick it up – was so charming to her he made the poor girl bright red with embarrassment. But it was enough. A dead giveaway. He's what you'd call Commando trained. A bare-handed killer.'

'Perhaps we are wasting your talent. An assassin indeed. I'm inclined to agree. Assassin of whom, one wonders? They'd hardly send him across and expect him to take a crack at Winston now would they?'

§ 9

It took days to reach England. A hop across Vichy France in a Swiss plane to Lisbon, and a two day lay-up at the Avis Hotel while they waited for the irregular American Clipper service to Poole, on the south coast of England. It was a mark of how much things had changed since the war, how much they'd changed since the fall of Holland and the loss of the KLM planes. It had been a daily service, the flying boats had connected fairly neatly with the steamers – some of them even bounced on via the Azores to touch down in Bowery Bay NY, within sight and sound of Manhattan – and you got your mail on time. Now there were queues of passengers, often more than a hundred, waiting day after day to cross the Atlantic or to skim the waves to England. Ruthven-Greene argued their priority over anyone short of a general and bumped them up the list and on to the next available plane.

Cal liked Lisbon. Its steep hills and streetcars put him

in mind of San Francisco, its sidewalk cafés of Paris. It was the antithesis of Zurich. Zurich was polite and businesslike in its teutonic fashion. The factions made appointments to see one another and observed a diplomatic regularity. Lisbon was nothing if not irregular. Lisbon in May, Lisbon at peace, even if everyone else was at war, was warm and sunny and a little careless. The warring sides passed each other in the street, rubbed shoulders in the bars and cafés, murdered one another in the alleys. It was new to Cal, and visibly old hat to Ruthven-Greene. On the second afternoon he had rummaged in his pockets for a light, ignored the book of matches on the café's kerbside table and nipped across the street to bum a light from a man smoking outside the café opposite. Reggie had chatted to the man for several minutes before he came back, scarcely suppressing a grin.

'Someone you know?' Cal asked.

'Yes. Old Dietrich from the German embassy. Usually pays to have a bit of a chat with the old sod. His boastfulness always gets the better of his discretion. One day soon they'll find his body floating in the harbour, and it won't be because of anything our lot have done. He came out with an absolute corker. Asked me about this bunker Churchill's having built under Glamis castle in Scotland – courtesy of the Queen's people, who own it – so he can hold the Jerries at Hadrian's Wall after they've conquered England. I don't know where he gets such twaddle, but I rather wish I'd made it up myself.'

Cal loved flying. He felt safe in the fat body of the little Boeing Clipper. He didn't get sick and there was something deeply reassuring about the throb of four robust-sounding piston-engined propellers close to the ear.

He watched the Spanish coast fall away as they flew on to the Bay of Biscay, swinging westward to avoid the

German-occupied French Atlantic ports – U-boat bases for the wolf packs that harassed shipping.

An unsafe thought crossed his mind. An unsafe question passed his lips.

'Supposing they fired on us?'

'Eh?' said Ruthven-Greene.

'By mistake, I mean.'

'Be the biggest mistake of the war so far. A diplomatic incident, old boy. It'd be like the last war – remember the sinking of the *Lusitania*? You and I would go down to the Jerry guns in the noble cause of bringing Uncle Sam into the war lickety-split.'

§ 10

After planes, Cal liked trains. They brought out the boy in him. Memories of long journeys across the wet flatlands of Pennsylvania and Maryland as his father shuffled the family between New York and Washington. Fonder memories of backtracks in the heart of rural Virginia as his father indulged him rarely in pleasure trips on the Norfolk and Western – riding for the fun of it – where trains the size of mountains moved at the speed of a horse and wagon, snaking through the countryside and crawling down Main Street in little towns for whom Main was the only street.

From Poole to Waterloo he could see nothing. The blackouts were drawn tight, and the compartments packed. Passengers sat four to a side.

Soldiers in uniform sat on their kitbags in the corridors, and a group of weary, dishevelled NCOs played poker in the mail van. The station porters yelled out the names of the stations at the tops of their voices – still people missed them.

He did not know what to say to anyone. Ruthven-

Greene said it all. Cal had rarely seen a man quite so affable, quite so banal – a master of inane chat – and he talked without, as Cal heard it, telling a single truth. Years of practice, he assumed – since Reggie could not tell the truth about what he did in the war he seemed to have achieved a believable cover so plausible he uttered it without any consciousness of it not being true. The fate of all spies, to believe one's own lies. Reggie chatted to the district nurse, to the naval lieutenant going home on leave, to the rural archdeacon going up to town to meet the bishop, and told them all he was an oatmeal buyer for the Highland Light Infantry. An army marches on its stomach, he said, quoting Napoleon, but a Scottish army marches on porridge, he said, making it up as he went along. And then he asked them a hundred nosy questions, recommended a few nightclubs to the Navy man, asked the nurse about her family and sang snatches of his favourite hymns for the clergyman. Cal nodded off to the sound of 'Jesus wants me for a sunbeam . . .'

At Waterloo Reggie nudged him and said, 'Shall we share a cab? You could drop me at the Savoy and then take it on to Claridge's.'

Cal demurred. He'd trust to the cabman's sense of geography. Reggie would tell him the Savoy was on the way to Claridge's even if it wasn't.

In the back of the cab as they crossed the Thames Reggie handed Cal a card with his name and the Savoy's address and telephone number on it and said, 'We've got tomorrow off. I suggest you get some rest, see a bit of the town and report to your blokes at the embassy on Monday. I'll see my chaps and give you a bell before noon.'

'My blokes?'

Reggie stuck his hand into his jacket pocket and brought out another of his many-folded bits of paper.

'A Major Shaeffer and a Colonel Reininger. D'ye know 'em?'

'I've met Shaeffer. On my last visit in '39. I've known Frank Reininger all my life. When I was a teenager he was based in Washington. My father sat on one of the House Defence Committees – Frank liaised. I guess you could call him my father's protégé. *E pluribus unum.*'

'Well he's the chap you report to.'

'Reggie – you could have told me that in Zurich.'

'Need to know, old boy, need to know. If Jerry had nabbed you, the less you knew the better.'

Cal was getting used to the jolts, the sudden reversals of tone and timbre – the instantaneous way the fact of war came home in a blunt sentence. Now, Reggie swung back the other way

'Uncle Sam does you proud doesn't he? Claridge's. Pretty damn swanky.'

'You're staying at the Savoy!'

'No, old boy. I'm *living* at the Savoy. And I'm paying for it. It's not the same thing at all.'

And back again.

'Had a nice little house in Chester Street, round the back of Buck House. Got blown to buggery just before Christmas.'

The cab swung off the Strand into the north forecourt of the Savoy. Reggie stepped out and took his bag from the front.

'Do you fancy a nightcap?' he said.

'Thanks Reggie, but I'd rather hit the sack.'

'Are you sure? You'll find a lot of your countrymen knocking about the place. I saw that newspaperman the other day – Quentin somebody or other. And wotsisname Knickerbocker. And Clare Booth Luce stays here too. You know, the woman from *Time*. Or is it *Life*?'

As if by magic, another cab disgorged Mrs Luce exactly as Reggie spoke her name. Cal saw him wave to her. She waved back. A smile. A glimpse of those familiar high cheekbones and too-prominent upper lip. That clinched it, if tiredness had not – the last thing Cal wanted was to while away an evening being Congressman Cormack's son once more for the benefit of the American press. He'd rather face a Panzer unit than the barbed tongue of Mrs Luce should it turn out that his father was currently out of favour with America's other First Lady. He told the cabbie to drive on and left Reggie lugging his bag, in search of porter, reporter and a stiff drink.

§ 11

Claridge's put Cal on the sixth floor – a large, comfortable room – table, chairs and a small sofa at one end, a big bed at the other, and its own bathroom. And all for four dollars a day. The window gave a good view of the western sky and, if the building opposite had been a tad lower, a better view across Grosvenor Square to Hyde Park. He could see a barrage balloon floating serenely over the square. Cal dumped his suitcase – in the absence of able-bodied bellhops (there'd been dozens last time, all in little red waistcoats, now all in khaki, he assumed) he'd lugged his own bags – and threw open a window. It was May 10th – it wasn't exactly summer, it wasn't even spring, it was plain chilly, but he wanted air, fresh and cool. There was a full moon in heaven tonight – he rather thought this was what the English meant by a bomber's moon. He'd no clear idea of what to expect in an air raid, but he found out soon enough.

He'd kicked off his shoes, thrown his jacket across the room and lain back on the bed. He was too tired to sleep, besides, the London air carried a whisper of anticipation on its wings. Forty-five minutes later he heard the wail of the air-raid sirens. He slipped on his jacket, grabbed his shoes and stepped into the corridor. He'd read about this. Wasn't this where everyone headed for the cellar until it was all over? Sang songs and drank sweet tea?

A maid was dashing along outside his door. He caught her.

'What happens now?' he said.

She stared at him. 'Sorry, sir, I don't follow . . .'

'I mean do we all get directed to the shelter?'

'Well . . . if you like . . . I can do that . . . but most people don't bother.'

'What do they do, then?'

'Well, sir, the women mostly put in earplugs and go to bed, and the men use it as an excuse to gather on the ground floor and play pontoon and drink half the night.'

Cal had no idea what to do now. He hadn't brought any earplugs and he'd never played pontoon.

'Is it safe up here?'

'God knows, sir. It's a modern building. Steel ribs an' all. But if Jerry's got your name on a bomb, well, goodnight Vienna. Look – you'll be as safe here as anywhere. Just don't use the lifts, eh? Takes an age to get people out of lifts if the electric goes off.'

She continued her dash and vanished down a rabbit hole. Cal put on his shoes and looked around for the stairs. It might at least make sense to find the shelter. He pushed open a swing door at the end of the corridor. The wallpaper and the wooden moulding vanished and he found himself in a shaft of concrete stairs, painted walls and steel railings, looking down the pit. He looked up. A glint of moonlight. There must be a door or a window up there. He climbed the stairs.

The door to the roof was open. He stepped out. A voice cried, 'Shut the goddam door! Don't want the whole goddam world to follow you up here, do you?'

A short, bald man sat on a folding canvas chair. A US Army greatcoat draped over his shoulders. Striped flannelette pyjamas and slippers peeking out from under it. On his shoulders two stars glinting in the light of the full moon. It was General Gelbroaster – General William Tecumseh Sherman Gelbroaster. In his mouth was an unlit cigar of a length to make Winston S. Churchill jealous, and across his knees a rifle of a length to make William F. Cody jealous.

Gelbroaster scanned the skies.

'You ever shoot buffalo, boy?'

'No, sir. A few ducks in the Ozarks. Nothing bigger than that.'

'I shot buffalo. When we had buffalo to shoot, that is. My daddy took me hunting with him the first time in '99. Nebraska. I was fourteen. Gave me this gun when I was sixteen.'

He paused, hoisted the gun and drew a bead on some imaginary object in the sky.

'How far up do you reckon these Nazis are?'

'I really don't know, sir. Ten thousand, maybe twenty thousand feet.'

Gelbroaster kept the gun tucked into his shoulder, his cheek along the stock, his finger delicately wrapped around the trigger.

'This gun'll fire a bullet more'n half a mile. What's that come to in feet?'

'About three thousand.'

Gelbroaster lowered the rifle.

'Damn. Damn damn damn!'

He looked straight at Cal for the first time.

'Have we met?'

'Yessir.'

'Washington?'

'Zurich, sir. Captain Cormack. Zurich consulate.'

'Cormack?' He looked Cal up and down. It felt to Cal like an inspection.

'You old Senator Cormack's grandson?'

'Yessir.'

That dated the general as far as Cal was concerned. A younger man, a man under fifty, would have been much more likely to ask if he were Congressman Cormack's son. His grandfather had retired in 1922.

'You new in town?'

'Got in less than two hours ago, sir. As a matter of fact, you sent for me.'

'I did? Well, I'm sure I had a reason.'

He chose not to remember the reason and scanned the night sky once more.

'Three thousand feet, you say? I'm never gonna get to hit one, am I?'

'Probably not.'

'Pity. In the last war I got three German biplanes over France. I was a young sharpshooter in those days. Took a shot at Von Richthofen, tore a piece out of his fuselage, but I couldn't bring him down.'

In the ear of the mind Cal heard Reggie's voice telling him to remember the *Lusitania*.

'Perhaps, sir, you should wait for the declaration of war?'

Gelbroaster considered this.

'That's a technicality, son. We haven't declared war, that's just a matter of time. But we're here. And there's a war on. Seems a mite unfriendly to our hosts not to lend a hand. If you're invited to a neighbour's house for dinner and the kitchen goes up in a whole mess of burning chicken fat, you help out with the buckets, don't you? Of course we could cut and run, like Joe Kennedy did. Moved his wife and kids out of London when the first bombs fell, got himself recalled at the first opportunity, and told all America that England was done for. Or we could stay and fight. Which is it to be? You a runner or a fighter?'

'I'm a fighter, sir. But as we've only the one gun between us I'd be happy to load for you.'

Gelbroaster rose up. Five foot eight inches of pure belligerence. No fool like an old fool. He pointed the gun skyward. Cal heard a whispered 'Geronimo' and then the boom of the gun ringing out like a hand-held howitzer.

'Sonsovbitches,' Gelbroaster said softly, and slipped the rifle into the crook of his arm. 'Glad to have you aboard, son,' he said to Cal, patted him on one shoulder and set off to the roof door.

The whine grew and grew. Cal had heard it the second the report of Gelbroaster's shot had died away. Still it grew. Stopped Gelbroaster in his tracks. He turned. They stared up. A German bomber bursting red and yellow flames – a billowing trail of black smoke – spiralling out of control, spinning down to earth some-where in the region of Hyde Park. Then a huge, woolly 'whumpff' as the plane and its unspent payload of bombs exploded.

Gelbroaster looked at the gun. Incredulity fading fast. Looked out at the orange glow on the western skyline where the plane had crashed.

'Maybe I'm younger'n I thought,' he said wistfully, then, lungs full and spirits rallied, he bellowed to the heavens, 'Root hog or die!'

Cal stayed. The bombers came in waves. He sat in Gelbroaster's chair and watched the *Blut und Eisen* version of July 4th light up the sky and shake the earth around him. Away in the south, London burnt fiercely. Closer to home he could see incendiaries bursting in buildings in the little streets of Mayfair, feel the weight of the nearmisses as high explosives crashed around him. He felt oddly free from fear. The rational part of his mind told him that the next bomb after a near miss could well be a direct hit, and while the hotel was a relatively sound structure, 'steel ribs an' all', he was in a most exposed position – and the rest of his mind overruled, in thrall to nothing more cerebral, nothing less visceral, than the thrill of it all.

Each part of the spectacle had its own colour. Ack-ack shells burst white in the night, little puffs of man-made cloud in an otherwise cloudless sky – and if they were close enough they showered shards of metal rain on to the streets below, adding atonal, clattering, tinkling music to the show. Tracer bullets fired by night-fighters shot across the sky, a dozen differing shades, like a pool rack dispersed by the cue ball, shooting red, shooting white, shooting green. Incendiaries burst blue and orange and then took on their hue from whatever they consumed. Oil and rubber burnt black. Wood burnt red and orange. And the searchlights roved like giant's fingers, crossing and criss-crossing and reminding him pointlessly of the opening of every Twentieth Century Fox movie he'd ever seen.

It was the English's own ack-ack drove him in. He watched a random pattern of shards hit the roof some thirty feet away, a hard rain, striking sparks, bouncing back, dancing like fireflies, racing towards him to stop only six or seven feet clear. He fell into bed in the small hours, curtains wide, to be woken by the light three hours later. For a moment he could not remember where he was. He had been dreaming of an Appalachian journey he had made with his father when he was ten, along the borders of Kentucky and the Carolinas, through the Cumberland Gap. He opened his eyes and could not place the cream walls and the chintzy furniture. Where were the knotty pine boards, the Shaker chairs? Then the smell focused him – cordite and burning, everything burning – paint, wood, rubber – and flakes of ash fluttering by his sixth-floor window. London burning.

He opened the windows and stretched out a hand. A wisp of ash landed on the palm of his hand, like catching an autumn leaf. It was paper, charred and weightless. The print still legible. The ghost of message and meaning. He blew gently on it as though on a dandelion head and watched it fragment to nothingness before his eyes, and as the tiny specks of grey wafted out over London he saw the city under a haze of ash, every breeze eddying by with the dust of a night's destruction, and over in the south the orange glow of sunrise. Sunrise? In the south-west? London burning.

He dressed quickly, skipped bathing and shaving, and went out. It was as though he had wandered into the art gallery of the half-waking mind. At seven-thirty on a Sunday morning London was a hive of activity, men in blue, men in khaki, backs bent to shovels and piles of debris, half in and half out of the half-houses, twisting and wriggling through the ruins, seeking out the trapped, the living, the dying and the dead – wires and pipes bursting from the ground like the spilt entrails of a gored beast, pools of water sitting motionless upon the tarmac, curls of grey smoke rising up into the spring sky from the brickfields of flattened buildings, engines of pumping, engines of rescue, engines of demolition, all the machinery of antiwar – and it was as though Bosch had met Breughel, Bosch had met and merged with Avercamp, in the limitless vista of the busy human landscape, the hurly-burly of a gruesome-beautiful urban-pastoral.

He drifted across Mayfair, down Half Moon Street, southwards, across Piccadilly and the Royal Parks, eastwards, and found himself an hour later upon one of the Thames bridges. The one by the Houses of Parliament that led to the big hospital on the southern bank. He could not remember its name, if he ever knew it.

Parliament had been hit. It was smouldering and smoking fiercely. He wondered what the English felt.

How would he feel if the Capitol had been blasted, the White House burnt? An Englishman told him. Just when he needed a native there was one ready to hand, drifting along the bridge from the opposite direction, pinstripe suit hastily pulled on over inch-stripe pyjamas – he could see the red and white flannelette sticking out from the cuffs, draped over sockless shoes like ludicrous spats. He too had neither washed nor shaved, and maybe not slept, he was eye-bleary and chin-fuzzy. He stared about him, another man in or out of the dream. He and Cal all but collided, back to back.

> This city now doth, like a garment, wear
> The beauty of the morning; silent, bare.
> Ships, towers, domes, theatres and temples lie
> Open to the fields and to the sky.

Cal took a stab at it. 'Byron?'

'Wordsworth. *Upon Westminster Bridge*. 1802. I don't think he meant "open to the sky" to sound quite so vulnerable as it does today, what?'

'I guess not,' Cal replied.

'You're an American?'

'I'm not wearing the uniform for fancy dress.'

'Eh? What? No. I mean, yes. Of course not. Sorry, there are so many uniforms in London these days. ARP, Home Guard, Heavy Rescue, Free French, Free Poles . . .'

'Free Americans?'

'Are you?'

'Just a joke,' said Cal.

'No but seriously, are you?'

'Am I what?'

'Here. I mean here to fight? "*Lafayette nous sommes ici*" and all that . . . whatever it was Pershing said?'

Cal was astounded by the question. Did he think America had quietly and unobtrusively declared war on

Germany? What answer did the man want? That he'd seen Gelbroaster unilaterally declare war only last night? That the rest of the nation might take a while to catch up with an old lunatic from Arkansas? Who would believe him? Or was he, a sockless civilian in jimjams, giving Cal, a man in uniform, the white feather? Was age – a man of fifty-five or so addressing a man of twenty-nine – was age the gulf between them, rather than nationality?

'I'm with the embassy,' he said, and knew it sounded like a cop-out, a truly lame remark.

'The embassy?'

He paused, looked about him.

'I see,' he said, with no sense arising in Cal that he saw anything but the devastation of the Mother of Parliaments that was bringing tears to the corner of each eye. He brushed them away and without looking at Cal said, 'You will excuse me, won't you,' and walked slowly back the way he had come, towards the great orange haze south of the Thames, the false dawn of conflagration. London burning.

§ 12

Reggie slept in on Sunday. He had no curiosity about the raid. Of course it had sounded like a big one, but when you've seen one you've seen them all. He had declined to take advantage of the Savoy's bomb-proof shelter, had bunged wax earplugs into his ears, several shots of malt whisky down his throat, and slept the sleep of the brave, oblivious to the booming guns and falling bombs. He awoke late, took breakfast in bed, soaked leisurely in his bath by cheating on the national bathwater limit and about noon felt ready for a stroll.

He headed for Chester Street, as he did once in every while, to gaze at the ruins of his house. He had bought the house in 1927 with the last of his inheritance. It was, in a way, his dream house, in that he had dreamt of such a house long before he was in a position to buy one – had dreamt about it when he was away from it, and dreamt about it now he had lost it. It fulfilled, and simultaneously thwarted, a persistent adolescent fantasy – that he would one day find the perfect place and somehow lose it – a bit like the lost domain of *Le Grand Meaulnes*. That his personal lost domain should turn out to be his own house was irony piled upon irony.

Now they were using it as an emergency water tank. Civil Defence had dug the rubble of the house out of the basement and flooded it. Of course, he still owned it. The site was his, and once the war was over he could rebuild. How do you rebuild a dream? This house had survived the imaginative flights and dire conformities of both his wives. Up on the first floor he could still make out the pattern of the wallpaper in his bedroom. His second wife had chosen it. It was such a pity. The Luftwaffe had managed to demolish his house and still the bitch's awful taste was left plastered to the wall for all to see.

'Reggie?' said a voice behind him.

It was his next-door neighbour, Clive Powell, a retired cavalry general from the last war. An old fool of the first order, a bow-legged believer in the efficacy of horse against tank who would not have been out of place at the charge of the Light Brigade. And he was wearing a uniform. What lunatic had taken him off the retired list?

'They brought me back, y'know. I'm in the Home Guard now.'

That explained part of it. The uniform was his old Great War cavalry khaki. His general's tabs removed and three captain's pips set in the epaulettes. Shoulder flashes, clumsily sewn on, spelt out Home Guard. Privately, Reggie thought the Home Guard the best place for men like Clive. They could still wear a uniform, they could prance around giving orders to men too old or, in a few cases, too young for the armed services, in the certain knowledge that they could do little harm. They were the front line in a battle that would never happen. The Battle of France had been a pasting for the British, the Battle of Britain the hard-fought, costly victory of the few. There would be no battle of London. All the same, he had to admire the old boy's modesty. Most generals would have held such a vast drop in rank to be an insufferable indignity and sat out the war in their clubs. Old Clive was doing his bit, at least.

'I've a platoon of railway clerks from Victoria station,' Clive went on. 'The odd porter, and a stoker, but mostly clerks. Just finished a morning's drilling. Absolutely bloody hopeless, but there you are. If the Hun ever make it to Victoria the worst they could do is sell 'em the wrong ticket. Send them to Penzance when they want to go to Preston.'

He broke into song.

'Oh, Mr Porter, what shall I do? Me Panzers are in Birmingham and me Führer's stuck in Crewe. Time for a cuppa, Reggie?'

Why not? thought Reggie. Humour the old bugger. After all, room by room the general-captain's house was identical to his own. All he had to do was sit with his cuppa, pretend to listen to the old boy's theories of how to win the war, mentally strip away the mounted heads of wildebeeste and gazelle, ignore the tigerskin rugs and the elephant's-foot umbrella stand, and paint onto those same rooms the colours of his dream.

An hour or so later, he had peeled off all his wife's excrescent wallpaper, redecorated in plain pastels and heard Clive's latest theory.

'Y'see,' Clive said, tipping the sugar bowl onto the tablecloth in order to draw an outline map of Europe with the thin end of his teaspoon, breaking up the last ginger biscuit on the plate and using its pieces to represent the capital cities. Rome, Paris, Berlin and Moscow dotted about on the sugar. There wasn't enough for London. Clive rummaged around in the biscuit barrel, prised out a gooey macaroon stuck to the bottom and plonked it down on England.

'First we take Italy from the Med, come up through the flabby gut of the Continent, knock her right out of the war.'

A silver teaspoon shot up Italy from the toe with all the savagery of a steel bayonet. Reggie ate Rome.

'We delay any invasion of France until the Russians are on board and winning.'

Reggie ate Moscow. He'd always wanted to do that.

'Then we land a vast seaborne invasion just where Jerry doesn't expect it – somewhere like . . . I dunno . . . Normandy . . .'

A row of determined cake forks hit the sugar near Caen. Reggie ate Paris.

'Then we catch the buggers in a pincer movement between the British and the Russian advances . . .'

The salt and pepper pots advanced across Europe like great silver tanks. Reggie ate Berlin.

'And that's exactly what would have happened in the last war if the Bolsheviks hadn't surrendered – could be we end up racing for Berlin. Of course, the Americans would be jolly useful if . . .'

Clive waved a hand in the air demonstrating an all too obvious conclusion. Reggie eyed London, the last biscuit on the map. That tantalising crispness, that elusive hint of almonds. Clive ended his gesture with his hand flat on top of it. He wolfed the macaroon before Reggie could make his move.

'Well? Whaddya think?'

Reggie made a mental note never to mention any of

this to anyone in case they thought him as cracked as he thought old Clive to be.

'Wizard,' he said, and brought a smile to the old man's lips. Pity about the macaroon, he thought.

Reggie waved bye-bye to Clive and drifted all afternoon. If he ever had to account for his movements that day he could probably have done no better than 'here and there'. He picked his way through the splendour and devastation of London and found himself oddly unmoved by either. When, he thought, you've seen your own house knocked off the face of the planet, you tend to take a bit of bombing in your stride. By six o'clock he was sorely in need of a wee dram and discovered that by pure chance his feet had led him to Pall Mall and to the steps of Pogue's – a gentlemen's club of which, again by pure chance, he happened to be a member.

As he went up the steps he bumped into his brother-in-law, Archie Duncan Ross, the elder brother of the first Mrs Ruthven-Greene, coming down.

'Archie, I was just going in for a snifter.'

Ross was shaking his head sadly.

'Complete washout, old boy – the Hun put one right through the roof, through five ceilings and into the wine cellar last night.'

'The swine! My God, the 1912 Margaux!'

'Broken glass and red puddles, I'm afraid. But there is good news.'

Reggie felt there could never be good news again. The 1912 Margaux – good God, the Nazis were ruthless. First his house, now the finest drop of claret in the city.

'I hear,' said Ross, 'That there is Krug '20 to be had at the Dorchester.'

Champagne always gave Reggie insomnia. Hence he had lived much of his adult life with insomnia. If it had ever crossed his mind that there was cause and effect operating between the two, then he might well have regarded it as a poor choice. Between booze and no booze, no booze was on a hiding to nothing. He had long ago learnt to while away the hours with a good book or, failing the availability of a good book, any book, preferably taken with a light snack and a cup of cocoa. His chosen snack was one of his favourites – cheddar cheese with Kep sauce. His chosen book was *The Flying Visit* by this chap Peter Fleming. He had been given the book by the author's brother, Ian Fleming – a colleague in the spook trade (Navy, mind, arrogant shits the lot of 'em, senior service as they always managed to remind you), and he had to admit, it was a bit of a hoot. You see, Hitler gets it into his head to fly over to Britain and bale out . . .

Reggie slept. Reggie dreamt.

He was in the middle of a large field. He was sitting behind the wood and glass partition of a railway-station booking office gazing out upon a railway designed very much after the fashion of Heath Robinson, involving a lot of gear wheels of varying size, a few hydrogen-filled balloons, several sets of bellows and an awful lot of much-knotted string – indeed, string seemed to be far and away the most common material in this technology. The single-line tracks stretched away to meet at infinity. A line of washing hung between the signals, a lazy Jersey cow munched grass between the tracks, a painted brown and white sign read 'God's Wonderful Railway' and was everywhere abbreviated GWR – it was even woven as a crest into his uniform, stamped in gold leaf on his pencil, wrought in iron into the legs of the platform benches, passengers for the use of. And high above it all a lone figure, gesticulating wildly, descended on a parachute. He landed with a bump on the wooden platform, his chute wrapped around the down signal, his backside flat on the planks and his legs splayed in front of him. He looked around him – the cow approached and proceeded to eat his hat. Then he noticed Reggie. Reggie couldn't help the feeling that they'd met somewhere before. Little moustache, bit like Charlie Chaplin, piggy little eyes and a great cowlick of hair across the forehead.

'*Eigentlich wollte ich nach Birmingham, aber Sie haben mich nach Crewe geschickt.*'

Reggie struggled with this. His dream-German was so rusty.

'Sorry old chap. Could you say that again a bit slower? Y'know, *langsamer.*'

The little man sloughed off the parachute, came across the platform and banged on the glass. For a foreigner he certainly knew a thing or two about complaining.

'*Dumkopf!*'

Well, that needed no translation.

'*Eigentlich wollte ich nach Birmingham, aber Sie haben mich nach Crewe geschickt!*' he said painfully slowly, and just as painfully and slowly Reggie worked it out.

'I wanted to go to Birmingham and they sent me on to Crewe.' Crewe? Where did the fool think he was?

'GWR, old chap. Exeter and all stations west. You know, Cornish Riviera Express. Torbay, Plymouth, the Saltash bridge – all the way to Penzance. Can't get to Crewe from here. You want the Somerset and Dorset Joint Railway to Evercreech Junction or Shepton Mallet. You'd have to change at –'

A fist crashed down on the counter.

'*Trottel!*' – which Reggie vaguely thought might mean 'idiot'.

Then the gun came out and the irate visitor banged off shots in all directions. Reggie ducked. The wall behind him splintered. The little man plugged a fat bloke capering across a beach on a railway poster bearing the cheery slogan 'Skegness Can Be So Bracing'. Reggie silently wished he was in Skegness right now, bracing or not. He felt no pain but wondered if he'd been hit when a ringing started in his ears. A persistent ringing that just would not stop.

Reggie woke. A creamy white telephone on the bedside table jumped about as though it had swallowed a Mexican bean. Reggie picked it up, ready to slam it down if it was Hitler calling.

'Reggie?'

This bloke certainly didn't sound German.

'Yes,' said Reggie.

'It's me. Charlie.'

Charlie? Charlie Leigh-Hunt – Reggie's right-hand man and a captain in the Irish Guards.

'Reggie? Are you all right?'

'Of course. I . . . I was just . . . sleeping.'

'Look. There's a flap on. I'm in the foyer downstairs. I'm coming up right away.'

'A flap?'

Reggie looked around. The room regained its old familiarity. There were his trousers hanging off the back of a chair by his braces. He knew where he was again. Imagine the disturbing effect if you woke up and spotted another bloke's braces. Didn't bear thinking about.

'A flap? Coming up? What's the matter? Hitler not landed in person, has he?'

'Oh God, you've already heard.' Charlie hung up. Reggie sat clutching the phone no longer quite able to say what was dream and what reality.

Reggie flung on his dressing gown and paced the floor. The minutes could not pass quickly enough before

Charlie knocked upon his door. He flung the door wide, the question bursting from his lips.

'Hitler's here? Where?'

Charlie kicked the door to.

'Not so loud. Do you want everyone to hear?'

'For God's sake, Charlie – just tell me!'

'It isn't Hitler, it's Hess.'

'Hess?'

'Deputy Führer Rudolf Hess. He took off from Germany late on Saturday in a Messerschmitt and baled out over Scotland around midnight. He was picked up at once and – you won't believe this – he asked for the Duke of Hamilton.'

'Hamilton? Hess? Picked up? By whom?'

'The Home Guard.'

Reggie was only seconds away from forswearing champagne for ever. He'd certainly think twice before finishing the day with a cheese sandwich again.

'The Home Guard? The Home bloody Guard?! What did they do?'

'Well . . . they sent for Hamilton actually.'

'I don't believe it. I do not bloody believe it!'

'You'd better. It's completely pukkah. And you'd better get dressed too. It's past nine and McKendrick wants to see us in thirty minutes. He sent me over to get you. He doesn't trust the phone at all where this is concerned.'

McKendrick was Gordon McKendrick, an Argyll and Sutherland Brigadier in a plain-clothes world where rank was all but invisible next to power – Reggie and Charlie answered to McKendrick, McKendrick answered to Churchill.

It was a fifteen-minute walk to McKendrick's office in Broadway – all the same they took a cab, across Trafalgar Square, along the bottom end of St James' Park and up Birdcage Walk into that corner of London that was inescapably Royal, military and, occasionally, secret. Palaces, barracks and spooks. Reggie sat in the back still fiddling with his collar studs and cufflinks, and still muttering, 'I don't bloody believe it', more to himself than to Charlie.

McKendrick looked as though he had lost a night's sleep – while Reggie had slept and snored and dreamed, Gordon had worked – his eyes watery, his little white moustache looking droopy, every vein in his large hands standing out as he locked them together on his desk. He spoke quietly in his soft Highland accent, as though he were trying not to wake someone in the next room. But that was Gordon's manner – he had long seemed to Reggie to subscribe to Teddy Roosevelt's dictum 'speak softly and carry a big stick.'

'It turns out that Hamilton had met Hess at some do or other in Germany. He's positive the man is Rudolf Hess, not some imposter or *doppelgänger*. And he is, to put it mildly, somewhat annoyed that Hess should think he'd have any pro-Nazi sympathies whatsoever. He got through to the Foreign Office yesterday afternoon. So happens the Prime Minister's Private Secretary Jock Colville was there at the time. The FO put Hamilton onto Jock, and Jock relayed the message straight to the PM down in Dytchley. I gather the PM was rather cool about the whole matter. Told Jock to get Hamilton flown down as soon as possible and he'd see him there. In the meantime he'd got a new Marx Brothers film he wanted to watch, and he wasn't going to let any Hess, real or fake, make him miss it.'

'Oh really,' said Reggie. 'They're awfully good. Is there a new one?'

McKendrick unlocked his hands, pinched the bridge of his nose, closed his eyes and ignored the question.

'Hamilton and the PM are on their way up to London now. Later today the Foreign Office are sending Ivone

Kirkpatrick up to Scotland to interrogate Hess. Kirkpatrick also met him in Berlin, so he can further identify Hess or not as the case may be. Hamilton'll go with him. This is where you two come in. You're to follow Kirkpatrick and watch. Do not tread on the FO's toes, just listen to everything that's said and be ready to step in when they get nowhere. Personally I think Hess will run circles round them, and the PM is of like mind. However protocol is being observed. We will give them their chance. But be ready – think of yourselves as . . . the watchers. Better still, the guardians. We'll use "guardians" as your codename if necessary. Hess is "Mr Briggs" from now on. Be ready by seven o'clock, a car will pick you up at your hotel and drive you out to Hendon aerodrome for the flight to Scotland. Now – any questions?'

Reggie always had questions.

'Wouldn't Five normally handle something like this?'

'Don't ask me about lines of demarcation. I couldn't honestly care less. The PM wants us to do it. Although I hesitate to tell you this, he asked specifically for you.'

Reggie hoped he wasn't blushing with pride.

'Where are we going exactly?'

'Buchanan Castle on Loch Lomond.'

'I see,' said Reggie. 'You tak the high road and I'll tak the low road.'

McKendrick pinched the bridge of his nose again and seemed infinitely weary.

'No jokes, Reggie. Please.'

'Are we listening out for anything in particular?'

'Yes.'

'Well – could you sort of give us a hint?'

'The Prime Minister has asked for confirmation of material gained from certain sources.'

This might as well have been gobbledegook as far as Reggie was concerned.

'Confirmation of what, sir?'

'Can't tell you that.'

'Well – what sources are we to confirm?'

'Can't tell you that either. Reggie, stop asking me damn fool questions and keep your ears pinned back. Report everything to me. If Hess confirms we'll have no difficulty spotting it. Now. Clear your desks, the both of you. Tie up any loose ends and be at the Savoy at seven.'

'On the matter of loose ends – what about my American?'

'What American?'

'Cormack – the chap General Gelbroaster put us on to. You know, the chap who worked Wolfgang Stahl?'

'What about him?'

'Well – we're supposed to be looking for Stahl right now.'

'Do we even know Stahl is in London?'

'No, but . . .'

'No buts, Reggie. This is the big one. Forget Stahl. Just concentrate on the job in hand.'

Out in the corridor Charlie said, 'Bit of a coincidence Jock Colville being at the FO just as Hamilton calls in with the news of Hess, don't you think?'

'No,' Reggie replied. 'I don't think. In fact, my fifteen years in the job has taught me that it pays to believe six impossible things before breakfast. Try it for half an hour a day. Begin with one impossible thing, Jock at the FO will do for starters, then work up to six.'

§ 14

On the same Monday morning Cal reported to the Embassy, a short walk from his hotel, just around the corner on the eastern side of Grosvenor Square. It had changed much since he was last there. It was changing as he watched. Teams of carpenters moved in and out with pre-fabricated partitions, carving larger rooms into smaller ones, desks were wheeled in and out on trolleys, metal chairs carried in in stacks. A face he knew met him – Captain Henry Berg. They'd been through West Point together, risen rank for rank together, and never found enough common ground to like one another. Berg was a born desk man. Cal nurtured secret dreams that, bifocal eyeglasses notwithstanding, he might be a man of action as well as a man of analysis. Even as Berg spoke the carpenters were erecting a new office around him.

'You gonna be here long?'

'I really don't know, Henry.'

'The colonel's asked for you to have a desk in here. Take the one by the wall. It's a pity we have to share, but as you can see, things are really hotting up. The staff has doubled since Christmas.'

Cal could see that. He didn't recognise half the faces that had passed in front of him. And he couldn't escape the sound of pique in Henry's voice as he used the word 'share'.

'I've got you an In-tray and an Out-tray. I've issued a request for a Pending, but really nothing should be pending long enough for you to need it.'

Cal stopped listening. Any minute now Berg would show him how the pencil sharpener worked and give him a key to the executive washroom. He wondered if this hive of activity spelt out the same message to Berg as it did to him – a nation gearing up for war.

'Can I use the phone, Henry?'

Berg pushed the telephone across the desk to him. Cal rang the Savoy and was told that Colonel Ruthven-Greene had already gone out. They didn't know when he'd be back. Odd, thought Cal, he'd've expected Reggie to be raring to start.

He found himself staring into nothing across the bent

back of a workman, busy hanging the door. Then the figure on the other side came into focus. A tall, gangly, middle-aged man. Frank Reininger.

Reininger grabbed his hand and shook it vigorously. Only Berg's presence saved him from the usual bear hug.

'Good to see you, Calvin. Henry here showing you around?'

'Yes sir – big changes, I see.'

'You're well? And your daddy?'

Reininger and his father went back a long way. Frank had always been a little blind to the tensions between father and son.

'Oh, he's fine,' Cal lied, without a clue as to his father's well-being.

'Come into my office. This isn't really my show. Deke Shaeffer just wants a quick word. He's in charge of security now – did I tell you that?'

Reininger steered Cal into another, far less makeshift room. FDR's portrait on the back wall, Woodrow Wilson and Teddy Roosevelt on the sides. Major Shaeffer sat behind an expensive, imported, antique desk. Reininger had paid for it to be shipped from Paris. It went where he went. Plywood was strictly for the other ranks.

Cal had never known Frank to be anything but the soul of bonhomie – but he'd never known Deke Shaeffer to smile and mean it. They were like chalk and cheese, a garrulous, thin man and a surly oaf built like Tarzan of the apes, but everybody said they were a first-class team.

'I just want to spell out the security implications of what you're doing,' Shaeffer said. 'And don't volunteer anything just because the pleasure of the chat carries you away. The general's playing this one close to his chest. All we've been told is that you're being loaned to the British. If the General sees fit not to tell us why, that's fine by me. Got it?'

65

This was obtuse in the extreme. They both knew what Cal did. He ran the Tin Man, whoever he was. He doubted it was true of Frank – but Shaeffer was putting official distance between himself and Cal.

'I'll put it as plainly as I can. I don't want any incidents.'

Cal looked at Reininger, but Reininger said nothing. 'Incidents?'

'Any incident. Especially as in "diplomatic incident".'

'Diplomatic incident? Major, the British asked, dammit, escorted me here. What could they possibly construe as a diplomatic incident?'

'I wasn't thinking of the British,' Shaeffer said. 'They're not the only ones in this war. And until we're in it, whatever the reality, let's at least have it look like we're neutral. You get yourself in trouble Captain and you're on your own. Capiche?'

'Absolutely,' Cal said. 'I capiche.'

Shaeffer flickered up a phoney smile, the merest flash of pearly teeth, got up and left – the audience, which was what it felt like to Cal, was clearly over. Reininger stayed. Got up, stretched, and sat himself down in the chair Shaeffer had vacated.

'He can't mean that, sir. He can't possibly mean that?'

Reininger sighed, a sigh meant to sound knowing and worldly.

'Calvin, I've known you since you were a boy. Behind closed doors I'm Frank. You don't have to call me sir or Colonel. And yes – Deke means exactly what he said. You're going to have to be very, very careful.'

'Sir . . . Frank . . . I find it very hard to believe that anyone in this embassy or the War Department in Washington seriously gives a damn what opinion in Berlin thinks of what we're doing. If they did, then perhaps we shouldn't be spying on them in the first place?'

'Well . . . that's just Deke's way. The guy's a frustrated diplomat at heart. But you're wrong all the same. What we do here matters mightily back in Washington. Not in the WD maybe, but up on the hill. Calvin, you just ask your daddy.'

Cal knew Reininger was right – every letter from the old man told him that – but the remark rankled.

'These days I tend not to ask my father quite as much as I used to.'

Reininger grinned.

'We all grow up. Eventually. And – you should understand this. Deke has a way of overstating things, but the embassy's been through turmoil since you were last here. We've had a clerk busted by the British for spying – I can't emphasise too strongly the effect of Tyler Kent's arrest on Anglo-Am relations. It was a transatlantic disaster. And we've had an ambassador practically demand to be recalled – and a new man appointed who's something of an unknown quantity. And on top of that – and strictly between the two of us – we have the General. Bright as a button and ornery as a jackass. Gelbroaster hates Joe Kennedy. And he doesn't care who knows it . . . if Kennedy hadn't gone back home I hate to think what might have blown up between the two of them.'

'I know,' said Cal. 'He told me.'

'You've seen him already?'

'At the hotel on Saturday night. Just sort of bumped into him.'

'Then you don't need me to tell you – as far as Gelbroaster's concerned we're already at war. Don't be misled by that. It's his policy – it can't be American policy. Right now, from now until the day FDR goes to Congress and asks to declare war . . . we are neutral and we act neutral. Which kind of brings me to the point. Calvin, you can't do this in uniform.'

Cal was nonplussed. From the global to the downright trivial in three sentences.

'I don't have anything else. They left me no time to pack. I've the uniform, a spare pair of pants and the usual stuff.'

Reininger stood up again. Stuck his left hand in his inside pocket.

'That's easily fixed,' he said. 'Take these and go to a fifty-shilling tailor.'

Cal took a small bundle of printed paper strips from him.

'What are they?'

'Clothing coupons. Should be enough there for a suit. Can't get one without 'em. Everything's rationed now. Try Soho – one of those narrow little streets the other side of Regent Street. If there's one shop there doing suits at ten bucks apiece there must be a hundred.'

§ 15

Across Regent Street at Mappin and Webb's jeweller's, down a dark alley – London had more than its fair share of those – along the side of a mock-gothic Victorian church and Cal emerged into a narrow Soho street of the kind he thought Reininger had meant. A couple of turns later and he stood in an alley off Carnaby Street facing the green, peeling shopfront of a fifty-shilling tailor. Above the door in faded gold lettering . . .

Lazarus & Moses Lippschitz Bespoke Tailors
by app't to
His Highness Duke Griswald of Transylvania
est 1891

and in the window in crayon on cardboard . . .

50/- a suit – You vant it ve gottit!

He pushed at the door. The pressure of his foot on the rubber mat triggered a bell somewhere in the deep recesses of the shop. Cal stood amid roll upon roll of dull, male-coloured cloth – the un-peacock hues of black, brown and grey, and the scarcely enlivening dark blue – the stripes of chalk and oxblood. Still the bell rang. Persistent to the point of annoyance. He stepped back onto the mat to see if a second step undid the effect of the first and out of nowhere a short, old, white-haired man in a yarmulke appeared at the speed of sound, pressed a button by the counter and the ringing stopped. The man smiled a small, fleeting, professional smile and looked over his shoulder.

'Mo! Mo! *Shmegege*. The Yanks have landed! *Mach schnell*!'

He turned back to Cal. Looked Cal up and down, measuring him with the eye as only tailors and undertakers could do. Cal looked back. A tiny man, less than five foot four – the yarmulke held on to his thinning hair with kirby grips, a rim of close-cropped white beard, a tape measure slung around his neck, a grubby waistcoat on top of a threadbare cardigan, pins stuck in all over it and chalk dust smeared at the rims of its pockets.

'Mo! Mo! *Mach schnell*, you *momzer*!'

Another man, identical in every respect to the first, scurried out from the back room. Eyed him up and down in the same way.

'Vot? Just the one? You said Yanks. All I see is one Yank. Vot use you tink is one Yank?'

'How should I know? All I said was come see. We gottem Yank. It could be 1917 all over again.'

The second tailor fixed Cal with one squinting eye, looking up at him.

'And how many you boys are over here?'

'I don't know, a few dozen I guess.'

'A few dozen! My Gott. Last time they sent whole regiments! How you expect to lick Hitler with just a few dozen?'

Cal did not want to say it. He was getting heartily sick of stating the obvious, but he said it all the same. 'We're not actually in the war, you know.'

'Not in the war! Young man, everybody is in this war! You tink Hitler will stop at Irish Sea? You tink crazy Adolf stop at Atlantic Ocean? You tink the brownshirts turn around when they see Statue of Liberty? Scared off by big green woman mit the torch an' the silly hat? Alla them Jews in Brooklyn – you tink the Nazis just gonna let 'em be?'

'Mo, Mo. Leave the boy be,' said the first tailor. 'Maybe he not here to invade France, maybe just want to buy a suit.'

'So? Am I arguin'? I was only askin'.'

'That's right,' said Cal, getting a word in edgeways.

'Vot's right? You here to invade France?'

'No, I'd like to buy a suit.'

'You want suit?'

'If that's at all possible,' Cal said.

'Gentleman wants suit!' the first brother all but yelled in the other brother's ear.

'A suit you say? He wants suit?'

And then to Cal. 'You want suit? You got coupons?'

Cal dug around in his pockets and found the clothing coupons Reininger had given him. Mo took them and riffled through them like a cardsharp, a glint of commerce in his eye.

'Larry, the gentleman got coupons!'

Mo? Larry? Cal was beginning to find something chillingly familiar in this routine. There'd better not be a third brother.

'Well, young man. You got coupons, the world is your

oyster an' we gottem pearls. Vot kind of suit you was wanting?'

Cal looked at the bewildering mass of rolls. One of the reasons he liked a uniform was that it saved a lot of decisions.

'Er ... what colour's in this year?'

'In?' said Mo. 'He wants to know vot is in. Khaki is in this year, that's vot's in!'

'Khaki I got,' said Cal.

Larry fingered the fabric of his battledress.

'Khaki? I call it sea green mit a dash of chestnut – nice schmutter though. I think you look good in blue.'

'Blue,' said Mo, 'with the double breasteds ...'

'And a nice pinstripe in pale grey,' added Larry. 'You look like a million dollars.'

'Blue and grey?' Cal queried.

'Grey and blue,' they answered, 'Blue and grey ...' A head shook, another nodded, a hand equivocated in the air to express balance – six of one, half a dozen of the other.

'OK.'

One tackled his buttons, the other zipped around behind him and they pulled off his battledress and flourished their tape measures.

'Mit this measure I fitted out Duke Griswald mit his burial outfit in 1888,' said Mo. Then Larry took up the tale and they alternated line for line in worst vaudeville.

'Finest suit we ever make.'

'Then the following year comes the pogrom, so we pack up the shop and come to England.'

'You know vot – not one single royal customer do we get.'

'We, who made suits for the Dukes of Transylvania!'

'The Prince of Wales – votta snappy dresser.'

'Does he come to us?'

'Does he bollocks!'

'So, I measure you mit the same measure I use on royalty!'

Cal tried to feel honoured and failed. 1888 was more than a lifetime away, Transylvania a nation that had ceased, if it ever had existed, to exist.

They both measured him. Two tapes around his chest.

'Forty,' said Mo.

'Thirty-eight,' said Larry, and each noted down his own figure.

Inside leg.

'Thirty-six.'

'Thirty-four.'

Waist.

'Thirty.'

'Thirty-two.'

And so it went on. When they'd finished on his sleeves Cal asked the obvious question.

'Do you guys have a method?'

'Method, schmethod. Sure we gotta method, we split the difference.'

Cal felt a slight frisson of misgiving. He could walk out of the shop now. He could walk right out and never look back.

'Could I get some shoes too?' he asked.

'Shoes? Next door is shoes. Isaac Horwitz. He sell you nice pair of shoes. You got shoe coupons?'

'No. Do I need shoe coupons?'

'These days you need coupon to blow nose or break wind. No coupon, no shoes.'

Cal looked down at his army-issue, brown roundies.

'Is no problem,' said the brothers.

'Nize blue suit.'

'Nize brown shoes.'

'Poifect!'

Somehow, Cal could not quite believe them, but it was

too late now. Besides, who ever looked at your feet? He slipped his battledress back on.

'When can I pick it up?'

'You come by Friday,' Mo said. 'We have it all ready for you.'

'Could you manage it any sooner?'

'For Uncle Sam and his dozen brave buddies,' Larry added, 'we make it Thursday.'

'Thanks,' said Cal, glad another English moment had passed, even if this was the Transylvanian version translated loosely from the Yiddish.

Mo scribbled down his address as he dictated it, but in the end Cal could not resist the nagging question.

'Mo, Larry? Where,' he asked, 'is Curly?'

Back home there would have been two possible reactions to this. The good-natured would smile or laugh, the sourpusses would tell you pointedly that this was the hundredth time they'd heard that joke this week, day or hour. The Lippschitz brothers looked at each other, more than slightly baffled, then they looked at him, then they looked at each other and shrugged, then they both yelled 'Curly!'

And from the back room a gangly, spindly youth of fifteen or so, plastered with acne, beardless but ringletted about the ears, appeared pushing a broom.

'Yeah, yeah, yeah. Don't get yer knickers in a twist. Now, wossamatter wiv you two?'

'Gentleman wants to see you.'

In the mind's ear Cal heard a wooden mallet bashing against the side of a skull with a hollow report.

'Thursday it is,' he said, and ran for it.

§ 16

The front desk at the Savoy handed Reggie half a dozen messages. All the same. 'Captain Cormack called – please call back.'

Up in his room the telephone was ringing.

'Reggie – where in hell have you been? I've been calling you all day.'

'Something came up. I'm afraid we may have to delay our little adventure for a while.'

'What?'

'Something rather important.'

'Reggie, what's up?'

'I can't tell you that, really I can't.'

'I know. You told me – we're not allies yet.'

§ 17

Walter Stilton was making his report to Thesiger. Thesiger had come up to town and phoned him in person from his hotel.

'Our Dutchman's in digs in Hoxton Lane. He's signed on at the local Labour Exchange. Gave his trade as printer and got a short lecture about the paper shortage and nobody needing printers any more. He's registered with the local nick, and he seems to know absolutely nobody in London. He spent yesterday afternoon in a café reading the small ads in the local newspaper.'

'Did you get a copy? Coded messages?'

'No sir – he was putting rings round items in the sits vac column.'

'He'll break cover. Sooner or later.'

'I'm quite sure he will sir, but in the meantime there is something useful I could be doing.'

'Which is?'

'Hess, sir.'

'My God, word travels fast. Is there anyone in England who doesn't know?'

'The Branch, sir – not England. We do get to hear things in the Branch. There'll be a team of our blokes going up to Scotland to interrogate Hess. I'd like to be one of them, sir.'

Stilton could hear Thesiger sigh. He had known even as he said it that it was an absurd request.

'If I could do this for you I would. If it were a matter of recommendations, you'd get mine. But I don't have the authority to assign you to that, really I don't. I don't even have the authority to forward your request. All I can say is if they wanted you . . . well . . . they'd have sent for you, wouldn't they?'

§ 18

Reggie called McKendrick from his room. One last try. Would Gordon even talk to him on an unscrambled line?

'I can't just dump the fellow, now we've got him here.'

'We don't need him. Briggs changes everything. This bloke your American knows is a sprat. We've got the kingfish now. The PM's told us to get Briggs to talk.'

'All the same, we can't just leave Jerry wandering around London – even if he is on our side.'

'I rather think you're going to have to, Reggie.'

McKendrick rang off. It was still only six o'clock. They had an hour before their driver was due. Reggie decided to nip down to the bar, and pass the hour over a drink with Charlie.

After his second whisky he could not but muse out loud.

'I mean, I can't just dump the fellow, can I?'

'Doesn't seem fair,' said Charlie, pandering.

'That's what the old man doesn't grasp – "fairness". Everything is contingent to Gordon.'

'I rather think that's the nature of war, total contingency,' said Charlie. 'However, I've an idea. There's Orlando Thesiger over by the bar . . .'

'Is he? Where?'

'Two tables to the left, chatting to Margot Asquith.'

Reggie strained his eyes. He could just make out the languid figure of Thesiger sprawled in a bucket chair, long legs crossed, knees jutting, head nodding gently, in perfect listening mode – listening to something old Margot was telling him, smiling, then laughing. She was known for her wit. She'd been outrageous since long before he or Thesiger were born.

'OK. I see him now. What's your point?'

'Well, before I got moved to Six, I had four months working for Orlando just after the fall of France. He spends his time quizzing suspected spies out at Burnham-on-Crouch. They fish them out of the water and Orlando has to decide whether they're kosher or not. They come across in rowing boats, on rafts and God knows what. Most of them are completely innocent, but every so often the Germans try and slip one through. As well as chaps like me, Orlando's got a bunch of Special Branch coppers working under him – they do the surveillance, arrests, all the legwork, that sort of thing. He must have someone who can look after your Yank. Show him around London, take him to all the likely places.'

'A German speaker would be useful.'

'A German speaker in the Met? You'll be lucky. Most of 'em hardly speak English!'

Reggie got to his feet.

'Well, I suppose it's worth a try. Do you think you're

76

up to entertaining the Countess while I buttonhole him?'

'Dunno,' said Charlie, 'but I've always wanted to try.'

§ 19

Thesiger caught Stilton the next day, just as he was leaving Scotland Yard. Hat and coat on, out of the door and halfway down the corridor when a constable called him back to the telephone.

'Do you still want a chance to use your German?' Thesiger asked.

'Hess . . . ?'

''Fraid not. But there's an American who needs your services. He's been brought in from somewhere or other, based at the embassy, and I gather they've given him a room at Claridge's. Name of Cormack. First name Calvin. A captain.'

'An American. I don't . . .'

'I can't tell you any more. In fact it isn't my show. It isn't even Five. You'll report to Colonel Ruthven-Greene at Six. You'd better get in touch with him straight away. Trust me. It's big. Bigger than anything you've done for me. It matters. And you'll be on the trail of a real live Jerry of your own.'

'A Jerry?'

'Yes, a wild card. A loose cannon, from what I can gather. Now, about our Dutchman, Smulders.'

'He's been up West a couple of times. Once to a printing house in Covent Garden. Didn't get the job.'

Stilton stopped. He'd said a word too much already. He hoped Thesiger would just accept it all at face value and ring off. Thesiger was not the sort of man to let a casual remark have a casual escape.

'A couple of times, you said?'

'One or two, aye.'

'You lost him. Is that what you're saying?'

It had been one of Stilton's constables, but it was a pathetic Chief Inspector who blamed his men. He'd bollocked the constable. If Thesiger now wanted to bollock him he'd just have to take it.

'Last night, as it happens. Just north of Oxford Street, close by the Marquis of Lincoln. Pitch dark in the blackout. Couldn't be helped. He was home before midnight. No harm done.'

'Walter, I don't want to make obstacles for you, but if you take on the American are you sure you can still handle Smulders?'

When Thesiger called him Walter it was usually a preface to him being put on a spot.

'It won't happen again, sir. We'll be watching him day and night.'

§ 20

Frederick Troy had arrived at Church Row, Hampstead, for an early dinner with his parents. His mother had insisted. They were so rarely in town these days, and Troy so rarely found his way out to Mimram, the country home in Hertfordshire, that she had taken to nagging him. Particularly if his brother Rod was on leave.

'How else am I ever to see my family all together?' she asked pointlessly. And once in a while it worked. Troy would have a day off that coincided with Rod's leave, and their sisters, the twins, Maria and Alexandra, would be whipped in from their conjugal homes.

'Dinner will be a little late,' said his mother as he kicked the front door shut and hung up his coat. He dutifully pecked her on the cheek – she stood, shorter than he, poised for the gesture as of right – before she finished what she had to say.

'Your father and Rod are in the study. We have a visitor.'

'Who?' Troy asked her vanishing back.

'You'll see.'

She was full of phrases like that. She was not past saying to a man of twenty-five, and at that a Scotland Yard detective, that if he asked no questions he'd be told no lies.

Troy looked in through the open study door. Rod was perched on the edge of a sagging, tatty armchair, an eager, argumentative look on his face. Troy knew that look. The keenness of argument, the triumph of intellect over adversity could lead him to a single-minded honesty that knew no tact. His father was behind his desk. Another blue notepad in front of him. A pencil behind one ear and a pile of balled blue pages tumbling forth from the upturned wastepaper basket. Today he had shaved. Today he had dressed. A stout man sat on the chesterfield with his back to Troy. All Troy could see of him was a thinning pate and the broad expanse of back in its brown striped jacket.

'No,' said Rod.

'No,' said his father, and then he noticed Troy.

'Freddie,' he beckoned him closer. 'You know Bert, do you not?'

Troy moved tentatively into the room – if they were arguing about Russia again, he was just going to leg it and leave them to stew – and the stout body turned to look at him. A round, ruddy face, a small moustache, beady eyes. It was Wells. Herbert George Wells. HG to the world, Bert to his friends.

'I was just saying,' he began in a high, strained, middling-posh English voice, 'who was it uttered the platitude about Russia – about the Soviet Union?'

'Which platitude?' said Troy. 'There've been so many.'

His father smiled at this. Rod didn't. Wells looked plainly puzzled.

'I meant,' he continued, 'the one about "I have seen the future and it works".'

'Don't say Shaw,' Rod chipped in. 'We've done Shaw.'

'I thought it was you,' said Troy.

'Me? Surely I'd remember if I'd said it myself!'

'Wasn't it in *The Shape of Things to Come*?' Troy persisted.

'No it wasn't!' said Wells, and Troy could see him reddening into annoyance. Wells could be such a crosspatch.

'You've said so much, Bert,' Alex said. 'Who could blame you if you forget?'

'I didn't forget it. I never bloody said it in the first place!'

Rod – ever the peacemaker, ever the inadvertent troublemaker, arbiter of truth, dispenser of English decency – stepped in with, 'Bertrand Russell? That thing of his. *Theory and Practice of Bolshevism*.'

Alex and Wells shook their heads and said a simultaneous 'no'.

Alex picked up the thread. 'Didn't Philip Snowden's wife do a book after her Russian trip? *Across Bolshevist Russia by Dog Sled* or something? About ten years ago it seemed that anyone who got to go there wrote a damn book about it.'

'If she had,' said Wells, 'would we any of us remember it?'

Polly the housemaid appeared in the doorway with a dinner gong. She looked at Troy, listened to the burgeoning argument, and froze, her big eyes wide, her hand poised.

'Just hit it,' Troy mouthed at her. And two of the Western World's greatest thinkers were gonged off.

He found himself seated between his sisters, Masha to his left, Sasha to his right. He hoped their affairs were going well. If they, in the absence of husbands who'd enlisted at the first blast of war's trumpet, were manless, they could be peevish beyond measure and would take it out on him. In their eyes he was still eight years old. They guarded him alternately viciously and preciously, as though his supposed virginity might somehow balance the spent currency of their own. Worse, sooner or later, since they knew no guilt, they would want to boast to him. He never wanted to listen. The last time, Sasha had described her unstoppable adulteries as her part of the war effort. Her mission to make English manhood happy. Those about to die got the chance to salute her.

'Got a girlfriend these days?' she said without preamble.

Troy said nothing.

Masha leaned over him.

'Didn't I tell you? He ditched that little WPC he was with, didn't you Freddie?'

Troy said nothing.

'Just as well,' said Sasha. 'Not your type. Honestly.'

'What is my type?' and he regretted instantly having spoken.

'Dunno. Just not wotsername.'

'You know,' said Masha, 'I've forgotten her name too. Milly or Molly or something?'

At the other end of the table, where Troy dearly wished he had been seated, Rod, their father and Wells had moved on from Russia to the only topic of the moment. The war. Rod had been holding forth for some minutes on the subject of a second front. Wells, having endured as much of his own silence as he could manage in the course of a single meal, said, 'Surely that's why he's here? Hess was sent to avert that possibility. To offer some sort of alliance and so pre-empt a second front.'

They both looked at Alex, as though this were his cue.
'A second front?'

'Second to North Africa, I meant,' said Rod.

'I know what you meant. But it seemed to me only the other day that we were fighting on half a dozen fronts at the same time, even if we do not call them fronts.'

'Were we, I mean are we?' Rod looked nonplussed.

'North Africa . . . we have barely left Greece . . .' Alex went on.

'And we have barely begun in Crete,' Wells added.

'The skies above us, and the waves below us, at least above us here and below those of our people stuck in the mid-Atlantic with German U-boats on the prowl.'

'That's five, four and a half really – I don't think you can have Greece and Crete in their entirety,' said Rod unhelpfully. 'There's not a British soldier in Greece, other than the POWs, and not a German one on Crete.'

'Not yet,' said Alex, 'not yet.'

'So what's the other?' Rod said.

'Iraq,' Troy said from the far end of the table.

'Quite right.' A nod of acknowledgement from his father. 'Iraq it was. Five and a half fronts – if you like. However, I cannot but think of it in terms of the last war. Eastern Front and Western Front. Sooner or later the pattern will reassert itself. And as to Hess being here: I don't know why he's here. I'd dearly love to be able to ask him.'

'Perhaps Churchill will let you,' said Wells.

Alex tilted his bowl, scooping at the last of a thin clear soup which Troy had found so tasteless as to be unidentifiable.

'Winston and I are no longer as close as we were. I

cannot remember precisely when we last spoke, but it must have been in 1939 or thereabouts.'

'It was just after your editorial on the Nazi-Soviet Pact, Dad,' Rod said.

Troy would not have bothered. They all knew when it had been. The row had been volcanic.

He felt hot breath upon his ear. Polly, clutching a bowl of steaming cabbage, was whispering to him.

'It's that Onions bloke from the Yard, young Fred. He wants you on the blower.'

Troy ducked out, feeling his mother's eyes upon him. Back in the study, the phone lay off the hook on his father's desk. He picked it up and heard Superintendent Stanley Onions' Lancashire growl.

'Are you free?'

It didn't matter if he wasn't.

'Body for you. A Mrs O'Grady, 11a Hoxton Street, phoned in. Lodger tripped and fell down a flight of stairs. Dead as a doornail. Better check it out. You never know.'

'You never know' just about summed up the working lives of two detectives on the Murder Squad.

Troy made his excuses in the dining room. Saw his mother rise and throw down her napkin, coming round the table to him.

'My dear, we have only just started the main course. Does Scotland Yard want you to starve?'

Her words all at odds with her gestures, she kissed him on both cheeks, escorted him to the door and made no effort beyond the formality of words to detain him.

'Is he still trying to write the same article?' Troy asked as he slipped into his coat.

'Yes,' she said. 'And he will tie us all in knots until he has done so. At the moment the idea is that he and Wells will write it together. I'll be amazed if it survives the evening. They'll be at each other's throats before the dessert if Rod doesn't stop stirring.'

'He doesn't mean to. In fact he doesn't know he's doing it. He just drops bricks.'

'Your faith in innocence would be touching were it not for your odd choice of profession.'

It was odd. And she'd never let him forget it.

§ 21

Cal dashed into Lippschitz Bros., slapped down two pounds ten shillings and grabbed the package the old men had for him.

'Don't you want to wait for a fitting?' they yelled after him.

'Don't have the time!'

It was a mistake. He stood in front of the mirror in his room at Claridge's and cursed the name of Lippschitz. The waist bagged, the jacket hung on him like something made for Cab Calloway to sport on Lenox Avenue, and the trouser cuffs let daylight onto his socks. He looked like a clown. Damn, damn, damn. And there wasn't a spare second to do a thing about it. He ran for a cab.

He was wondering why Stilton had suggested a pub and not Scotland Yard or the American Embassy, wondering how he'd know Stilton if he saw him.

It was too easy. He pushed open the saloon door of the Green Man in the Strand. A man leant against the bar, chatting happily to the barman in an accent Cal could not place, one hand in his trouser pocket, one elbow on the bar, looking for all the world as though he could hold the posture all night if need be.

'Not so much as a whizz or a bang for five days. 'Appen it's over,' he was saying.

'More like Adolf's saving it all up for a big one. I've heard say the next'll be the biggest we've seen.'

'Jack, you are a miserable sod, you always look on the black side. Try being an optimist. Like I said, 'appen it's over.'

Jack gave this a second's thought, then slapped his hand on the bar. 'Touch wood,' he said, then he looked at Cal, as though waiting for his order. Stilton's eyes followed and found Cal.

He was a big man, as tall as Cal himself, but sixty or more pounds the heavier, and every inch the London bobby. A nondescript, voluminous brown macintosh, a trilby hat perched on the bar next to his pint, shiny boots – polished until they gleamed like ebony – and a plump, reddish, fiftyish face, framing bright brown eyes and a big, bushy, wild moustache – the only un-neat thing about the man. Peeping from beneath the macintosh were the folds of a dark, striped suit – better by far than the work of the fifty-shilling tailor Reininger had sent him to – knife-edge creases in the trousers, cuffs neatly resting upon the tops of his boots, not hovering at half-mast around the ankles like Cal's.

He straightened up. Stuck out a hand.

'Stilton. Walter Stilton. You must be Mr Cormack.'

Cal shook the hand. Tried once more to place the accent and couldn't.

'Do I look that much like an American?' he asked.

'You said it, lad, I didn't. Now. What's your poison?'

'A pint,' said Cal, hoping it was what was expected of him.

'Pint o' what?' Stilton replied, piling on the confusion.

'What do you have?'

The barman answered. 'Bitter, mild, stout . . .'

Bitter sounded . . . well . . . bitter. Mild sounded pathetic. Had to be stout.

'Fine,' said Stilton. 'Jack, bring 'em over. Mr Cormack an' me'll be in the snug.'

The snug turned out to be a room the size of a closet, partitioned from the main bar by an elaborately etched glass door. He guessed that Stilton wanted privacy. The snug was empty, but then so was the bar. Thursday evening was clearly not their rush hour.

'I've not been told a lot, you understand. Just the basics. You'll have to bring me up to date as best you can.'

Cal stared at the poster on the wall above Stilton's head. A caricature of Hitler, all cowlick and toothbrush moustache, had been worked into a repeated motif for wallpaper – little Hitlers spiralling down the poster – and the caption 'Walls have ears'. He'd seen posters much like this dotted all over London in the last few days: 'Walls have ears' – 'Careless talk costs lives' – 'Keep Mum She's Not So Dumb' – and no one seemed to pay a blind bit of notice.

The barman set a pint of black stuff in front of him. Stilton put a few coppers on the table and waved Cal down when he reached for his wallet.

'Cheers,' said Stilton.

Cal sipped at his pint. It tasted like mud. It was so thick you couldn't see through it. He must have pulled a face.

'Not to your taste, lad?'

'No, no,' Cal lied. 'It just takes a bit of getting used to. So many things do.'

'Now – to business. About this Jerry we're after. Colonel Ruthven-Greene got on the blower to . . .'

'The blower?'

'Telephone, lad. I left a message for him at Broadway. He called me back. Filled me in. Told me to lend you a hand.'

Cal wondered again about the English. Reggie had

'filled him in'. Over the telephone? A little Hitler caught his eye.

'Scrambler, o' course,' Stilton added, as though he had read Cal's mind. 'He called me on a scrambler.'

'Did he say where he was?'

'Where he was?'

'I've been calling him at the Savoy since Monday. I got through to him once. It's Thursday now. We've lost the best part of four days.'

'Can't help that, lad. They didn't bring me in till Tuesday. It was yesterday before Colonel Ruthven-Greene called me back and . . .'

'OK, OK. I know it's not your fault,' Cal conceded. 'Perhaps you had better tell me what you have to tell me.'

He listened while Stilton told him what he knew, nodded, said 'yes' when it seemed necessary, feeling all the time that the little Hitlers in the wallpaper were watching him, only him, and that if he looked up quickly he would catch the beady eyes upon him.

At the end of it Stilton asked simply, 'D'ye have any questions?'

'Do *I* have any questions?'

'Well. Do you?'

'If you put it like that – yes I do. Can we find him?'

'If he's in London we'll find him.'

'That's part of the problem. Reggie was convinced Stahl would come to London. He could be here now.'

'He could. But not without we know about it. Now . . .'

Stilton rummaged in an inside pocket. Found his wallet, pulled out a piece of paper and stared at it.

'Would this be anything like your man? Six foot or more, light hair, blue eyes, thirty or thereabouts. Weight about thirteen stone.'

'Thirteen stone?' Cal said, feeling slightly stunned by the speed with which Stilton had changed course.

'Thirteen stone. About one hundred and eighty pounds.'

'Six foot, blond, one eighty. Yes, that could be Stahl.'

'D'ye reckon he could pass for a foreigner?'

'He is a foreigner.'

'I meant, could he be taken for Swiss if he tried to pass himself off as one? To a Swedish crew, I mean.'

'Of course. He's an Austrian. Both countries speak German. I don't think the finer points of a German accent would be all that obvious to the Swedes, or to the English for that matter.'

Stilton spread the sheet of paper out on the table.

''Appen this is him, then. On the seventh a Swedish merchantman was anchored overnight off Hull waiting for the tide.'

Stilton paused almost imperceptibly, changed tone, threw in the next line almost as an aside.

'Hull's a big port up Yorkshire way. About two hundred miles north of London.'

Well, thought Cal, I asked for the High School geography lesson, didn't I?

'Next morning Immigration and Special Branch sail out with the pilot to check out the crew. Matter of routine with neutral shipping, these days. One man was missing. Erich Hober, aged thirty, signed on in Stockholm. Papers showed he'd shipped out from Danzig before that.'

'Missing? How does anyone go missing from a ship at sea?'

'Easy lad. They'd be within sight of land. Hull's a good way up an estuary the size of the Thames. They'd not be at sea, they'd be in the dredger channel. A good swimmer could slip over the side and make for the shore.

If that's what this chap did, he'd have eight hours' start on us. He'd've been in London before they were even looking for him in Hull.'

Cal had that sinking feeling. The one that had set in with Ruthven-Greene's last phone call. Stahl had got here before him. Stahl was doing whatever he had come to London to do. And Cal had been dumped. Fobbed off with a pensionable policeman who spoke a language that baffled him with every other sentence.

'That could be him. It sounds like him.'

'Good, now all we've got to do is find the bugger.'

Stilton downed most of his pint, a dusting of froth on the ends of his moustache, smiled at Cal. Cal left his beer untouched. Good God, they'd given him a grinning fool.

'Where,' he asked, 'where do we even begin to look in a city of five million people?'

'More like six and a half, lad, and we look in all the right places and ignore the wrong ones. I know what you're thinking. And I wouldn't blame you. But tracking Jerries is my job. My speciality. I've narks in every immigrant quarter in the city. You'll find the refugees tend to gravitate to the pubs and restaurants around their own exiled governments. And the poorer they get, the further they fan out. A bit like tribes around the wigwam. I've Poles in Putney, Czechs in Bayswater, Norwegians in Kensington, French in Piccadilly, a few Dutch here and there and a handful of Belgians. There's nowhere this bloke can go and not surface sooner or later, and if he surfaces in the wrong quarter, tries a bluff too far, then they'll spot him, and we'll get a tip off. A lot of these people hate each other – that's Europe for you after all, ten centuries of hating each other – but they've one thing in common. They all hate Jerry. There are times I think they hate us too – most of 'em learn just enough English to order a meal.'

'Then you'd better leave the talking to me. I've got my specialty too. German.'

Stilton was grinning at him again. One bushy eyebrow slightly up.

'Where d'you learn the lingo?'

'Family. My grandmother's family were Germans. Moravians. There's a lot of Moravians in the Southern States. We all got German handed down to us along with the family bible. It was a good start. I polished it at school. And I've spent the last two years and more in Zurich.'

Stilton was nodding now, not grinning quite so much.

'Well, lad . . .' he said at last, and Cal knew he'd come to hate being called lad. 'I do envy you. I learnt mine in Cottbus.'

'Cottbus? What's Cottbus?'

'German prisoner-of-war camp, lad. Prussia. 1916–1918. I learnt it the hard way. I've picked up Polish and Czech on the streets of London. A damn sight more fun, I can tell you.'

Just a little, Cal felt humbled.

'So,' Stilton resumed. 'He can pass for Swiss. He'd hardly be still using that as his cover though. What's his next best ticket?'

'Czech. Sudeten Czech. Bilingual. German-speaking as well as Czech. That could explain any oddities in the accent. He could maybe lose himself in a Czech district. Or Polish at a pinch. He could pass for a Pole to you and me, but I doubt he'd fool a real Pole. And of course Austrian. Pretend to be what he really is. You didn't mention Austrians in your list.'

'Oh there's Austrians all right. Jews mostly. Could he pass for Jewish?'

'I don't know,' said Cal. 'What does a Jew look like?'

'That's rhetoric, I take it?'

'Pretty well.'

90

'Then I'd say it's got a damn sight less to do with what he looks like than what he says and what he sounds like. If as you say he's going to have to lose himself, he has to blend. I couldn't blend into Jewish culture, could you?'

'Probably not. I'd mess it up at the first "maseltov".'

Stilton scribbled in his notebook with a pencil stub, mouthing the words as he did so. Cal felt as though they'd both just tested each other – and passed.

'There's one or two blokes I could get hold of this evening if you've the time.'

'I've all the time in . . .'

The barman cut Cal off.

'Stinker! Your man Dobbs on the dog an' bone!'

The barman lifted up the wooden flap of the bar to let Stilton through.

''Scuse us, lad,' Stilton said over his shoulder. 'Telephone.'

Telephone? 'Dog an' bone'? He'd only just learnt 'blower'.

He tipped the rest of his pint into the pot of a ragged aspidistra. It needed a drink more than he did. When he returned Stilton's expression had changed. He was angry – controlling it, but angry.

'Change of plan, I'm afraid. I've got to go to Hoxton. You'd best come with me. It'll mean missing my Czech nark, but he'll not say a dicky bird without me there. 'Appen we can salvage some of the evening a bit later.'

He grabbed his hat and swept out, clearly expecting Cal to follow. 'Dicky bird?' Word? Word! Good God, that was it – the English talked in rhymes.

Out in the street, Stilton yanked open the driver's door of a large four-door Riley Kestrel and pointed Cal to the other side.

'Or did you think you were going to drive?' he asked rhetorically.

He pressed the starter and the car jerked out into a street all but empty of traffic. They'd driven a mile before either of them spoke again.

'What's in Hoxton?' Cal asked, hoping for an answer.

''Nother Jerry,' Stilton said tersely. 'An agent they've sent over. But we were on to him from the first. He'll never get to do what he's come to do.'

'You think he's a spy?'

'Most of 'em are. But not this one. This one's a killer. Sent over to bump off some poor bugger.'

Cal wondered how to phrase the next question. A piece of the puzzle, the first, had just landed on the board. The last thing he wanted to do was alarm Stilton, risk him clamming up.

'You sure?' he said simply.

'Oh aye, I'm sure. But we'll stop him. Whatever it is, we'll stop him.'

'Why are we going to Hoxton now?'

'My man Dobbs. He's watching the boarding house. He rang to tell me there's police in the building.'

'Is that a problem?'

Stilton snorted with laughter. 'Oh, it's a problem all right. The last thing you want is the boys in blue trampling all over the shop in their size tens. Wot larx, eh?'

Cal let this one sink in. He thought he'd got the gist of it. The Branch were political police. And they regarded the criminal police as a nuisance. In this scenario, he and Stilton were the Feds, racing to take over from a county sheriff in some hick town in the mid-west that had been lucky enough to trap Dillinger. Slang was OK. He'd get used to it. He was in the picture. The big picture. It might not be so bad after all. Stilton might not be so bad after all. But he'd no idea what the man meant by 'Wot larx'. It didn't seem to rhyme with anything.

Hoxton Street was long, narrow and not particularly straight. It snaked its way from Shoreditch station almost to Dalston, fizzling out and changing names just short of the Grand Union Canal. Halfway up it stood the Red Lion public house, and opposite the Red Lion stood Mrs O'Grady's Boarding House – its trade announced by a hand-written card in the ground floor window: 'Furn. rooms avail. for respec. gents. No gippos.' Outside the house was a small black car – a Bullnose Morris. By the Bullnose Morris was a nervous, pacing, slyly smoking policeman, a cigarette cupped between his fingers, the glowing tip facing backwards, as though this simple precaution might make his illicit action the less obvious.

'Put that bloody fag out!' Stilton roared as he and Cal got out of the car.

Dobbs dropped the cigarette and ground it underfoot. Stilton pointed at the Bullnose Morris.

'Troy?' he said.

'Upstairs, boss. I couldn't stop 'im.'

'Save it, lad. I'll listen to your lies later.'

He led off, into the house. Cal followed. Inside the door, a large, stout, worried woman in a pinafore stood waiting, looking up the stairs. She turned when they entered.

'Oh Mr Stilton, thank Gawd it's you. What a to-do! What a to-do!'

Stilton ignored her display. Grief or fear or whatever.

'First floor, is it?' he asked, and headed up the stairs. Cal followed. Smiled at the woman. In return she told him once more what a to-do it was.

He stood behind Stilton, looking past him into the landing of the next floor, where a second staircase led to the floor above that. A man in a black cashmere overcoat was bending over the body of a big man – barefoot, vest and trousers – crumpled at the foot of the stairs, the arms, legs and neck jammed between the wall, the banister rails and the floor at unnatural angles – as though someone had picked up Pinocchio and just dropped him. The young man was talking to a white-haired man of sixty or so – a doctor, repacking his bag and looking at his watch.

'All I'm saying is that nothing like this can ever be open and shut.'

'It's as simple as this, Sergeant. He's at the bottom of the stairs, the carpets are worn to buggery and he's got his neck broken. I can't see the mystery in that.'

The younger man stood up. He looked tiny to Cal. No more than five foot six or seven – a mop of thick black hair falling across his forehead, so that he was forever sweeping it back with one hand, and shining, black eyes in a pale face. He looked like a freshman student. Far too young to be a cop.

'You're wrong,' he said bluntly. 'The neck isn't just broken, it's twisted. We need a full post-mortem to determine the cause of death. We need –'

And there Stilton cut him short.

'Thank you, Mr Troy. Good of you to step into the breach. But this is a Branch matter, and I'll take over now.'

'I was just trying to tell the doctor, sir –'

'I've spoken, lad. It's my case.'

'He's one of yours?' said Troy with a nod at the corpse.

'Yes.'

'Then I'll leave you to it.'

Troy walked out. For a second they exchanged glances. Cal found himself looking straight down into the black eyes as he passed, ebony mirrors reflecting back

94

at him – and then he was gone. Down the stairs, past Mrs O'Grady still lamenting such a 'to-do'.

Stilton now bent over the body.

'Bugger, bugger, bugger.'

The doctor clicked his bag shut, took one more look at his watch.

'Important, was he?'

'You could say that. Now, before you dash off to whatever's made you look at your watch three times since I came into the room, cause of death. A professional opinion, if you please.'

The doctor actually blushed a little. Not so stupid as not to know when he was being bawled out. Cal slipped in behind Stilton as he stood up to tackle the doctor and looked at the body for himself.

'Neck's broken. Death was instantaneous. No marks to indicate any struggle. Your man on the door says he saw no one come or go. Only other person in the house was the landlady. Ergo, I conclude the poor sod tripped on the top step, tumbled all the way to the bottom and broke his blasted neck. Happens all the time. Houses like these are death traps. If it wasn't for the war we'd have 'em all shut down as health hazards.'

'Thank you. You can get off to your dinner now. It was your dinner you were anxious not to miss wasn't it?'

The doctor said nothing. Picked up his trilby, jammed it on his head, last symbol of his damaged pride, and left. Stilton bent to the body again. Side by side with Cal. Cal had only ever seen a body once before, his maternal grandfather laid out in his casket – black suit, combed hair, mortician's make-up, eyes shut. This man's eyes were shut. He was almost prepared to bet that the young cop had closed them himself. In seven years as a soldier he'd never heard a shot fired in anger, unless it was Gelbroaster's the other night, and he'd never seen a body that had just collapsed instantly into death like this. The

95

heap that was death. A grim human puzzle. Take these parts, these tangled limbs, and rearrange them into human form.

'You seen many corpses in your time, Mr Cormack?'

'No,' said Cal. 'No, I haven't.'

'This is one Jerry I'd hoped to see live just a while longer. Long enough to find out what he was up to.'

They found Troy outside, leaning against the bonnet of his car, collar up. Hands deep in his pockets.

'Was there something else, Sergeant?'

Troy stood upright. It made little difference to his size up against Stilton, but it indicated the right amount of deference to rank.

'You know that's no accident, don't you?'

'Mebbe.'

'I'd recommend a full PM and Forensics out at Hendon. Whoever he was, and I'm sure you know better than I, he needs the works.'

'I've handled suspicious deaths before, lad. I've seen dead bodies before.'

'And I see them all the time. Forgive the plainness of this, sir – but murder is my business.'

'Thank you, Sergeant. 'Appen you're right. And right now we should both be about our business. Dobbs!!!'

Stilton strode across the road to where Dobbs was hastily stepping on another butt.

Troy opened the door of his car. Looked straight at Cal.

'Are you working with Mr Stilton?'

'I guess I am,' said Cal.

'Then I wish you luck,' said Troy.

He drove off. Cal could hear Stilton bawling out Dobbs. Half London could hear Stilton bawling out Dobbs.

'You were in the pub. Weren't you? In the Lion.

Supping ale when you should have been watching the door!'

'Boss, it was so quiet. Nothing was –'

'While you were wetting your slimy gizzard, someone slipped in and topped the bastard. Do you hear me Dobbs? We've lost him. He's dead. Or did you think the Murder Squad sent Troy out to check his ration book? You stupid, stupid bugger!'

'Honest, boss, it won't 'appen again!'

'Too bloody right it won't. 'Cos if it does they'll be using your bollocks for target practice down at Bisley. Get in there now. Calm down old Peg before she bursts a blood vessel. Get hold of the meat wagon and get matey carted off. Do a house to house. Talk to the whole damned street. When you've done all that, get back to the Yard. Write out a full report of everything you've seen and done in the last seventy-two hours and have it on my desk before you go home tonight. Do I make myself clear, Mr Dobbs?'

When he came back to Cal, there was the whisper of a grin beneath the moustache.

'That looked like fun.'

'Oh it was Mr Cormack, I enjoyed every second of it.'

'Good. Because I have a little advice for you.'

Stilton laughed out loud.

'Come on, lad. Let's hear it.'

'That young cop is right.'

'I know damn well he's right.'

'Then why did you ignore him?'

'Let's just say I don't like being taught how to suck eggs by the likes of Frederick Troy. He may be Scotland Yard's *wunderkind*, but as far as I'm concerned he's still wet behind the ears.'

'Then you'll order a full autopsy?'

'Of course.'

'The Works?'

'You're beginning to learn the jargon. But why do you ask?'

'This is the bit you won't like.'

'Try me.'

'This dead German was a hit man, right? An assassin?'

'A Dutchman, but yes, an assassin.'

'What kind of man gets the drop on a trained killer?'

'I don't know. You tell me.'

'Another trained killer?'

'You think there's another one?'

'One? Maybe. Or do you have a whole bunch of trained killers on the loose?'

It was Stilton's turn to look at his watch.

'We've missed my Czech for tonight. Do you fancy a spot o' dinner?'

'You know a good restaurant?'

'I wasn't thinking of a restaurant. I was thinking – would you like to come home? Have something to eat with me and the wife?'

Cal said nothing. He was almost too startled to speak. He'd primed himself for an eruption of bad temper, and he wound up with an invitation to dinner. He'd never been inside an Englishman's home before. He'd heard they all thought of them as castles.

'You can tell me your theory on the way over to Stepney.'

Stilton grinned over the word 'theory'. Cal accepted silently and got back into the car.

§ 23

Cal had no grasp of London's geography, but even the walk around London last Sunday morning, after the big raid, had told him that it lacked order. Following your nose only worked if you weren't going anywhere. What

London needed was a grid. True, the Washington streets he'd grown up with had nothing as romantic as Piccadilly or as historically obscure as Rotten Row – the best they could come up with was a prosaic Avenue C or M Street, and you'd never while away a lazy five minutes wondering about the origins of 'M' – but they led somewhere. Major L'Enfant, Washington's genius, had taken the stripes off the flag, drawn them as a grid across a swamp in Maryland, thrown the stars at them, one for each of the fifteen states at the time of the city's inception, and where they hit declared a road junction and linked up the diagonals. What could be simpler? An easy-to-use city, with a few statues thrown in.

It was scarcely beginning to get dark as Stilton steered him across the urban chaos that was the East End, but blackouts were already being pulled tight in the houses they passed. One or two of the oncoming cars had put on their dim, hooded headlights. In real darkness, enough to see each other coming, not enough to see where you were going. A sense of caution seemed to have grown into the British motorist as a consequence. Cal doubted that Stilton clocked more than twenty miles an hour the whole way. He realised he would come to crave real darkness soon enough.

'You've said nowt,' Stilton said after about ten minutes of crawling along the half-empty streets.

Nowt? Cal tried to think of a rhyme, the key to meaning, unwilling to admit he didn't know what the man meant.

'You were going to tell me your theory about the killing.'

'Oh, I see. Let's get back to Stahl for a moment. I, I mean we, don't know what Stahl is looking for. We don't know why he doesn't simply come in. It's been implicit from the start that he's running. But running from what?'

99

'From the Germans, of course. I should o' thought that's pretty bloody obvious.'

'Sure, and if he's running, why shouldn't they be chasing?'

'Eh?'

'If Stahl has been blown. If Germany knows he's an American agent – then they'd try to kill him before he told us whatever it is he has to tell us. They'd have sent someone after him, wouldn't they?'

'Smulders?'

'Was that the guy's name?'

'Said he was a Dutchman, a master printer from Delft. He may well have been Dutch. There's plenty of Quislings around.'

'Suppose it was Stahl he came to kill?'

Stilton said nothing to this. Cal could almost hear him thinking.

'You mean like a hypothesis?'

'Sure . . . if that helps, think of it that way.'

'OK. I'm listening.'

'The hypothesis is that Smulders came to kill Stahl.'

'If you say so.'

'And if he did, then the implications are serious.'

'Eh?'

'Think about it. He came after Stahl. Came to kill Stahl – but wound up getting killed.'

'OK – I get your drift.'

All the same Cal spelt it out to him.

'Suppose Stahl got to this guy before he got to him. And at that right under the nose of your man Dobbs. Think what it means. It means Stahl's one step ahead of the Germans and two steps ahead of us. If he doesn't want to be found . . .'

Cal let the sentence trail off.

'There is one thing,' Stilton said after a while. 'We lost Smulders. Just for one night, you understand. But for more than two hours we'd not a clue where he was. If he encountered Stahl in that time . . .'

Now Stilton had no conclusion to his sentence.

'Doesn't bear thinking about, does it?' said Cal.

Stilton paused again. Another breathing, thinking space as he pulled the car off Mile End Road and headed down towards the river.

'Mind – like you said, it's just hypothetical . . .'

'If you say so.' Cal echoed his own caution back to him.

'You know, Mr Cormack, you're not as green as you are cabbage-looking.'

Now what the fuck did that mean?

Stilton stopped the car in a side street. Pulled up the handbrake between the seats.

'Are we there?' said Cal.

'Welcome to Jubilee Street.'

They got out. Stilton dug into his pockets looking for his keys. Cal looked around. For all he had seen in the last few days, nothing had prepared him for what he now saw. He had seen public ruins, ruins on the grand scale. Public places blasted into vacancy, open to the sky. This was different. These were homes, human habitations. And in all the street only one house still stood. Alone in a desert of rubble stood the home of Chief Inspector Walter Stilton. A big, five-storey double-fronted house, once the centrepiece of a late Victorian terrace – that surely, was the Jubilee celebrated in the street's name? Even his passing knowledge of British history covered Queen Victoria's Golden Jubilee of 1887 – and its windows were patched in cardboard, its paint peeled back to raw elm, and its walls were jagged as a row of rotting teeth, where they had once locked neatly into the house next door. But there was no house next door. Next door, in the literal sense, looked to be the best part of quarter of a mile away. What remained of the surrounding houses appeared to be sunken pools. Cellars into which the structure of the houses had collapsed upon impact from a bomb – 'pancaked' was the local jargon – only to fill up with rain in the days and weeks that had passed. Cal had learnt on Saturday night just how flimsy – how unexpectedly flimsy – London was. He'd watched bombs slice through houses from top to bottom like they were made from nothing more substantial than tinfoil. Unexpected – because London was old. Older than America. Older than his family home in Fairfax County – and that had withstood a three-day siege by the Union Army. London, so elegant, so redolent of lived history, seemed to him to be no more than an Anacostia shantytown. Hitler huffed, Hitler puffed and he blew your house down.

Over the slaughtered houses a tall factory chimney stack was visible – as prominent among the ruins of the East End of London as the Washington Monument in the great fields of the Mall. How had they managed to miss it? Whatever the Luftwaffe left standing propelled Cal to wondering how? Why? Why this building? Why not that? Why wasn't London razed from East to West and North to South. How did they stand it, how did they survive, how, put simply, did they live?

'It's nowt grand, you'll understand,' said Stilton fiddling at the lock with his key chain. 'We live plain.'

The door, warped in its frame, jammed. Stilton muttered ''alf a mo' and put his shoulder to it. The door scraped across the linoleum with a shriek and Cal found himself in a long corridor, with stairs ascending and descending, and the steamy smell of cooking wafting up from below.

'That you, Stinker?' a woman's voice yelled.

'Who else would it be? You're not expecting your fancy man, are you?'

''E don't comeround Thursdays!'

Stilton clumped down the wooden stairs, Cal trailing after, into a huge kitchen. Hot with cooking, a dozen aromas mixing in the air. A fat, fiftyish woman in a flowery apron, grey hair pinned up in a bun, stood by a large cast-iron cooker, the like of which Cal had not seen before. It was four or five feet across, and six or seven pans stood bubbling on two giant hotplates, their covers hinged back against the chimney breast. She flipped a couple of pan lids. Stirred their contents with a wooden spoon.

Stilton crept up to the woman, hugged her around the waist. Lifted her gently off the ground and whispered in her ear. She prised him off less than gently. Rapped his knuckles with her spoon and said ''Ands orf. Can't you see I'm busy?' Then she noticed Cal.

'You daft so-an'-so. You didn't say we'd got visitors.'

One hand unconsciously smoothed down her skirts where Stilton had ruffled them, the other clutched the dripping spoon.

'This is our Mr Cormack. Mr Cormack is a Yank. First one we've ever had. Mr Cormack, the missis. Our Edna.'

'How do you do, Mrs Stilton?'

Before Edna Stilton could answer Stilton said, 'You can fit in another for dinner, can't you Ed?'

'Comes the day we can't! O' course we can. But you're early, Stinker, I'm all behind tonight. What with Kev and Trev home, and Kitty says she'll be along later, there's been a lot to do. You'll have to make yourself scarce for half an hour. I can't be doin' with you under me feet.'

Out in the street once more Stilton said, 'We'll go for a swift half.'

'A what?'

'We'll go to the pub.'

'Again?'

'I don't mean the same pub. There's plenty of pubs.'

It was, Cal knew, a classic British understatement. They were, Stilton professed, just 'nipping round the corner', but this still entailed passing what looked to Cal like a perfectly decent pub. But pubs, as he was learning, were a matter of ambience and nuance. It was not for the uninitiated to pronounce.

'We'll kill twenty minutes in the Brickie's Arms,' said Stilton. 'You're going to love this. A real treat this time o' night.'

Stilton pushed at the door of a blacked-out, glazed-brick and red-tile building on the next corner. Inside it was warm and moist and brown. The room was not large, but it was pretty well full, and it existed in nondescript hues of brown, from the oak and mahogany of the furniture to the dirty sawdust on the floor and the nicotine mist on the ceiling, to the faded, featureless pattern in the forty-year-old wallpaper. It might once have been red, but it was brown now. Above the bar a portrait of the Prime Minister took pride of place and contributed the only splash of colour with its trailing ribbons of red, white and blue.

'Evening Stinker,' said the barman. 'What'll it be?'

'Two halves o' best. You don't want stout again, do you Mr Cormack? I doubt Eric's got an aspidistra to water.'

Cal did the merest double-take at this and accepted the offer.

'Chief Inspector . . .'

'Call me Walter, lad.'

'Why do they call you Stinker?'

Stilton grinned. 'It's not what you were thinking.'

'I wasn't thinking anything.'

'Cheese, lad. Cheese. Where I come from, up north, Derbyshire way, they make four or five varieties of cheese. Two of 'em called Stilton. A white one and a blue one. The blue does niff a bit.'

'Niff?'

'Stink.'

'Derbyshire?'

'Aye.'

'So you're not a cockney?'

'Nay lad, or did you think I talked like this for the fun of it?'

'I thought you talked like that guy on the radio.'

Stilton took this quizzically.

'What guy on the radio?'

'The late-night guy. Priestley. J.B. Priestley.'

'No, no. He's Yorkshire. Not the same thing at all. They still live in mud huts in Bradford. Now, the wife's a cockney though. She was born in that house we live in, and all her brothers and sisters along with her. And all our kids too.'

They carried two brimming halves of best bitter to a table. Three chairs, one of them occupied by a morose-looking man with a glass of flat beer in front of him, as though he had spun it out since opening time and now given up on it.

Stilton knew him. Made the introductions.

'This is the sheriff, Station Sergeant George Bonham. He runs the local nick, don't you, George? Mr Cormack. Our Yank.'

Bonham looked up. Did not smile, did not object to their presence.

'We saw your protégé today, George.'

'Me what?'

'Protégé. The *wunderkind*. Sergeant Troy.'

Something resembling a smile rose and withered on the man's face.

'I've not seen him in a while,' he said. 'Not since . . .'

He left the sentence unfinished. Stilton elbowed his

beer. A minute passed with neither of them speaking, then Bonham bent down under the table, picked up a policeman's helmet from the floor and stood up. Cal was in awe. At six foot and more he was quite accustomed to being one of, if not the tallest in any room. But this man had to be six foot six, and that was without the silly hat.

Bonham muttered goodnight and vanished.

'Was it something I said?'

'Nay, lad. It was me. I was only trying to cheer him up, but I should have known when he and Troy last met. His wife's funeral. Ethel Bonham copped it in the Blitz just before Christmas. George is taking it very hard. I shouldn't have mentioned Troy. Troy was his boy at the local nick, trained him up from nowt. Now he's the darling of the Yard, just when old George needs him.'

'I had kind of meant to ask you about that.'

'About what?'

'Well, the Blitz, the street. Your street. How many people died?'

'Oh, I see. One, as a matter of fact. Just the one. Mrs Bluit at number 72. But she was ninety. Died in her sleep. When the all clear sounded, there she was, stretched out in her bed. Stone dead. Natural causes, the doctor said. Her house lost its windows and its roof and most of one wall, and in the end Heavy Rescue bulldozed it before it could fall on anybody, but there wasn't a mark on her.'

'I don't get it. It looks like . . . like Armageddon.'

'Everyone else was down the tube station at Liverpool Street. Now, don't get me wrong. The Jerries blew the street to buggery. We were lucky. It was December, day after Boxing Day – same raid as killed Ethel Bonham. I reckon there was more'n a bomber a minute for the best part of four hours. That makes about two hundred and fifty planes. Biggest raid I'd ever heard till last Saturday. Now, if it'd been September, then it might've been a different story. We weren't expecting 'em then. Everybody'd pulled out or sent their kids to the country in '39. By 1940, when nothing much had happened, they were drifting back. Last September we weren't ready. We lost a lot of people. There's plenty of folk 'round here lost someone. George, if he'd just snap to and take a look around him, would realise he's not the only one, that everybody in Stepney Green knows how he feels. Everybody's lost someone. Or everybody knows somebody who's lost someone. We've lost more civilians so far than soldiers – and that includes Dunkirk.'

Cal let this one settle. He'd never felt more like an outsider.

'You know,' he said, 'I'd hate to have to explain that back home.'

'You don't have to. That's why we've got Ed Murrow.'

Cal heard the silent touché in Stilton's remark. They'd touched swords again.

'I am trying, you know. I know that to the English I represent a rich, complacent nation with no commitment to the war. I know that to the English I'm "Yank" or "lad" – but I'm trying.'

'Would you rather I called you Captain Cormack?'

'No. I'll settle for lad, and only because I don't think I could ever stop you. But my name's Cal.'

Stilton roared with laughter and slapped him on the back. As the breath burst from his lungs, he could just hear the barman calling for order.

'Right, shut up you lot, the bugger's on again!'

The room fell silent. A crackle of static filled the air, someone tuning a wireless set, then the burble, hiss and hum of a station found and the first words of speech upon the airwaves.

'Garmany calling, Garmany calling.'

The room went mad. A deafening explosion of noise.

'Garmany calling, Garmany calling. Haw bleedin' haw bleedin' haw!!!'

A noise rippled forth like a thousand farts as every man in the room stuck his tongue between his lips and blew a Bronx cheer. Two jokers in Wellington boots, their trousers stuck into the tops, marched up and down in front of the bar with black combs pressed to their top lips, the other arm out to the heavens, legs kicking higher and higher with every goose's step.

Two short, fat men nipped smartly in front of them.

'I zay, I zay, I zay. Mein hund has kein nose!'

'Your hund has kein nose. How does he smell?'

'Like ein true-bred Aryan!'

They stomped off holding their noses. Their entire audience yelled 'Phwooarrr!' and another thousand farts rippled forth.

§ 24

One end of Edna Stilton's kitchen was occupied by a vast round table, the other end by Edna Stilton. She stood in front of the cooking machine she called 'me Aga', stirred, grumbled and served, while her daughters scurried back and forth between the cooker and the table. Around the table a baffling array of faces greeted Cal, a serial chorus of 'pleased to meet you, I'm sure', and no amount of bonhomie from Stilton would make introduction or remembering any the easier for him.

'My girls, Rose and Reenie.'

Two women Cal put at about his own age – late twenties – looking like younger versions of their mother, smiled at him from the far side; a flutter of the eyelashes, a coy tilt of the head. One in an ATS uniform, the other, the coy one, in a maternity smock. Stilton worked his way clockwise round the table.

'Tom. Our Rose's husband.'

A short man in a neat black suit – thinning hair, tight lines around the eyes – a good few years older than his wife.

'Ministry of Works,' he said, as though sharing a confidence. A limp handshake followed.

'Our Mr Bell. Top floor front. Organist at the Gaumont cinema in the Haymarket, Mondays to Saturdays, and at St George's-in-the-East, Limehouse, on Sundays.'

A thin man, a neglected man, a threadbare man, leather elbow patches on an old tweed coat – his socks probably needed darning too. He reached over, held out his hand to Cal. A reedy voice – the perfect organist down to his larynx and tonsils.

'I'm more of a Bach man than a Bing man,' he said, straining for joviality.

'And then there's Maurice, our Reen's husband. Pilot Officer Micklewhite.'

A big man, as big as Stilton – all women marry their fathers? Cal had already forgotten which was Reen and which was Rose – a pale blue RAF battledress draped across the chair behind him, black braces and a blue shirt on which he'd popped the collar stud.

'Based at Hornchurch,' he said by way of explanation. He might just as well have said Timbuctoo. Only when he added, 'So close, it might as well be home,' did Cal draw the conclusion that Hornchurch must be somewhere near London.

'Our Miss Greenlees. Our Joanie.'

The woman blushed scarlet behind spectacles as thick as milk bottles.

'First floor back. Clerk to the Registrar of Births, Marriages and Deaths, Finsbury Town Hall. So if you ever want to get married in a hurry, Mr Cormack, you know where to go.'

Stilton hooted at his own joke. If it were possible the poor woman blushed the more – a female Mr Bell, spinsterly, spidery and forty. They were what some families might have called 'paying guests' – though he could not conceive that his would need or use such a term – but to Stilton they were 'the lodgers'.

'The twins. Kevin and Trevor.'

Cal shook hands with two young ratings in naval uniform. Short hair, ruddy skin, firm grips. On the back of the door above their heads, two flat-top blue Navy caps bearing the simple inscription 'HMS Hood'.

'Our Vera.'

A big, bold, blonde young woman of twenty or so. No maidenly blushes, no flirtatious, fluttering eyelashes. A manly handshake, and a terse 'take me as you find me' tone of voice.

'And last and least, our youngest – Terence.'

A spotty seventeen-year-old.

'Tel,' the boy said. 'And I'll be enlisting next year.'

From the far end of the room his mother spoke.

'Over my dead body. I got four kids in uniform. That's quite enough for one family.'

Cal looked around the room. Mrs Stilton set a large pie in the centre of the table, and seated herself opposite her husband. Cal counted up. They were thirteen at table. Two lodgers, two sons-in-law, the Stiltons them- selves, six children and only three of them in uniform. Surely she knew how many kids she had in uniform? But there was a fourteenth, unoccupied place. On the far side of Cal between young Tel and his father.

'I'm not waiting,' Stilton's wife said. 'She'll be late for her own funeral, that one.'

And no further explanation of 'she' was offered.

Dishes circulated. A mess of hot cabbage. A bowl of butterbeans doused in oily margarine. A slice of pie.

One of the boys in uniform reached for the dish.

''Ands orf! Manners! We got guests. I don't want you showing me up! Mr Cormack, do help yourself.'

Mrs Stilton beamed at him, glared at Kev or Trev. Cal helped himself to a small portion of the as yet unnamed pie. Whatever it was, it smelled great.

Kev and Trev duly served, one of them began to tear his piece of pie apart with knife and fork.

'What's up, son?' his father asked.

'What's up? What's up? I ain't got no meat in my bit! That's what's up!'

He and his twin looked accusingly at their mother.

'No, you ain't,' she said.

'Wot?'

'You ain't go no meat. And neither's nobody else. It ain't a pie with meat. It's a pie without meat.'

The bonhomie of paterfamilias that had threatened to set like rictus on Stilton's face vanished as he prised up the crust of his portion and confirmed the bad news.

'It's called Woolton pie. There's carrots and parsnips and a nice white sauce and lots of goodness.'

'Goodness. Wot the bleedin' 'ell's goodness? I want meat. What's a bleedin' pie without meat?'

Mrs Stilton moved quickly for a big woman. She leaned across her daughter and son-in-law and whacked each of the twins across the backs of both hands with her wooden spoon. Fast as a tommy-gun.

'Wossatfor?'

'That's for language – 'ow many times I have to tell you? We got guests. Mr Cormack don't come here to hear you swear. Now eat up or put it back. 'Cos it's all you're gettin'! And if you wanted meat you should have handed over your ration books like I asked you the day you both come 'ome on leave. I spent half the afternoon down the butcher's. Queuin' in the Mile End Road. You know what I got? Quart o' pound o' bacon. That's what I got.'

The other twin, nursing a bruised knuckle and a grievance, spoke for the first time.

'Woss wrong with bacon pie then?'

'Bacon pie. Without eggs? I never 'eard of such a thing. No. Bacon's for your dad's breakfasts. He gets up every day at the crack o' dawn and goes out to earn the money to keep this family together. You expect me to send 'im orf without a good cooked breakfast inside 'im? Course not. You eat your pie. Like I said. It's full of goodness.'

The repetition of 'goodness' – a word in which none but Mrs Stilton seemed to believe – reduced the table to a silence. Pilot Officer Micklewhite broke it.

'Will you be joining us, Captain Cormack?'

'Joining you?'

'The war,' said Micklewhite. 'Will the States be getting stuck in with us? Shoulder to shoulder?'

'Nah. They'll be late just like the last time,' muttered one of the twins. A look from his father shut him up.

'Manners, Maurice. Captain Cormack can't be expected to answer questions like that.'

Cal looked quickly around the table. Every man in the room, Vera too, was looking back at him. It didn't look as though he could duck the question except by hiding behind Stilton's intervention – but then he'd no wish to duck it, he'd heard it too often, it was time to take it at the flood.

'It's OK, Walter,' he said. 'I'm happy to answer. I can't speak for America, I can only speak for myself. In the last week I've been asked the same question by complete strangers. A guy in the street, standing on Westminster Bridge. The tailor who made the suit I'm wearing. I said nothing. I rather wish now I'd spoken. England seems to need to know. I can't say I blame England. But – I'm here. I'm in the war. I'm with you. Maybe not shoulder to shoulder. And right now not in uniform. But I'm here.

As far as I'm concerned I've been fighting this war since I was posted to Europe in 1939. If you want me to answer for my country – well, I guess I began by resenting the question – I was wrong and I don't any more – but all the same, all you'll get is my personal opinion.'

'Which is?'

'We'll be in this war by Christmas.'

Cal could scarcely believe it. They cheered and stomped. Everyone but the Stiltons themselves, who seemed baffled and bemused by the behaviour of their children, not quite sure if it was 'manners' or not. And as the hubbub died, one pair of hands clapping, and a figure in the doorway he had not seen before. A tall redhead with deep green eyes, clapping him fiercely and smiling ear to ear.

'Well said,' she said. 'Whoever you are.'

Cal rose, the only man in the room on his feet, while Edna Stilton scuttled back to the stove for a warm plate.

'I already said. Be late for your own funeral, you will.'

'My eldest,' Stilton resumed his list. 'Katherine.'

The young woman advanced on Cal – a bluish-black uniform he couldn't quite place. Sergeant's stripes on the sleeve.

'Kitty,' she said. 'Kitty Stilton.'

After the motley array of Stilton daughters, nothing had prepared him for the woman he now met. She put her sisters in the shade.

'Calvin Cormack,' he said softly.

She unbuttoned her tunic and threw it onto a chair behind them. She smoothed down her skirt, making Cal acutely conscious of her figure. Edged her way between Cal and her father.

'Inch up, Dad. I'm not sitting next to Tel. He'll pester me to death.'

Tel protested. She ruffled his hair. He squirmed. Stilton moved up and made room for her. She and Cal sat down together. Edna Stilton stuck a plate in front of her.

'Woolton pie,' she said, almost as a warning.

'Great,' said Kitty, not even looking at it.

Cal heard the table dissolve into half a dozen conversations and felt relieved that he was no longer their focus. Kitty Stilton chatted to her father, and as her mother gathered up plates from the first course and dished out bowls for the next, she turned to him and said, 'Well?'

'Well?' he said.

'What's the uniform you say you're not wearing?'

'United States Army. I'm a regular. A captain. And you?'

'You mean you don't know?'

'I'm sure I've seen it. I just can't place the uniform. I can't even tell if it's blue or black. Are you a Wren?'

She laughed, a hugely engaging laugh, devoid of mockery, genuinely amused that he had to ask.

'I'm a copper. A sergeant in the Met. Didn't my old man tell you?'

'I'm sure he'd've gotten round to it.'

'And there was I thinking he boasted about me to every eligible man he met.'

She paused, glanced down at the unadorned fingers of Cal's hands.

'And you are eligible, aren't you?'

And, not waiting for an answer, got up to help her mother serve.

Cal had a friend in Zurich who pointedly removed his wedding band when he went out to pick up women. It left a ring of paler skin on his finger as blatant as a tattoo – it all but screamed 'married' – and he never failed to score. Cal could not imagine putting on a wedding band, but then he could not imagine anyone who had put one on ever wanting to take it off.

Kitty returned to the table, plonked down what

114

appeared to be a hazard to shipping in off-white, dotted with black spots that could be raisins or detonators.

'Right,' said Edna Stilton. 'You know what else I got at the butcher's? Suet. That's what I got. I got the last bit o' suet in the shop. So you lot get spotted dick. Only watch out for the sultanas, on account of I've had 'em in the cupboard since 1932. You break a tooth, you've only yourself to blame.'

From the look on the face of every man present – Stilton sat with his spoon upright in his fist; 'those about to eat salute you' – Cal was aware that, whatever it amounted to, spotted dick was to be regarded and received as a treat.

Cal put it down to the length of the evening – the light if somewhat chilly May nights. Whilst he would gladly have accepted that the social day was over and gone back to his hotel, the Stiltons would not hear of it. They adjourned to an upstairs room. Turned on the radio.

'You can't go now,' they all seemed to protest in unison. 'Billy Cotton's on the wireless.'

This meant nothing to him. A band Cal privately thought not a patch on Benny Goodman or Duke Ellington piped up and the twins took turns twirling a blushing but unprotesting Miss Greenlees across the carpet. She was a far better dancer than either of them, as she proved when Tom-from-the-Ministry took their place and matched her skills with his. No one involved him in the dance, no one 'asked' him to dance or hinted that he should ask any one of the endless Stilton daughters. Perhaps they'd reached the boundary of good manners – he would have hated to do it but could scarcely see a way to say no. Instead he listened to Edna Stilton regale him with the lives of absent lodgers. Her house, it seemed, had always had a floating population; several generations of clerks, librarians and shop girls had passed through. An extended, inconstant family.

'O' course this time last year there was rooms going begging. Nobody wanted 'em. Everybody'd packed their kiddies off to the country. But we lost so many houses since the Blitz started that a good room's become hard to find again. Mr Bell – he lodged at number thirty-eight with Mrs Wisby. Got bombed out. We took him in when old Mr Trewin went to live with his daughter in Weston-super-Mare . . .'

Cal stopped listening. Stilton had lit up his pipe and appeared to be in a huddle with his daughter Kitty. Cal guessed from the intent look on their faces that they were discussing work. He could hear nothing in the smothering cloud of music and laughter of what they were saying, but when Stilton looked right at him he saw his chance and took it.

'I think I should go now, Walter. It's been a long day.'

Stilton got up, tapped out his pipe on the side of the fireplace.

'Then I'll run you back.'

'No. It's OK. I'll get a cab.'

'Not in this neck o' the woods you won't. Like I said, I'll run you up West.'

Kitty was looking at Cal – still perched on the edge of her father's armchair, one arm stretched out along the back, one leg swinging gently.

'Don't worry, Dad. I can give Mr Cormack a lift. No bother,' she said.

Stilton protested, 'He doesn't want to ride –'

She cut him short. 'Dad, I'm going home to Covent Garden. It's hardly out of my way, is it?'

Then she turned to Cal.

'Up West? What hotel you in? Claridge's? All the Yanks is in Claridge's.'

Only when she reached down a black motorcycle helmet from the hallstand did Cal realise the exactitude of the word 'ride'. But he was trapped now, in the web of his own sense of 'manners'. He said his goodbyes – thanked the Stiltons for their hospitality and followed Kitty into the night. A large Ariel motorcycle – 500 cc at least – was leaning on its stand at the kerb. Kitty hitched up her skirt.

'Let me kick 'er up, then you hop on behind. You ever ridden pillion?'

His 'no' was drowned out as she leapt bodily off the ground to land on the kickstart, and the bike fired up.

'You put yer arms 'round me waist! You got that?'

Cal did as he was told, stretched a leg over the pillion seat and slid on behind her, wondering, as she yelled 'tighter', if this was as dangerous a venture as she seemed to think it was.

Kitty had none of her father's sense of caution. It was now pitch dark, but she throttled up the motorbike and roared through the City of London at sixty miles an hour. Past the Bank of England, over Holborn Viaduct, to streak along Oxford Street before zig-zagging across Hanover Square to Claridge's.

When she finally stopped Cal's legs were shaking, his fingers were numb, and he felt his hair must be standing on end like Elsa Lanchester's in *The Bride of Frankenstein*.

He hadn't a clue what to say to this woman. Southern manners took over, he offered her a frozen hand and said, 'It's been a pleasure.'

'I do like a feller wot can talk posh,' she said, and had to grin before he realised she was taking the mickey.

'You and my dad'll be working together then?'

'I guess we will.'

'Then we could be havin' a lot more "pleasure".'

She kicked the bike back to life. Cal headed for the door, the elevator and bed.

He flicked on the bathroom light and pulled the door three-quarters shut so that a sliver of light cut across the bedroom carpet. Just enough light to see what he was doing. If the Germans could spot that maybe they'd earn the shot. He drew back the curtains onto a moonless, cloudy night. Threw off his jacket, loosened his tie and wished half-heartedly for a bottle of bourbon. It had been another day in which he had got nowhere. Some part of him wished for the spectacular distraction of an air raid, and the part of him that furnished guilt for all occasions stepped on this as though upon a cigarette butt tossed into the gutter.

There came a gentle tapping on his door, and when he opened it there stood Kitty Stilton, helmet in one hand, a large white envelope in the other.

'Dispatch for Captain Cormack,' she said and grinned.

'Is that what you told them downstairs?'

'Yeah. Actually it's yesterday's *Evening News* stuffed inside an old envelope. But Claridge's ain't the sort of hotel where they let a man stroll in with a strange woman.'

'Even one in uniform?'

'I might not always be in uniform. Now – you goin' to ask me in, or do I have to stand here all night?'

Cal swung back the door. Closed it behind her. She dropped the envelope and helmet on an armchair, stood in the window for a second, looking out as he had done.

'It's a bad habit,' he tried to explain.

She turned, her face entirely in the shadows – visible only from the buttons on her tunic, downwards.

'Wot is?'

'Looking out for the planes. Expecting to see them. Wanting to see them.'

'Oh. We all do that. If you see 'em you're torn between the thrill and the knowledge that some poor sod's copping it, and if you don't you think Hitler's saving it all up for the big one.'

'So I've heard.'

Kitty picked at the buttons of her uniform. Sloughed off the tunic, scraped off her lace-up shoes, heel to toe.

'I was wonderin',' she said, 'if you fancied a bit?'

'A bit?' he said, not understanding.

'Well. To be honest, I was wonderin' if you fancied the lot.'

A zipper slid at one hip and the blue skirt pooled at her feet. She stepped lightly across the floor in stockinged feet and a slip. Locked her hands behind his neck. Even barefoot, she was only a couple of inches shorter than he – and just a couple of inches away.

'The lot?' he said, understanding perfectly.

'The works,' she said, and smooched him.

§ 25

In the morning Cal woke early. He lay in bed, Kitty asleep, one arm stretched across his chest, red head buried in the sheets, and wondered again about the famous English reserve. After the third bout, when he had begun to think her inexhaustible, he had put the question to her.

'What happened to the famous English reserve?'

And Kitty had answered, 'Don't you know there's a war on?'

But then, he had learnt in less than a week that that was pretty much their answer to everything.

The telephone next to the bed rang. Cal slid from under Kitty's arm and picked it up.

'Captain Cormack? Chief Inspector Stilton in the foyer for you, sir.'

Cal looked at Kitty. Looked at his watch. Good God, it was only seven thirty. Did the man never sleep?

'I'll be down in ten minutes,' he said.

'Kitty, Kitty.'

He shook her.

'Kitty, wake up. For Christ's sake, wake up.'

She opened her eyes, the lids fluttering blearily.

'Wossatime?'

'It's seven thirty.'

'Zatall? I'm not on till noon.'

She pulled a pillow over her head. Cal snatched it away.

'Your father's on now!'

'Wot?'

'He's in the lobby right now.'

She sat upright, hands flat on the mattress, breasts swaying.

'He's never coming up?'

'No – but I've got to go down.'

'Fine – bung out the "do not disturb" and I'll get some kip.'

She took back her pillow, pulled up the sheets and ignored him.

Cal took the lift down to the lobby, showered, shaved and dressed in less than seven minutes, rubbing at his chin and knowing he looked about as shaved as a singed pig. He wondered about the Stilton sense of 'manners' – a word so potent both Stilton and his wife had used it as a one-word reprimand last night – the cockney equivalent of 'good form'? What was good form when greeting a man whose daughter you'd just spent a long night fucking? What if sex inscribed itself on your forehead like the mark of Cain? From the open lift doors he could see Stilton at one of the tables, a large map spread out in front of him. On either side of the Atlantic, the moment had only one clearly good form – deceit. Lie and hope nothing showed.

Stilton was eating – toast and jam – a cup of tea stuck on top of the map. A young woman sitting opposite him – glasses, hair up, a pleasing smile and intense eyes.

'Hope you don't mind,' Stilton said. 'We ordered breakfast on your room number.'

'That's fine. I hardly ever eat breakfast.'

'Nor me,' said the woman.

'I was forgetting meself. Captain Cormack, Miss Payne. Our sketch artist.'

'Sketch artist?'

'We don't have a photo of our man. We can't go around London expecting to find him on a description, now can we?'

Cal sat down in the third chair. A waitress asked him if he wanted anything and he asked for black coffee. He brushed away the mark of Cain and waited for Stilton to explain.

'It's dead easy,' he began. 'You tell Miss Payne what Stahl looks like and she'll draw him.'

Instinctively, Cal looked around. He'd never get used to this – this public airing of things and names he'd learnt to see as secrets. Perhaps it wasn't just Stilton, perhaps it was the British? The habitual cry of 'Don't you know there's a war on?' was a necessity – most of them seemed to forget so readily. Perhaps it was all of them? Miss Payne hadn't batted an eyelid, just sipped at her tea.

'How long will this take?'

Miss Payne answered, 'About two hours.'

Stilton set down his cup, wiped his lips on the back of his hand, stuffed the crumpled map into his macintosh pocket and got up.

'I'll drop by about eleven.'

That was more like three hours.

'You mean you're going without me?'

'Got my Czech bloke to find, haven't I?'

'Walter?'

Cal followed him to the door. Caught up with him in a few strides and buttonholed him.

'Walter. I didn't come all this way to sit by while you chase –'

He couldn't say it. It went against all his training to utter Stahl's name out loud.

'Walter, we have to do this together.'

'Aye, lad. And we will. We'll get stuck in. We will. Straight after lunch. We'll get right on it. But we do need that sketch.'

He clapped Cal on one shoulder with the flat of his hand – an avuncular brush-off.

'Wot larx, eh?'

Wot larx? What was the man talking about?

He went back to the table. A silver pot of coffee had been set out for him. Miss Payne had her sketch pad propped against the table. A row of sharp pencils. A vicious looking penknife. A huge, putty-coloured india rubber eraser. She smiled at him. A silent 'ready-when-you-are'. Cal sighed a silent sigh. Poured himself a coffee. Miss Payne was following the movements of his hands, like a cat at a tennis match.

'Is anything wrong?' Cal asked.

'I don't suppose your coffee would run to two, would it? I'm not really a tea sort of person.'

'Of course,' he said, and she slopped her tea into a handy aspidistra and stuck out her cup.

'Walter's a tea man. Could drink it all day, I've no doubt. But I do so miss a good cup of coffee. And that really does look like a good cup of coffee.'

She sipped and sighed. A look of real pleasure on her face.

'Why didn't you just order coffee?'

'Reserved,' she said, looking at him across the top of her cup.

'Reserved for whom?'

'For Americans.'

'For Americans?'

'Coffee isn't actually on the ration. After all, most English people don't care for it, anyway. And generally one can have as much as one wants. But just lately it sort of comes and goes. A bit of a bean famine. Especially since Jerry flattened the coffee stores in Old Compton Street on Sunday morning. One hears rumours – there's coffee to be had in Barnsley or Bakewell or Banff, the sort of places one wouldn't go to more than once in a lifetime if at all. Quite why is baffling – I mean, why Barnsley? Why not Highgate or Chelsea? When it last got short, about three weeks ago, your embassy took to supplying coffee beans to those hotels that billet embassy staff. A bit goes to the Savoy, but most of it comes here. Officers only, of course. Those of us that can't swallow the taste of dandelion and roast barley – what the Ministry of Food laughingly calls ersatz coffee – are terribly envious of life here. I have a girlfriend who's hung around here since the end of April trying out every accent from Mae West to Vivien Leigh in *Gone With the Wind*. Never works. I almost got arrested. I tried to do Marlene Dietrich in *Destry Rides Again* – forgot she was German, you see. When I called her "dollink" the waitress called the police.'

'But you are the police.'

'Strictly for the duration, dollink. No Season after all, and one must do one's bit.'

Cal sipped guiltily at his own cup, then set it down and pushed the pot across the table to her.

'Help yourself,' he said.

'Thanks awfully. You're a brick. Now shall we make a start?'

'How, exactly?'

'Just describe the chap to me, that's all.'

Cal tried to think of words that would convey Wolfgang Stahl to the ears and hands of a woman who'd never seen him and never, until now, had to imagine him. What Stahl looked like had never mattered to him. What Stahl *was* had been the axis of his work for two years.

'Stuck?' Miss Payne asked.

'A little,' Cal said.

'Why not . . . why not think of your chap as a type? Tell me what type you'd sort of put him into.'

'Sort of?'

'You know . . . roughly.'

'He's an Aryan.'

'Ah, one of those, eh? Odd when you think about it. I mean. How did they arrive at blue-eyed blonds as a racial type? Hitler's short and dark and looks like Charlie Chaplin. Goebbels is short and ugly and looks like a rat. And as for Goering – well is that what Billy Bunter grew up to be?'

'Who?'

'Never mind. I'm rambling. Aryan it is. Look, why don't you sit where Stinker sat, so you can see what I draw. We'll get on a lot better that way.'

Cal moved around the table. Pulled the chair closer to look over her right shoulder as she worked, caught the waft of her perfume, watched her hands fly across the paper as he talked.

Two hours later Miss Payne had worked her way through twenty or more pages, and a version of Stahl had appeared on the pad. She'd had to draw the scar above the left eyebrow half a dozen times before Cal saw Stahl come to life. She'd taken a coloured pencil and added a dash of blue to the eyes, and then, when Cal had said 'Too bright', rubbed a little charcoal in with the tip of her pinky finger. It was Stahl. Not a hard face, but a face that had rendered itself hard. Not a face so much as mask, he thought.

Miss Payne was holding the sketch at arm's length and squinting at it framed against the bank of elevators when

Cal saw the doors open and Kitty emerge, looking clean and fresh and vital – the opposite of the blanket bed-beast he'd left a few hours ago. She waved – a cheery smile – a hammy wink of the eye. Good God, what was she thinking of? Then he caught sight of Miss Payne, waving back and smiling.

'Old Stinker's daughter,' she said. 'Quite a character. Rules weren't made for our Kitty. Now, is this the bloke or isn't it? I may not be Picasso – but then, if I was, I suppose no one would ever recognise him with his nose under his armpit. Any chance of another pot of coffee?'

§ 26

Came a lull in the day. A message on his desk told him to collect a bloodstained dress and a shoe from Forensics. They could just as easily send them, but Troy saw an opportunity to indulge a copper's nosiness. He drove out to Hendon, to the Metropolitan Police Laboratory, in search of Ladislaw Konradovitch Kolankiewicz, the Polish beast, one of the lab's senior pathologists – a protégé of Sir Bernard Spilsbury, an exile of indeterminate age, extraordinary ugliness and foul, fractured English that Troy had long ago come to regard as a form of colloquial poetry.

He was scrubbing up. Hairy arms sluiced under the tap. A corpse under a sheet on the slab. A young woman in white perched on a high stool. Flipping through a shorthand notebook and reading bits back to Kolankiewicz.

'Displacement of first three vertebrae, resulting in severance of spinal column from ... brain stem ... would appear to be result of ... I'm sorry, I can't read my own writing.'

Kolankiewicz elbowed the taps, turned round to argue and noticed Troy.

'Ah, smartyarse. What brings the *Plattfusswunderkind* to my lair?'

'Nothing much,' said Troy. 'Just a hunch.'

'Ah! Copper's hunch. That and three ha'pence would just about buy me cup of tea. Now, pretty boy, since you were last here we have a new addition to death's family. Mrs Pakenham, my lab assistant. She joined us in the New Year and is now learning shorthand – the hard way – as the War Office saw fit to call up my stenographer.'

The young woman stopped reading her notes and scratching her head with the pencil.

'Sergeant Troy,' said Kolankiewicz. 'Brighter than your average flatfoot, but still total pain in arse.'

This was mild. Kolankiewicz was minding his manners. The woman must be good. It could not last. He relished the English language with all the fervour of a convert. It held no traps and no taboos as far as Kolankiewicz was concerned. 'Fuck' was never far from his lips at the worst of times, and those were all the times he and Troy had had between them.

The young woman looked up. The merest flicker of a smile. A cut-glass English voice.

'Anna,' she said. 'Anna Pakenham.'

It was a little like looking into a mirror. A short, slim woman, thick black hair – pulled back with a working-day severity – pale skin like his, and eyes like his – black as coal.

'Frederick Troy. Murder Squad.'

It sounded like the most unattractive calling card in the world – indeed, Troy kept calling cards without rank or job just to drop on the silver plate without causing alarm – but she said, 'I'll suppose we'll be seeing a lot of you, then?'

No, he thought. Kolankiewicz had got through so

many stenographers and assistants since the war started. This one would not last. They none of them did. She'd volunteer for the ATS or the WRNS or go off to wear jodhpurs and dig spuds in the darkest shires. A pity. Married or not, she was a looker.

'You get sick of the sight of him,' said Kolankiewicz. 'Now, whatever it is, spit it out.'

'I was wondering about a body. A Dutchman found dead in Hoxton Street last night.'

Kolankiewicz whipped back the sheet.

'This fucker?'

Troy found himself staring once more at the unearthly, drained, white-beyond-white corpse of Jeroen Smulders, fresh stitching loosely holding incisions Kolankiewicz had made. He glanced sideways at Mrs Pakenham. She was not reacting, either to the corpse or to Kolankiewicz's lapse into plain speaking. She had the makings of a good Kolankiewicz assistant. Blanch not at the bodies nor the beast.

'Yes. That's him. Are you done? Do you know how he died?'

'This not your case, Troy. That big bastard Stilton, the one with the silly accent, sent him over. I had him on the phone at crack of dawn this morning.'

'I know. I checked with his office. I'd just rather know for myself than wait for him to tell me. It *was* my case. I was the one who was called out to the scene. I have a feeling about this one.'

'Two hunches in two minutes? I'll have arrowroot biscuit with my tea. Anna?'

'It says ... violent pressure on the head and neck, clockwise twisting of the neck, evident in subcutaneous bruising. At least I think it says "clockwise". I'm terribly new to shorthand.'

The contrast between the formal, procedural English

of an autopsy, and Kolankiewicz's colloquial mode never ceased to startle Troy.

'Enough?' he was saying. 'Enough for a nosy rozzer?'

'I was wondering about the hands.'

'Hands?'

'Hands.'

'What about his hands?'

'If you fall down a staircase conscious you try and stop yourself. You grab onto something. You flail about. Chances are there'll be marks on the hands. Bruised knuckles. A torn nail.'

They both looked at Mrs Pakenham.

'Nothing,' she said. 'No bruises. Nothing.'

'And,' Troy went on, 'if you fall down dead, you don't. As simple as that really.'

'He was dead, believe me, Troy, he was dead.'

'And?'

'I tell you what I tell Stilton. The killer was right-handed. Taller than this bloke, but not necessarily stronger. It's more of a knack than brute force. Snap a neck in a single movement. Death was instantaneous. A pro job. You happy now?'

'Happy?' said Troy. 'No, I'm not happy. I just have a feeling that this one will come back to me.'

'Three hunches! I'll have buttered scone and jam dollop too.'

§ 27

That afternoon Alex Troy was in his study. He would have liked to take a walk on the heath, but it was unseasonably cold for May. He would have liked to meet the world, if only for half an hour, but the telephone rang and the world came to him.

He picked up the phone.

'Alex? It's Max.'

A short syllable to introduce a short man with a long handle – Max Aitken, Lord Beaverbrook, proprietor of the *Daily Express* and Minister of State, until recently Minister of Aircraft Production, in Churchill's government.

'I held a lunchtime briefing for the Fleet Street editors at Claridge's today. I half expected you'd be there.'

So, that's what ministers of state did. They gave briefings.

'Half? You are such an optimist, Max. Perhaps if you were to expect me a sixteenth or a thirty-second you would be less disappointed in me.'

'I was wondering. Would you care for a drink at my club tonight?'

Beaverbrook usually asked him round for one or both of two reasons. He knew something you didn't and wanted to lord it. What, after all, was the point in being a lord if you could not lord it? – as far as Alex was concerned this might as well be the Beaver's motto in life. Or he had some crackpot theory he wanted to air, partly, as with the first reason, to remind you that he was close to the powers that be, and partly because it was not the sort of thing he could air in his newspapers without being guilty of the kind of rumour-mongering and defeatism the government deplored in the common people and would deplore the more in one of its own.

The last time they'd met had been May Day. Max had bored him silly with 'The balloon's up. We're backs to the wall now, Alex. The war has turned ugly for us. I'd say two or three days at the most. Invasion is imminent.' – when it transparently wasn't. It made Alex wonder how much the Prime Minister really told him. Bugger all, it would seem. That he could not see for himself was shocking. The RAF had won the battle for Britain. Won it with the planes the Beaver had churned out as Minister of Aircraft Production. A job that had enabled him to rally the nation's housewives into giving up their pots and pans to be melted down into aeroplanes. Alex had never been certain whether this was anything more than a morale-building stunt – 'Women! You too can do your bit!' – but ever after he'd thought of Beaverbrook as Lord Saucepans. There probably was a Beaver Brook, somewhere in the wilds of Ontario, probably several, along with Moose Gulch and Wild Ass Pass – they none of them managed to sound real when appended to the word 'Lord'.

Alex had no desire to go to the Beaver's club – to any of his clubs, the Carlton or the Marlborough, the former political, the latter royal in basis.

'How about *my* club?' he said.

'The Garrick? Fine,' said Beaverbrook.

They fixed a time and rang off.

Alex was going by the counter-theory of that applied by single women: 'Never invite him in. Go back to his place, then you can always leave. Far easier than throwing a man out.' He was taking Beaverbrook to his club – watering hole of old hams and young pretenders, where a distraction could always be arranged without the necessity of walking out, and where they were unlikely in the extreme to meet any other 'gentlemen' of Fleet Street – but, then, that was precisely why he had joined, to escape the 'gentlemen' of Fleet Street.

§ 28

Stilton's three hours had become half a day. It was close to three in the afternoon before he returned to Claridge's. Cal had sat in the lobby, watched Lord Beaverbrook's entourage breeze in and out like visiting pashas, read every newspaper he could get his hands on and drunk coffee till he felt he was floating on the stuff.

'Jesus Christ, Walter. Do you know what time it is?'

'Aye, aye. Couldn't be helped. Might've known it would be a waste of time in daylight. But I had to look for my Czech – Hudge. The sooner we find him the better.'

'But you didn't find him? Is that what you're saying?'

'No – a bit of a night owl really. Still. There's always tonight.'

Cal looked at his watch.

'You're not telling me we have to wait for darkness – in May, in double summertime? I've been stuck on my butt all day.'

'Oh – there's things to do, don't you worry. Now, did Poppy – that is, Miss Payne – get done?'

Cal handed over the sketch that had cost three pots of coffee, a morning of his time, a stream of London gossip and much of his tolerance of flirtatious upper-crust English women with names like Poppy. Stilton looked at it.

'Is it him?'

'Oh, it's very him.'

'Good – let's nip over to the Yard shall we?'

§ 29

Beaverbrook always reminded Alex of a monkey. He had a monkey's round face, wide mouth. A monkey's stature. A monkey's sense of mischief. Most people bore passing resemblance to their own caricature – Beaverbrook was the spitting image of David Low's cartoon – no caricature, no exaggeration seemed too grotesque. The big head on the little body, the grin that seemed to split it like a watermelon struck with a shovel.

He was in the foyer of the Garrick, being helped out of his overcoat when Alex arrived.

'You missed a good lunch,' said the Beaver.

'No, I missed a free lunch. And I find I can never afford your free lunches.'

Beaverbrook laughed at this and let Alex, by much the older, slower man, set the pace as they went upstairs to the bar, a panelled room lined with portraits of long-dead hams, a patina of age and cracked glaze across most them – indeed, as Alex often thought, across most of the members too. He was not a club man. It was too English a notion. But since one had to belong somewhere, this was better than most, oblique as it was to his own calling. When he was seated, had got his breath and ordered a drink, he said, 'What was the occasion?'

'Hess. What else?'

'I suppose you told Fleet Street to dampen it down?'

'No, quite the opposite. Winston wanted to make a statement. I talked him out of it last night. I think we should all speculate, each paper with a different angle. Make as much of this as possible, throw out every possible reason Hess could have for what he did. Get the maximum possible propaganda value out of it.'

'A licence to lie, Max?'

'I wouldn't put it that way. Shall we say a licence to gild the lily?'

'Words, words, words. You were still asking them to lie. You're asking me to lie now.'

'Think about it, Alex. Why do you think he's come? Don't you think that's an honest question? Don't you think that's an honest question to put before your readers?'

'No. I do not. It's no more honest than the German papers. On Tuesday they all carried the same headline to the letter – Hess in Tragic Accident. The accident being the long-awaited onset of madness.'

'Do you think he's mad?'

'I've no idea. I met him just the once and that was years ago. But it does seem that until he finally tells someone what he's up to, then both sides will find equal cause to dismiss him as mad.'

There was a pause. Alex could almost hear the Beaver timing it like the true ham he was.

'I asked Winston if I could see Hess, you know.'

Ah. At last the nub. Beaverbrook was rubbing his nose in it.

'Did he say yes?'

'He didn't say no.'

At the back of his mind Alex felt vaguely certain he'd heard this repartee before somewhere.

'What did he say?'

'Later. He said later. When the Foreign Office are through with him.'

'Well Max, there you are, another scoop.'

Beaverbrook did not react to the sarcasm.

'Who have they sent?' Alex asked.

'Kirkpatrick.'

For a second all Alex could think of was a young American journalist who'd been in London covering the war for one paper or another – Helen? Hannah? H-something Kirkpatrick. Then he remembered – Ivone Kirkpatrick, the diplomat at the Berlin embassy who'd come to the attention of the British press when he'd been stuck with the unenviable task of translating for Chamberlain at Munich.

'He's not the man for the job.'

'Do you know him? He's considered an expert on Berlin.'

'No, I've never met the man. But it's not a job for a career diplomat. It's an expert in interrogation they need, not an expert on Berlin. They should send in the toughest nut they have. An English Yezhov or a Beria, if there is such a beast. Ernie Bevin on a bad day. And if that doesn't work I would not be at all surprised if Winston didn't just put the bugger up against a wall and have him shot.'

Beaverbrook grinned, Beaverbrook chuckled, Beaverbrook guffawed. The monkey face split from side to side – head back, eyes popping. It was unthinkable – but Churchill might just do it. The wave of laughter subsided in him. He wiped the corner of one eye and indulged in another meaningful pause.

'If you were interrogating Hess now, what would you want from him? If you could ask him just one question, Alex, what would it be?'

And yet more – Beaverbrook was rubbing his nose in it at the same time as he sought to pick his brains. Alex saw no point in lying to the little sod. There could only be one plausible answer.

'I would want to know the intentions of the Third Reich towards Russia. To be precise, I would want the date and the battle formation for Hitler's invasion of the USSR. I would want to know when the lunatic proposes to lead his country into mass suicide.'

'Do you really think it would be that? Most of my Cabinet colleagues seem to think Russia would last three weeks. A month at the most.'

'Have a little faith, Max. Think of Russia's power to resist. Almost a passive quality. But what a power! Remember Napoleon. Read *War and Peace*. It will be suicide on the grand scale. If Russia comes into this war, then Germany is doomed. And Russia will pay the price in suffering that we British seem to have been spared thus far.'

'We British,' said Beaverbrook, grinning. 'A Canadian and a Russian.'

It seemed to Old Troy to be neither statement nor question. He answered in kind.

'We British. A couple of wogs. A baron and a baronet – rewarded for nothing more significant than our wealth and influence. What a curious country this is.'

Sarcasm was so often wasted on the Beaver.

§ 30

'The Yard', as in 'Let's nip over to the Yard', was a cheering phrase – a movie cliché to rank with 'Let's form a posse' and 'Come out with your hands up, we've got you surrounded.'

In reality it had meant more sitting on his butt while Walter had the sketch copied by Scotland Yard's photographic section. Cal had dreamt of a day when you could stick a piece of paper in one end of a machine and get a copy out the other end in two seconds. It was like something out of H. G. Wells or Aldous Huxley. It went with food synthesisation and the Feelies. He even had a name for the machine – the Instant Image Replicator, very catchy. If he knew the first thing about science he'd've doodled a sketch and dashed to the patent office. Instead he had sat, getting angrier and angrier, until Walter reappeared with a bundle of photos, stuck one in his hand and said, 'Pubs're open.'

In the car, heading north up the Charing Cross Road, he said to Stilton, 'Does everything take place in pubs?'

'Pretty well.'

'How many are there?'

Stilton laughed. 'God knows. I've never counted and I couldn't begin to guess. Mind, I did once count every pub, church and chapel in the town I grew up in. As I recall, thirty-five pubs and seventeen assorted churches and chapels.'

'For how many people?'

'Not a lot. A few thousand.'

'Jesus. Is that what the English do, sin all Saturday and repent on Sunday?'

'Pretty well,' said Stilton.

When they pulled up in front of the Marquis of Lincoln, Cal asked 'Why this one?'

'The one time we lost Smulders, it was a few yards from here. It gets its fair share of refugees. Time to ask who was in that night.'

Considering the public house appeared to be the pivot of English social life, Cal was surprised they were not more friendly. More friendly, more clean, more warm – more everything. By and large this one did little to alter his first impression of the night before – they were grim places. Worse still, a bit of mugging to the wireless notwithstanding, they were joyless places. The wall of faces that now faced him across the ranks of half-empty pint glasses on every table looked to him like gargoyles. The barman was no exception – a nose like Punchinello, bright enough to light his way home and constitute a breach of the blackout regulations.

Stilton called him 'Ernie' and beckoned to him.

'Mr Stilton. What brings you in, might I ask?'

'Business, Ernie, business. Were you on, Monday night?'

'I'm on every night.'

Stilton laid the sketch of Stahl on the bar.

'Was this bloke in?'

'Dunno,' said the barman.

Stilton put a photograph of Smulders next to it.

'Nor 'im. Look Mr Stilton, why don't you ask some of the regulars? They got nothing better to do than look who's new and who ain't. Me, I'm pullin' pints all night.'

Stilton turned to Cal, said, 'Have a seat for five minutes. I'll just have a word with this lot.'

Cal watched him move from table to table, watched his face run a gamut of hammy theatrical expressions, each one donned and doffed like a *Commedia dell'Arte* mask. One man needed to be cajoled, another bullied and another wheedled. It took him ten minutes or more, but one way or another every look of suspicion with which they greeted him was overcome or outflanked. Stilton moved among these shabby little men – and it was men, not a woman in the place – like a colossus among the threadbare remnants of a tatty, defeated army. The weight of the word sank into Cal's imagination. There was misery here. For the first time the English looked defeated – as he had thought when he first walked in, joyless. He'd often heard the phrase 'crying into your beer' – maybe that's what beer was for?

His attention came to rest on a couple in the corner. A blind man and his minder. A stout old man in a ragged blue overcoat. A few wisps of white hair seemed to stand up on his skull as though blown by the draught. His eyes were lost behind glasses that were not simply dark, but utterly opaque. Stilton was making his way across the room to them now. Cal followed, picking his way between the whispering, surly faces at the tables.

'Well, if it isn't Mr Potts,' said Stilton.

The blind man spoke to his minder, a surprisingly cultured voice, 'I know that step better than I know that voice. The heavy tread of Old Bill. I take it the constabulary are in tonight, Leckie?'

'It's me, Walter Stilton. I just wanted a quick word.'

'Always at your service sir,' Potts answered. 'Anything for the Met, Chief Inspector.'

Walter set the two pictures on the table, 'I'm looking for two men. One or both of 'em might have been in on Monday.'

Cal whispered. 'Walter, this guy is blind!'

'Trust me,' Stilton whispered back.

The man sitting next to Potts was his logical oppostite. A tiny man, his shoulders only slightly higher than the table, his eyes wide and bright, a mass of red hair spiralling off in all directions. Now, he whispered to Potts.

'No, Mr Stilton. Leckie says we have not seen them.'

'Monday. It's Monday I was asking about.'

Leckie whispered again.

'We were here Monday but we don't remember. But Leckie says we know a man who might.'

Another whisper.

'Hudge,' said Potts. 'Hudge was in Monday. We are certain of that. Leckie has reminded us. We distinctly heard his lopsided shuffle. And then we heard his cough. No two men cough alike. Did you know that, Mr Stilton?'

'A useful tip, I'm sure. About what time?'

'Nine. It was nine, wasn't it Leckie? And it was busy.'

'Did Leckie see who Hudge was with?'

Another whisper.

'We think he was alone and . . .'

One more whisper.

'. . . and we think it's your round. A pint for Leckie and a large malt for yours truly, Chief Inspector.'

Stilton grumbled, bought them each a drink, scribbled in his little black notebook and left, looking to Cal quite pleased with himself.

'Hudge?' Cal said, when they hit the street.

'My Czech nark. I do like it when two bits meet in the middle.'

'What's a nark?'

'A grass – a stool-pigeon. Needless to say, nobody else is sure of anything. Some thought they recognised 'em, nobody was certain. And nobody would say they saw 'em together. That lot might be dozy, they might even be lying to us, but Hudge, he's in it for a living. If there was something going on in there on Monday he'll have seen it. He's a pro – one of me regulars, you might say.'

'Then surely you know where he lives?'

'I did. I went round there today before you were up. Nowt but rubble. Must have caught a packet last Saturday. Only one thing I know for sure, he was still alive on Monday.'

'And there's been no raid since?'

Stilton nodded.

'So where do we go from here?'

'The shelters. We do the shelters tonight.'

He looked at his watch. 'It's half past six. Meet me at the Yard at ten, and we'll do the rounds.'

'The rounds?'

'Aye. Back East. We'll do the Stepney shelters. Bound to be in one of 'em.'

§ 31

Cal flopped onto the bed, eased the top button of his pants. He wished he could sleep. Stilton had given him the best part of two and a half hours. Maybe he could sleep. He closed his eyes. It wasn't going to work. He thought about calling room service. A shot of spirits. That could do the trick. Then the phone rang.

'Calvin? It's me. Kitty.'

'Hello Kitty.'

'Wossup? You sound flat as my Aunt Flo's Yorkshire pudding.'

'I'm lying down. Your old man kind of ran me ragged today.'

This was a lie. It was not the day or the man that had worn him out, but the night and the daughter.

'I could soon fix that. I get off at nine. I could be over there in a flash.'

'Kitty, I don't know how to say this, so maybe I should just say it as it comes. I know there's a war on, and I figure the war does strange things to the way people behave. Men and women. But before we leap into bed again, don't you think we should talk?'

'Woss to talk about?'

'I don't know. That's just the point. I don't know you and you don't know me. We met yesterday and we went straight to bed!'

'No we didn't. We had dinner with me mum and dad first!'

'That's hardly getting to know one another. Kitty, I just think we should try to get to know one another. I think we should talk.'

'Don't you like it with me, then?'

'It's not a matter of like or not like. It's a matter of what I'm used to. You're rewriting the rules. That takes some grasping. Let's meet and let's talk, as soon as we both have the time.'

'Like I said, I get off at nine.'

'And I have to meet with your father at ten.'

'Great. That's bags o' time. I'll see you in the Salisbury at quarter past nine. We can have a drink and a natter.'

This wasn't what he meant. He wished he could tell her so.

'The Salisbury?'

'A pub.'

'Another one? I thought your father had already dragged me through every pub in London. Good God, how many are there?'

'Thousands, but this particular one's in St Martin's Lane, on the right as you go down. See you there. Quarter past nine. OK?'

'Kitty, I'm kind of pubbed out.'

'Yeah – but just for me, eh?'

He felt he couldn't win this one. His idea was to talk,

to discuss, for want of a better word, the protocol of their relationship. Her idea was to prop up a bar and chat to him for half an hour.

'I'll be there.'

He listened to the dial tone as she rang off. Lay back on the pillow. He wanted to sleep. He wanted Kitty. He wanted Kitty and everything she had on offer. Why the guilt? What bendable but unbreakable moral imperative had his childhood seared into his character?

§ 32

Just over two hours later, Troy pushed open the door to the Saloon bar of the Salisbury. It was the nearest public house to his house, a minute's walk away from the tiny Georgian terrace he had in Goodwin's Court, on the opposite side of St Martin's Lane. He was looking for Charlie – his oldest friend, they'd met on their first day at an English public school they had both loathed – and they'd stuck together ever since. About the time Troy had joined the Metropolitan Police Force, Charlie had come down from Cambridge with a third in Arabic and had joined the Irish Guards. For the first few years Charlie had shown up in uniform more often than not. Now he was a secret agent, of what precise variety he had never said and Troy had never asked, he wore civvies. Being a spook suited him. He looked like a ladykiller in or out of uniform – well over six foot, a mop of blond curls, dazzling blue eyes – and whilst it was a truism of war that a uniform attracted women like moths to a candle, Troy had never once seen Charlie disadvantaged by the lack of it. He could pull a woman as she handed him the white feather.

Charlie was sitting in a booth on the Cecil Court side, flicking through the *News Chronicle*, a whisky and soda at his side. He looked up as Troy sat down, eyes bright, a broad smile across his lips. He lit up, a hundred tiny physical responses – all the visible muscles expressing. Charlie was the most affectionate person – man or woman – Troy had ever known. He was clearly, genuinely delighted to see Troy. Troy might well have reciprocated – few people meant as much to him as Charlie – but he did not have the vocabulary of such affection, physical or verbal. He had not the facility with honesty. As his brother Rod put it, he was 'a colossal fibber' – it was second nature to him to guard the truth, the truth of his own emotions not excepted – and, if nothing else, it made for a dedicated copper.

'Freddie? What'll you have?'

Troy hardly drank and asked for a ginger beer.

'Bollocks. You want ginger beer you can buy your own. Have a drink, for God's sake. Even if it's only a half.'

Troy asked for Guinness. Charlie buttonholed the bloke clearing the empties and ordered half a pint of the black stuff. Troy would leave it sitting on the table, the white head slowly deflating into the black, and with any luck Charlie would never notice.

'How's tricks?'

'Not much fun,' said Troy. 'The only good body to show up in a while got nicked from me by old Walter Stilton.'

'Father of the luscious Kitty, eh? She's standing at the bar right now.'

'What?'

'Next to the tall bloke in the awful suit. See, looks like it was cobbled together by Flanagan and Allen in a Crazy Gang sketch at the Palladium. They were there when I came in. The chap sounded American to me.'

He'd know Kitty anywhere, from any angle. She slipped her arm through the man's. Gave him a kiss on the ear. Troy wondered if she knew he was there. If Charlie had told her who he was meeting. But the Salisbury was twenty yards from Troy's front door. Who else would Charlie be meeting? Kitty inched closer. The light between their bodies vanished as she melded her affection into him, fitting the curve of her waist around the man's hip. Troy stared, willing the American to turn around. He did. It was the same man he'd seen Kitty's father with last night. Time to change the subject.

'You've been out of London. You must have. Or you'd have been nagging me to come out for a drink before this.'

'Indeed I have, o'man. But I can't say where or why for reasons of national security.'

This was nonsense, or the prelude to a gag. Charlie was the most indiscreet man alive. He couldn't keep a secret to save his life.

'Come off it,' Troy said simply.

'Let's just say a quick trip to the land of bagpipes and haggis, a quicker trip back to a large unnamed fortress not a million miles from here in which Richard III murdered his nephews, all because of a chap who's name begins with H and ends with ESS, but who is known to us in the trade as Mr Briggs.'

Troy tried not to laugh. If he did Charlie would get the giggles and collapse in a heap of helpless laughter. This was typical of the man. The unutterable blurted out in a flippant sentence. Matters of national security. Of course he should not have told Troy that Hess was in the Tower of London, but Troy could not think of the force on earth that could stop him. Short of a firing squad.

'Chatty, was he?'

'Doesn't breathe between paragraphs. Talk? The bugger never shuts up. Alas, he doesn't say anything that matters. I've just witnessed four days of the party line. I think he came here genuinely believing that Hamilton would introduce him to the King and a bunch of senior Tories, and then they'd all get together, dump Churchill and do a deal with Hitler. He even asked for a copy of *Three Men In A Boat* – if that's his vision of England, then Mr B. is a chronic fantasist who seems to believe in some sort of ancient Tory heartland that's only waiting for the moment to make peace.'

'Well,' said Troy. 'He's right about that. That's why we locked them up.'

'Quite – but I rather think his invitation to join forces against the Soviet horde might have found itself out-weighed by the opening of the flat or the start of the hunting season. "Mad" does not begin to convey Rudolf Hess. Barking, barking, barking. No matter what question the blokes from the FO put to him, he found some trite bit of Nazi spiel that covered the issue neatly. I tell you, Freddie, it reminded me of nothing quite so much as getting stuck on the doorstep with a very persistent Jehovah's Witness.'

'You should introduce him to my father. They'd be well matched.'

'We'd probably get a damn sight further with your old man putting the questions than we have with these types from the Foreign Office. However, I think hell will freeze over before the boss lets your father within a mile of Mr Briggs.'

'Who is the boss?'

'Reggie Ruthven-Greene. Do you know him?'

Troy shook his head. Charlie flagged down the clearer again and ordered another whisky and soda, pointed at Troy's untouched Guinness. Troy shook his head, lifted the glass to his lips and put it back without taking a sip.

Charlie said, 'This had better be my last. I have to meet Reggie about five minutes ago. Look, I won't be far out of London once old Briggs is fixed up, and I can be back any time there's a break. You're single again, aren't you . . . ?'

'Single?' said Troy, as though the word meant nothing to him.

'You know what I mean . . . spare . . . without a woman! Why don't we get together one night next week? Do the town. Check out operations on the totty front.'

He belted back his whisky in a single gulp and was on his feet before Troy could answer. But Troy never would answer. He'd just say 'Of course', and when Charlie phoned up divert him from the plan or plead the 'job'. Charlie always wanted to check out the totty front, but he always ended up 'doing the town' without Troy.

The American and Charlie collided in the doorway. An 'Excuse me' deferred to an 'After you, old chap', they hesitated for ten seconds and then the American slipped out and Charlie waved his cheerio and followed. The coincidence of them leaving at the same time left Troy staring at Kitty Stilton's back. She turned, stuck her hands in her coat pockets and sauntered across the floor towards him.

'Fred,' she said by way of greeting.

'Sergeant Stilton,' said Troy with all the neutral inflection he could muster.

'Your mate coming back, is 'e?'

'No. Yours?'

Kitty pulled back the chair Charlie had sat in.

'Ain't you gonna buy a girl a drink, then?'

Troy buttonholed the clearer. Asked for a gin and lime.

'I'm not a bleedin' waiter, y'know.'

Kitty opened her coat, let him see the uniform beneath and thrust out her chest.

'For the boys in blue?' said Troy, and the man muttered a grudging 'Awright'.

Thirty seconds later he slammed a glass down in front of Kitty, spilling half its contents and stuck out his hand for the cash.

Kitty sipped at her drink.

'S'made with cordial,' she said. 'Don't taste the same.'

'I expect they can't get fresh limes any more.'

Troy tipped his Guinness into the aspidistra pot.

'Could you do me a favour?'

'Course.'

'I bumped into your father last night. He's still treating me like a pariah . . .'

'A wot?'

'An outcast. He talks to me with thinly disguised hatred. I wonder if you might put him straight. Tell him the truth.'

'What truth would that be?'

'That you dumped me, not I you. He seems to have got it into his head that I trifled with your affections.'

Kitty sniggered through her gin and lime, and succumbed to a fit of giggling and choking.

'And while we're on the subject of loose ends, you still have a key to my house.'

'Ain't got it on me though, 'ave I? Besides, you still got all my records.'

'Come and get them. I've no wish to deprive you of them.'

'Right now?'

Troy paused – this had the makings of a Kitty trap.

'Isn't your friend coming back?'

'Nah – he's got to meet my dad. They got work to do. He'll be gone all night.'

No – she could not mean what he thought she meant. They were past that. She had dumped him. She'd made that perfectly clear.

§ 33

Troy opened the cupboard under the gramophone and removed a stack of records – all the things Kitty liked and he didn't. Dance bands with inanely exotic names – Orpheans, Melodians, Waldorfians – or inanely stupid – Syncopating Syd and his Tyrolean Accordionist Ensemble, Ali McDonald's Ocarina Wizards. He'd tried and failed to get her to listen to Duke Ellington or to Art Tatum. Ellington had 'got something', but she'd never put him on the turntable of her own choosing, and Tatum was 'just a racket' and 'ruined a good tune'.

A record slipped from the top as he reached the table. Kitty caught it or it would surely have shattered on the floor.

She held it in both hands and looked at the label, fingers brushing across the grooves, tracing out the words on the label.

'It's *Riptide*,' she said. 'Al Bowlly and Lew Stone.'

She hesitated, staring down at the record in the dim light.

'Lovely Al Bowlly,' she said. 'Poor, lovely Al.'

Al Bowlly had been killed in an air raid in the wee small hours one Thursday morning the previous month. A land mine had floated down, taken out a large slice of Jermyn Street and Mr Bowlly with it. The women of London still mourned him. England's greatest crooner. A womaniser extraordinaire. Troy wondered if Kitty knew this. If she did it probably didn't matter to her. A romantic ideal, that unfleshly object – while the real man, the flesh beneath the ideal, had had half the women he'd ever met. Kitty was weeping, softly, silently for Al Bowlly. Troy said nothing.

'Could we play it?' she asked.

Troy wound the gramophone. It was easier by far than

finding anything to say to her. He was glad she'd caught it, though the rest he could willingly have seen smashed: *Riptide* had that certain something. He was particularly fond of that long, slow introduction before Bowlly came in. It had an inescapable intensity. After it Bowlly's voice could only be a let-down. He had always sounded to Troy more like a man in his seventies than his forties. He had never understood the appellation 'the English Crosby' – he sounded nothing like Bing Crosby. Troy much preferred the women singers – Elsie Carlisle or Greta Keller. Yet – the song was pleasing. Its structure delighted him. It was all verse. No chorus. The song did not repeat itself. Just when any other song would rehash all it had said so far, the band came in again and Bowlly sang no more. It was startling to realise the song was over. It had made its statement – made a song of its precisely captured emotion, but not a 'song-and-dance' of it.

Kitty was shuffling around the room in a slow, sad dance for one. Caught in her own little riptide.

She came to rest in front of him – still tearful – and, though the taller, managed to rest her head upon his shoulder.

'When was it, Fred? When was 'e killed?'

'It was the seventeenth, I think. A month ago to the day, all but a few hours.'

Her arms slipped around his neck. Troy braced himself immovably. I won't dance. Don't ask me. He half expected her feet to resume their half-hearted shuffle. They didn't. She swayed gently, leant into him, and aimed her words somewhere into his chest.

'So this is the anniversary of Al's last night on earth?'

'I suppose so. If you think a month is any kind of an anniversary.'

It was three months to the day since she'd dropped him, but he wasn't going to tell her that. He wasn't counting.

'I been lucky in this war. So far. I never lost anyone. None of me family. All me old boyfriends are still alive. Two of 'em even made it back from Dunkirk. I knew people who died – the bombs and that – but they weren't people I lost. I just knew 'em, sort of. Al Bowlly dying was like losing someone. Really it was.'

She was right. She had been lucky. They'd both been lucky. But Troy would not have been the one to say so. They could lose all, lose everyone before this war was over. To say so seemed rather like inviting it.

'I don't want to spend the night alone,' Kitty said. 'Not tonight of all nights.'

Troy said nothing. He'd heard her say this before. It was line one of Kitty's chat-up routine.

Kitty took his right arm and slipped it around her waist. Troy did not move. She wriggled until he could escape no longer the obligation to enfold her shoulders with his left. She looked at him, eye to eye, as she stooped. Her cheeks were still wet. She kissed him lightly, and buried her head in his shoulder, singing softly to herself.

'Riptide. Caught in a riptide, torn between two loves, the old and the new. Riptide. Lost in a riptide, where will it take me, what shall I do?'

Troy said nothing. Telling Kitty what to do had always been a waste of time.

§ 34

'St What?' said Cal.

'Alkmund. It's Saxon. And it's a whopping great church, one of the biggest in Shoreditch. They cleared out the crypt last November. Got rid of the dead to make room for the living.'

Stilton had stopped the car. Cal got out into another urban desert. The church stood like a redwood in wilderness – little else did, for what Cal estimated to be a couple of blocks in any direction.

'Is it safe?' he asked.

Stilton stared up at the spire.

'Probably not. But where is, apart from down the Underground? Half a million tons of masonry held up by flying buttresses and prayer. Thing is, it feels safe – it's well . . . reassuring.'

'Give me sacred steel and God's good concrete any day. We going in?'

Outside the main porch they passed a group of people sitting on a tomb. Cal heard the plummy tones of upper-class English voices. He'd heard that the English all 'mucked in', as they put it, but this lot were not the sort who looked as though they'd spend the night in a crypt except as a gag at Halloween. They were overdressed, as though they'd slipped out in the interval from a West End theatre, and they appeared to be sipping wine and eating sandwiches. Stilton's feet clattered on the stone steps ahead of him.

'Leeches,' he said, cryptically.

'Leeches?'

'Well – mebbe not. More like voyeurs. Ghouls. Toffs coming East from Mayfair to see how the other half live.'

'Die, how the other half die,' said Cal.

'Aye – whatever. Can't stand the sight of 'em. They should all have summat better to do.'

The crypt was on a scale Cal could not have anticipated – somehow he'd thought the word implied low and small. This was a cathedral beneath the streets, a cavern twenty feet high stretching into an infinity of half light, criss-crossed by arches, fragmented by alcoves. And full of people. Cal could not begin to guess. A thousand seemed arbitrary but suitably large. A sea of humanity pinpointed by flashes of light – a cigarette being lit, a portable stove fired up – punctuated by a thousand different noises and a dozen different smells. It hummed, literally and metaphorically. Only when Stilton shook him by the arm did he realise he'd stopped, and was just staring – not, he hoped, open-mouthed.

'I know what you're thinking.'

'Do you, Walter, do you?'

'How can people live like this?'

'Well – how can they?'

'Believe me, Calvin, this is a damn sight better than it was last autumn. Then there'd be two and a half thousand people crammed in here. That was before the government had the sense to open up the Underground at night. Mind, they only did that 'cos folk from round here defied the authorities. Went in and wouldn't leave. There was talk of 'em even being turfed out by the coppers. You can imagine how well that went down. But it's fine now. Us and the toffs. We understand one another a bit better. A few ghouls notwithstanding.'

Stilton pointed upwards with his finger, back towards ground level.

'What's the smell?' Cal asked. 'It's pretty … pervasive.'

'Chemical lavvies, lad. Imagine how pervasive the smell was before we had them. Now – let's be getting on.'

'Sure. What do I do?'

'Wait here till I find Hudge.'

'Wait? Walter, I've spent a week waiting.'

'Do you know what Hudge looks like?'

'Of course not.'

'Then leave this bit to me. I'll not leave you out when I think there's summat you can do. Trust me.'

Stilton took out his torch and walked off into the crowd. Cal felt stranded again. High and dry in a cavern

151

that smelled like an accident in a high school chem lab. If Walter wanted him to wait, he'd do it outside. He didn't much want to feel like a voyeur either.

On the surface, the small group of late night revellers had broken up. Only one woman remained, still perched on the tomb with, he noticed for the first time, a leather, squarish shoulder bag and an armband on her black jacket bearing a discreet red cross.

'Are you lost?' she said in an accent that rhymed lost with forced.

'No, we – I mean the Chief Inspector and I – are looking for someone.'

'Good Lord – I say, you're an American, aren't you? You're the first American I've had pop down to see me.'

He hadn't popped down to see her. He'd come up into the night for a breath of fresh air.

'All sorts of chaps pop down, but I don't think we've had an American down here since, well . . . since the autumn. Ed Murrow came. The chap who broadcasts for CBS. Do you know Ed Murrow?'

'We've met. I wouldn't say I knew him.'

She hopped off the tomb. A small woman, no more than five feet tall.

'Daisy Hopton,' she said cheerily.

Daisy, Poppy. Did the English upper classes name all their daughters after flowers?

'Calvin Cormack. Would that be Miss or Missis Hopton?'

'Neither, darling – Lady Daisy, actually.'

'You're married to a lord?'

'No, Daddy's one. Lord Scowbrook. That's in Derbyshire. I don't suppose you've heard of it?'

''Fraid not. Do you have estates there?'

'No. Not so much as an allotment or a shed. All our land's in Devon. But then all the Duke of Devonshire's is in Derbyshire, so it all sort of comes out in the wash.'

Cal had heard of the Duke of Devonshire – who hadn't? Half the women he met in Washington before the war wanted to marry a duke's son or an earl's. He knew one who'd memorised the name and title of every eligible eldest son in Debrett's. Being a congressman's son didn't count for much among the belts and garters.

'Look, there's bags left over. Would you like something to eat?'

It was tempting. Walter had eaten his breakfast. He'd skipped lunch just waiting for him to show.

'Sure.'

'A little smoked salmon and a glass of sherry perhaps?'

She unwrapped a sandwich for him. It was white bread. White bread was scarce. It was prized.

'You just have to know the right people,' she explained.

Cal sipped at his sherry, looked around at the ruins half hidden in the darkness, felt the mixture of chemical sterility and human heat still wafting up the stairs from the crypt.

'What exactly do you do here, Lady Daisy?' he asked.

'I sort of run a first aid post. I have my little bag of tricks, as you can see. And I have a tin trunk full of bandages and iodine and . . . stuff . . . yes, stuff, I've got lots of stuff, stuff of several different kinds, I should think. Absolutely oodles of stuff.'

'And you tend to the wounded?'

'Sort of.'

'Sort of?'

'There hasn't been a raid for almost a week, and if people make it in here, they usually arrive before it starts. Short of a direct hit we don't get a lot of injuries. I've taken splinters out of fingers, bathed a few cuts, but the biggest thing I've ever done is set a broken leg in a splint. Between raids they tend not to want to know me. I believe "fiercely independent" is the cliché. Does tend to make one feel a bit redundant.'

'Then why do you do it?'

'Well, one has to do one's bit . . . and besides . . .'

Poppy Payne's words came unbidden to Cal's lips.

'Besides, there's no Season.'

'How very perceptive of you, darling. Yes, that's it in a nutshell. No Season. I mean, one would get awfully bored wouldn't one?'

'And in the meantime?'

'And in the meantime I pursue this exercise in democratic futility.'

This threw Cal. He'd not the faintest idea what the woman meant. Just when he thought he'd got her pegged as a do-gooding social butterfly she tossed in a polysyllabic from an Economics Major. He thought better of saying anything.

'I mean,' she went on, 'you hear all this guff about all being in the same boat. How the Blitz has formed us into a classless society. Isn't true, of course. In fact it's complete roundies.'

Roundies? Almost involuntarily Cal glanced at his shoes. He'd always called them roundies – it was military school slang. Complete shoes? It didn't make sense?

'Excuse me?'

'Bollocks, darling. Complete bollocks. And you still don't know what I mean, do you? Men's roundies – balls, darling, complete balls. We're one nation, strictly for the duration. We tolerate one another without liking one another. When this war's over the poor will probably eat us.'

They were eating smoked salmon and white bread and sipping dry sherry. Suddenly it seemed to Cal less like a novelty and more like a skirmish in the great British class war. Now, he'd really no idea what to make of this woman. Kitty wasn't exactly simple – but compared to this she was simplicity personified.

'Your copper's taking his time,' she said.

'A lot of people to look at.'

'Who are you looking for? A criminal of some sort? God knows there's enough of them down there.'

'No – a nark, I believe that's the term.'

'A nark?'

'A Mr Hudge.'

'Darling, why didn't you say so?'

'You know him?'

'Little chap, no taller than me? Club foot? Sort of clumpy limp?'

'I don't know. I've never met him. Walter never described him. I just know the name – Hudge.'

'Actually, darling, it's Jaroslav Hudcjek. But Hudge is generally all most people can manage, so Hudge it is. I know Hudge, everyone knows Hudge, although I think the news that he's a rozzer's nark might come as a bit of a shock to more than a few people round here . . .'

'You could always keep that to yourself.'

'Discretion is my middle name, darling – or at least it would be if it weren't Phoebe. As a matter of fact I even know where the little blighter lives.'

'So do we. Got bombed out on Saturday.'

'And by Tuesday he'd got himself somewhere else. I'm way ahead of you, darling.'

'And you know where this somewhere else is?'

Daisy Hopton led him out of the churchyard and pointed off to the east, towards the only building still standing in the rubble desert. It reminded Cal of Jubilee Street where Stilton lived, but the devastation was the greater and the contrast the starker. This was a slender house, that at some point had been in the middle of a terrace. Standing alone it looked perilous, as gravity-defying as the tower of Pisa. As though someone had swept away everything else and at the end thrust a knife into the ground as a marker. He found himself wondering what kept it up.

'He lives there?'

'You bet. Everyone else got bombed out, the last family left in January, but when it was still standing after Saturday's raid Hudge decided it was charmed. After all, everything else got flattened months ago, and then pounded to dust only last week. It does look miraculous. Dead lucky, he reckons. You'll find him in there somewhere.'

As a child, Cal had been force-fed books. It was a maxim of his father's that they should not forget the old country, be that old country the Scotland of his father's family or the Germany of his mother's. What his wife thought of this no one thought to ask. Cal, meanwhile, grew up on a diet of the Brothers Grimm, Goethe, Fontane, Scott and Robert Louis Stevenson. Stepping into the silent gloom of Hudge's chosen ruin he could not help but remember the scene in *Kidnapped* when David Balfour visits the House of Shaw and his Uncle Ebenezer sends him in darkness to climb a topless staircase. Cal set foot on the stairs, knowing they too might be topless, or middleless, and at any moment could send him crashing to earth. He wished for a torch. Tomorrow he'd go out and buy one, if regulations still permitted.

The stairs were intact, as far as the second floor. A chunk of the outside wall was missing – he walked twelve steps on a wooden hill without any visible means of support, and, in a blacked-out back room on the second floor, found what he was looking for. A naked light bulb dangled from the ceiling by a twisted thread of cable. A hammock had been strung across the room from nails banged into the wall at either end. Above this a large black umbrella diverted overspill from a leaky cistern away from the head of the sleeping occupant, a short club-footed man, clutching a book to his chest. Cal looked at the book. *Tractatus Logico-Philosophicus* by Ludwig Wittgenstein. He'd no idea people still wrote books in Latin. Less that anyone might actually read them.

He must have made more noise than he thought. The eyes opened and a hand grabbed the book, trying to pull it from his fingers. The eyes opened wider. A rapid sentence in indecipherable Czech. Cal let go of the book, and the little man clutched it to his chest like a child grasping a torn shred of comfort blanket.

Cal spoke no Czech – it had always seemed to him to be one of the alphabet soup languages – but this could hardly be a problem. Most Czechs spoke German, surely?

'*Herr Hudcjek. Ich bin Captain Cormack. Amerikaner, mit Scotland Yard.*'

'Waaaaaaaaaghhhhh!!!!!!!'

Hudge rolled from the hammock screaming, banging around the room, his ironshod foot clattering down upon the floorboards. Wittgenstein landed in the dust, pages splayed. The umbrella flew off and landed down in a corner.

'Waaaaaaaaaaaagggggghhhhhhhhh!!!!!!!!'

He seemed to be circling – he certainly wasn't making a dash for the door, and at the speed he travelled a dash was probably beyond him. Cal stepped in and headed him off, arms outstretched in what he hoped was a placatory gesture.

'*Ich komme von Scotland Yard. Ich arbeite mit Walter Stilton. Verstehen Sie? Mit Walter Stilton.*'

Hudge collapsed in the corner. His hands fell upon the umbrella, which now became a shield between him and Cal.

'*Nicht schlagen Sie mich!*'

What? 'Don't hit me!' What on earth was he on about?

A flick of the wrist and the umbrella was transformed from a dripping parachute into a cudgel, with which Hudge began to beat Cal, yelling all the time, '*Nicht schiessen, nicht schiessen.*'

It was like being hit with a rolled-up newspaper, soft and sodden. The blows fell upon his head with a sound like slapping meat. He backed away, blinded by the spray of water in his eyes, all but deafened by the rising volume of '*Nicht schiessen*'. He backed into a pair of big hands which grabbed him, turned him and shook him.

'What the bloody hell's going on?'

'Walter?'

Stilton shoved him aside, bent down to Hudge in his corner and spoke softly to him in Czech. Hudge replied in Czech, looking all the time from Stilton to Cal and back again.

'No,' Stilton said in English. 'Not German. American.'

Hudge stared silently at Cal. Then he muttered a long sentence to Stilton, still unwilling to speak English. Stilton looked over his shoulder at him.

'He thinks you're Gestapo.'

'What?'

'You woke him up and spoke to him in German. You daft bugger. Did you want him to have a heart attack?'

Stilton came back to him, one hand on his arm, pulling him away from Hudge into a conspiratorial huddle, a whispered conversation.

'He was in one o' them camps. Oranienburg, the one near Berlin. He taught theology in university – one morning in 1934 they just came for him. Chucked him in the camp, beat the shit out of him for four months, then turned him out. Jobless, homeless, broke. He got the message. He was on a train to Calais before you could

158

say Lili Marlene. And you have to sneak up on him and talk to him in German.'

'Jeezus, Walter. I didn't know. Why didn't you tell me?'

'How was I to know you were going to go wandering off on your own?'

'Maybe if you didn't leave me out of things I wouldn't have the time to?'

'Well – now isn't the moment to include you. He's scared to death. Even says you look like a Nazi.'

'Must be the glasses.'

'I'm glad you can see the funny side. Because if his dog hadn't been killed on Saturday night it'd've ripped your throat out at the first *umlaut*! Now. Either stand still and say nowt or bugger off outside. Which is it to be?'

'I'll stay.'

'Good.'

There was one chair in the room. Stilton set it upright, blew the dust off it and helped Hudge onto it.

'We need a little help, old son.'

Stilton whipped out the photographs of Stahl and Smulders.

'Did you see either of these blokes in the Lincoln last Monday?'

Hudge stopped glaring at Cal and looked. Another rapid sentence in alphabet soup.

'In English, Hudge. For the sake of our friend here.'

'Friend,' Hudge said, as though Stilton had just introduced him to a new philosophical concept.

'Oh yes. Definitely. Our friend. My wife thinks the sun shines out of his arse.'

'The younk one. He was talk to Fish Wally. He write something down. Then he go. Maybe half hour later the old one come. He chat only few minute. Then he too go.'

'And Fish Wally?'

'He stay till chucky out. He buy me drink. He got money.'

'Did he say anything about these blokes?'

'No.'

Hudge looked at the photos again.

'The younk one. Something not right. I think it the scar on eye. Cannot be sure. Maybe scar. Maybe not.'

'Well Calvin, whatever you have to say, say it in English and smile.'

Cal thought he'd have to drag his voice up from his belly. He couldn't remember when he'd last felt so self-conscious.

'It's just a sketch,' he bleated.

Hudge looked again.

'Ja. Just so. Sketch.'

Hudge reverted to Czech. Stilton pointed at the book and motioned to Cal to pick it up. Cal dusted it and brought it to Hudge. He took it, clutched it to his chest once more.

'Thank you,' he said to Cal. 'Not forget?' he said to Stilton.

'Oh no,' Stilton replied. 'We won't forget.'

Clumping down the stairs Cal whispered, 'What won't we forget?'

'The dog,' said Stilton. 'I told him we'd get him a new dog.'

They crossed the rubble plains to the car, Cal trying all the time to think of the right words to apologise to Stilton.

'I'm sorry, Walter. I goofed.'

Stilton was silent for a few seconds, then said, 'We both did. But I'll do you a deal. You take your cue from me – whatever we're doing – and I won't leave you standing at the boundary. We're a team, Calvin. Time we started to act like one.'

Walter throttled the Riley into life. They'd driven a quarter of a mile before Cal said, 'Where are we going?'

'Fish Wally's house. He passed through Burnham more than a year ago. Real name's Waldemar Wallficz. He's a Pole. He was a civil engineer before the war – built bridges. But he was in the reserve. He went to fight the Germans – blew up bridges. And when the Germans won he was one of a band of diehards who wouldn't surrender. Most of 'em did die hard. Wally didn't, he escaped. Went east. Crossed the line. Dodged the Russians as well as the Germans. He says he walked across the ice from the Baltic coast to Finland.'

'Good God, do you believe him?'

'Well – he's got the worst case of frostbite I've ever seen. And the Squadron Leader saw fit to turn him loose. He's lived a mile or so up the road ever since.'

'Do you still – what's the word? – observe him?'

'I don't – he's clean. I've no doubt about that. He's supposed to report to the local nick from time to time, but then they all are. Most of 'em do. Some of 'em don't.'

The car took the hump of a narrow bridge, swung left into a maze of tiny streets and two-storey houses, right at an old Victorian school and pulled up.

'We there?' said Cal.

'Yep. Chantry Street, Islington.'

They got out. One side of the street – the odd numbers – was intact, bar a few broken windows: the other side, the evens, wasn't. It was in pieces. Some houses stood, some didn't. None of them seemed inhabited. It was almost familiar. Cal was getting used to this. Could you go to any borough in the east and find most of it missing?

Stilton was leafing through a wire-bound spiral notebook, muttering 'Bugger, bugger, bugger.'

161

'Odd or even, Walter?' said Cal. 'We have a fifty/fifty chance.'

'Here we are. Wallfiçz. 20 Chantry Street ... oh bugger!'

They found number 21 and stood with their backs to it. 20 was a heap. And there wasn't much more of the house next door.

'Saturday night's got a lot to answer for,' said Cal.

'No. This is older. This looks like it happened weeks ago.'

In front of the ruin of number twenty-two an iron manhole was set in the pavement. A head appeared from it, level with Stilton's boots. The dusty blonde head of a child. A filthy child. A child from *The Water Babies*, looking as though it had just been sent up to sweep the chimney. Stilton squatted down.

'What are you doing down there at this time of night, young lady?' he asked.

'Who wants to know?'

'I do. Chief Inspector Stilton CID.'

'Dad says not to talk to coppers.'

'Would that be because you're looting?'

'Looting! I ain't nicked nuffink! It's our house, this is. Dad sent me to get a bucket o' coal.'

'Bit young to be sent down a manhole, aren't you?'

'I'm ten! Besides, Dad don't fit. Nor do none of me bruvvers. 'Ere, cop hold of this.'

Cal took the bucket from her as she pushed it up. Then her head and shoulders filled the manhole. Her hands found the rim and she flipped herself up to the pavement with the skill of a practised gymnast. She was in a vest and knickers, and black from head to foot.

'Tell me,' Stilton went on. 'Did ye know the bloke who lodged next door?'

''Ow much?' said the child. 'You want me to grass someone up, it'll cost.'

'A tanner.'

'Bob.'

Stilton stuck his hands in his trousers pocket and dug out a few coppers.

'Ninepence,' he said, counting them out one by one.

The child stuck out her hand and said, 'Done.'

'Now. Did ye know him?'

'Wot? 'Im wot lived wiv Mrs O'Rourke?'

'If she lived at number twenty, yes.'

'Yeah, I knew Fish Wally.'

'The raid? A while back, was it?'

'It were in March. Day before me birthday. Mum'd saved up flour an' marge an' neggs for ages to make me a cake, then 'Itler blew it to bits. I din't get none of it.'

'And Fish Wally – he was still here then?'

'Oh yeah. We was all down the shelter, when the street got blown to bollocks. Dad told Wally he should come and live with us at Mum's sister's till 'e got fixed up. But 'e wouldn't have none of it. Dug around in the rubble for a day or two. Found his razor and his spare trousers and off 'e went. Dad says 'e ain't seen 'im since.'

Cal could see that Stilton wanted to say 'Oh bugger' again but, however foul the child's vocabulary, could not bring himself to add to it.

'You know,' he said, 'I think it's time you were in bed. And I think it's time I had a word with your dad.'

§ 35

Troy wondered what time it was. He was not like his father – a man who could awaken at any time, instinctively know what time it was, calculate how much was left to dream and go back to sleep for a precise period of time, be it ten minutes or four hours. More often than not Troy did not sleep. It was still dark, darkish – Kitty

163

stood in outline near the foot of his bed, caught in a sliver of moonlight where Troy had peeled back the black out. He watched her roll a stocking up one leg, back bent, one leg ramrod straight, the other bent into a curiously balletic, attractive pose, toes on point as she eased out the rucks at the knee, passed hand over hand up her thigh and hooked it onto her suspenders. He watched her. She watched him. As dispassionate as could be. Not a flicker on that disarmingly pretty face. He felt as far from her affections as . . . as if he were light years away – away from her warmth, away from heat and light. Aphelion. It was a too-familiar moment. The pure detachment of the woman from the man. He knew it too well. With any other woman it would be him looking on so detachedly. She dressed without a smile. Left without a word.

§ 36

At breakfast in Claridge's next morning Cal found two men eating his breakfast: Walter Stilton and a face he thought he vaguely knew, stuffing itself with tea and toast. Stilton got up, clapped him on the shoulder as though greeting him at a private party he was hosting – when in fact it was pretty much the other way round.

'Calvin. You'll remember our man Constable Dobbs?'

Ah – the copper Stilton had 'bollocked' in front of him a few nights back.

'Sure,' he said.

'Bernard,' said Dobbs. 'Bernard Dobbs.'

Cal pulled up a chair.

'Tell me, Walter. Do you think the War Department budget will run to three breakfasts in a single day? I'm kind of peckish after last night.'

Dobbs froze mid-munch. His teeth locked onto the

toast, his eyes flickering between Stilton and Cal. Too much brass around a single table for his own comfort. Then Stilton gave him his cue, roared with laughter and waved at a waitress as though he'd been eating at Claridge's all his life. Dobbs munched on in relief.

'I've worked out a plan,' Stilton began. 'Belt and braces.'

'What? Belt and what?'

'It's an old saying up north. Belt and braces. What the nervous man does to keep his trousers up – wears both belt and braces – you call 'em suspenders, least they do in Hollywood – that way if one snaps your trousers still stay up.'

'I see,' said Cal, not seeing, wondering at the power of gravity in the north of England.

'Bernard, here. He's going to stand guard outside the Lincoln. We know Fish Wally goes in there. If he spots him he calls in to the Yard. It's routine stuff, but it might just work. Besides, our Bernard's good at standing outside boozers, aren't you Bernard?'

Dobbs avoided meeting Stilton's gaze.

'And us. We do the streets and the caffs.'

'What streets?' said Cal. 'What caffs?'

'Well – if I'd been bombed out I'd go back to my own. If you see what I mean. It's possible Wally has gone back to the Polish bits of London. It'd make sense. He'd be more likely to get fixed up that way. They'd look after him. Get him another room. Slip him a bob or two till he's found his feet. So you and I are going to tramp the beat in Polish London.'

'Putney?' said Cal.

'Well remembered, lad. Putney it is. And if that draws a blank we'll look across the other side of the river in Fulham.'

'Walter, how long will this take?'

Stilton laughed. 'How long's a piece of string?'

§ 37

A more appropriate question might have been, 'How long is a piece of elastic?' Four days later, they had tramped, as Walter so accurately put it, the streets, cafeterias and public houses of Putney – meeting suspicion, hostility, curiosity and, on occasion, hospitality – to no avail. Cal could not conceal his sinking spirits. He could not tell, any more than he thought Stilton could, whether these motley refugees of Mittel-Europa were co-operating or lying. No one had seen Fish Wally. No one would admit to having seen Fish Wally.

They crossed the river with a sense rising in Cal that in fanning out, their chances had been thinned and diminished. He wondered if they were ever going to find this Fish Wally, and if they did, would they ever find Wolfgang Stahl?

They sank a pint, as Walter termed it, in the World's End public house at the foot of the King's Road – through Fulham and almost out the other side into Chelsea.

'Walter. We're on a hiding to nothing.'

'No. We're not. This is what it's like. Not all police work is like a shoot-out with Clyde Barrow. This is what it's like. Routine. Often as not, routine is what pays off.'

The routine of his days was not matched by his nights. He could not predict when Kitty would turn up. On the fourth night she was already in his bed when he got home.

'How did you get in?'

'The maid. She's taken a liking to me. Used her pass key.'

Kitty lay underneath a single sheet. She wasn't wearing a nightdress. He could see her nipples pushing up the sheet, the dark patch of red pubic hair. They still

166

hadn't 'talked' – she tossed the word back at him as though describing some sort of perversion he wanted her to indulge in. He'd given up all hope of a serious conversation with her. What was the point? The woman was irresistible. He could tumble into Kitty and nothing else mattered.

§ 38

What Stilton needed was divine intervention – *deus ex machina*. What he got was a tip-off. A telephone call just as he was contemplating a mountain of paperwork on his desk at the Yard and preparing to give up on it and go home.

'It's me. Joe Downes.'

Stilton said 'Yes' while he racked his brains.

'You came round my gaff last week and told me I was a lousy father for sending me daughter down a coal hole at midnight.'

'Oh aye – I remember you now.'

A surly git who'd not had the courage to look him in the eyes when he'd taken the black imp back to him.

'You was asking about Fish Wally.'

'You've seen him?'

'*I* haven't. It was the missis. Says she bumped into him down Covent Garden this morning. Says he's taken to spending his nights at St Martin's.'

'What?'

'I said –'

'I heard what you said. I meant which St Martin's?'

'St Martin-in-the-Fields. What other one is there?'

'I don't believe it,' Stilton said, more to himself than Downes.

'That's what I told the missis. Still, we're even now, you and me, aren't we?'

'Aye lad, we are. Just mind how you go with the nutty slack.'

§ 39

Cal knew at once that this was different. St Alkmund's, whatever the stink, however much it looked like some hellish gothic vision, had had women and children – women cooking, women putting children to bed, children playing, children refusing to be put to bed, while men played cards or shoved coins up and down a board with the same glee with which Cal used to race frogs. St Martin's held naught but men – and they played no games. By comparison it was quiet, not silent, constant interruptions, shouting and cussing, meaningless interjections – and off to one side, in the shadows, standing alone, an upright, crazed monologuist conversing with person or persons invisible.

And the smell – if St Alkmund's had been chalked up to the cliché 'humanity', how could St Martin's be less than human? It reeked of beer, sweat and dirt – the penetrating cheesy smell of the unwashed, great or not, that could put a dead skunk to shame.

'Walter, do we have the right place? This is a dive – it's a shelter for bums and drunks.'

'I know,' said Stilton. 'Surprised me too – but that was the tip-off. Down with the down-and-outs in St Martin-in-the-Fields.'

A young curate approached them – the permanent smile of the righteous rictus-stapled to his lips.

'Can I help you? It's not often we get a visit from the Constabulary these days.'

Stilton didn't bat an eyelid at this. Just flashed his warrant card and said, 'D'ye know Fish Wally?'

The young priest beamed. 'I should have known. Our

Mr Wallfiçz. There he is, right at the back under the pavement arches.' He pointed down the crypt. Cal and Stilton stepped over the prostrate, drunken, incontinent bodies and headed towards the glow of a kerosene lamp.

A ragged man sat bolt upright on an upturned crate. Half a dozen newspapers scattered around his feet, another clutched in hands that seemed to Cal to be more claw than flesh, the arc of the lamp shining upon on it. But he wasn't reading it. He stared off into a lost middle distance, lost in some landscape of the mind.

Stilton waved a hand in front of his eyes. Fish Wally blinked once and said, 'Stilton? Long time no Stilton. I had heard you were looking for me.'

Stilton pulled another beer crate closer and plonked himself down on it. Cal stood back, half in the shadows, outside of the small circle of light, watching.

'If you knew I were looking, why didn't you call me? For that matter you were supposed to tell us if you moved digs – but you didn't, did you?'

Fish Wally looked lazily at Stilton, heavy-lidded eyes half closed.

'The answer is the same to both questions. I have other things on my mind.'

'Such as?'

'We're about to be invaded. That may mean nothing to you. You come from a complacent race. We Poles have seen it all before – I somewhat more recently than 1066.'

'All the same, you should have told us. You don't want me reporting this to the Squadron Leader, do you?'

'Do your worst, Stilton. He knows I am kosher. And so do you. You have found me – you have the larger part of my attention, for the while at least – what else matters?'

'Since you ask . . .'

Stilton laid out the photos across his knees, on top of Fish Wally's newspaper.

'These two were in the Marquis of Lincoln, Monday last. So were you.'

Fish Wally picked up the photographs, angled them into the light.

'The young one – the blond one. He asked me to help him get a room. The older one merely said he might have to move in the foreseeable future. I told him to tell me later – I do not deal in maybe. I never saw him again.'

'You're sure it was them?'

'The scar on the blond puzzles me. It is a likeness this sketch, no more – it has not caught the man.'

Stilton twisted his neck to look up at Cal. The first acknowledgement he'd made of his presence since they crossed the room.

'Never mind,' he said to Fish Wally. 'It's him, isn't it?'

'Yes – it's him.'

'And the older one?'

'Definitely him.'

'Good – now, did you get the young one a room?'

'Of course. I took him to my cousin.'

'Your cousin?'

'My cousin. Why else did you think I came to London? Did you think I washed up on these shores like Gulliver in Brobdingnag? Stilton, I told you last year I had family. I have a cousin Casimir – been here since 1932. A naturalised Englishman. He lets rooms. I send him people from time to time. Mostly I send him Poles. But we would consider any refugee.'

'I'm not addled, Wally – I remember you had a cousin. I tried to find him three or four days back. I don't recall that he let rooms.'

'In those days he didn't. He had one room on Fulham High Street. Things changed after the fall of France. You know that as well as I. We have lived in a new world ever since. The blond man said he was Czech. Sounded Czech to me. So we arranged to meet outside the London Palladium just after closing time. I took him round to Cash Wally.'

'Cash Wally?'

'Casimir – Casimir Wallfiçz. Hence, since yours is a tongue that must mangle what it cannot spell, "Cash Wally". A man aptly named. A greedy man in every respect. A mean man. I live on the handouts he gives me and the work I can pick up.'

Fish Wally held up his mangled hands.

'You will appreciate, Walter, that is not much.'

'And where does Cash Wally have this house of exiles?'

'23b Marshall Street – the one in Soho. As you would say, spitting distance from the Palladium. I even know the room number. He is in four – the second-floor front.'

Stilton quickly scribbled down the address.

'And you Wally, where are you living now?'

'I have a new room in Drury Lane.'

'From Drury Lane you could shelter in the tube at Holborn or Covent Garden or the Aldwych. Why on earth would you want to come down here? If your cousin pays you a wage and you've a room of your own, why here, why down here with the drunks and the tramps?'

Fish Wally looked off into the crypt – stared a moment at the ranting monologuist, then fixed his gaze on Stilton and sighed. It seemed to Cal that through his precise, cultured English he was talking to Stilton as though he were an exasperating child to whom he must state the obvious once too often.

'I like it here. It reminds me of the last time I saw Poland. Before the Germans came we were workers. Teachers, engineers, policemen even. After the Germans came we were fighters. Then we lost. We became runners. Some of us ran all the way to Hungary, some of us ran all the way to the sea. I stayed with my unit. Thirty of us, retreating north, we tramped five hundred miles on foot, dodging Germans every step of the way. Those who fed and housed us the Germans shot – so we took no food or shelter. We lived off the land. And when the winter froze the soil, we starved. We sank to the bottom of Poland. And most of us died there, and some of us went mad. I saw half a dozen comrades turn mad as hatters. My last sight of my brother Stanislaus was him standing in a Polish forest ranting at the trees like that witless idiot over there. We became raggedymen, all of us raggedymen. We looked, we sounded, we smelt no different from this lot. We were the dregs of Poland, the last scum of a scorched earth. "And I alone am escaped to tell thee." To tell thee, Stilton, to tell the Squadron Leader. You took me in. England took me in. And I sank to the bottom of England. And so you find me here, as deep as I can go. And now it is England's turn. Soon England will fall before the Panzers. Tell me, Stilton, how deep can you go? Try it – learn. I am here to replenish my sense of reality. I have lived too easy this last year or more. I have a pillow for my head and coins to jingle in my pocket – but I can go deep, straight to the bottom. One day soon we will all know this madness. How deep can you go, Walter?'

Outside Cal said, 'What was that about?'

'My fault, lad. I shouldn't have asked. Not as if I haven't heard it before. It's pretty much what he said day after day when we had him out at Burnham-on-Crouch last year. It's . . . it's Wally's vision, I suppose. He's cast himself as the wandering Jew. At least the Catholic version of it.'

'Or Ishmael. "And I alone am escaped to tell thee." That's *Moby Dick*. I know, I skipped to the last page when I realised I was never going to get through it all.'

'Oh,' said Stilton, a bit dismissively. 'I'd just assumed he was quoting the Bible. No point in skipping to the end o' that, is there? We all know how it ends.'

§ 40

Marshall Street was as close to the heart of things as could be. Regent Street was only few yards west, Oxford Street a few yards north. Stilton drove in silence. There was a new tenacity to the man – just when Cal thought they'd both been flagging, the prospect of getting close to the quarry had invigorated him. He wished he felt the same. He thought of the prospect of meeting Wolf again with a mixture of sadness and fear. He voiced none of it. Better by far to let silence prevail. Anxieties could only alarm Stilton – as would questions, and there was one question he was biting back. If he'd been the one to talk to Fish Wally, he'd've asked why total strangers came to him for help, and how they knew where to find him. Could be Fish Wally might not know the answer, but that did not invalidate the question. It nagged. It burst the logic of pursuit they had set up for themselves. Walter, after all, had been emphatic. Wally was clean. And if they really were only minutes away from catching up with Stahl, what did it matter?

23b Marshall Street was a ramshackle house, but at least it still stood. Cal estimated it to be about as old as his country. They were probably laying these bricks as Jefferson pondered life, liberty and the pursuit of happiness. Three items currently in short supply.

The door looked rotten, as though one good kick from Stilton would send it flying from its hinges. It wasn't locked. Stilton pushed gently at it – a miasma of steam and frying fat filled the air.

'Reckon we caught Cash Wally at his trough,' Stilton

173

whispered, and walked softly towards the back of the house with Cal treading on his heels. The trail of steam led them straight to the kitchen. It was a filthy parody of Edna Stilton's kitchen. A big room, a centre table, strewn with dishes waiting to be washed. A patina of grease on every surface, into which months of dust had settled, giving solid, inanimate household objects an illusion of life – they had fur, so they might breathe or move also. In the fireplace stood a three-legged gas stove, propped up at its fourth corner by a pile of bricks. And on the hob a pan of potatoes boiled furiously, while three sausages nestled deep and crisp in a cooling pan of lard.

'Good God,' Stilton said softly. 'How can he live like this?'

'And where is he?' Cal added. 'It's like we've pulled up alongside the *Marie Celeste*.'

Stilton beckoned to Cal, they stepped into the stairwell.

'Is our man likely to be hostile?' he whispered.

'Walter – I've no idea. He's on our side. If that makes any sense.'

'Then we play it by ear.'

Cal rather thought that this was what they'd been doing for a week already. He followed Walter up the stairs, step for step, pausing as he paused at every crack and creak to listen for any response. The house was deathly silent, much as Cal resisted the adverb.

Stilton stood on the far side of the door. He rapped on it. There was no answer. There was no sound of any kind. He rapped again. Then he turned the doorknob and pushed. The door swung in onto an empty room, banging back against the wall. Cal put his head round the door jamb. Stilton leaned in from the other side.

'Bugger,' Stilton said.

They stepped into the room. In complete contrast to the kitchen this room had been cleaned and dusted. The bed stripped. Every surface wiped. You didn't need Sherlock Holmes' magnifying glass to know there'd be no fingerprints. Stahl had left no tracks. Not a scrap of paper, a burnt match or a bus ticket. It looked to Cal like a thorough, professional job. This man meant to vanish.

All the same, Stilton peeked under the bed, opened the closet, pulled out the drawers in the dresser and uttered the conclusion Cal had reached minutes before.

'He's flown the coop. Not so much as a toothbrush or a pair of socks.'

'Always one step ahead of us,' said Cal.

They heard the slam of a door downstairs. They looked at each other. Stilton all but tiptoed to the landing. The sound of someone banging about in the kitchen drifted up the staircase.

Stilton put a finger to his lips and set off down the stairs. At the next landing Cal grabbed him by the arm and whispered, 'Let me do it.'

'It's not Stahl – that would be too good to be true,' Stilton whispered back.

'No matter. We're a team, aren't we? My turn.'

Stilton yielded silently and let Cal pass. Down to the ground floor on feet of glass. A gentle twist of the door handle, and a sudden thrust. A spidery, thin man in a tatty sweater, all elbows and knuckles, his hair standing up as though galvanised, was seated at the table in front of a plate piled high with mashed potato, the mash peppered with sausages – and a brand new bottle of the ubiquitous British brown sauce clutched in his hand ready to gloop.

'Casimir Wallfiçz?' Cal said breezily.

The man stared at him, his hand still poised over the base of the bottle ready to give it the baby-bottom slap that would send the sauce gushing over his feast.

'Wod?'

'You are Casimir Wallfiçz, the proprietor of this

establishment?'

'Proprietor?' Cash Wally said, a much more heavily accented voice than his cousin's. 'Proprietor be buggered. Is my house, I own it lock, stock and sausage. Now who you and what you want? As if I couldn't guess.'

'Calvin Cormack, US Intelligence. My colleague, Chief Inspector Stilton. You don't mind if we join you?'

Cal snatched the plate from him. Slammed himself down in a chair and said, 'The guy in number four. He checked out. When?'

'How should I know?'

Cash Wally reached for the plate. Cal held it away from him at arm's length, like a schoolyard bully teasing a child.

'You know, Casimir, I think you know damn well, because you don't strike me as the kind of guy who lets his lodgers do moonlight flits. Besides, you've two pound notes and a ten-shilling note stuck behind the clock on the mantelpiece, so somebody's just paid their bill.'

Cash Wally tried to look stubborn. He succeeded only in looking hungry. Cal picked up a sausage and bit into it. From the look on his face, Cal might just as well have bitten into Wally. It was agony, the tortured passion of the eating man.

Cal wolfed the sausage. Cash Wally moaned out loud. His head shook from side to side, his eyes rolled. As Cal finished the second, Cash Wally beat the table with his hands and screamed.

'No. No. Nooooooo!!!!'

Cal took up the third sausage, worked it around in the neck of the sauce bottle, worked up a good head of gloop, and pointed at him with it. He dared not look at Stilton – so much as a smile from Stilton and he knew he'd corpse.

'Wally. You've one sausage left. Now, you see this man here? This is Walter Stilton. One of the finest trenchermen in Scotland Yard. And he skipped lunch today. He's a particularly hungry policeman. This is your last wienie. If you don't tell me everything and right now, I'll toss this wienie in the air and you'll see the Chief Inspector catch it in his teeth like Pavlov's dog. Then I'll turn him loose on your mash. Very partial to a plate of mash, is the Chief Inspector. Now – the Czech guy. The guy who said he was Czech. When did he go and where did he go?'

Cash Wally put his arms on the table, his head resting lightly on them. It seemed to Cal that he was stifling sobs.

'He left about four o'clock this afternoon. I don't know where he gone. He gave me extra ten bobs just to say he never been here. He said at the beginning he would not be here more than ten days. Believe me – I do not know where he gone.'

Stilton spoke from the far end of the table, the brusque informality of the Metropolitan Police, the dull inevitability of procedure observed. 'And did you tell the local nick you had an alien here?'

Cash Wally raised his head, red of face, bleary of eye, 'Aliens? We're all aliens. What one more mattered more or less?'

Cal didn't doubt the sentiment – the pain which shot through his words, and the continental contempt for the very notion 'alien'. He felt for Cash Wally – just a little – he also felt certain he'd got pretty much the truth out of the man.

He looked at Stilton, wondering if he felt remotely what he was feeling himself. 'Well, do you want this man's wienie?'

'No,' said Stilton. 'Let him have his banger. I think we've got all we're going to get.'

'So do I.'

Cal stuck the sausage back in the mountain of mash

and shoved the plate towards Cash Wally.

'Eat up, Mr Wallficz. Nothing's going to happen to you. But you'll do as the Chief Inspector asks, won't you? You'll report every new foreigner to the police. Right?'

'Right,' sobbed Cash Wally. 'Foreigners. Police. Police. Foreigners. Right.'

They sat in the car. Stilton seemed to be waiting for something. If only, Cal thought, for his own anger to subside. He'd looked grim from the minute they left Cash Wally's kitchen.

At last he said, 'Y'know, I didn't think you had it in you. But I have to say ... well done.'

'You don't think that maybe it was a little cruel?'

'No I don't. In fact he's lucky I didn't wring his neck. We check the local station reports every morning. If he ran a straight house and listed his foreigners we might have picked up Stahl days ago. As things stand we're back to square bloody one. I think I'll send the uniforms round in the morning just to see he gets the message. No – you played the bugger just about right. I couldn't have done it better meself. Mind, I've never thought of myself as a trencherman before.'

He was smiling as he said it. The anger had passed. They were on level ground again.

'So? What do we do now?'

'What do we do now? We go back to Stepney and pray my missis has stuck summat tasty in the oven. You've had two bangers. I've had nowt.'

§ 41

There was a note on the kitchen table. Cal felt Stilton must have seen it a few thousand times in the course of a thirty-year marriage – 'Your dinner's in the oven.'

Stilton took a tea cloth, opened the lower oven and

pulled out a dish half full of something indeterminate and crisp.

'Dunno what it is,' he said. 'But it smells a treat.'

'It's fish pie, Dad.'

Reenie Stilton appeared in the doorway, and eased her pregnant bulk onto a kitchen chair.

'My Maurice got a twenty-four-hour pass, so him and some of his mates went fishing out past Southend somewhere. Came back with two lovely whole cod.'

'Past Southend? That's a restricted area.'

'Leave it out, Dad. Who do you think Maurice is going to spy on? Old fellers diggin' lugworm? You just be grateful you got some supper. Rest of us ate hours ago.'

Stilton dished up. The greens were boiled to death and dried out, but Cal could have eaten seconds and thirds of the pie. It was fresh and spicy and it hit the spot. Stilton ate with a practised fork action that improved his elbow speed and upped his rate of consumption. He was scraping the dish before Cal was halfway across his plate. And he'd never thought of himself as a trencherman.

'Where's your mother?' Stilton said as Reenie plodded across the floor to stick the kettle on.

'Went round to old George Bonham to give him a bit o' cooked cod. Reckons he don't eat proper any more. Then she was going on to Aunt Dolly. Her Dennis is constipated again, and you know they always ask for Mum like she was the family witch-doctor. She'll dose the little sod.'

'You know, Walter,' Cal said, 'the house certainly seems empty.'

'Kev and Trev are back at sea. They sailed a day or two back, I should think. Rose and Tom have got their own home to go to, though most of the time you'd never know it.'

'Tel's gone down the Troxy,' Reenie chipped in, leaving Cal to wonder what a troxy was.

'And Vera's gone with Mum.'

Over the hiss of the kettle Cal thought he heard a motorbike engine putter down to nothing. The missing name from the list. He heard the door slam. A slight pause in the steps along the hallway as she hung up her helmet – then a rush of feet dancing down the stairs – and the kitchen door burst open. Kitty's hair bounced the way it always did, springy on her blue collar. Her eyes flashed, the way they always did. If she was surprised to see him sitting there, she didn't show it.

'Late again,' said Reenie. 'I don't think there's any left.'

'Wot?'

'You shoulda got here on time. You're on reg'lar shifts. You don't work daft hours like dad. I reckon Captain Cormack's had yours.'

Kitty looked from Cal to her father to the empty dish and back again.

'Wot? You greedy so and sos. You ain't left me a mouthful!'

'Manners,' said Stilton, as Cal knew he would. 'Captain Cormack's a guest in this house.'

'I know,' Kitty sneered. 'Mum thinks the sun shines out of his –'

'Kitty!!!'

Kitty turned her back on her father and wheedled her sister.

'Reen, be a love and take a look in the larder. A bit o' bread and cheese. Anything.'

'Walter,' Cal said softly. 'What does that mean? About the sun shining –'

'Don't ask, lad, don't ask.'

Upstairs the door slammed again. Stilton muttered that he ought to fix that door one of these fine days, asked Reenie to bring his tea up and told Cal he was just off for a word with the missis. Reenie slapped a meagre sandwich on the table in front of Kitty and said, 'You make the tea, bossy boots. My fibroids are killing me. I'm off for forty winks.' And Cal found himself alone with Kitty. Somewhere upstairs the telephone began to ring.

'So, superman. It's not enough that you get to eat me every so often. You've got to eat me dinner as well.'

'Kitty – for Christ's sake!'

'Wot you doin' 'ere anyway? I was coming over to see you a bit later.'

'I'll be there. We kind of hit the buffers this evening.' The phone rang and rang. Kitty had slipped off a shoe and was running one stockinged foot up the side of his trousers towards his groin.

''Bout what time?'

'Kitty – I can't tell you how uncomfortable this makes me. Your mother could walk in at any minute.'

Kitty shot to her feet as though stung and yanked at the kitchen door.

'Will somebody answer that bloody phone!'

Then she folded her arms and glared at Cal.

§ 42

Stilton was saying 'Yes, love.' It was what he always said when he didn't much want to listen to what his wife was trying to tell him. He picked up the phone.

'Boss. It's me. Bernard.'

Instinctively Stilton looked at his watch. It was past ten. He tried to remember where Dobbs was supposed to be. Where he had left him. He ought to know and he didn't.

'Yes, lad.'

'I been outside the Marquis of Lincoln. Waiting for Fish Wally.'

Oh bugger – he'd forgotten to pull Dobbs off watch when he'd received the tip-off about Fish Wally. The poor sod had been standing there for the best part of a week, and for the last few hours, at least, to no purpose.

'Aye, well you can knock off now, Bernard. I found Fish Wally hours ago.'

'I'm not there now, boss. I trailed him.'

'No, Bernard, I said, I've already talked to Wally. Go home, lad. Get some kip.'

'No, boss, I'm not talking about Fish Wally. I mean the other feller. He came by the boozer at opening time. I followed him.'

'What other feller?'

'The one in that sketch.'

'Stahl?'

'Yes – Stahl.'

'Bernard, where exactly are you?'

'Cleveland Street, boss. Where it meets Warren Street. Corner house.'

Stilton bounded down the stairs, bellowed 'We're on again!' at Cal, grabbed his macintosh off the back of the door and ran back up the stairs.

The speed of it all left Cal standing, half in, half out of his chair, an untouched cup of steaming tea in front of him. An untouched steaming Kitty, too.

'I . . . er . . . I guess this means I don't know what time I'll be home,' he said lamely.

'I know,' Kitty answered. 'You're on again. So we're off. Thanks. Thanks a million.'

§ 43

Troy sat up in bed reading one of his father's newspapers. The old man had used the editorial column in the day's *London Evening Herald* to air his views on the matter of two nations. There was not an editor in the land who, sooner or later, did not have recourse to Disraeli's phrase. Two Nations, Trojan Horse, Phoenix from the Ashes – all the overworked clichés of journalism. Troy was amazed he got away with it. He had not put his name to it, but Troy knew his father's prose style. Whilst overtly calling for Britain to pull together as one nation he was also pointing out at every turn that it was, inevitably, two nations, that the war was not the leveller that most of Britain now chose to pretend it was, and that the nation, undeniably, was riven with inequalities. We die together, we do not live together. Had it been less subtle it would have provoked the authorities to fits of rage, and the old man would find himself hauled in front of some ghostly committee accused of defeatism. But Alex Troy was nothing if not subtle.

The front door slammed. It had to be Kitty. Only Kitty had a key. But it was unlike her to storm in, Kitty crept in. Always trying to surprise him.

She appeared in the doorway of his bedroom. Leant against the door jamb and stared at him. He had no idea what had made her so pissed off. He knew it wasn't him. It was, he thought, an anger all but spent – drizzled down into exasperation, *sehnsucht* and want.

'Come back for another fuck?' he said.

'Don't use that word. I've told you before, I don't like it. I don't want to hear it. I know it's how they talk in your house. Those sisters of yours are foul-mouthed. But it's not the way I was brought up to talk.'

Kitty kicked off her shoes, not caring where they fell.

Turned her back on him and yanked at the silver buttons of her tunic. Kitty had not clicked with his sisters. It was unfortunate they'd ever met. They could not but look down upon a working woman – for her part, they weren't 'ladies' and never would be. Kitty had a fair range of abuse and insult, but she drew the line at 'fuck'. Troy didn't think his sisters knew there could be a line.

Later, after the act she would not name by its bluntest single syllable, she was restless. Sprawled half on him, half off him, but unsettled. Troy opened his eyes. She looked away.

'About this American of yours,' he said.

'Wot?' Prising her head off his chest to look down at him. 'Wot about him?'

'I was wondering. What's he like?'

'You seen him. That night in the Salisbury. Tall, skinny, speccy, bit bald at the front. 'Bout my age. Not exactly a looker, but . . . you know.'

'I didn't mean what does he look like. I meant . . . what's he like?'

Kitty turned her back on him, swung her legs to touch the floor, looked back at him, arms out, hands resting on her knees, back bent, breasts pendulous.

'Wot do you mean wot's he like? You never asked before.'

'I was curious.'

'Nosy more like.'

'Then indulge me.'

'You want to know why I'm with him, don't you?'

'To be precise, I want to know why you're *not* with him.'

She stared at the ceiling, dug her fists into her waist, arched her back and stretched her neck, breasts flattened out against her ribcage. A faint snap of cartilage as she unbent and looked back at him.

'Well, since you ask, he's –'

Stilton looked at his makeshift posse. The tall, speccy American. The short, sly, lazy London copper. He knew what duty and regulations demanded of him – that he take Dobbs into the house on Cleveland Street with him. But he also knew what he had promised the American. Besides, if it came to a bit of the rough stuff, Cormack looked as though he might handle himself a sight better than Dobbs.

Dobbs pointed up at the top-floor front window.

'He's in there. I watched the blackouts being drawn. There's an old couple on the ground floor, but nobody on the first or second floors. Bloke on the third went out to work about half an hour ago. I had a quick word with him – a bus driver on the 73 – says he thought the top floor was empty until today.'

'Back way out?' Stilton said.

'There's a door to the mews at the back, but the only way out of the mews is back into Warren Street. From the corner here you can see every way in and out.'

'Good lad. You stay put. Me and the Captain are going in.'

They took the staircase in silence. It seemed to Stilton so like a repetition of what they had done in Marshall Street only a couple of hours ago that it needed no explanation. No one answered the door, and when Stilton pushed it in, it too banged against the wall of an empty room. But this room hadn't been stripped and wiped – it was even more like the *Marie Celeste*. A burning cigarette lay on the side of an ashtray, curling wisps of smoke drifting towards the ceiling. A folded newspaper on the tiny dining table. A slice of toast with two bites out of it. A half drunk cup of tea.

'I don't get it,' he whispered to Cormack. 'We'd have met him on the stairs.'

Cormack pointed silently at the ceiling and stepped out onto the staircase once more. The stairs narrowed up to a small door set in the roof, scarcely bigger than a hatchway. A chink of moonlight shone through it. The wind caught it, and the gap seemed to open and close as though winking at them. Cormack started up the last flight. Stilton put a hand on his shoulder and held him back.

'Nay, lad. I came prepared. You didn't.'

He reached into the long pocket of his trousers, pulled out a full-length Metropolitan Police truncheon and whacked it gently into the palm of his hand.

'Walter,' the American said softly. 'Do you really think we need that?'

'Dunno. But he's running, isn't he? That doesn't bode well. Bloke who's running from you can like as not turn on you.'

Cormack gave way. Stilton led off up the stairs and pushed gently at the door. There was a half moon in the sky, enough light to see by. He found himself on a flat roof high above Warren Street, facing a forest of chimney stacks. Stahl could be behind any one of them. He took a cautious couple of steps, then another and another and stood on the grey plain of roofing lead wondering which way next.

From behind the second nearest chimney stack a figure in a black hat appeared. He ran towards Stilton, so quickly, so quietly, Stilton had no time to react. He felt himself rooted to the spot as Stahl closed on him. Then he saw the arm swing up from his side and the glint of moonlight on metal – the gun in his hand.

Stilton felt a blow between his shoulder-blades – a shove that sent him sprawling, face down on the lead roof. Then a bang like the sound his Riley made when it backfired. He raised his head, like a Tommy peeping over the top into no-man's-land, he thought, just in time to see Stahl hit the roof, flat on his back, dead. The wind caught the black hat and blew it out over the rooftops of London. He turned, flipped onto his backside. Cormack was staring intently at the body, his arm fully extended, clutching a gun. For a few seconds neither of them moved, then Cormack lowered the gun and looked at Stilton. Stilton was struggling to get one foot of leverage. Cormack crouched down – the hand that held the gun loose at his side, the other pushing him gently back down.

'Sit awhile, Walter. We both should.'

Only now could Stilton hear the rasp of his breathing, see the deep rise and fall of his chest.

'You've not done this before?'

'No – but I'm trained for it. Had to be a first time. Almost inevitably. Or did you think that because I wore glasses and did a desk job I somehow wasn't a real soldier?'

'Dunno what I thought. What is that thing? A cannon?'

'Smith and Wesson.'

Cormack's right hand disappeared beneath his coat and the gun vanished into a discreet holster somewhere in the small of his back.

Stilton nodded at the corpse.

'He's dead?'

'Yep.'

'You're certain?'

'He didn't leave me a lot of choice.'

'Well – that pisses on the chips doesn't it?'

Stilton struggled up, Cormack stood and lent his hand.

'How's that?'

'Stahl. You just killed Stahl. All these days looking in every nook and cranny of the city and we end up with another stiff.'

'That's not Stahl, Walter.'

Stilton took a few heavy-footed paces towards the body.

'Looks damn like 'im to me.'

Cormack stood next to Stilton, looking down. Tall, blond, thirtyish, a neat hole in the forehead leaking blood.

'It isn't Stahl. Looks more than a little like him, but it isn't. If it were, we'd be lying there instead of him.'

'Could you see it wasn't him when you shot the bugger?'

'No – but like I said, he didn't leave me much choice.'

'So the only way to be certain was to kill 'im. If you got 'im it couldn't be Stahl – if he got you it was?'

'That's about the size of it. 'Cept it was you he was aiming at.'

'Jesus Christ. Jesus Christ,' said Stilton. 'If he isn't Stahl then who the bloody hell is he?'

The crunch of a boot made him turn before Cormack could answer. A fire-watcher in a blue blouse and a tin hat was crossing the roof from the house next door, striding towards them with all the importance of half a uniform built into his cocky swagger. A bantam of a man, in his sixties, short, wiry, the moustache almost as big as he was.

'I 'eard a bang.'

He flicked his torch on and off, saw it reflected in the dead eyes of the corpse.

'Allo, allo, allo. What's all this then?'

Stilton whipped out his warrant card, held it up to the man's torch, shot Cormack an eyeball order as his hand reached beneath his jacket once more.

'I could book you for nicking my lines, you realise. Got to be a copper to say "allo, allo, allo".'

The man stared at the card.

'You're a copper?'

'I didn't print it meself, if that's what you think. Chief Inspector Stilton, Scotland Yard.'

'Like I said, I 'eard a bang. It's me job to investigate things that go bang.'

'If you don't bugger off, it'll be your head that goes bang against my fist. This is coppers' business. Go about your own business and say nowt to nobody.'

'Charming,' said the fire-watcher, but he left all the same.

'Can you trust him?' Cormack said softly.

'God knows, but the sooner we call out the binmen for this one the better.'

'Binmen?'

'Cleaners – blokes who come out and take care of things like this.'

'Shouldn't we just dial 999?'

'Not on your nellie. Nobody's to know about this. If this gets out how can I ever boast to you again that there's no spies in London we don't know about? Thing is, I meant it at the time. I'd've put a fiver on it to be true – but there you are. I was wrong. No, this gets buried. I tell my people. You tell nobody – and in return I won't mention you were the one with the gun.'

This last sentence was uttered in a closely conspiratorial stage-whisper.

'It's perfectly legit, Walter. I'm a serving army officer.'

'You're a serving army officer out of uniform. If that cockamamy suit's the new American uniform, then I feel sorry for the lot of you.'

There was a pause. Stilton looked at the door again, making sure no one else was about to emerge armed with a torch and a daft question, half expecting to see Dobbs.

'I have to leave you alone with him. I have to go and call my people, you see.'

'That's OK. I understand.'

'Could you bear to touch him?'

'Touch him?'

'Someone's got to go through his pockets.'

'His pockets?'

'Papers and that.'

Stilton searched for the right word and came up with the all too obvious. 'Clues,' he said, as though it were a technical term and somehow the arcane nature of it might be lost on Cormack.

'That's OK, Walter. I can look for "clues".'

'I'll be about ten minutes. I'll leave Dobbs out front to keep an eye open. Let's just hope the buggers don't take all night about it.'

§ 45

Left alone, Cal sank down, his back against a chimney stack, his weight balanced on the balls of his feet. He was not accustomed to death, but the body of a dead German – he had to be German, didn't he? – held no terror. He looked at the face. Yes, he was very like Wolfgang Stahl – and now he understood the hesitation that both Hudge and Fish Wally had shown about the sketch. There was no scar over the left eye.

He began with the gun. Picked it up with the tip of thumb and forefinger. A Browning automatic. A gun very like his own, a medium-bore service weapon. What did you expect? said a voice in his head. A Luger? He sniffed the barrel. It hadn't been fired recently. Stilton would have been its first victim. The stream of blood from the hole in his forehead had covered his face. He did look like Stahl under the crimson glaze. Now the blood had reached his shirt, which soaked it up like blotting paper. Cal unbuttoned the jacket and looked for an inside pocket. A plain black leather wallet. A packet of Player's Capstan. He opened the wallet. Letters – all from one Mavis Tookey of Riverside Villas, Leigh-on-Sea. A photograph – a girl in her late teens, presumably the aforementioned Mavis. And a handful of official documents. A National Identity Card. A War Office letter indicating Deferred Service. A Ration Book. All in the name of Peter Robinson – a name he took to be as anonymous here as John Doe might be at home – at an address in Cardiff. The Germans were past masters at this sort of thing. It would be a simple task for them to fit out this assassin with a plausible cover. They'd even given him the stub of a return ticket to Cardiff. The letters were probably real. There probably was a 'Peter' in some stalag in Germany, from whom they'd been stolen, and poor Mavis in Riverside Villas would never know the use to which her affections had been put. A sentimental moment seized him: to return the letters to Mavis, to put heart and head back together. Then the unsentimental sharp edge of reality – they'd got number two. The Germans had sent a two-man team to take out Stahl – one in the open and one undercover, left jab, right hook – and they'd got both of them. It improved the odds on Stahl's surviving long enough for them to blunder into him. He'd have to think hard how to explain this to Walter. It was the sort of thing that Walter's decency and plodding logic might have difficulty with.

He was reading Mavis's letters – moved far more by this thin strand of life than he was by the lumpen fact of death at his feet – when Walter returned with two men and a sackcloth body bag.

'You get everything?' he asked simply.

Only when he flopped face down onto his bed in Claridge's and felt the bulge in his pocket did Cal remember that he and Walter had said an exhausted good night, fixed a time for the following day and parted, without Cal handing over the package.

It was not a Kitty night. No telephone call, no gentle tapping at his door. He'd made her mad, but he couldn't help that. He was glad. He needed the break. All the same it was of Kitty that he thought as he read the love letters of an English girl in an English seaside town to an Englishman in God-knew-where. He fell asleep. Still in his trousers and shirt, still clutching a letter, knowing what he missed – the simple, understated restraint of the way she signed off – 'luv ya xxx.' He didn't think Kitty knew the words.

§ 46

Around dawn Troy felt Kitty slide from his bed, heard the rustle of her slipping back into her clothes, the wooden groan of a drawer being prised open.

'Need a hanky. You don't mind, do you?'

She plucked out one of his F-embroidered handkerchiefs. Troy said nothing.

Then the gentle click of the Yale engaging on the front door, and the roar of her motorbike ripping up the blackout in Bedfordbury.

Kitty roared home to Covent Garden. All of three streets away. She needed sleep before her shift. She'd got next to none in Troy's bed. It was less than three hours later when her father phoned to murder sleep.

§ 47

Cal was using Walter as his alarm clock. If he said he'd be there at eight thirty, he would be. Cal would get a call from reception, on the dot. Walter would order a second breakfast on Cal's room number and happily wait for him. When he awoke at nine, he knew something was wrong – but all he could do was wait. For once, he'd be up and shaved and Walter would have to forego a second breakfast at his expense. He listened to the news as he shaved. The *Bismarck* was still loose in the North Atlantic. The battle for Crete dragged on – the British were getting hammered. Ever inventive, the Germans had mounted an airborne invasion, floating their soldiers in on parachutes. Nothing like it had been seen in the history of warfare. On the first day the British had picked them off like pheasants driven towards their guns by beaters. But the Germans had soon got the hang of it – Crete was going to fall.

At ten he switched on the radio again in the easy hope of further developments. He'd missed the opening headline, and it was so hard to tell from the tones of a BBC announcer just what you were listening to – the good, the bad or the indifferent . . .

'. . . at six a.m. this morning the *Bismarck* and the *Prince Eugen* were sighted in the Denmark Strait and engaged by His Majesty's ships *Hood* and *Prince of Wales*. HMS *Hood* opened fire at 26,000 yards . . .'

Good God, that was the best part of fifteen miles.

'. . . but failed to find the range of the German ships. HMS *Hood* was hit by a salvo from the *Prince Eugen*, and on returning fire the *Bismarck* too was hit. After several exchanges of fire, the *Hood* was hit amidships by a shell from the *Bismarck*, exploded and sank. It is believed the German shell penetrated the ship's magazine. The search is now under way for survivors. *HMS Prince of Wales* withdrew from action after receiving several direct hits. There are reports of casualties.'

The understatement was staggering. Was it the Navy or the British? You can't say nothing, at the same time you can hardly tell the truth, so you end up with the half-truth of unhysterical understatement that becomes a lie in itself. 'There are reports of casualties.' Too calm. It was a time to get hysterical. What casualties? Men blown apart? Men blinded and maimed? God, he'd hate to be British this morning. You'd have to be stoic this morning. To be British . . . and then Cal remembered where he'd seen the name *Hood* before. Two sailor caps hanging on the back of the kitchen door in the big basement at Jubilee Street. Walter Stilton's boys – Kev and Trev – served on the *Hood*.

He wanted to call Walter. To telephone him. To tell him. He wanted to call Kitty. To tell her what? But he had neither of their numbers. They came to him. One by day and one by night. He was not in control of this. They were.

Patience. All his training had taught him that. He went down to the lobby at lunchtime. Good form had vanished into the occasion. A radio was stuck on one of the tables – half a dozen or so residents clustered round it. He knew the type. Old men – Claridge's seemed half full of well-heeled widowers at the best of times, old buffers who'd never learnt how to open an egg and could not bear the fuss of a housekeeper. A certain type of old man who wouldn't leave for the country when the bombs started to fall. Most likely this lot were old soldiers, veterans of the last German war, determined not to miss this one even if it meant staying through the Blitz.

'Bloody hell,' said an old boy with a pure white handlebar moustache. 'Three? Three, out of all those men!'

He turned to Cal as he approached.

'D'ye hear that, young man? Three survivors from the *Hood*!'

Three? Out of how many? What was a battleship's crew these days? Eight hundred? A thousand? Fifteen hundred?

Cal didn't ask. The broadcast switched to the weather reports. Somebody flicked it off and the *ad hoc* gathering of old men split up and headed for their separate tables. It must be a sign of shock for an Englishman not to want to hear the weather report, even in this embryonic summer of feeble sunshine and habitual drizzle.

Handlebar moustache was the only one left. He was sitting, head down, death-dreaming. He twitched, raised his eyes again and noticed that Cal was still there. For a second Cal wondered if he was going to be handed the 'white feather'. The old man stuck out a hand.

'Gresley,' he said. 'Ernest Gresley. Rorke's Drift, Ladysmith, Mons. They retired me after Mons. Too old, they said.'

Cal shook the hand. There was a tacit invitation to join him. The old man was older than he thought. He'd stated his credentials, rattled off his résumé – and he must be eightyish to have seen Rorke's Drift. Cal was in awe of the old boy. He was fascinated. This man had fought as a redcoat. The uniform had scarcely changed from the Battle of Long Island in 1776 to the Zulu Wars a hundred years later. Imagine being back in Washington and being able to say he'd met with a real redcoat.

But he had no idea what to say to this. Stating his own credentials was pointless. He'd encountered the enemy only once in his life – and that was last night. He could not hold his own with this. He couldn't sit and make small talk with an old redcoat. It was an English day. Let them have their day. He knew it was shitty behaviour, but he muttered an 'excuse me' and left. An entire crew lost. Good God, they didn't need his two cents' worth.

He found himself in Soho – killing time. He sat in cafés, watched the English hunched over their newspapers, spread the width of tables, nicotined fingers stabbing down at the paper – the strategy of the Cafeteria Corps. After a couple of cafés he knew there was unanimity among the armchair warriors – we, it always was 'we', were going to get the *Bismarck*. The Earth was not big enough to hide her. He bought a copy of the *Evening Herald*'s early edition – the loss of the *Hood* was, it seemed, a body blow. If Dunkirk had been victory snatched from the jaws of defeat, then this was plainly irredeemable by propaganda. Fourteen hundred men had died on the pride of the fleet, and the *Bismarck* had steamed away from the battle. There was an article, an obituary for a ship, written by Alexei Troy – he'd heard that name before somewhere, hadn't he? – recalling the twenty or more years in which the *Hood* had sailed the world as an ironic ambassador for peace; how the *Hood* had flown the flag in all the old ports of empire, and how he himself had seen the largest battleship afloat glide through the Golden Gate into San Francisco to the roaring cheers of an old enemy. And then how its first taste of action had been the unenviable, ignominious sinking of the French fleet at Oran after the surrender. Fourteen hundred men had gone down with the *Hood*. And with the British still in pursuit of the *Bismarck*, the death toll could not but rise.

Early in the evening, he was lying on his bed. The telephone rang and announced Sergeant Stilton. He could hardly believe this. What was Kitty thinking of? He found out soon enough.

She was in civvies, a plain black two-piece. Her face scraped white with misery. Eyes red and watery. A handbag, scarcely big enough to hold a handkerchief. He'd never seen her with a handbag before. He'd never seen her out of uniform before. He'd seen her strip it off *ad libidinum* – but she'd never arrived wearing anything else.

'You gotta come home with me. I can't stand it no more. I been there since breakfast. It's driving me mad.'

'Kitty – I can't intrude on your family's grief.'

'Intrude ain't got nothing to do with it. If you come they'll pay attention to something outside their own misery. If something doesn't snap 'em to we'll all drown. Just get your coat and come with me, please.'

'Kitty – it's been less than a day!'

'It's been thirteen bleedin' hours. I counted every bleedin' minute of 'em. An' I can't take no more. Get yer coat!'

They caught a cab outside the hotel. Cal had half wondered on the way down whether he'd find her motorbike outside – but she flagged a cab and said, 'You'll have to pay. I got no money.' He was happy to pay. Anything was better than the thought of driving up to Jubilee Street on the back of that motorbike. It seemed an indignity pushed to an insult – an insult to Walter and Edna Stilton and their two dead boys.

'Who's there?' he asked.

'What?'

'At your parents'. I mean, is the whole family there?'

'An' the rest. Half the neighbours. Me mum's sisters been there most of the day. The vicar been round. That was nice for me mum. Told her Kev and Trev was 'eroes. Me dad wouldn't talk to him. Atheist me dad is. Me mum cries all the time an' me dad puffs on his pipe and says nothin'. Would you believe it, he's been married to her for thirty-odd years an' 'e don't know what to say to 'er? Vera's taken over the kitchen. She's in her element. And she's in control. Miss Greenlees makes a thousand pots of tea and keeps askin' everyone if they want more. She's shot through a fortnight's tea ration in less than a day. If she asks me again I'll clock 'er one. They don't need me. Really they don't. They got all the fuss one family can 'andle. But I can't duck out of it. I only got out by tagging on to the aunts when they left. But I got to go back. They won't let me duck out.'

'So I have to duck in?'

'You got it. That's exactly what it is. I need you. Right now I need you.'

They were emotive words, uttered wholly without emotion. He was not a necessity in her life. He was a convenience.

§ 48

Walter was standing in the hallway when they arrived. The telephone pressed to his ear, saying 'I see' over and over.

Kitty waited till he'd finished.

'News, dad?'

'Aye. That mate o' mine at the Admiralty. Those three blokes the Navy picked up. A midshipman, a signalman and an able seaman. No leading seamen.'

For a moment Cal was not there. They could neither of them see him or acknowledge him. Then Kitty said 'That's it then. We know now, don't we.'

Walter disappeared into the parlour to shatter his wife's last hope. Kitty led Cal down the stairs to the basement, pulling on his hand like a child dragging a reluctant father to the shops.

Vera was at the range, swapping pans around like a juggler. Grim-faced, stripped of make-up, sleeves up and tearless. Losing herself in her own efficiency. Miss Greenlees hovered with the kettle until Vera swore at her and snatched it away.

'I was only going to make a cup of tea. I'm sure Captain Cormack would like a nice cup of tea.'

'He'd love a nice cup of tea,' said Kitty. 'We both would.'

'Jesus Christ,' said Vera. 'How much bleedin' tea do you have to drink to bring back the dead?'

She slammed the kettle onto the hob. Miss Greenlees fled in tears. Cal wished he could follow her.

'Vera, for God's sake . . .' Kitty began.

'Don't Vera me. She's been wittering on at me all day. You sloped off, you sly tart. You've had a break from her. You've had a break from all of 'em. Don't start on me!'

'I did not slope off!'

'You sloped off all the way to Claridge's. You been up West. If that ain't slopin' off I don't know what is. You left me 'ere on me jack jones to get a meal for us all. Kitty, you're me sister, me own flesh and blood, and you're about as much use as a fart in a colander.'

Walter appeared in the doorway.

'Will you two shut up. This is meant to be a house in mournin' – or had neither of you noticed?'

The women turned their backs on him. Walter's attention turned to Cal.

'The missis'd like a word, Calvin. If you've a moment.'

Cal had not anticipated this. He had come for Kitty. He'd sink back into the wallpaper. No one would notice him. No one would ask anything of him.

'I've all the time in the world, Walter. But I've no idea what I can possibly say.'

'You don't have to say anythin' lad. Let our Edna do the talking. You're a servin' soldier, after all. That's what matters to our Edna. Just to be able to talk to another man in uniform. Someone as knows what it's like.'

Cal followed, wondering what on earth he could do for Edna Stilton to fulfil the notion Walter had dreamt up. He'd never been in the Navy – he wasn't actually in uniform – as in better days Stilton was wont to remind him – his experience of combat was clandestine, grubby compared to the heroics of the Royal Navy. No one would ever boast of what he and Stilton had got up to last night. For himself, he wasn't sure he'd ever tell anyone.

Edna Stilton was leafing through a photograph album. Stilton eased him gently forward with a hand between the shoulder-blades. Then Cal heard the door close softly, looked around and found himself in a room he hadn't seen last time. A formal room – Victorian in the weight of its furniture and the universal hues of brown and black. The 'parlour' – that was what Stilton had called it. It had the air of a room scarcely used. Like the ballroom in his grandfather's house – the dustsheets came off once a year.

'Mrs Stilton?'

She looked up. Sad and smiling at the same time.

'Captain Cormack. It's very good of you . . .'

'Calvin, please . . .'

'I was just looking at some snaps of my boys.'

Cal peered over. Black gummed corners sticking the snapshots down to a coarse grey paper, heavy as blotter. Two shorn pre-adolescent boys in swimming trunks, facing the camera with four rows of bright teeth. A castle made of sand.

'That was Southend, 1923. The year they got nits and I had to shave their 'eads.'

She turned a page, then another and another. Came to rest on the twins in uniform, a cigarette stuck to each lower lip, beer bottle in hand, one of them with his head back, roaring with laughter.

'That was the year they enlisted. 1934.'

Cal pulled up a footstool and took the crick out of his back. He felt like a child next to Mrs Stilton, her bulk sedate in the depths of an overstuffed armchair.

'You're a reg'lar aren't you, Calvin? Not like Maurice. Maurice is only in for the duration.'

'Yes. I've served eleven years if you count West Point.'

'What's that? Is that like Aldershot?'

'More like Sandhurst, I guess.'

She nodded at this, turned another page. A formal shot. The boys in dress uniform standing to attention.

'The vicar was round.'

'Yes, I heard.'

'Reckons they was 'eroes. Told me and Kitty they died a hero's death.'

This was the moment Cal had dreaded. His own feet of clay. He had no idea what to say and less of what to be.

'But they was reg'lar. "That's the thing with reg'lars," he said. "They lay down their lives for their king and their country." '

She stared off into nothing for a few moments. Then she looked straight at Cal.

'Was that why you joined up?'

And he could see no moral or merit in lying to her.

'No, Mrs Stilton. I'm no hero. I joined up to escape the ties of family. The obligation to go to the right university after the right school, and to cheat the career my folks had mapped out for me. It was a selfish act on my part. I had no thoughts of heroism. I had hoped to get through it all without ever coming face to face with an enemy. It was always meant to be something temporary. I saw myself doing something else within a few years. I'd no idea what, but I never imagined I'd still be a soldier on the eve of a war. Not everyone's a hero. Not everyone can be like your boys.'

'Heroes?'

'We're not all cut out for it. Your boys were . . . special.'

'An' you didn't want to be a hero?'

'Never entered my mind.'

'I'm pleased to hear you say that. I'd much sooner remember them the way they were – a pair of scallywags looking out for the next fag and the next likely girl. If I thought they was really heroes I'd never have understood 'em. They joined up to get off the bloody dole queue. 'Scuse my French.'

She closed the book flat on her lap.

'Vicar always was a silly old sod. I remember during the General Strike him saying we'd all go to hell 'cos we'd broken God's law and it was God as allotted us our station in life. You hang on to your life, young Calvin. I don't think I believe in dead heroes. Now – has no one offered you a cup of tea? There's nothing like a nice cup of tea.'

Her arms were poised to push herself out of the chair when the door opened and, as if on cue, Stilton appeared with the tea tray.

'There's nothing like a nice cup of tea,' he said, and Cal knew he was trapped for the duration of the English Tea Ceremony.

§ 49

Vera cooked as well as her mother. Cal had no idea what it was, but there was plenty of it. A dash of meat somewhere, he thought it might be mutton, but healthy portions of carrot and lentil. All the same it was a spartan meal, in that neither Stilton nor his wife nor the lodgers came down to eat, and the awkward recriminating and self-recriminating gathering around the kitchen table consisted of Cal, Kitty, Vera, Rose, her husband Tom, the roundly pregnant Reenie, and the boy Tel.

Cal aimed for neutrality, as heads bent over plates in what he could only think of as an angry silence.

'Is Pilot Officer Micklewhite on duty?' he asked of Reenie. Reenie and Rose were the tearful ones, always on the verge of grabbing a handkerchief and dashing from the room. Reenie looked up at him, eyes red-rimmed.

'Beg pardon?'

'Maurice – I meant, I guess Maurice is on call?'

'Yeah,' she said. 'He can't get away, you see. They could scramble any time.'

And in saying this the implication of her own words came home to her. She sniffled and dug around in a pocket for her hanky.

Vera's voice cut through the sniffles.

'You'll have to move back now. You know that, don't you?' Cal wondered to whom she was speaking, but Kitty answered all the same.

'Wot? Wot do you mean?'

'I mean you, fancy pants. You'll have to move back. I can't manage this house on me own. It's time you recognised that you can't shirk your responsibilities no more.'

'Wot? Me? Why me? Why not Rose or Reen?'

'Why you, 'cos you're the eldest, that's why. Besides, they're married. They got blokes and kids of their own to look after. I can't look after me mum as well as Dad and Tel.'

Tel chipped in, 'You won't 'ave to look after me. I don't need no looking after. I'll be in the Navy next year.'

Then both the sisters turned on him.

'Not bloody likely!'

'Wot?'

'You're going nowhere,' said Kitty, aiming at him with her fork. 'Hasn't this family lost enough already? You can just wait till you're called up, and even then you won't have to go. Not after this. It'd be cruel to take you as well as Kev and Trev. If you join the Navy now it'll break your mother's heart.'

'That's not fair!' – the cry of younger siblings everywhere. 'You're making me stay at home just so you can go on swanning around up West.'

'That's got nothing to do with it. I work up West.

Bow Street ain't exactly the Mile End Road, you know. I can't roll out of bed and be at work ten minutes later! Will you lay off. Will you all just lay off! I am not moving back, and that's final.'

Vera gathered up plates, an oversized show of bustle, as much noise as she could make. And when she'd dumped everything in the sink, she faced Kitty across the width of the kitchen and uttered the single word, 'Bitch.'

Kitty pushed back her chair and yanked open the kitchen door. Cal sat nonplussed. He'd never seen anything like this. In his family it simply didn't happen. His sisters would never call each other a bitch, they'd simply point out that one was being boring – the greatest sin the family knew of, to be boring.

'Calvin!' Kitty said from the doorway.

Out in the street it was already dark.

'Will you take me home?' she said.

'To Covent Garden? Sure. I'll get us a cab at the end of the street.'

'No. I meant to your place. To Claridge's.'

'To Claridge's?'

'I can't stay here. Not with that lot. And I don't want to be on my own. So just take me home with you, will you.'

'Am I ever going to see where you live?'

'You wouldn't want to, really you wouldn't.'

§ 50

Afterwards. Lying in the bed. Lights out, windows open, curtains flapping. A single sheet pulled over them, Kitty with her head on his chest, one hand splayed across his belly. Cal said 'Are they always like that?'

'Like wot?'

'Angry.'

'Oh, that. Yeah. I think it's the only way Vera and Tel have to show emotions. Like they don't have the vocabulary for all the others, so they use the one they know. Vera's as cut up as the rest of us, but it's the only way she's got to show it, to take it out on Miss Greenlees and me and young Tel.'

It was the most analytic statement he had ever heard Kitty make.

'Doesn't let you off the hook though, does it?'

'You mean I lost me temper too?'

'That . . . and the fact you can't bear to be there.'

'If you lived with 'em you'd know.'

'I do know. I told your mother much the same thing while you were in the kitchen with Vera. She asked me why I joined up. I told her, not in so many words, but I told her I'd done it just to escape my family. It's not unique to the English. You joined the cops, I joined the army. Amounts to pretty much the same thing, really.'

Kitty propped herself up on one elbow. He couldn't see her eyes but he knew she was looking at him.

'You slyboots,' she said.

'Slyboots.' He weighed up the phrase.

'Answer me this, then. You wear them bifocals – specs to read – specs to look at objects more than about thirty feet away – how did you ever get into the army in the first place? You can't be better than A4 with peepers that bad.'

He was wearing his glasses now. He'd put them back on within a minute or so of rolling off Kitty. He could get by without them and a lot of the time he had to – but he could see her the more clearly with them. He'd made love to her out of focus – in the afterglow he rather wanted to be able to see her. He put his specs on much as most men lit up a cigarette. Unconsciously he pressed a finger to the bridge and shoved them an infinitesimal fraction further up.

'Well?' she said.

'I cheated.'

'You cheated!?!'

'I had a friend sat the eye test a little ahead of me. He has what's called an eidetic memory. You know what that is?'

'No.'

'Means he sees things as pictures and takes them like a camera. When he wants to remember something he just summons up the picture. Anything from the arrangement of flowers in a vase to pages of print. He can hold thirty thousand words of text in his head, without even thinking of them as words. He just sees a block of images.'

'That's amazing.'

'He sat the test two hours ahead of me. Came out, drew all the eye charts for me and I learnt them by rote – the hard way. Passed A1.'

'That's amazing. I never met anyone like that.'

Cal had, he'd known two people with that gift. One was Billy Blick, who'd helped him into the army. The other was Wolfgang Stahl.

§ 51

In his room in a London lodging house, Stahl could not sleep. He lay on his cot oblivious to the noises of an uneasy household of single, displaced men – grunting, arguing, farting, fighting – the walking wounded of life, not war – and stared at the ceiling. Image after image flashed onto it, the family trees of battle formation: Army Group North, von Leeb, 21 Infantry Divisions; Army Group Centre, von Bock, 32 Infantry Divisions; Army Group South, von Runstedt, 63 Infantry Divisions. If that didn't put him to sleep he'd start on the Panzers.

§ 52

Cal was woken by the phone. Eight-thirty. Walter time. Except that it couldn't be Walter. Not today. It was. He shook Kitty.

'Get up. For God's sake, get up!'

'Wossmatter?'

'Your father's here.'

'So?'

'This time he's coming up.'

Cal tugged her naked into the bathroom, resisting all the way. He turned on the taps.

'What are you doing? Leggo!'

She jerked free of him, and he slammed the door with his backside, pressed against the panel.

'Stay here. The noise of the water should smother any sound you make. Just stay here!'

He slipped out, dashed around the bedroom. Pulled on his robe. Gathered the scattered clothing Kitty had peeled off and thrown down the night before. He shoved the bundle at her through the bathroom door, but she grabbed him by the arm and pulled him in.

'We don't have to hide.'

'I don't,' he said. 'You do. Or would you rather your father found us like this?'

'Like what? Calvin – I'll be thirty this summer. He can't possibly think I'm a virgin.'

'Do you really want what he might think to be confirmed this way?'

They could hear Stilton knocking at the door now. She lowered her voice.

'They can't nag me about not being married at twenty-nine and expect me to be a virgin, now can they?'

'Get dressed and stay quiet. I'll get rid of him.'

207

He opened the door, feigning sleepiness, when even the hairs on his head stood to attention.

'Walter?'

Stilton pushed past him. Pacing the middle of the room. Antsy in a way Cal had never seen him before. Then he seemed to sniff the air. Oh, God, Cal thought, what is it – her scent, or worse, the reek of illicit sex?

Stilton snapped to, plonked himself down in one of the bucket chairs by the window. 'We've work to do,' he said. 'Things we both forgot.'

Cal stood still. Pretended to scratch his head until he realised that this could only make him look like Stan Laurel.

'Walter, are you sure this is a good idea? Isn't this a little too soon?'

'Work's the best remedy I know of. I'll be fine. Don't you worry about me.'

'The family, Walter. Aren't there things to be ... to be ... arranged?'

'Like what?'

'Like ... a funeral?'

'You need bodies for a funeral. My lads are five hundred fathoms down in the Atlantic.'

Of course – it was a stupid remark.

'Walter, would you give me a few minutes to get myself together?'

'Aye – I'll read the morning paper. But chop chop all the same.'

In the bathroom Kitty had settled into the bath and was soaping herself lazily, a hand gliding the length of one arm, cupping one breast, nipple up, lips pursed to blow bubbles off it and create one of the simplest pleasures known to man – soapy tits. Cal wished he could ignore this, wished she'd stop what she'd started. He sat on the lavatory seat, eyes on her body, mind struggling back towards the remote outposts of common sense.

'D'yer get rid of him?'

'Er . . . no, he's staying. I'll have to get dressed and go out with him. You'd better stay here until you hear me slam the door.'

'And . . .'

'And I have to shave.'

'You can't go out all icky-fluffed from bed. Why don't you get in with me? I'll soap yer todger.'

'Kitty. You just lost two brothers. Your mother's up to her eyes in grief. Your father's in the next room telling me he wants to bury himself in his work . . .'

'Yeah. But we're still alive, aren't we? I think you should get in with me. I think you should get it while you can.'

'Is that your life's motto in a nutshell, Kitty?'

'Pretty much. You getting in or not?'

Cal said nothing. Whipped the razor across his face, brushed his teeth, dearly wished he could piss in front of a woman, but found he couldn't, went back to his bedroom and threw on his clothes.

'I remembered,' Walter was saying. 'We never got round to what our man had in his pockets.'

Cal took an envelope out of the desk drawer and set it on the round table in front of Stilton. Stilton put on his reading glasses and spent five minutes peering closely at the late Peter Robinson's documents.

'What conclusion did you reach?' he asked.

'Walter, could we discuss this over breakfast?' said Cal.

Stilton looked at his pocket watch. Cal had hit him where it counted.

'I don't see why not,' he said.

There was a clunk from the bathroom. Cal ignored it. Stilton did not appear to have heard. Cal slammed the door after them as loudly as he could. Stilton glanced at him but said nothing.

With a cup of coffee inside him and six floors of steel and concrete between him and Kitty, Cal felt much more like answering questions. Through a mouthful of toast and marmalade, Walter asked the same one again.

'What did you make of it all?'

'They sent a two-man team. We got lucky. The man on the roof was an assassin, just the same as Smulders – sent to kill Stahl. Only this one they landed from a U-boat on some bleak stretch of coast, rather than send him in pretending to be a refugee. Could be they hoped we'd be so taken up with Smulders we'd never notice this one. He called himself Peter Robinson, by the way.'

'Aye, I saw. Forensics reckon there was nothing about his clothing to suggest he was German. British labels. Phillips replacement rubber soles on his shoes. An Ona condom still in its foil packet lost in the lining of his jacket. Home and Colonial linen handkerchief. Remains of London bus tickets in the dust in the bottom of his pockets, a bit of old Fry's chocolate paper stuck to 'em. They'd kitted him out down to the fluff. What did you reckon to the paperwork?'

'I've never seen an ID card. But the Germans are first-rate at this sort of thing. If Robinson was sent by the Abwehr, and I might add that is only one possibility, then Canaris's back-room boys would have seen to it he got the best.'

Stilton swilled tea, Cal stared at him, wondering if he really had taken the one possibility at face value. Privately, Cal thought it much more probable that Admiral Canaris knew nothing of these men, that they had been sent by Heydrich.

'Oh, they're very good,' said Stilton. 'You ever seen food coupons?'

'Clothing – yes. Food – no. I eat here or I eat out. In either case, off the ration.'

Stilton passed him the ration book.

'Are they obviously bad?' Cal asked.

'No, no. They're not. They're good. Thing is, they're too good. Ration books are inky and messy. The perforations have gaps where they won't tear. This is perfect.'

Cal looked at it, without any clear notion of what he was looking for.

'You mean they slipped up?'

'You tell me?'

'They wouldn't. If they'd seen a current British ration book they'd have copied it exactly.'

'And if they hadn't?'

'I don't follow.'

'ID cards don't change. The ration book's changed a few times – when the ration changes, or at least when they add a new item to it, it does. Cheese went on only a week or two before you got here.'

The wistful, sad look of a trencherman denied passed across Stilton's face.

'Meat went down to a shillin' per person. I ask you – a bob's worth a week.'

Cal nodded, trying to fake sympathy with a man who regularly ate two breakfasts. Stilton picked up his thread again.

'Could be the Abwehr can't keep up. Can't get hold of 'em as fast as we can print 'em.'

'I still don't follow.'

'I think our chum bought it here. I think it might be the one thing he couldn't get in Germany. I think it's a local forgery.'

'Why? Why would anyone fake food coupons? Seems like a lot of trouble for nothing.'

'When you've been here a while, Calvin, you'll eat your words. And when you've been on the British diet for a while, you'll think your own words a damn sight tastier than a sausage made up of the worst scraps in a butcher's shop and a handful o' sawdust. O' course there's villains forging coupons. They're like anything else in a society made up of scarcity – a tradeable, and therefore a nickable and fakeable commodity.'

'You mean we've got a lead?'

'I'm pretty certain we could find the bloke who made this ration book. But that doesn't lead us to Stahl, does it? Just lets us follow the trail back to Robinson.'

'Or,' said Cal, 'to the point where his trail crosses Stahl's.'

'Eh?'

'Hasn't it puzzled you how easily Stahl and Smulders found one another?'

'If they found one another . . .'

'Indulge me a little longer, Walter. We've proceeded for a week or more, now, on the assumption that Stahl killed Smulders. If we hadn't we would not have found Robinson, would not have mistook him for Stahl. We thought we were following Stahl.'

'Go on.'

'Stahl found Smulders before Smulders found him because he's using the German network.'

Stilton raised a bushy eyebrow at this but said nothing.

'He's using what he knows. It's a terrible risk, but if he wanted to stay underground it was what he had to use. All the contacts the Germans have in London. At least all the contacts he knew about – and of course, Stahl being Stahl, he'd have made it his business to know.'

'I don't like the sound of this . . . this . . . network.'

'Don't get me wrong, Walter, I don't mean Germany has infiltrated on the grand scale. I'm not talking about a vast, secret Fifth Column. I'm talking about sending agents abroad with a few names, someone who might give them a room without too many questions, someone who can fake a ration book. That's all.'

'I know what you mean. I just don't like it. Short of a network of spies, you're saying Jerry picks up on that element in society that'll do anything for half a crown and a bag of peanuts – they're using the scum of London, the forgers, the tea-leafs, the dips I spent most of my early days locking up. I've seen some right villains in me time, but I'd've said most of 'em were patriotic when push comes to shove. And push came to shove at Dunkirk. We've had our backs to the wall ever since. I'd like to think there was a scrap of decency even in the worst of men.'

'A couple of rotten apples, Walter, that's all. Not the whole damn hogshead.'

'Jesus Christ, Jesus Christ.'

'May not even be English. Look at that woman caught last year passing information to the Germans at the Russian Tea Rooms.'

'What woman?'

It occurred to Cal that he'd boobed, that the British people, and that included Chief Inspectors of Police, had been told nothing about the arrest and trial of Tyler Kent of the US Embassy, and Anna Wolkoff of the Russian Tea Rooms in Kensington. It was common talk in the world in which he moved but, as this conversation was revealing to him, the outrage to which Walter could be provoked showed how different their worlds were.

'About a year ago,' Cal went on, 'a Russian exile was found to be a German agent. That's all. It's no big deal.'

'And?'

'And now she's serving time in Holloway.'

'You mean there was a trial?'

He seemed both surprised and hurt not to be in the know.

'Walter, you know . . . secrets.'

'Secrets,' Stilton repeated as though the word meant nothing to him.

'You know, maybe somebody just called for the "binmen"?'

'Touché,' said Stilton softly.

Cal picked up the ration book again.

'A local forgery, you say?'

'I'm almost certain of it.'

'Do you know the local fakers?'

'No, but I know a man who does. There's a bloke at the Yard deals in little else. If you could give me a couple of hours, I could 'appen have a word with him.'

''Appen?' Cal mimicked.

Stilton looked guilty.

'Aye. I'm not dumping you, honest – but there's things best said copper to copper.'

'That's OK, Walter. I understand. There's something I could be getting on with anyway. Why don't you pick me up around lunchtime?'

Cal went back to the sixth floor and found his something wrapped in his dressing gown, drying her hair.

'You see him off then?'

'Kitty,' he said. 'We can't go on like this.'

'Like wot?' she said.

§ 53

Inspector Drew held the ration book up to the light. Then he took a large magnifying glass from the top drawer of his desk, and scrutinised it. It was a full minute before he spoke.

'It's as though he'd signed it. The silly sod.'

Stilton said nothing. He liked Drew. He was his opposite as a copper – young, technically trained, a desk and paper man, a meticulous man with a field of expertise at his fingertips, not the shoe-leather, brown mac and make-it-up-as-you-go-along copper he knew himself to be. More than he liked him, he admired Drew. It was hard not to. In his way he was the English, the civilised version of that lunatic Pole Kolankiewicz out at the Hendon lab. You admired Kolankiewicz, you respected his talent, but you'd never say you liked him.

'It's perfection. What the Ministry of Food aspires to and will never attain. So silly. It would be a piece of cake for him to make a messy one, but no – he has to turn in a work of art.'

'He?' Stilton said. 'Who's he?'

'Forsyte. Lawrence Forsyte. It's his work. I've no doubt about it. Best in the business. Least he was till I nicked him in '37. Five to seven years for forging five-pound notes.'

Stilton found this confusing.

'We didn't have ration books in 1937. And this is bang up to date.'

Drew put the paraphernalia of his trade down and chewed a moment on the end of his pencil.

'Walter – what I have to tell you must go no further. You do understand that, don't you?'

''O' course.'

'Forsyte served less than three years. He was paroled in January last year.'

'Then it's time we yanked on his leash. He could go down for another stretch for this, as well as the one he hasn't finished.'

'No, Walter. That's just it. He can't and he won't. Forsyte works for us now. Or to be more accurate, for your lot.'

'The Branch?'

'Not quite – but you do have the same masters. Penny dropped now, has it? Good. Larry forges all the German stuff we need to send our chaps into occupied territory. Travel permits, identity cards. They've even got him at work on Reichsmark notes. Whatever he's done, he's pretty well untouchable.'

'What he's done is forge ration books. If that's for the war effort I'm a monkey's uncle!'

'Well – I'm sure he'd say the temptation was too great. I keep an eye on him, of course. Helps to let him know he's not entirely ignored by the Forgery Squad. But most of the time they use your colleagues in the Branch as nothing more than go-betweens, and the truth is they let him do what he wants – orders, naturally – and with that kind of freedom he'll dabble in this sort of thing just to see if he can do it. I shouldn't think it bothers the spooks – if they have to turn a blind eye to it, then of course they will.'

'I took this off a dead German agent two nights back. How do you explain that? Is that dabbling?'

'I don't explain it. And I'm inclined to take it as seriously as you do.'

'Then you'll tell me where I can find him?'

'If I do – two things. First, you never got his address from me, and second, you can threaten him all you like, but you can't pull him. Shout at him, let him taste the back of your hand, tickle his ribs with a truncheon, if you like, but if you go after Forsyte all you've got is one big bluff.'

'Story of my career,' said Stilton.

Even now Drew was still thinking about it, teeth clamped onto his pencil, little flakes of yellow paint sticking to his lip.

'OK. He has a printing shop in Silver Place. Nothing

more than an alley at the end of Beak Street. You'll find him in the cellar.'

'I'll find him? You mean you're not coming?'

'Sorry, Walter. You're on your own. Whatever you do when you get there, I don't want to know. And if he picks up the phone to Military Intelligence, I shall want to know even less.'

§ 54

They arranged to meet mid-afternoon. It seemed simple enough to let Cormack find his own way there. What could go wrong? It was, as Stilton pointed out, 'ironically close to Marshall Street' and Cormack had said, 'That's not irony, Walter, that's just coincidence.' All the same the American had got there ahead of him. Stilton rounded the corner from Lexington Street to find him sprawled on the pavement, feet in the gutter, head down on the slabs. He stirred his boots and, as much as a portly policeman could, he ran, reached the body, seized a shoulder and turned it over.

'Walter, this guy is unbelievable. He's down there forging twenty dollar bills!'

Then Stilton spotted the fanlight at pavement height, opening into the cellar. He hoped he wasn't red in the face – he knew he was breathless – hoped Cormack couldn't see what a fool he'd just made of himself. He tugged at the knees of his trousers, stuck his backside in the air and bent to peer through a century of grime into the cellar. At some point the fanlight had been painted over from the inside, but it was flaking now, and there were half a dozen peepholes into the world below the street.

'Look along the wire in the middle of the room. Those

green strips of paper are twenty dollar bills – and those big white ones ... aren't they –'

'Fivers,' Stilton said. 'Five-pound notes. The bugger's gone back to printing fivers! This bloke's a one-man crime wave. I'd love to nick 'im. It's going to be a temptation not to. How you get a wrong'un to talk without the threat of arrest, God knows. I've all the power of a friendly fireside chat.'

'I think the FBI might have a few things to say to him themselves.'

'Let's get in there. I feel like a penniless kid at the sweetshop window.'

Stilton hammered on the door. The bolts shot back and an over-refined voice said from the dark interior, 'You're early. I wasn't expecting you till tomorrow. But as you're here ...'

The door swung wide, they found themselves following a man's back down the cellar steps, still not having seen his face, a smell of oil and ink and the clatter of printing presses.

Forsyte stood behind his desk, still not looking at them, filling a small attaché case. A five-pound note brushed Stilton's hat as he passed under it. The blasé-ness of the man made his blood boil. Five-pound notes – the ink not even dry – pinned up with clothes pegs like the Monday wash – and he didn't seem to give a damn who saw.

'There's six *Ausweisses* in the names you asked for. Half a million in Reichsmarks and there'll be another two hundred thousand tomorrow. I don't know what's so urgent, but perhaps next time a telephone call?'

He looked up at them, clearly feeling none of the confusion they felt themselves. He was thirtyish, a thin moustache, prematurely grey above the ears – and Stilton was right about the voice. It was, he thought, posh with a long 'o', the fake culture of an upper-crust accent by lower-class pretensions. Hence the fondness for a loud waistcoat and a bow tie. They went with the over-articulation and the prolonged vowels. Was nothing real about this man? Was he as phoney as his currency? Perhaps he wore false teeth and a cardboard collar?

'You were expecting me?' Stilton said.

'I was expecting a policeman. You're a policeman. You look like every Special Branch copper they've ever sent as a bagman. If not, you've missed your vocation and I'm about to send for a real one.'

He reached for the telephone. Stilton and Cormack stepped forward with the synchronicity of Busby Berkeley dancers, but it was Cormack who spoke first.

'That won't be necessary. Calvin M. Cormack, FBI.'

He flashed his Virginia driving licence before Forsyte's eyes for a split second, and snatched a twenty-dollar bill off the line above his head.

'Double sawbucks, huh? Uncle Sam's going to be mighty pissed with you. Whatever arrangement you have with the British won't cover this. Run off all the fivers you want: mess with United States Treasury and you're in big trouble.'

Forsyte stood frozen, the telephone still in his hand. Stilton took it from him and laid it gently back in its cradle.

'Agent Cormack's working with us on this one,' he said softly.

'The President is personally concerned about this. Do you understand me, Larry? Mr Roosevelt is personally concerned. Now, how many have you printed?'

Forsyte had gone pale. The accent slipped at the speed of a landslide.

'Only what you see. Two dozen. It's not what you think . . .'

'Tell that to J. Edgar Hoover.'

Cormack turned to Stilton and winked hammily at him. 'Chief Inspector, cuff him.'

'No, no . . . it's . . . just an experiment.'

'An experiment?' Cormack said.

'Just to see if I can do it. Like a lab test. Purely academic.'

'Academic? Do we arrest academics, Walter?'

'Depends,' said Stilton. 'Depends what's on offer.'

'Eh?'

'You scratch my back, lad, and I'll scratch yours.'

Forsyte sank into his chair, the weariness of the cornered written on his face. He pinched his nose, sniffed loudly and said, 'OK. You can cut the Flanagan and Allen routine. Just tell me what you want.'

Stilton stuck the ration book on the desk.

'Yours, I believe.'

Forsyte didn't pick it up. Looked at it where it lay and said, 'So?'

'Another little lab test, perhaps?'

'If you like.'

'But this one leaked into the street. This one's been bought and sold a few times, hasn't it? What I want is the name of the bloke you sold it to. You did sell it, didn't you? I mean, you're not giving them away out of the goodness of your heart, are you?'

Forsyte stared silently at them. Cormack plucked another bill off the line, pulled his glasses to the end of his nose and said, 'Work this good could get you ten to twenty in Sing-Sing. Federal Offence. Worse than not licking the seal on an airmail letter or forgetting the date of President Taft's birthday. Think about it, Larry.'

'I printed six. I have four still. I sold two. A chap came along and made me an offer.'

'And?' Stilton prompted.

'A Pole.'

'And does this Pole have a name?'

'I don't know his real name, but they call him Fish Wally.'

§ 55

'I think I'm going to kill him,' said Stilton. 'The sly, two-faced git. D'ye remember what he said? He said he lived off "whatever I can pick up". Even held up his hands to make it seem like it was almost literal. And what's he doing? Flogging ration books to German spies. I'll murder the little sod!'

'Walter,' Cal said. 'Do you really think this changes anything?'

They were sitting in a café in Endell Street, just around the corner from Drury Lane and the home of the much-abused Fish Wally. Stilton slurped at his tea. Cal tried – he found tea solved less than you'd think.

'How do you mean?'

'You said all along that the guy was kosher. Your Squadron Leader passed him. He's lived here the best part of eighteen months without attracting suspicion. Maybe he works his little fiddles without knowing who's working him.'

'Oh – I get it. This network you were on about this morning.'

'Wally doesn't have to know he's part of it to be part of it. The other side just need to know that he operates under the counter.'

'Calvin, he's not stupid. He's a clever man, an educated man.'

'He's also half crazy. I think he's just got known as a man who can fix you up with a room without too many questions. The ration book was a bonus. Wally had just acquired them, saw a potential customer in our Mr Robinson, and did the deal.'

'Thing is, who else did he deal with? Has he still got the other book or did he flog that too?'

'Only one way to find out.'

Stilton abandoned his tea and pushed it away from him. In Cal's experience Stilton never abandoned anything, cold coffee, the crusts on toast, the scrapings in the bottom of the pan – any pan – he hoovered up the lot. From the look on his face Cal deduced he didn't much relish what he had to say next.

'I'll have to pull him, feel his collar, you know that.'

'Of course.'

'Tek 'im down the Yard and give 'im the works.'

'The works? I think this is where I came in.'

'Aye – more's the pity, it's where you go out.'

'What do you mean? You're dumping me again? I thought we worked Forsyte pretty well back there. I felt we were a team for the first time.'

'So did I. You've the makings of a good copper. But I've got to pull Wally by the book. Down the Yard, in an interrogation room. I can't take you with me.'

'Why? I mean, why not?'

'Copper's stuff. And you're not a copper. Wally may be half crazy, you're probably right. But I know Wally, he'll not decide to talk because we pinch his sausages or bluff him with your driving licence. I'll need to stick 'im in a cell and sweat him. He really hates being locked up. You're not on the force, lad . . . it wouldn't be . . . it wouldn't be right. This is something I have to do with Dobbs, and believe me Calvin, if I could choose you instead of that dozy pillock I would.'

Cormack gave up on his tea, shoved his cup and saucer to clink against Stilton's. A cheerless toast in brown scum that had tasted of shoe-leather.

'How long?'

'Overnight. Doubt it'd be longer. And I'll tell you the minute we get a lead.'

'Cross your heart and hope to die?'

§ 56

They parked the car out of sight and hung around the street corner. They could not see the door, and no one using the door was likely to see them – but Stilton and Dobbs could see the window of Fish Wally's living room on the ground floor of a sturdy, purpose-built block of turn-of-the-century flats, the like of which had been built the length and breadth of London fifty-odd years before for the benefit of working men and their families. Rabbit hutches, Stilton called them. Two poky rooms and take your baths in the kitchen. His old mate George Bonham lived in one back in Stepney. He and his wife had raised three kids in one. Stilton wondered how they did it. On the other hand, they were bijou accommodation for the single villain.

Wally was not home. Stilton was waiting for the blackout to be drawn. Then they'd nick him. It was Stilton's turn to watch. Dobbs leaned against the wing of the Riley, looking pale and sleepy. Stilton was angry enough without this provocation.

'Bernard – you nod off now and I'll roast you on me truncheon like one o' them Ayrab shish kebabs.'

Dobbs did not seem to have heard him. Stilton stepped back a few paces and shook him.

'Eh?' said Dobbs.

'Have you been at the beer again, laddie?'

'What? What chance have I had, boss? We been stuck here since before opening time. I was just feeling a bit dicky, that's all – I'll be fine now.'

Stilton stepped back to the corner just in time to see the blackout being drawn over Wally's window.

'We're on,' he said softly.

Dobbs yanked the ignition keys from his trouser pocket and eased his backside off the car.

'Not so fast,' Stilton said. 'I want him to get his coat off, I want him to get his slippers on – kettle on, knees under the table, rolling ciggy. I want him to feel safe in his little nest before I drag him out of it and throw him in a cell.'

'He's really got your goat, hasn't he, boss?'

'Understatement, Bernard, understatement.'

Stilton let ten minutes pass, looked at his wristwatch and said, 'Bring the car right up to the porch and leave the nearside back door open.'

He strode off, macintosh flapping, trilby pulled down firmly. Once inside he tapped gently at Wally's door, the friendly-shy knock of a neighbour wanting to borrow a cupful of sugar.

Fish Wally came to the door, yawning and smoking simultaneously, a fag glued with spittle to his lower lip. Stilton knocked the cigarette away, seized him by the arm and bundled him inside. The kettle sang on the hob, his baccy pouch lay open on the oil cloth, the cat occupied pride of place in the armchair – and Wally wore his slippers.

'Stilton! What you –?'

Stilton grabbed the other arm and, in a gesture born of years of practice, slapped the cuffs on his wrists and clicked them closed.

'For God's sake, Walter – what do you want?'

Stilton found Fish Wally's shoes under the table and threw them at him without a word. Wally took the hint, wrapped his crab hands around them and slipped them on. Stilton turned off the gas, opened the wire-mesh cold-larder above the sink, found a few scraps of fatty meat wrapped in greaseproof paper and dumped them in the cat's bowl.

'You going to tell me what this is about? Or do I have to guess?'

Stilton took his coat off the back of the door and threw that at him too. The door slammed behind them, Stilton dragging Fish Wally by the scruff of his neck, down to the car and bundled into the back seat. Only when Dobbs had slipped the car into gear and set off down Drury Lane did Stilton speak.

'You are not obliged to say anything, but if you do . . .'

'For Christ's sake, Walter – do we not know each other better than this?'

Dobbs crunched the car through the gears at the junction with the Aldwych, the metallic scraping filling the silence. Then Stilton said, 'I thought I knew you, Wally. Now I'm wondering just who the hell you are.'

§ 57

Fish Wally sat by himself in a cell at Scotland Yard, still in the handcuffs. Stilton checked his watch, Dobbs flopped down on a wooden bench in the corridor.

'Let's give him an hour on his jack jones. Tell the uniforms to leave well alone. No cups of tea and no chit-chat.'

'Wh . . . wh . . . whatever you say boss.'

Stilton leant down and looked at Dobbs all but eye to eye. He'd gone deathly pale. And he could hardly put a sentence together.

'Bernard – if I didn't know better I'd swear you were one over the eight.'

'I sh . . . sh . . . should be so lucky.'

'I'm sending you home, laddie.'

'I'll get a cab.'

'Bollocks – I'll whistle up a squad car. Go home and go

to bed. If you're no better by the morning just give me a bell. I think you're coming down with summat.'

Stilton put an arm around Dobbs and lugged him up to the ground floor. He seemed to go completely limp, as though someone had just cut his strings.

Back in his own office, he took out his little black notebook and the desk file he was supposed to type up regularly. He'd typed in nothing since the last time he was in Burnham-on-Crouch with Squadron Leader Thesiger. He couldn't be arsed at the time and he could not be arsed now. Wally would be sitting down there, that seemingly unshakeable philosophical stance getting more wobbly by the minute. There was one thing Stilton could do that Wally couldn't, and it would give him a nice edge in an hour or so – he could catch forty winks and get down there feeling a damn sight fresher than 'me laddo'. Stilton slept. Forty winks became eighty winks. One hour became two.

'Walter, are you going to stop playing games now and tell me what this is about?'

Stilton leant across the table and unlocked the handcuffs. Fish Wally rubbed at his wrists.

'That Czech bloke you sent me after . . .'

'I heard – you lost him. Is that my fault?'

'That Czech bloke you sent me after,' Stilton said slowly and emphatically, 'was a German.'

Fish Wally was galvanised. Head up, eyes wide. Perhaps Cormack was right. Or Fish Wally was a better actor than he'd ever thought?

'What?'

'A German – an Abwehr spy.'

'I don't believe you.'

'Suit yourself.'

Stilton got up and left. As he locked the door a young constable appeared with a cup of tea.

'Nowt for him. I'll have that.'

'But guv'nor, regulations –'

'Bugger regulations. He gets nowt till I say so.'

An hour later he came back. Wally was on his feet at once, shouting in his face.

'I didn't know! How the hell you expect me to know? You think I deal with Germans knowingly? You think I don't have every reason in the world to hate Germans? What kind of a man do you think I am?'

'Like I said. I don't know any more.'

'Pah!' A wave of the arm, a puff of Polish contempt, but Fish Wally sat down again and faced Stilton.

'We're making progress, I see.'

'Meaning?'

'An hour ago you didn't believe he was German.'

Fish Wally glared. He seemed to think it wiser to say nothing. Stilton took out four little paper books and laid them on the table between them as though he were playing patience. Four Ministry of Food ration books.

'I got these off Faker Forsyte this afternoon.'

Fish Wally tried a 'So?' but it lacked total conviction.

Stilton put a fifth, slightly tattier book next to the others.

'I took this one off the German last night. The bloke you told me was Czech. The bloke you fixed up at your cousin Casimir's doss house.'

Fish Wally shrugged. A silent 'So?'

'Did you sell it to him?'

'Why don't you ask him?'

'Not to mince words, I took it off the body . . . the corpse of that German.'

Fish Wally flinched at this.

'I'll ask you again. Did you sell it to him?'

'What if I did?'

'Wally, I might expect remarks as stupid as that from the average London tea-leaf . . . but if that's what you want. Firstly, it's illegal to trade in counterfeit documents. Second . . . you're a British resident now. We took you in. It's ingratitude, it's treason if you want it plain.'

'Treason? Ingratitude? Good God, Stilton, what do you want from me? I am no traitor. I am a poor man. Worse –' He held up his hands again '– a broken man. I have a living to make where I can. But why should I betray England?'

'So you did sell it to him?'

'Yes. But treason was no part of it. I believed him to be Czech. Another victim. Like me.'

'How much did you touch this victim for, Wally? Ten bob? A quid? Two quid?'

Fish Wally said nothing. Met Stilton's gaze without blinking.

'Faker Forsyte says he sold you two ration books. What did you do with the other?'

'He told you that? He's a liar.'

'Have it your own way.'

Stilton left again. He could keep this up all night if he had to.

Around midnight he flipped the peephole on the cell door. Fish Wally was pacing the floor, restless and caged. Seconds out, thought Stilton, round three.

He set out the photographs once more. Smulders and Stahl.

'I know,' said Wally. 'These you showed me at the crypt. I told you the truth then. I saw them both. I told you everything I knew. Do not fling these in my face and call me a liar.'

'You didn't mention the third bloke.'

'What third bloke?'

Stilton pointed at the sketch of Stahl.

'A third bloke who looked pretty much like this bloke.'

'I told you. I saw no third bloke that night. This bloke

is this bloke. Him I sold the book to. Him I took to Cash Wally.'

'Not necessarily the same night.'

Stilton could almost hear Fish Wally thinking, wondering how much he could admit to without digging himself a deeper hole.

'Wally – why do you think any of these blokes come to you?'

'I'm known,' he said. 'Cash Wally is a misanthropist, a recluse. Hates humanity with a vengeance. Trusts only money and food. He needs me to help out. I'm known as Cash Wally's cousin. In immigrant circles word spreads.'

'I'm not talking about immigrant circles. I'm talking about these blokes. Germans.'

'No – the older one, he is Dutch.'

'No, Wally, he *was* Dutch.'

'You killed them both!?!'

'Let's just say they're both dead. And Dutch or not, he was a German agent. We'd been watching him since he landed.'

'I don't believe you. Go on, get up and walk out again. Every time I call the bluff you walk out.'

Stilton leaned on his elbows, that bit the closer to Wally, his voice dropped to pianissimo.

'They come to you, Wally, because you're known. Known to the Abwehr as well as the immigrants. You're part of their network, whether you know it or not, whether you like it or not. They've been using you to place their agents among immigrant groups in London.'

He knew he'd hit home. He knew Fish Wally would not call him a liar again. He was pale, his skin sagged like a punctured balloon. It was as though he had only to prick up his ears to hear the air hiss out of him. He knew Stilton was telling the truth. Stilton knew that he knew.

He croaked out, 'Stilton, what do you want?'

'The third bloke. Probably came to you a day or two

before these two. You sold him a ration book and you found him a room, right?'

Fish Wally said nothing.

'I asked you about him. This is him.'

Stilton tapped the sketch of Stahl with his index finger.

'I asked you about him. You sent me to the German. I had no picture of the German. I was asking you about this bloke.'

Fish Wally picked up the sketch. Looked at it for more than a minute.

'I had always thought there was something wrong. The scar. The German had no scar. Do you have a pencil?'

Stilton took one from his breast pocket and gave it to him.

'This one you call the third man. He had a scar. Not as pronounced as your sketch would have it. But he looked nothing like this.'

Fish Wally's crab hands clutched the pencil awkwardly, but the tip flew across the paper with the facility of a skilled draughtsman. A thin, dark moustache, darker hair.

'And here and here.' Fish Wally tapped each temple. 'Bald. The rest of the hair was black, turning to grey. I would say he was forty or more. Not the twenty-something you have here.'

'And you sold him a ration book?'

Wally nodded.

'And you got him a room?'

'Yes.'

'Where?'

'Cash Wally was full that day. I sent him to the Welsh Widow in the Holloway Road.'

Stilton ordered tea for Fish Wally. When he got back about twenty minutes later, Fish Wally was swilling the dregs and asking for more. He looked at the sheet of foolscap Stilton held in his hand and said, 'So, now we hit the bottom, eh, Walter? Now you charge me.'

Stilton took a fiver and a fountain pen from his pocket and pushed them across the table to him.

'What's this?'

'Your wages. Just sign here. You're one of us now.'

'Eh?'

'From now on you tell us everything. Every foreigner, whether you think he's suspicious or not, that comes to you, you tell us. Sign, before I change my mind. Sign now. It's this or spend the rest of the war in chokey.'

Fish Wally picked up the pen and read.

'What am I signing?'

'A receipt for five quid.'

'Ah.'

'And the Official Secrets Act.'

TROY

§ 58

Walter Stilton ate with relish the inner organs of beasts and fowls. He was more than partial to thick giblet soup, the toughness of gizzard held no fear for him and stuffed, roast heart no symbol. When he could get it – when his wife had queued half a morning to get it – he loved liver slices fried in breadcrumbs – but most of all he adored to start the day with grilled mutton kidneys, faintly piss-tanged to the palate – a breakfast, if not fit for a king, then sweetly fit for a Chief Inspector of the London Metropolitan Police Force.

He moved softly about the kitchen. It had been light since before five and first light woke him better than any alarm clock. Tangible light in the basement room, the promise of the heat of the day beyond its windows. Summer mornings such as this made him peckish. He'd eat his plate of grilled kidneys, washed down with strong, sweet, milky tea, silently reading last night's evening paper. And when he had done he would pad about the kitchen in his socks, shirtless, the braces hanging down his back like the reins of some giant and unruly toddler, making tea and toast for his wife. He was always first up – had been since the first morning of their marriage. It was a habit of his father's. Handed down. A Derbyshire miner, at work before the world was awake, he would always light the fire, feed himself and take breakfast to his wife. It was the only domestic chore he would undertake – so it was with Stilton. He'd never washed so much as a cup and saucer in his married life, but he'd stoked the Aga and made breakfast every day of it.

A saucer of milk for the pusscat, then softly up the

stairs to the first floor. Edna was awake, windows open, a curtain flapping gently in the summer breeze. Stilton set down the tray upon her knees and said nothing. He'd run out of things to say to her. And there was nothing she asked of him.

'Will you be late home?' she asked.

'Hard to say, love.'

And in that the routine of conversation in the wake of the death of their children varied not one whit from the routine of thirty years and more. They neither had the vocabulary to prolong the manifestation of grief.

Stilton dressed. A clean shirt aired on the Aga's front rail. The collar stud eased in with a practised thumb. His Metropolitan Police Bowls Team tie. His shiny black boots, the pusscat weaving between his legs and lashing out at the laces as he did them up.

Looking at himself in the mirror of the hallstand – a silent voice in the head telling him to look like a copper, shoulders back, a tug of the hatbrim, trying for the glint of steel in the eyes – he heard the creak of bedsprings in the room above and the plump thump of his plump wife's feet on the floor. Daybegun. He pulled the door wide, the morning light reflecting brightly off the broken facade of the house opposite, and stepped out into the last day of his life.

§ 59

As Walter Stilton stepped into the street Sergeant Troy was awoken by a telephone call from his father, a man who would never accept that his son did not 'do' mornings unless duty required. As a boy he had known his father to bumble into his bedroom in the pitch-darkness of pre-dawn with some philosophical conundrum on his lips. Today was a day just like those old days. Troy had long since learnt to move from sleep to waking without transition – one second sound asleep the next wide awake and firing on all cylinders.

'What was it Berdyaev used to say about Russia?' Alex said without greeting, without so much as a syllable from Troy.

Lately – the last ten years or so – his father had tended to treat Troy as an extension of his memory. A substitute for his own failing powers. He had made Troy read so much as a child – all those prolonged, sickly weeks off school – that his education was warped by the old man – he knew things no one of his generation or education might ordinarily be expected to know. Alex would ask Troy things he could not ask Rod. It depressed Troy to think that his father was still grinding away at his Russian piece. If he hadn't finished it by now? And what had become of his collaboration with Wells?

'What exactly about Russia? He banged on about so many things.'

'It's in *The Soul of Russia* – or at least I thought it was. I cannot find it. Books without indexes should be banned.'

'That's probably what first narked Hitler.'

Alex ignored this. 'He was, as you put it, banging on about the Russian Mission.'

'Oh,' said Troy, 'that. The Light from the East. It's not Berdyaev – well, not just him, it's most of the old ones. It's in Dostoevsky. Perhaps even in Tolstoy, and you might recall your dad had more than a bit of a bee in his bonnet about the Holy Russian Mission.'

'Holy?' said Alex as though the word meant nothing to him, one atheist talking to another.

'The Great Civilising Mission westward, how Russia as the keeper of the flame of Orthodoxy, the original true faith of Christ, would ultimately be the salvation of the decadent West, by which they meant anything west of Lvov. Of course they were right, in a way.'

'What way?' said his dad.

'There was indeed a Russian mission west – it just wasn't anything to do with Christ or Orthodoxy or Holy Mother Russia. It was born in 1917 and it died at the end of Frank Jacson's icepick about nine months ago.'

'Permanent Revolution,' said Alex. 'The earth-shattering theory of the late Comrade Trotsky. How very cynical of you, my boy.'

He rang off. Troy wondered if he'd pushed the old man too far. He was fed up with things Russian, but Trotsky's murder had run a shudder through the Troy household. If, his mother had protested, the arm of Joseph Vissarionovich Stalin reached all the way to Mexico, then who in Europe was safe? Troy's father had remained unruffled. He was, he pointed out, no threat to Stalin, no renegade Red and, better still, no exiled White. Stalin would not bother with him. Rod had strongly urged him to seek official protection, to talk to Churchill, and the old man had firmly and impolitely refused.

Troy looked at the clock and felt lazy. He could go back to sleep for another hour, perhaps two. He was on the late shift and would not see his bed again before midnight. Besides, Kitty had not been round for a day or two – it would be just like her to turn up tonight; so he decided to sleep while he could.

§ 60

Cal passed the morning lying on his bed blowing smoke rings. It was the sum total of what he had learnt in two years at military academy. He rarely smoked, but when he did it was a sign of tension or boredom or both. A letter had come from his father, from New York – what was he doing in New York? – via Zurich. Postmarked

April 23rd. The mail was speeding up. He had read it over breakfast. It filled him with despair.

> Plaza Hotel
> Grand Army Plaza
> New York

Dear Son,

America took a giant step today. The people spoke. Thirty thousand attended the New York America First Rally to hear Lindbergh speak. If FDR ignores this he's a fool. This is the voice of America. This is the voice of the people.

There were few things he hated more than having his father address him as though he were a voter rather than his own flesh and blood. Then the tone changed – a cloying confidentiality that had him yearning for the old man to get back on the stump.

Of course I stayed off the platform. Let Lindy do the talking – as much as I could. The man is not the brightest bear in the woods, and God knows what he'd've said if I hadn't written most of the speech for him. He was all set to sock it to the Jews. I told him 'There's no votes in criticising Jews, in New York City of all places.' Hymietown, for Christ's sake. As long as we can keep him clear of anti-Semitism he'll do fine. Just the figurehead we need. Perhaps we can let him rip when we get out West – nobody there gives a damn one way or the other about the Jews.

What we have to get across is the conspiracy – there's no other word for it – between the British and the White House, between FDR and Winston Churchill to bring America into this war, against the wishes of the people, by any reasonable pretext they can drum up. That's what America First has to expose . . .

Cal stopped reading. Conspiracy? The old man was getting crazy. Poking around under the bed with a shotgun.

He passed the afternoon drifting. Hating Walter for his absence. Drifting. From the leafy squares of Mayfair into the West End. Peering in the gentleman's outfitters of Jermyn Street – wishing Frank Reininger had given him enough coupons to go in and ask them to measure him for a shirt. Thinking of Reininger he made his way back to the embassy – passed an hour waiting to see if Frank showed up. He didn't. Berg did, greeted him as though his presence was an affront – 'So you finally decided to show up.' Cal said 'Fuck you, Henry,' and left.

He found his way to a café in Brewer Street. It was dismally quiet. Two old men shoving halfpennies up and down a marked board, just as he'd seen men doing that night in the crypt of St Alkmund's, the radio on merely as a background burble. Then, the volume soared as the proprietor turned it up for the news, and a bloodless BBC voice announced the sinking of the *Bismarck*. What little chatter there had been stopped. Cal could count the beating seconds by the sound of his own heart. Half a minute passed this way. He was surprised. He'd half expected cheering or someone to get up and sing 'Land of Hope and Glory'. At last one of the old men picked up a halfpenny and said, 'That's that, then.' And the other just said, 'Yus.'

He ate alone at the Bon Viveur. A table for two – a dinner for one. He figured to time his return to Claridge's for the end of Kitty's shift. With any luck they'd meet in the elevator. He'd persuade her to come out. Postpone the inevitability of sex until they'd been out somewhere. A club, a bar, some-where.

When he collected his key at the front desk the clerk

handed him another letter. It looked like Kitty's writing – that childish, half-formed hand he'd seen on her odd notes to him. The scrawl was hereditary. The letter was from her father.

> Been trying to get you on the phone for a couple of hours. Thought you'd be around. Meet me in Coburn Place N1 at 10.30 tonight. It's an alley between two pubs, the Green Man and the Hand & Racquet. Don't be late.
> Hoping this reaches you, one way or another.
> Yrs.
> Walter Stilton
> PS Wot larx!

The address meant nothing to Cal. He asked at the desk – they silently handed him a street map of London. He found Coburn Place. Only with difficulty. It was tiny – it lurked under the L of ISLINGTON, sprawled across the grid in letters half an inch high. The two pubs weren't marked on the map, but a music hall close by was – Collins' Music Hall. He'd look for that.

'How long would it take to get to Islington?'

'By taxi, sir?'

'Sure.'

The clerk spun the map to face him. Cal lifted his finger.

'Less than half an hour. Perhaps fifteen or twenty minutes.'

It was 10.05 now. Cal ran to the front door and told the doorman to hail him a cab. He'd be lucky to make it. Don't be late, Walter had written. But better late than never.

Late it was. In front of King's Cross railway station the damage of May 11th was still being patched up. A water main exposed – a deep trench in the road, a dozen workmen up to their ankles in brimming water, a lone policeman waving at the traffic and directing them all south, into Finsbury, a loop past Farringdon station, through Clerkenwell and into Islington from the other side. Cal sat with the street map open, trying to follow their route by the frequent flick of his cigarette lighter, glancing all too often at his watch.

Late it was, and later. At 10.40 he paid off the cabby by Collins' Music Hall and found Coburn Place, bent between the two public houses, zig-zagging right and left. He almost fell down the open cellar hatch of the Hand and Racquet. He struck his lighter with the ball of his thumb, held the cap open against the spring and moved slowly on with his left hand on the bricks as though to trace out his trail would somehow lead him back like Ariadne's thread.

Flickering, miasmic light – enough to see five paces ahead; enough, too, to see the leather soles of a pair of shoes that lay on the cobblestones not twenty feet beyond the cellar. He dropped the lighter – got down on his hands and knees and groped about on the stones. Found it, struck the flint and struck it again, and in the yellow light found himself looking into the dead eyes of Walter Stilton.

'Jesus Christ.'

He let his thumb off the lighter – sank into darkness, wondering if he'd seen what he knew he'd seen, wondering if he had the courage to look again.

He flicked the flint. Walter was lying on his front down the length of the alley – the right side of his face lay in a pool of blood, the left looked up at Cal. One arm outstretched, the other lost beneath the body. His hat lay a few feet ahead, angled against the wall, as though it had spun off him like a loose hubcap. And there was no doubt about it. The man was dead. His third encounter with violent death, and already Cal knew the sight and fact of death with unquestioning certainty.

The pool of blood was still spreading. Cal's knees were wet with it. He got to his feet. Heard his heart roar in his ears, a pulse as loud as a jackhammer throbbing in his head. Above it all he heard the sound of a lavatory flush, saw a brief flash of light as a door opened up ahead of him, and a man emerge from the gents buttoning up his flies. Whoever he was he had not seen Cal – he pulled on the back door of the Green Man and vanished.

Cal followed. In the light of the pub he looked down at himself, Blood on his trousers and on the hem of his jacket. All over his hands. He wiped them on his trousers. Surely everyone was looking at him? Surely everyone could see him, dressed like a scarecrow, drenched in blood? In the fug of tobacco smoke and the roar of people chattering, heads turned at the sight of a stranger, but none of them seemed to think him worth a second glance. One woman looked him up and down as though appraising him, and still didn't see the blood.

He made his way to the bar. The barman was busy. Cal tried to seize his attention, and found his voice had gone. He managed to say 'Excuse me' in a shrill, unnatural voice, and was told to 'Hold yer 'orses. Can't you see I'm on me own?'

It seemed like an age. The barman served two other men and leaned on one elbow in front of Cal.

'Right, young man. What's yer 'urry?'

'Phone,' Cal squeaked. 'I need a phone.'

The barman reached under the pumps and stuck a bakelite telephone on the bar.

'A drink while you're 'ere?'

Cal asked for a brandy and dialled 999.

'Police, Fire or Ambulance?' said a young woman.

'Police,' Cal croaked.

The barman was looking at him now; at the optics, his back to Cal, he turned at the word 'police'.

The police operator came on. Cal realised he had no idea what to say. He knew exactly what he meant but he could not think of the form of words.

'Stilton,' he said almost involuntarily.

'Beg pardon, sir?'

'Chief Inspector Stilton's been . . .'

The barman seemed to have frozen, his hand still holding Cal's glass of brandy under the optic. The next word would surely galvanise him.

'Murdered. He's been murdered. Coburn Place. Islington. Behind the Green Man.'

The barman dropped the glass. The roar of the night-time drinking crowd stopped as though it had been one voice. By the time the glass hit the floor, it tinkled into a cavernous silence.

'And you are?'

'I'm sorry?'

'Your name, caller, your name.'

But they were all staring at him now. A woman not six feet away was looking from his bloody trousers to his face and back again, mouth open, silent. She was not silent for long. She screamed. The roar of the crowd returned – the volume doubled. Cal slowly put the phone back on the cradle and headed for the door. The crowd parted in front of him. All except one big man, stood between him and the door, inspired by some civic sense or the pure, unsullied bravado of the drunk.

'Gertcha.'

'Excuse me,' Cal said softly. 'My friend just died.'

'Gertcha,' said the drunk, and Cal dropped him with a right-hander to the belly and pushed him aside.

He knelt by the body. A dozen heads crowded the doorway, a shaft of light cutting into the blackness of the alley. Walter had to be covered. As ever, he was wearing his brown mac regardless of the weather, but to prise it off him seemed so disrespectful. Cal took out the street map, unfolded it to its fullest and spread London, all the way from Brentford to Limehouse, from Highgate to Streatham, over Walter's head and back. It seemed fitting. A shroud for a London bobby.

He ignored the gathering crowd at the back door of the pub, oblivious to its mounting murmurs and wept silently for the life of Walter Stilton. Late was never. He'd let the man down. He'd let somebody kill him. He sat motionless, his back against the wall, his forearms across his knees, eyes fixed on Stilton's body, somewhere around Chelsea Bridge. Walter was dead. And dead was all. Dead was everything. Total. Cal had died with him. His death was all-embracing.

An age passed. He found his tears dried. A torch flickered up the alley from the street end, feet neatly sidestepping the open cellar, and then the beam tilted down into his face. Then the man knelt down next to him.

'Are you OK?'

'What?'

'You're not hurt?'

Cal knew the voice, and as he leaned in knew the face. It was the same young copper he and Stilton had encountered in Hoxton Lane. Sergeant Troy.

'No. No. It's Walter. He's dead.'

Troy peeled back the map to look at the face and head.

'Gunshot. Side of the head,' he said too matter-of-factly, then added, 'He'd've felt nothing, you know.'

'Sure,' Cal whispered pointlessly.

Troy stood up. Held his warrant card in front of the torch.

'Where's the landlord?' he cried to the crowd and the barman shuffled foward, pale of face, a glass cloth still in his hands.

'That'll be me,' he said, as though he doubted it himself. 'Atterbury. George Atterbury. Green Man.'

Troy addressed him with a calm no one else seemed to feel.

'Call an ambulance,' he said. 'And then call Scotland Yard. Whitehall 1212. Ask for Special Branch and report the death of Chief Inspector Stilton. Gottit?'

But the man was staring at the body, at what little was visible of the big man, the legs and feet protruding from beneath the map – the fingertips of one hand pointing down the alley like a contrived clue.

'Eh?'

'Stilton. S-T-I-L-T-O-N!'

The barman jerked into life.

'O' course,' he said. 'O' course. The Yard, the Branch, Stilton.' And ran back into the pub.

Troy waved the crowd back indoors, searched with his torch for a few cobblestones free of Stilton's blood and sat down next to Cal.

'How long?' he asked simply.

Cal pulled at his sleeve, looked at his wristwatch. It was 10.55. It was fifteen minutes since he had groped his way up Coburn Place. It felt like hours.

'I found him at . . . 10.40. I guess it was 10.40. I looked at my watch as I . . . as I got out of the cab. I was late. I was supposed to meet him here at 10.30.'

Troy looked at his own watch.

'You're running slow. It's eleven now. I'd say poor old Walter's been dead less than half an hour.'

Cal thought Troy meant something by this. He'd no idea what.

'I . . . er . . .'

'You just missed the killer, it seems.'

'Jesus,' said Cal softly.

'You saw no one?'

'No. Of course not.'

Cal wondered why he had said 'Of course not'. It just rattled around in his ears. It made no sense. But then, so little did. Why had Walter wanted to meet him here, in this black hole? Who had he met first?

'Look. You're absolutely covered in blood,' said Troy. He took out his handkerchief and wiped away the blood from Cal's chin, from his cheeks, where his tears had mixed with Walter's blood. It was oddly maternal. The human touch. Cal began to feel that he was alive, that the shock of death was somehow less than total. His mind locked onto the idea of Troy – clung to him as to a floating leaf.

Troy asked him no more questions. Flashed his torch around occasionally, as though looking for something he couldn't find. It seemed that he too was simply waiting. And a couple of minutes later the screech of brakes in the street confirmed the thought. Three big coppers, two in uniform, strode down the alley, torches swaying up and down the narrow space like searchlights.

'Troy?' said the plain-clothes copper.

Troy got to his feet.

'Chief Inspector Nailer. Special Branch. I'll take over now.'

Cal grabbed at Troy's coat.

'I thought . . .' he began, and Troy seemed to read his mind.

'I can't investigate. This is Branch business. I'm Murder.'

'Somebody murdered Walter.'

'Walter was Special Branch. They look after their own.'

'When you've quite finished, thank you, Mr Troy!' Nailer roared.

Troy told Cal he was sorry and risked more wrath by saying goodbye and patting him on the shoulder. Nailer waited a few seconds, as Troy's footsteps echoed down the alley, and then in a voice like brimstone said 'Now who the fuck are you?'

§ 61

It was past four in the morning at Scotland Yard before it dawned on Cal that he had been arrested.

He had let himself be driven to the Yard, sitting silently between the two uniformed bobbies. He'd let himself be led compliantly into a brown and cream interview room of intimidating plainness. He'd answered all their questions. At least, all those to which he had answers. And, of course, he would not name Stahl as the axis on which the whole mess pivoted. Maybe there were too many 'I don't knows'? And he had turned out his pockets – a few pounds in sterling, a few scraps of paper – nothing that could identify him clearly – Troy's blood-stained linen handkerchief – and his gun, wedged between his back and the waistband of his pants. Cal looked apologetic as he hefted it out and laid it quietly on the table.

The first guy had been friendly. A young man. About his own age. A Detective Sergeant. Called him sir.

'Do you have a licence for this, sir?'

'I'm a serving army officer. It's standard issue to have a sidearm.'

The sergeant took out his handkerchief and flipped out the magazine. The bobby in uniform sitting by the door stared as though he'd never seen a Smith and

Wesson before – maybe he never had. Then he sniffed the barrel.

Everything Cal had was taken away, and then they said there'd be a wait.

They took him to what he assumed was going to be another interview room, and only when he found himself face to face with a cot, palliasse and seatless lavatory did the reality hit home. He turned, the faintest words of protest on his lips, but the door had already closed and all he heard was the key turning in the lock. He gave up instantly and almost gratefully. Fell face down on the straw mattress and slept.

They woke him at 8.30. A cup of gagging-sweet milky tea. Cal would have drunk pig's piss if they stuck it in a tin cup and called it tea.

He had begun to smell. Worse, so had the dried blood on his clothes. A crisp brown stain covering most of his pants, the hem of his jacket, and the pockets where he'd wiped his hands.

'I need to wash,' he told the constable. The man came back five minutes later with a jug of cold water which he tipped into the enamelled iron basin bolted into one corner of the room.

'Any chance of getting my suit cleaned?'

'Where do you think you are, Hopalong? The bleedin' Ritz?'

Cal drank the foul national drink and thought over the insult. Was that how they saw him? A national cliché?

Twenty minutes later they escorted him back to the interview room, washed, but unshaven and feeling he must look like a tramp. Nailer took over. Nailer was not friendly. Nailer was downright hostile. Nailer had not slept, grey bags under his eyes, a fuzz of grey bristle to his chin. Cal had slept the sleep of the dead.

'From the top, if you would,' Nailer said plainly.

From the top? Cal hesitated. He knew what he meant.

He just could not quite believe they wanted him to say it all again. Nailer lit up a strong, untipped cigarette and blew smoke over Cal. He wasn't Walter – not a man cut from the same cloth – a thin, angular man with bloodshot eyes and pinched nostrils. Not a mark of good humour or fellow-feeling upon him. A stringbean of a man, with lank, dirty grey hair and a lifetime of nicotine scorched into his fingertips.

Cal told him everything. And there his troubles began.

'You were working with Walter?'

'Yes.'

'Since when?'

'Since . . .' He could not quite remember. 'It was after the big raid. Maybe the Thursday or the Friday after. The raid was the tenth wasn't it?'

'Why doesn't Walter mention this in his notes?'

'What notes?'

'The ones he types up from his police notebook.'

'I've no idea. I saw him scribble in his little black book from time to time. Surely . . . ?'

Nailer was shaking his head.

'His notebook's missing.'

'Missing from where?'

'From the person of Chief Inspector Stilton.'

This baffled Cal.

'What?'

'His pocket, Mr Cormack. The folding notebook should have been in his pocket. We all carry them. At all times.'

'Maybe the killer took it?'

'We're looking into that. In the meantime, who else could vouch for you? Who else knew about your work with Walter?'

'Well . . . Walter's man Dobbs, for a start.'

Nailer and his constable looked at one another quizzically.

'"Walter" . . .' Nailer had a way of putting inverted commas round a word as he uttered it. 'Walter didn't tell you then?'

'Tell me what?'

'Bernard Dobbs had a stroke day before yesterday. He's unconscious in hospital.'

'Jesus,' said Cal. 'No. He didn't tell me. But you'll appreciate. An awful lot has happened lately. In fact . . . I don't think I've seen Walter since the day before yesterday.'

'Till last night, you mean. Who else knows you?'

'My people at the embassy.'

'Names.'

'General Gelbroaster. He sent for me from Zurich. My immediate superior at the London Embassy – Major Shaeffer and his superior, Colonel Reininger.'

Nailer left him alone with another silent uniformed bobby for company. Half an hour later he was back.

'I got this Major Shaeffer on the blower.'

'Good,' said Cal.

'Not good. He says you weren't working for him and he's never heard of Walter Stilton.'

Cal recalled now what had not occurred to him once in the course of the night – 'You land in trouble and you're on your own. Capiche?' It had never crossed Cal's mind that Shaeffer would go so far as to disown him. But he had.

'Superintendent. I think there's been some kind of misunderstanding here . . .'

'No there hasn't. He was clear as daylight. He doesn't know why you're in London. He knows nothing of any mission you say you're on.'

'Did you check with Gelbroaster?'

'The General's in Washington.'

'Reininger?' Surely Frank wouldn't just dump him for the sake of diplomatic neatness?

'On his way to Ireland.'

'So nobody's backing me up?'

'Get smart, Captain Cormack – you've been thrown to the wolves. And I'm the one with the big teeth.'

'There are other people who know I was working with Walter.'

'Such as?'

'Edna Stilton. Her daughter Kitty. They both met me.'

Cal had not thought this a provocative remark. When Nailer got up from his chair and grabbed him by his shirt front, he was genuinely surprised.

'Shut your stinking gob – you toerag! Don't ever mention the name of Edna Stilton to me again. That woman's a saint! If you think I'm calling her or her family the day after their man got blown away by some cheap hoodlum with a shooter, you can bloody well think again! That woman's in mourning. Her world just came to pieces. And you have the fucking nerve to suggest I call her? Get this through your Yankee skull – the embassy don't know you – Walter makes no mention of you in his notes – you're in the shit, and you're going to have to come up with something better than that!'

Nailer dropped him back in the chair, shirt-buttons popping off. Yankee? My how the world had moved on since then.

'The letter,' Cal said.

'What letter?'

'The one Walter sent me. Telling me to meet him in Islington.'

'Where is it?'

'Your . . . your man . . . Sergeant Dixon. He took all my papers.'

Nailer sent for Dixon, and in front of Cal they sifted the papers from Cal's pockets – everything he had turned out for Dixon last night and watched him slip into a cellophane bag. There was no letter.

'Try again, Captain Cormack.'

'I must have lost it. But he sent it to me. How else would I know to find the pub in Islington, either of those pubs?'

'You tell me – but in the meantime, I'll tell you that if this is the best you can do, you're going to find yourself in hot water pretty damn quick.'

'There is someone else who could alibi me.'

'Name?'

'Ruthven-Greene.'

'Who's he?'

'MI6. He's the man put me in touch with Walter. Reggie Ruthven-Greene.'

Another wait. This time, most of the day. At noon he was taken back to his cell, and half an hour later a meal of cold, greasy meatloaf and mashed potatoes was served to him. It was five before Nailer sent for him again.

Nailer's face never seemed to give anything away – he had two expressions, surly and angry.

'Well?' said Cal.

'There's good news and bad news. This Ruthven-Greene bloke appears to exist. But he can't be found. He's incommunicado, as they say.'

'I don't believe this. I do not believe this. I've given you half a dozen names. Every one of these people knows me.'

Nailer put him back in the cells. Another two hours passed in silence. Then he was taken back to the interview room again. Nailer stood on the far side of the room, saying nothing, watching Dixon. On a clean, clear table Dixon set out the objects in the case, one by one, with a care and precision in their placing that forced Cal to look for meaning where there could be none. It was like checkers for the advanced student – little cellophane bundles, each piece an utterly unknown quantity.

'Right,' Nailer said at last. 'You recognise this lot?'

'What is this, a game?'

'Right, it is – Kim's game. Or don't you Yankees read Kipling?'

There it was, that word again. Red rag to a tired bull.

'You know, Chief Inspector, I could get mightily pissed off with you.'

The blow took Cal by surprise. The back of Nailer's hand to the mouth – a split lip and the taste of blood.

'Look!'

Cal looked. A pile of paper, a few pounds in change and notes, about fifty or so dollars in his billfold, his key ring, his driver's licence, the bloody handkerchief – from somewhere they'd retrieved the map of London he'd covered Walter with: one of his thumbprints stood out clearly, a bloodstained spiral in New Cross, now ringed in blue pencil. And his gun, split into component parts, the holster, the clip and the bullets flipped out and set next to it.

Nailer held one of the twenty-dollar bills up to the light. Cal felt like an idiot. He'd just pocketed them without thinking, that day in Silver Place.

'The ink's run on this,' Nailer said. 'Now, what would an honest American soldier want with a phoney bank note?'

Cal said nothing. He could think of nothing that would sound remotely plausible.

Nailer picked up the gun with two fingers wrapped in a grubby handkerchief and held the barrel out to Cal at face height.

'This gun's been fired recently.'

'Three or four days ago – if you want to call that recent?'

'When exactly?'

'The night before the *Hood* was sunk. I don't remember the date. Twenty-third or twenty-fourth, I think.'

'One bullet short in the magazine.'

'I fired one round – yes.'

'At whom?'

Cal didn't know. And if he did – how could he explain it to Nailer? That he'd shot a man on a rooftop in the middle of London, and left Walter and his 'binmen' to dispose of the body?

'I can't tell you that.'

'Just like you can't tell me who the Jerry was you claim you were following.'

'It's my job,' Cal said.

'And this is mine. Dixon, take Captain Cormack's fingerprints.'

Dixon set a blue inkpad next to the row of little cellophane bags and Cal let him roll his fingertips across it and then onto the numbered boxes of the print form. It was like being a child again. Literally in someone else's hands. As the thumb of his left hand pressed into the pad, Cal found himself fixed on the corner of a handkerchief, visible through its transparent wrapping. An 'F,' neatly embroidered in scarlet thread. It must be Troy's initial. Walter had called him Frank or Fred or something.

'Wait a minute!'

Nailer was at the door, his hand already grasping the handle.

'Well?'

'Troy. Troy knows me. He saw me with Walter.'

'Captain Cormack, I saw you with Walter. He was dead. He was dead when Troy saw you with him!'

'No – I mean before that. The day Walter and I met. He was called out to a case in Hoxton. Troy was there too. Walter took over the case from him, just as you did last night. He asked me if I was working with Walter. I told him I was.'

Cal could hear the desperation in his own voice. He was beginning to feel no one in London would ever admit to knowing him. Nailer took out his notepad and jotted down a couple of words, then paused with his pencil on the pad.

'When d'ye say this was?'

'The day Walter and I met. The Thursday or Friday after the big raid.'

§ 62

It was night – at least it felt like night, every cell in his body told him it was night, but the light was on continuously and there was no window to show the true state of light or darkness in the world outside his cell – when Nailer sought him out again. Cal swung his feet off the cot and set them on the floor. Nailer had come in and the duty cop had locked the door behind him. Cal wanted to stretch, but he felt safer sitting. Nailer was clutching a plywood chair, which he plonked down a few feet away from Cal. He sat down and leaned back. Lit up a cigarette and did not offer one to Cal.

'It's not your day,' he said cryptically. 'Not been your couple of days, I'd say.'

'Just tell me what you mean, Chief Inspector.'

'Troy. Set off for Cheltenham early last night. Called out on a murder enquiry. Hadn't arrived when I phoned through. And I've heard nothing back. Looks as though our Sergeant Troy no more wants to know you than your own people do.'

'I see,' said Cal, aiming for a neutrality of tone he did not feel.

'Son – why don't you stop wasting my time? Every alibi you offer is a total red herring. Your gun had been fired. One bullet. That's all it took to kill Walter Stilton. You even admit it's your gun. Your prints are all over it. Your thumbprint's there in Walter's blood on that map of London. You're the only person seen going up the alley at the time of the murder. Why don't you just come clean?'

'I didn't do it. Even you don't think I did it. Why would I kill Walter? The man was kindness itself. I knew him for – what? Ten days? Ten days, and I'd reckon him one of my closest friends and one of the most decent, generous-spirited men I've ever met. Dammit, Walter treated me better than three-quarters of my own family do. I had no reason to wish him any harm.'

Nailer exhaled a cloud of smoke over Cal and let it disperse as though he cherished the symbol.

'Captain Cormack – when I catch a man at the scene of a murder with a smoking gun in his hand, I don't ask about motives, I ask about facts. And where facts are concerned you're remarkably short of answers.'

'The gun was not smoking. And it was not in my hand, it was in its holster. If I killed Walter why did I then call the cops, cover the man's body and wait for you to arrive?'

'Why? Because you're clever. The music hall was just emptying, people milling around everywhere – you stood no chance of getting out unseen, so you tried a bluff. Pretended you'd found the body. It was a nice try, I'll give you that. Not many blokes have the nerve to sit with the corpse of a man they've just killed, but I've known one or two ruthless bastards try it. Who knows – other coppers might have bought it. Mebbe Sergeant Troy might have been daft enough to swallow that one. I'm not.'

'That's ... that's preposterous ... that's the biggest load of horseshit I ever heard.'

Nailer dropped the butt of his cigarette to the floor and ground it out with his heel.

'Horseshit it may be ...' (Good God, the man was actually smiling) '... but it's enough to hang you.'

Cal looked at Nailer. Tried to read the expression in his eyes.

'Chief Inspector, you don't think I killed Walter. You know I didn't kill Walter. So what's all this about?'

The smile wiped itself away.

'What's it all about? I've a dead copper on me hands. That's what it's all about. One of our best men knocked off on the streets of London. Do you think I'm going to make a daily report to the Met Commissioner and tell him I've no suspects? That I've no one in the frame? Do you think I'm going to have half the villains in London laughing up their sleeves saying we can't look after our own? No, Captain Cormack. Not bloody likely!'

'So I'm in the frame?'

'Right now – you're all I've got. You were there. Armed to the teeth, covered in Walter's blood – and nobody's vouching for you. Right now, Captain Cormack, you're it.'

Cal moved a little closer. He could smell the beer on Nailer's breath – mixed with the familiar halitosis of a country that seemed yet to invent dentistry.

'You call that justice?'

'No – I call it more than justice. I call it the honour of the Met.'

Nailer moved close to Cal, their faces only inches apart, and dropped his voice to a whisper of discretion.

'Don't get me wrong, young man – if I have to stitch you up to save that honour I'll do it, and there's not a court in the land would prove me wrong.'

'You know,' Cal whispered back, 'when you're

through with the Met, I think there could well be a vacancy for you in Chicago.'

Nailer doubled him neatly with a belly blow, and when he fell off the cot booted him in the balls. Cal heard the door slam as though it had closed inside his skull. He rolled over, threw up, and wished he'd never spoken.

§ 63

Troy got back to the Yard tired and bored. Cheltenham had been a complete waste of time. An accidental death of some interest to a provincial coroner, but none at all to Scotland Yard. It had been a rough night – a room in a pub full of drunken squaddies on embarkation leave. Let us piss away this night for in the morn we piss away lives in blood and sand in North Africa. He planned to make a quick verbal report to Onions, a mad dash through the paperwork piling up on his desk, and then have an early night.

'Did Enoch Nailer get hold of you?' Stan asked as Troy was trying to slip out of the door.

'Nailer? What would he want with me?'

'It was something to do with Stilton's death.'

'He's got my report. I typed it up before I logged off, the night Walter was killed.'

'Well, he was looking for you this morning. I thought he'd rung Cheltenham and left a message for you.'

Onions roared for Madge, his secretary. A sour-faced woman in her mid-thirties stuck her head round the door.

'D'ye still have a note of what Chief Inspector Nailer was wanting?'

Thirty seconds later she put a memo sheet on his desk and left without a word to either of them.

'Ah . . . I remember now. He's holding some bloke for

the murder of poor old Walter. Bloke says you can vouch for him.'

Troy was baffled.

'What bloke?'

'An American, name of Cormack.'

'Stan, Cormack found the body. He was the one dialled 999. He was sitting with Walter when I got there.'

'Mebbe,' a typical Onions word. 'But for the last thirty-six hours he's been sitting in a cell downstairs. Turns out he had a gun on him. You didn't search him, did you?'

'No,' said Troy. 'No, I didn't. I had the publican call the Branch straight away – and they sent Nailer. I just sat with Cormack until Nailer got there. Cormack didn't kill Walter. He was in shock. He was in tears.'

'And that's his alibi? It seems he's telling Enoch that you knew he was working with Walter all along. Not that Enoch's ready to believe him – he isn't.'

'I saw them together a couple of weeks ago – you sent me to a body in Hoxton Lane. Walter unceremoniously turfed me off the case. The American was with him.'

'That's all? Did you talk to him?'

'I can't remember.'

'OK, I'll tell Enoch. Mind – it doesn't prove much, does it?'

§ 64

Troy had never done anything like this before. He had earned the enmity of one or two of his superiors by being right once or twice when they were so clearly wrong – but he'd never deliberately set out to interfere in a case being conducted by a senior officer, to whom he was not assigned, and who was, moreover, a leading light of the

Special Branch, who as far as Troy could see were special merely in that they were the only bunch of plodding thugs allowed through the doors of Scotland Yard without being clapped in irons. It would require careful handling.

He killed thirty minutes in the canteen in the hope of catching one of the few Branch coppers he knew personally – Sgt Peter Dixon, who'd started at the Yard the same day as Troy. He got lucky. Dixon came in, took his cup of oily tea and sat at another table, eyes closed, as though sleeping upright, without even noticing Troy. Troy took his tea over, and sat opposite Dixon. His eyes flickered open.

'Freddie – long time no wotsit. How's murder?'

'You tell me, Peter. I hear you've got the case I was turfed off.'

'Oh – the Yank, you mean. By God, it's a rum one – running me ragged. Says he and poor old Stinker were on a secret mission together – would you believe he's asked half the nobs in Britain to speak for him? Either they won't or they can't be found. Even asked for poor old Bernie Dobbs. I suppose you've heard he's asked for you? Says you knew he was working with Walter.'

'I know, I've just told Onions what I know. I saw Cormack and Walter together on the sixteenth. But as Onions said, I don't know what it proves.'

'Bugger all, as far as the Boss is concerned.'

'You think he won't let him go?'

'No. It's rum. I tell you, Fred, it's rum. Nailer's taking this one personally. It's not as though he and old Stilton were mates. They weren't. It's more . . . there but for the grace of God . . . as though the Boss thinks it could have been him. I've never seen him like this. He's worked himself up into a right tizzy.'

'What does he think he's got?'

'Two eyewitnesses saw him go up the alley . . .'

'Peter, that's hardly surprising, as he was still there when I arrived. In fact it's hardly evidence. There's more than one way into that alley.'

'Through the Green Man, you mean? A London local? On a Tuesday, just about the flattest night of the week? Just try walking through a local London boozer on a Tuesday and not being seen or remembered. If you wanted to commit murder that would be asking to get caught, wouldn't it? You'd be setting foot in a nest of nosy-parkers just waiting for something or someone to break the monotony.'

Troy silently disagreed with this. He'd learnt early on in his time as a copper just how unobservant people could be.

'You questioned them?'

'Freddie – you teach me how to suck eggs and I'll clock yer!'

'All right. So what did your eyewitnesses see?'

'Hold your horses . . . thing is, they didn't see anyone else. Boss attaches a lot of importance to that. The way he sees it, we've got a foreign soldier, out of uniform, none of his own people vouching for him – that's just downright peculiar, but the Boss thinks it means something – and the gun. It'd been fired, y'see. That's the clincher. Catch a bloke with a smoking gun in his hand and you've got him . . . well . . . red-handed, haven't you?'

'It wasn't smoking, Peter. I think I might have noticed that.'

'Been fired recently, all the same.'

Troy found an Onionsism useful. 'Doesn't prove much, though, does it?'

Dixon shrugged and slurped noisily at his tea. Thought about it.

'You seem pretty convinced of this bloke's innocence,

considering you met him only twice. Do you know something you're not letting on, Fred?'

The man was more awake than he seemed. It was not a question Troy wanted to answer, so he didn't.

'If the boot was on the other foot, Fred, and it was your case, would I be sitting here telling you that catching a bloke with a discharged gun concealed about his person doesn't prove much?'

'Concealed?' said Troy. 'Concealed where?'

'Clip holster, back of his waistband. Just hooks onto the trousers. And there's one other thing.'

Dixon leant in close as though about to reveal the deepest secret. Troy followed, almost nose to nose.

'Boss ever finds out you got any of this from me, you'll be going to the next policeman's ball with yer knob in a splint!'

Back in his office Troy tackled that which might prove much. He called Kolankiewicz at the lab in Hendon.

'Did you do the post-mortem on Walter Stilton?'

'No – Spilsbury was asked to do this one in person.'

Troy supposed it was an honour accorded the fallen – to be cut open by the best pathologist in the land.

'All I got was ballistics.'

'You mean you've got the bullet?'

'Yep.'

'And?'

'And what?'

'How does it compare?'

'To what? – for Chrissake – they sent me nothing to compare it with yet!'

Troy went back to Onions.

'I need to talk to Nailer.'

'You know where to find him then, don't you?'

'I mean ... I need you to arrange a meeting with Nailer and Major Crawley.'

Crawley was the Superintendent in charge of Nailer –

Onions' opposite number. A former regular soldier, he was always referred to by his military rank – except among the constables, to whom he was inevitably 'Creepy'.

'What?'

'Nailer's sitting on evidence. He hasn't asked for a ballistics test on the gun you said Cormack was found with.'

'You can't call that sitting on evidence. Ballistics isn't everything.'

There were ways in which Onions was an imaginative copper and ways in which he was thoroughly a man of his generation.

'Yes it is,' Troy insisted. 'Set up a meeting and get Nailer to bring the gun.'

Onions had been at best half attentive to the conversation. Now he pulled back. Put down his pen, ceased his jotting and looked squarely at Troy.

'Oh God, Freddie. Don't make me do this. Don't make me tread all over Crawley's toes.'

'Stan – if I stick my nose into Nailer's case without you standing behind my shoulder he'll blast me into the middle of next week.'

'Freddie – don't make me do this.'

§ 65

It was the middle of a luke-warm afternoon, May drifting towards June, by the time Onions assembled his cast.

Troy sat to one side of Onions' desk, watching the *dramatis personae* take the stage. Onions, big, broad, blunt and Lancashire – on his feet glad-handing Crawley – an austere, upper-crust copper with the throttled vowels of the Edwardian age, hair almost a coiffure, a pencil-line moustache written on his top lip – and Nailer, like every

Special Branch copper Troy had ever met, unimagina-tively neat, but unimaginatively plain. The sort of copper happiest in boots, bowler and macintosh. The sort of copper who was careful to tip the dust out of his turnups at least once a week. But he looked awful, as though he was strained to breaking by this case – his eyes limpid and bloodshot, the plain, good suit now creased and crumpled as though he had slept in it, at odds with the near-military precision of his character. Dixon was right, he had worked himself into a 'tizzy'. He looked to Troy to be teetering on the edge. All he needed was a nudge.

Crawley seated himself, crossed his legs and set a box folder on the desk in front of him. Nailer sat, conven-iently, as far away from Troy as he could.

'This is irregular, Stanley,' Crawley kicked off. 'I do hope you've something positive to contribute to our case.'

'A bit irregular, Dennis, but hardly a revolution. You've a murder on your hands. And when one of our own goes down in the line of duty it's up to us all to rally round, wouldn't you agree?'

'Quite,' said Crawley, much as Troy might have said himself. Then, 'I read the memo you sent round about the suspect, naturally.' And turning to Troy, 'I gather you're offering an alibi for the man, sergeant?'

Now they were all looking at Troy, and Troy was wishing Crawley had not used the word 'alibi'.

'I knew Cormack was working with Chief Inspector Stilton, yes. I can't say that I'd call that his "alibi". By coincidence I was also the officer called out to the scene of the crime. What I saw has not led me to conclude that Cormack is the murderer. I felt it was time I . . .' (What, for God's sake, was the euphemism for 'blew you bastards out of the water'?) '. . . time we . . . pooled our knowledge.'

'I see,' said Crawley noncommittally. He jerked his head sharply left as though stung by an insect. 'Enoch?'

Nailer rattled it off. Terse, precise and fuck you. 'I found this Yank . . . standing over the body . . . a recently fired gun in his possession . . . I have two eyewitnesses who saw him go into Coburn Place about twenty minutes before . . . he was the only person to enter the alley in the timespan we're concerned with . . . and no one, 'cept you, is vouching for the man . . . his line is that Walter summoned him there by letter . . . needless to say he can't produce the letter . . . you don't have to be Agatha Christie to solve this one.'

'Might I ask who your witnesses are?'

'Couple of streetwalkers . . . pair o' prozzies . . . working Islington Green. They reckon they were stood there from about quarter to ten, and they were still there when I got there. They say he walked right past them – inches away.'

Another involuntary twitch from Crawley. Clearly, he wasn't too happy with this as testimony. No barrister in his right mind would relish putting a prostitute in the box and asking her to swear a credible oath.

'Did they see anyone else?' Troy asked.

'I've already said they didn't.'

'I mean anyone, anyone at all. You said they were there from about 9.45 and were still there when you arrived. That's well over an hour, nearer an hour and a half. Who else did they see go into Coburn Place?'

'Nobody – they saw Cormack, that's what matters! How big do you want the letters, Mr Troy? They saw Cormack!'

This was inverse logic. Cormack was found in the alley. Ergo, he had at some point gone up it. This scarcely needed witnesses. What mattered was what the two whores did not see.

'They can't have been that alert, then, can they? I went

up the alley twenty minutes or so after Cormack. If they didn't see me, who's to say who they might have missed twenty minutes earlier?'

'It's who they did see that matters.'

'Has it occurred to you, sir . . .' It seemed to Troy the right moment at which to throw in a 'sir'. 'Has it occurred to you that for a prostitute to admit to you that she was off the street for any length of time might be seen by her as an admission of prostitution, and that the reason they told you they were there without break was because they did not wish to admit openly to prostitution in front of a policeman? They weren't there when I went up the alley. Either they were being dozy – which I doubt, since their trade depends on spotting the single men – or else they weren't there, and if they weren't there when I got there, who's to say where they were at 10 or 10.30? Most turns take less than five minutes, they could have had three or four men in rapid succession and still have kept their patch on the street. But Walter's killer probably needed less than one minute.'

Nailer went from grey to red. Troy had done more than he meant to do; he had begun the logical demolition of the man, and it wasn't over yet.

'That isn't the most important thing. Of course they missed the killer –'

Crawley was looking hard at Troy, his discomfort self-evident.

'– But they would also appear to have missed the victim.'

'What?' said Crawley.

'Quite simply, sir, where were they when Chief Inspector Stilton went up the alley?'

It was so obvious, it was little short of calling Nailer stupid. Crawley tacked away from it. If Troy had been in his position, he thought, he would too – he would bat for his man.

267

'There is, of course, the matter of the gun.'

And it was the intervention Troy had been all but praying for. For one of them to bring up the gun made it so much easier for him to say what he had to say.

'Quite, sir, and I must say I'm baffled at the weight of evidence you seem to attach to it.'

'I don't follow, sergeant.'

'Am I right in thinking that you've asked for no ballistic tests?'

The merest exchange of looks between Crawley and Nailer. Crawley spoke.

'We've only the gun and the spent bullet that's lodged in Chief Inspector Stilton. We don't have the cartridge case to match up.'

This was old-fashioned thinking. This was the way ballistics had been until about nine or ten years ago. They could match cases; they had the greatest difficulty in matching or comparing bullets – even now it was a far from perfect science, but it was doable, and to a policeman of Troy's generation it was the first thing one would ask to be done.

Nailer chipped in again. 'Ballistics isn't everything.'

Troy looked at Onions. He could have sworn the man blushed, ever so slightly, at the way Nailer betrayed their ages in the word-for-word repetition of what he had said himself. 'I was on Murder for two years myself under Mr Onions' predecessor. In my day if you caught a bloke with a gun in his hand at the scene of a murder you didn't need to ask for the man in the white coat, you knew. Walter Stilton was shot just above one ear'ole. I should think you'd've noticed that for yourself. And I should think that when you've been in the job more than eighteen months, when you've done a bit more than spit and cough, when you're not still wet behind the ears, you'll know. When a small-bore bullet passes through that amount of bone it'll bend – of course it'll bend. A fat

268

lot of use a bent bullet is. Where are you then, with the men in their white coats?'

Troy had always admired punctuality. It was a mark of civilisation – even in one so thinly civilised as the Polish Beast. Madge stuck her head round the door and said, 'Professor Kolankiewicz is here, Mr Onions.'

'Kolankiewicz? I didn't send for him,' Stan said blankly.

'I did,' said Troy.

'You little shite!' Nailer exploded. 'You've fitted me up!'

'Perhaps if you weren't so keen to fit up the American, I wouldn't have had to.'

Nailer got out of his chair, his right arm raised as though he'd thump Troy if there weren't a superintendent and a desk between them. Crawley calmly pushed him back into it.

'Mr Troy, I'll thank you to treat my officers with more respect,' he said without raising his voice. 'Chief Inspector Nailer has served over twenty years in this force and deserves better.'

He turned his attention to Onions.

'I deplore such tactics, Stanley. However, now that Professor Kolankiewicz is here we may as well see him.'

'I agree,' said Stan. 'And Freddie, keep yer gob shut.'

Kolankiewicz bundled in, homburg pushed way back on his head, pockets bulging, a copy of the *News Chronicle* under one arm. He was not a serving police officer. Rank held no terror for him. He pulled up a chair, plonked it down next to Crawley and said 'Which one you coppers got the gun?'

Troy could have sworn he heard a soft 'Oh Jesus' escape Onions' lips. Crawley simply twitched again and jerked his head towards the box file on Onions' desk.

'It's there. Sealed in cellophane. The suspect's fingerprints are all over it.'

Kolankiewicz tore off the wrapper like a small boy attacking a Mars bar. He sniffed the barrel.

'Smith and Wesson. Been fired.'

Nailer sighed at the obvious. Kolankiewicz ignored him and stripped the wrapper off the holster. A small black triangle of tough leather, a stainless steel clip on the flat side. Kolankiewicz sniffed that too.

'It's a closed holster,' he said. 'Unusual. It would complicate things.'

'How?' said Onions.

'Bloke shoots some other bloke. Unless he stands around like Wild Bill Hickok blowing smoke off the barrel and boasting to every bugger that he's Deadeye Dick, he puts it back in the holster straight away. In an open holster the barrel would protrude, the gases would be allowed to disperse at what I would term a normal rate. In a holster like this . . . well, you might as well put a cork up the barrel. Gases are trapped. Makes it difficult to say when the gun was fired. All you can say is that it was fired.'

Onions fixed his gaze on Crawley.

'Does this help, Dennis?' he asked without a trace of sarcasm.

Crawley gave a far straighter answer than Troy knew Nailer would attempt. The man might be a colossal prig, but he was honest.

'It . . . er . . . it complicates matters. Cormack has admitted that he fired the gun five or six days ago . . . of course it would help if he told us at whom . . . but he's claiming some sort of diplomatic immunity on that one.'

'You want my professional opinion?' Kolankiewicz said. 'That's why you got me here, is it not? My opinion is that if you had sent me the gun the night Stilton died we might be in a better position to judge, but as things stand I will say now that I cannot say with any reliability when this gun was fired. It is perfectly possible that this Cormack is telling the truth. But there is yet more.'

He tore the wrapper off the bullets and set one of them upright on the desk. He tugged at the bulge in his coat pocket and pulled out a large wad of cotton wool. A few seconds probing with his fingers and he set a second bullet, distorted and shapeless, next to the first. Every copper in the room looked at it. Nailer could not restrain a grin, the small man's smirk of petty triumph.

'As you boys can see, is bent to buggery. However . . .'

Kolankiewicz picked up the unspent bullet, whipped out his spectacles, and eyed it closely.

'. . . It is the same calibre. Point 32, with full metal jacket made for a .35. The spent bullet I have shows a right hand twist, which is what it'd have if it too had come from a Smith and Wesson. There are not many .35 handguns. In fact Smith and Wesson are one of the few firms ever to make them. A small gun, 22 ounces, more powerful than their .32 – that's what I'd call a handbag gun – not as powerful as the Colt .38 or the Browning 9mm, but still some stopping power. I shall have to compare the bullet that killed old Stinker with a test shot. It's all in the rifling – the twist.'

'But,' said Nailer, 'it's bent to buggery! You said so yourself.'

'Trust me. I'm a smartyarse.'

It occurred to Troy that working for the Branch did not often bring Crawley into contact with the old immovable object that was Kolankiewicz. He spoke to him as though he'd been accosted by a particularly rude fishmonger who'd had the sheer neck to ring at the front door clutching six months of unpaid accounts. It came effortlessly, unconsciously perhaps, to men like Crawley to use a tone of voice that directed you to the tradesman's entrance.

'Let me understand you. You're saying you *can* run tests on this?'

'Yes. Difficult, but not impossible, so yes.'

Troy heard Stan draw in breath as though about to speak. But Nailer spoke first, reddening once more with anger and exasperation.

''Scuse me sir, but this is bollocks. We shouldn't be playing around with useless blobs of lead with what we've got. He was there, he had a gun, and he's no explanation that adds up to piss in a tea-strainer as to why he was there or why he was with Walter at all. This immunity he seems to claim, this mission he says he's on – it's all bollocks. He did it. I know he did it. The Yanks know he did it. He's a villain and they've disowned him. I say forget the damn tests and charge him now.'

It was a speech that left every man in the room, save Kolankiewicz who did not appear to be listening, slightly stunned.

Crawley jerked his chin off his chest, slowly turned to face his Chief Inspector and said, 'Enoch, are you quite serious?' in the same tone in which he might have said 'Are you quite mad?'

'Charge the bugger, charge him now!'

Onions turned to Troy – the injunction of silence lifted.

'Mr Nailer,' Troy began. 'Does the phrase "diplomatic incident" mean anything to you?'

Nailer did not answer. He glared at Troy.

'Has it occurred to you that far from being disowned Cormack might merely have fallen foul of the internal politics in what is known to be a very factional embassy, and that when they finally work out the mess he's in they'll want him back in one piece? You've held him for a couple of days. It's his rotten luck that of all the English people he's named I'm the only one available to speak for him, so you've had a romp watching his alibis topple like ninepins. But tomorrow or the day after the Americans will tire of playing games and they'll ask for him back.'

Nailer glared still, and it seemed to Troy that he'd not understood one word of what he'd just said.

Crawley stood, stiff-necked, adam's apple bobbing in his collar – head of house and captain of the first eleven rolled into one.

'I'm fed up with this. I'm putting an end to it now. Mr Kolankiewicz, do your tests and send me the report.'

Publish and be damned. Nailer said nothing. Troy said nothing. Onions muttered the platitudes of rank. Chairs scraped back. Legs stretched. Kolankiewicz was out of the door in a flash, closely followed by Troy and Nailer.

Past Madge's office, at the head of the stairs, Nailer tapped Troy on the shoulder. He was not about to let him go easily. The finger that tapped the shoulder now prodded him in the sternum.

'You cheeky young bugger! I've been a copper since you were in nappies. I've been a copper more'n twenty years –'

'Then,' Troy cut him off, 'it's a pity that in twenty years you've learnt fuck all.'

An inarticulate noise burst forth from Nailer – nothing clearer than 'Wuuurgh!' He lunged at Troy, fist clenched, missed and fell against the wall – purple in the face, a blood vessel in his forehead throbbing furiously. Troy ran down the stairs, chasing after Kolankiewicz.

He caught him on the ground floor, short, fat legs hurrying against the grain of his character.

'You're off to Hendon? I'm coming with you.'

'You are welcome, my boy – but it is not to Hendon I go.'

'Where then?'

'You want your proof, don't you? The death of a fellow flatfoot bothers you as much as it bothers Crawley's creeps, does it not? Then we should go to the top. You may believe in the necessity of good forensics, but Nailer is typical not only of many of your colleagues but also of the Metropolitan Police bureaucracy. You know how I got my first comparison microscope? I built it myself. In 1934. I'm still using it – and in all the equipment with which the misers at the Yard have supplied me, there is nothing that I would grace with the words "state of the art".'

'So?'

'So we go to the top man. Tell me – have you ever met Mr Churchill?'

§ 66

Troy had never met Mr Churchill, but he had long wanted to. It was an irresistible invitation. He followed Kolankiewicz at a cracking pace. It seemed the little lunatic really had the bit between his teeth. Out of the Yard, across Whitehall, and down Downing Street.

At the end of Downing Street he turned right across Horse Guards Parade, over the Mall, up Carlton House Steps into Lower Regent Street, across the Haymarket, right into Orange Street, and at the junction with St Martin's Street he stopped outside a small shop. If Troy's knowledge of geography served him aright, they were at the back of the National Gallery, and if his knowledge of the underworld served him aright, pretty well opposite one of the most notorious brothels in London.

'You understand, I hope,' Kolankiewicz was saying, 'that we're going private. You'd better have your chequebook on you.'

'Don't worry,' said Troy. 'It'll be worth a few quid to wrap this one.'

Kolankiewicz yanked on the bell. A black-coated

gentleman's gentleman opened the door to them, a figure from another era, perhaps Dickensian – he put Troy in mind of Wemmick, this was how he'd always seen Wemmick – and if not Dickensian, then certainly of the other century.

'Mr Chewter,' Kolankiewicz said.

The man's Victorian face cracked into a smile. 'Professor Kolankiewicz. My, but it's been a while. Is the Guv'nor expecting?'

'No. But if he is free I would be grateful for an hour of his valuable time.'

Chewter cranked the handle on the side of the phone and announced them.

'Professor Kolankiewicz, Guv'nor and –'

He turned to Troy.

'Sergeant Troy,' said Troy, and then added, 'of the Yard,' as though explanation were needed.

'Quite all right. Would you gentlemen care to go up?'

Chewter opened the cage door on an impossibly small lift. Troy found himself all but belly to belly with Kolankiewicz whilst staring down at the top of his head. The lift stopped at the second floor, and there stood another short, stout man, wiping his hands on an oily rag to extend one dry if grubby hand to shake Kolankiewicz's. He looked every inch a Churchill – the girth, the thinning hair, the jowls – but with a moustache, and the best part of ten years younger. Even Lord Haw-Haw had been known to confuse them.

'You've brought me a new copper, then, Ladislaw.'

Nobody called Kolankiewicz Ladislaw. There were people at the Yard who'd known him since he first landed in England who probably did not know his Christian name.

'My old friend Sergeant Frederick Troy, my even older friend Bob Churchill.'

They shook on the dubious connection of lasting friendship with the Beast of Lodz.

'Troy,' Churchill said. 'One of the Devon Troys?'

'No,' said Troy. 'Hertfordshire.'

'Oh, I see. One of the Alex Troys. I knew your father once upon a time.'

Troy loved the expression, as though the two had met in some distant fairy tale – the constant tin soldier and the ugly duckling. It often seemed to Troy that his father had stepped out of something no more nor less credible than a fairy tale of his own weaving.

'I'm a Dorset man meself. That lot over at Blenheim are a junior branch of the family. Now – what can I do for you?'

Kolankiewicz held up Cormack's gun. Churchill took it from him.

'Good Lord, a Smith and Wesson .35. Haven't been made for about twenty years, been a while since I saw one. Small, dark and brutish,' he said, and led the way through to the front room.

Troy had never seen anything like it. Every surface, every wall, held guns, guns by the dozen – guns in racks, guns in bits, and guns not yet built – walnut stocks, gunmetal barrels, leather cases. Down the length of the room ran a large table covered in red baize and littered with some of the most beautiful shotguns Troy had seen. The workmanship was exquisite. But all in all, it was pretty much what he might have expected to find on the premises of the finest gunsmith and ballistics expert alive. On a bench behind the table was a large, ugly, black, greasy machine gun as testament to the times in which they lived. They had clearly interrupted Churchill in the business of stripping down his Bren gun.

Churchill seated himself at the head of the table and whipped out the magazine from Cormack's gun.

'Automatic with a seven-shot magazine in the grip, a large pistol grip relative to the barrel size, as you can see.'

Troy did see. The pistol reminded him of nothing quite so much as a spud gun – a childhood toy capable of propelling a chunk of raw potato all of six feet.

'Spring recoil mechanism with a hidden hammer. They stopped making ammunition for this last year. Full metal jacket bullet – lead centre with guiding sheath. Six grooves in the barrel giving a right hand twist to the bullet. You've a spent bullet from this, I take it?'

Kolankiewicz handed him the wodge of cotton wool. Churchill put a jeweller's glass to his eye and looked at it.

'Victim died, did he? Head shot, I suppose?'

Troy answered. 'Yes. A policeman, as a matter of fact. I saw the body. The entry wound was just above the right ear.'

'Exit wound?'

'Wasn't one. The bullet was recovered in the post-mortem.'

'Well – bone does that to a bullet. I suppose you want a comparison?'

'If it's possible.'

'Oh, it's possible all right. Did you recover the shell?'

'No – I was the second person on the scene, and it had gone. I think we're dealing with a scrupulous killer.'

'Well – they're few of them scrupulous enough. If you ever join the other side, Mr Troy, and find yourself clutching a smoking gun, destroy it. That'd be my advice. Now, if you gentlemen would care to join me in the cellar, we'll bang off a few rounds.'

Kolankiewicz stepped into the lift. Only when Churchill tried to follow him in did it become clear that it would not hold two bellies of such rotundity. For a few seconds they jiggled around like a pair of hippos in a hat box, until Troy said 'We could all walk,' and they descended the steps to emerge below street level in a converted wine cellar.

'This is the set-up,' Churchill said, pointing off at a tunnel leading out under Orange Street. 'We've fifteen hundred-gauge, twelve-bore cartridge cases, packed with cotton wool. Behind them, iron plate, behind that a few tons of rubble. We could fire an elephant gun at this lot without ricochet.'

'Why fifteen boxes?' Troy asked.

'Largely,' said Churchill, 'because I've yet to find the gun that can fire a bullet through more than a dozen. Mauser'll penetrate eleven or twelve, standard issue Webley no more than five or six. If, as you say, this bullet penetrated a human skull and spent itself in the cranium, then I'd say no more than two boxes.'

'Can we simulate the effect of passing through bone?'

'Indeed we can.'

Churchill picked up a square piece of oak. It looked to Troy to be about half or two-thirds of an inch thick. Churchill slotted it in front of the first case. Then he clipped the magazine into the butt of Cormack's gun, and handed it to Troy.

Troy had no idea what to do.

'I'm not really a gun person,' he bleated.

'Just point it and fire.'

Troy held the gun at arm's length, just like they'd taught him at Hendon in his obligatory weapons training. That had been in 1935. He had not held a gun since.

'No, no,' said Churchill. 'Not like that. Use your body.'

'My body?'

'That thing between your arms and your legs.'

Churchill took the gun from him, tucked his elbow into his hip, the gun-butt wedged into his belly, swung to face the boxes and fired, all in a single swift, almost graceful motion – startling to see in such an ungainly-looking man. Not only that, he'd hit the first box dead centre. If the box had had a target scrawled on it, this would have been a bull's-eye.

Churchill walked down the tunnel to the second box, and flipped down the wooden side. He rummaged around and eventually said, 'Nothing doing.'

The same pattern repeated itself with the third and fourth boxes. At last his hand emerged from the fifth, clutching a white ball of cotton wool, and inside it the bullet. He peeled back the layers and showed the spent bullet to Troy.

'It's intact,' said Troy. 'It isn't bent at all!'

'We'll fire another just to be sure.'

Churchill banged off a second round, hitting the oak barely half an inch from the first, and retrieved the bullet from the fifth box again.

'Now,' he said, grinning like a schoolboy, 'the fun really begins.'

On a bench at the far side of the cellar stood Churchill's comparison microscope. He was not the inventor of this device, but he had modified it and refined it. And, as much as was possible when dealing with a body of men as naturally conservative as the English police, he had popularised it. He had proved its worth over the last ten or more years from the witness box at the Old Bailey. He had argued its merit in the pages of the *Daily News* only to find himself answered by a lengthy correspondence in the *Mail* from no less a figure than Bernard Shaw. All the same, men as sceptical as Onions or as ignorant as Nailer still deprecated its role. The only other such microscope Troy had ever seen was Kolankiewicz's, which, compared to this, looked like it had been cobbled together from a Meccano kit. This was big, like a pair of binoculars on stilts, feeding two images into a single eyepiece. Churchill set the bullet that had killed Walter Stilton on the left hand plate, and one of the test bullets on the other. A flick of a switch and both specimens were flooded with light.

'Before I do anything,' Churchill said, 'just take a look.'

Troy peered down the microscope. It was a blur, the shapes did not match.

'OK?'

Troy didn't have a clue what was OK and what was not.

Churchill took over. One eye at the eyepiece, his left hand at the plate that held the deadly bullet. He changed the angle of the light. He twisted a mirror to the right of the bullet, and changed the alignment of the plate.

'Take another look.'

This time the bullets were in alignment, the bent bullet miraculously unbent by the mirror. The two did not line up perfectly and the composite image was still blurred. Then Churchill turned a wheel at the base of the microscope and suddenly the bottom halves of both bullets fused into one.

'Ignore the centre where the bullet's bent. And for now ignore the top. Just concentrate on the bottom. Well, what do you see?'

'The rifling. The twists. They're curling in the same way, a bit like bindweed, but they don't match.'

Churchill turned the wheel the other way. The top of the bullet came into focus. The markings no more matched than they had at the bottom.

Churchill looked again. 'Of course,' he was saying, 'there's a limit to how much you can compensate for damage with mirrors, but as long as you can get a section of the twist lined up ... Bob's your uncle, if you'll forgive the boast. It's a lengthy process to be able to say a pair of bullets match, but a bit quicker to say they don't. And these two don't match at all. No doubt about it, fired by two different guns. The gun you brought me did not fire the fatal bullet.'

'Would this hold up in court?' Troy asked.

Churchill feigned outrage, 'Mr Troy!'

'Sorry – I'm being dense. What else can you tell me?'

'Depends what you want to know.'

'Well . . . why didn't the test bullet bend, why did it fire through five boxes when you estimated two?'

This did not seem to require any thought on Churchill's part. The answer was on the tip of his tongue.

'Granted identical weapons, I'm inclined to conclude a different load. The bullet that killed your chap was probably fired on a low load. A bullet designed for work at close quarters, but otherwise practically useless. In fact, about as effective as a popgun. That's why it distorted when it hit bone and the test bullets didn't when passing through oak. Of course, you'll appreciate that oak and bone don't behave exactly the same . . . but then . . . I don't have a heap of skulls lying around just to test bullets.'

Troy was intrigued. 'Why would anyone want a low load?'

'Well,' Churchill mused, 'if you know what you're doing with any handgun you won't try and shoot someone at a hundred yards. You'd be better off at six feet. Most handguns outside the hands of marksmen are pretty inaccurate at much beyond a few feet. Jesse James once emptied his Colt .45 in a bank raid, at pretty well point blank range, and missed every time. So having to get in close is no real disadvantage – and you have the added bonus of knowing that you won't kill the chap on the other side of your target by the bullet passing right through the target – and of course, "popgun" is really rather apt. That's what it'd sound like, a sort of popping. You want to shoot some poor devil where there are likely to be people around . . . well, with any luck no one would hear, and if they did they'd think little of it. A car backfiring would make a damn sight more noise.'

'And is that in any way standard issue?'

'To whom?'

'American soldiers.'

'No. Not at all. The gun itself isn't standard – it's all but obsolete, but it's light and it's small and I expect one or two might choose it for that reason. The standard issue is the M1911A1 .45. And that's made by Colt, not Smith and Wesson. Now, modified bullets, that is . . . shall we say . . . that is quite something. Low loads, soft heads, that sort of thing. That's someone who really knows what he's at. I'd say it was a professional's choice – someone who carries a gun because he means to use it, not simply someone who's issued with it as part of being a soldier – someone who kills professionally – and I don't mean in the course of battle. I mean dirty work. All in all you got lucky, Sergeant Troy. If the man who modified this shell had also notched the head to make it fragment you'd've whistled for your match – and the professor here would be rooting around in the victim's brains for half a dozen fragments of lead. All the king's horses wouldn't have put it back together then.'

'So perhaps he wasn't so professional after all?'

'Don't ask me too much about people, Mr Troy. It's guns I know about.'

It seemed to Troy that Mr Churchill had been so long and so detailed in his report that if he, Troy, could only sum it up succinctly it would be the clearer to him, the clearer to everyone.

'It's an assassin's weapon,' he said at last.

'Exactly,' said Churchill.

'Could we get this down on paper?'

Troy sat at a high, old Imperial typewriter, its roll more than a foot and a half across, and typed onto foolscap as Churchill dictated. When they were done

Churchill shook his hand and Troy asked, 'How much do I owe you?'

'On the house, Mr Troy. Just remember me to your father, and remind him that he bought a gun off me in 1928. If he should ever choose to make it a pair . . .'

'Of course,' said Troy.

In the course of the last hour, Troy thought he had scarcely heard Kolankiewicz say so little. He ascribed it to professional courtesy in the presence of a master. Something he would never be in Kolankiewicz's eyes. Kolankiewicz had him tagged as a 'smartyarse' – not the same thing at all. Walking back to the Yard, Kolankiewicz had a simple question for Troy.

'You picking this case up now?'

'Picking it up?'

'It is your clear intent to bump the idiot Nailer off the case. I merely enquired if you now proposed to appropriate it yourself.'

'No – absolutely not. I've been trying to drop the damn thing not pick it up. And I don't want to bump Nailer off it, I just want to get Cormack out. Once that's done Nailer can find out who's really done it.'

'A pity. What this case needs is a real smartyarse.'

'Not this smartyarse.'

'Then you don't want to know what I think next, do you?'

Troy thought about it.

'No – I don't. Tell it to Nailer.'

'Your reluctance to stick your proboscis further into the death of old Stinker wouldn't have anything to do with your hot/cold love affair with his delightful daughter, would it?'

That was the thing about Kolankiewicz – just when you thought you were home free he had another surprise for you.

Troy had finished his paperwork. Later than he had hoped. He looked at his watch. Eight thirty. He opened the centre drawer of his desk and, as was his habit, dumped the day's work into it in a single sweep of his arm. It would stop Onions reading what was on the pile if he happened to stroll in unannounced – exactly as he did now.

He parked himself by the unlit gas fire, a man who could never shake off the habit of winter, struck a match on the sole of one shoe and lit up a Woodbine.

'Well,' he said through a waft of cheap tobacco.

'Well?' said Troy.

'You did it. The American walks. The Major read your report and told Enoch to turn him loose. It's not over, mind. We'll want to know a thing or two from the Americans, when they get round to answering questions.'

'Good,' said Troy, hoping that was that and that he could just go home. But Stan was musing, drawing slowly on his fag and musing.

'How do you see your career panning out, Freddie?'

It struck Troy as an odd enquiry. Untypical of Stan. Stan had picked Troy up from the Divisions, transferred him from Stepney to the Yard, made him a Sergeant at the age of twenty-four. He had every reason to be grateful to Stan. Stan *was* his career.

'Dunno. I never think about it. I'm happy with you, if that's what you mean? Happy in Murder.'

'Happy in Murder,' Onions mused. 'I don't think I've read that one.'

Troy smiled. Stan was right. He had inadvertently invented a very likely title for a whodunnit by one of those lady novelists who seemed to dominate the genre in the thirties.

'I meant,' he said, 'that I've no desire to move.'

'You don't fancy a job in the Branch then?'

'That's the last thing I want.'

'Just as well. You made several enemies today.'

Troy got the message. It wasn't an enquiry, it wasn't a ticking off, it wasn't even a warning. It was a statement.

'And I get the feeling they'll not be the last you make on your way up.'

'You're unhappy with that?'

'No. No. I backed you today. And I'll back you when I think you're right.'

Onions paused. The clincher could not now be far away.

'But I'd be happier still if I thought you were telling me all you knew.'

§ 68

Troy walked home in the creeping, thin darkness of late May. Not so much night as a veil across the day. Troy walked home, feeling for the first time that day that he was free of Cormack, feeling for the first time in a while that he might also be free of Kitty. Home the back way. Along William IV St, into the curve of Chandos Place and up Bedfordbury to the end of the narrow alley that was Goodwin's Court, and Troy's home. It was a mistake. Halfway up Bedfordbury, by a block of Peabody Dwellings, the sound of marital strife blew out of an open first-floor window and cut the air.

'You spent it? You spent it all? You miserable bugger! You miserable drunken bugger!'

He knew the voice well. His near-neighbour Alice McArdle. And she could only be talking to her husband, Ardle McArdle – and she was exaggerating. Ardle McArdle was a happy drunk – as a rule. On the occasions when he wasn't he'd been known to knock Alice about. Troy had booked him once, flattened him twice, dunked him in the horse-trough in Chandos Place on half a dozen occasions, and on two or three had prevented Alice from almost murdering him by confiscating the rolling pin. McArdle was only miserable when confronted, as now, with the consequences of having spent his pay packet on beer, and the onset of sobriety.

As a young copper, learning his job through the soles of a pair of size-six, unbendable police boots, pounding the paving stones of Stepney and Limehouse, Troy had on many occasions wondered what the role of a copper was. To nick villains: well, that went without saying. George Bonham, his station sergeant and mentor ('Wot?' had been Bonham's only response to Troy's use of that word) had defined the job for him. 'This is what we do. This is what coppers are for. If we're not this, what use are we? As a copper you're sort of a village wise man, an elder, and age's got nothing to do with it – comes with the pointy hat, when you put it on that's what you become – the village wise man – like it or lump it.' After six months on the beat Troy had fed the line back to George, revised it. 'We're witch doctors,' he said. 'People expect us to be able to do what they cannot do themselves. A sort of magic. It's not that we're better than they are – we make them better than they are themselves.' 'Bloody hell,' Bonham had said, and left it at that.

Troy stopped. Looked up at the flapping curtain in the open window. Felt the onrush of copper's magic. Pricked back his ears. There was a key phrase in the rise of Alice's rage.

'I'll swing for you, you bastard!'

At which point she would begin destroying the family crockery piece by piece, beating Ardle about the head with it until there wasn't a plate left to smash, and her drunken husband collapsed to the kitchen floor.

Troy dashed up the stairs. The voice in his head that might have told him he'd already played the boy scout today, and shot the bolt of his white magic, silent in his head.

Alice had McArdle cornered in the kitchen – a couple of dinner plates shattered at his feet. She had her back to Troy. He grabbed her by the shoulder as she lunged at her husband once more.

'Alice!'

She spun round – the weapon in her hand sliced through Troy's shirt, and tore a gash in his chest two inches below the nipple.

Troy clutched his ribs with his right hand. Watched the blood seep between his fingers, saw Alice's mouth open silently in shock. He looked at her hand still poised in the air. She'd stabbed him. Stabbed him with a potato peeler.

McArdle staggered to his feet just as Troy staggered backwards, bumped into a kitchen chair and sat down with a thump.

'Jesus woman, you've killed a copper!'

Alice had her eyes fixed on Troy's bloody shirtfront. Then she held up the potato peeler like a crucifix presented to Christ, dropped it and screamed. The gust of whiskied breath told Troy what he should have known all along. She was as pissed as her husband.

McArdle rinsed a dishcloth under the tap and came back to Troy with the dripping, smelly, grey mess, intending to apply it to the wound.

'Do you want me to get septicaemia?' Troy asked. 'Why don't you try and shut Alice up? I'll be fine.'

Alice had resorted to a mantra of 'Jesus, O Jesus, O Mary Mother of God.'

'Alice woman. Will you shut yer gob! Mr Troy says he'll be all right.'

Troy would only be all right if he got himself out of there and home. He got up, shaky on his feet, light-headed and made his way to the door. The next time, he'd let them murder each other.

Out in the street he took a breather against a lamp-post, not at all sure whether he was going to throw up or not. McArdle leaned out of the window.

'Are you sure you'll be all right Mr Troy?'

'Fine,' Troy lied. He'd only be all right if he got home and got to a doctor.

Fumbling with the key at his front door, he could feel the blood reach his legs – the wound must be deeper than he thought. He fell into an armchair next to the phone and dialled Scotland Yard. Whitehall 1212.

'Is Mr Kolankiewicz still in the building?'

The constable on the desk said he'd ring round and call him back. Troy wriggled out of his jacket, pressed a cushion to his chest and lay still. A couple of minutes later the phone rang and he heard Kolankiewicz's voice say, 'What's up? I was just leaving the Yard in search of a plate of tripe and onions and a bowl of hot plum duff with custard.'

'I need . . . I need your professional services.'

'Oh fuck, Troy – not again. I stitched you up only last year. You already look like Boris Karloff playing Frank-enstein's monster. Call your physician.'

'And get signed off sick? Not on your nelly. Pick up a bag of tricks and get in a cab!'

§ 69

'You mean I can go?' Cal knew he sounded incredulous.

'Yep,' Dixon said. 'On yer bike. If that means anything to you.'

Cal had been two days in his bloody clothes. He felt he

288

must smell like a slaughterhouse. As Dixon handed him his possessions one by one, he said 'I can't walk though the streets like this.'

'No. You can't.'

Dixon took his macintosh off the peg on the back of the office door. The ubiquitous bobby's mac – just like the one Walter Stilton had worn.

'I'll want it back, mind.'

'I'll send it back in a cab.'

'Sign here.'

Cal slipped his arms through the coat and glanced down at the form Dixon had put in front of him.

'It says "all personal effects".'

'So?'

'My gun?'

'You want your gun back? I've been told nothing about that.'

'Have you been told not to give it to me?'

Dixon thought about this.

'Not as such.'

'Then surely it's part of "all". Come on Sergeant, you know I'm a serving soldier. You've seen my dog-tags, you've talked to the embassy. All officers have sidearms.'

'It's evidence.'

'Of what? You just said you're letting me go. If you had the slightest suspicion that I'd killed Walter you wouldn't be letting me go, now would you?'

Dixon opened his desk drawer. Took out the gun, its clip and its holster. Scooped up the bullets in one hand and dropped them down on the desktop like a pocketful of marbles.

'Four left,' he said. 'I gather Mr Troy used a couple in his test.'

'Troy. Troy tested my gun?'

'Troy got you out of chokey Mr Cormack. And you say I told you that and you'll get me shot,' Dixon said.

'Not funny, Sergeant.'

'Not meant to be, Captain.'

§ 70

Cal thought about handing Dixon's coat straight over to the cabbie who dropped him at Claridge's, but the idea of crossing the lobby in the rotting remains of his Lippschitz Bros. suit was intolerable. He needed, and there was no better word for it, camouflage.

As he picked up his key the desk clerk said, 'You left this the other night, sir.'

'What?'

The man already had his back to Cal, his hand flashing across the rows of pigeonholed guest mail. When he turned he was clutching the torn envelope containing Walter's note.

'We weren't at all sure you had finished with it, sir.'

Cal was almost dumbstruck. All, well most, of the evidence he'd needed to shove in front of Nailer and it had been here all the time – he'd simply dashed out and left it on the counter.

'I'm afraid I lost your map,' he said softly.

'It doesn't matter,' the clerk replied.

In the elevator going up to the sixth floor Cal quietly, almost reverently, took out Stilton's note and unfolded it.

'Wot larx!' He was always saying that. He'd never say it again, and Cal still hadn't got the foggiest idea what he meant by it.

He rang room service, ordered a large Scotch, and ran a bath.

Then he rang room service back.

'Could you make that a fifth of Scotch?'

'Do you mean a half bottle, sir?'

'Sure. Whatever. Just tell the maid to let herself in and leave it. I'll be in the bath. Oh – and ice. I need ice.'

The English never thought of ice, or if they did, as with so many things, they thought small.

A quarter of an hour later he was lying back in the suds and heard the door click. Only innate, unshakeable modesty stopped him yelling 'Bring it in here' to the maid – he felt far too tired to move even for a glass of Scotch. He closed his eyes, listening for the second click of the door as the girl left. It didn't. She was taking a long time about it. He opened his eyes and found himself gazing at Kitty, Kitty clutching a tray, a bottle and a glass of ice.

'Bumped into the maid in the corridor. Relieved her of this. Only one glass though.'

She set the tray down in front of the mirror, shook his toothbrush out of the bathroom tumbler and poured for them both.

As she handed him the glass she said, 'Calvin, where the bleedin' 'ell you been?'

'You mean you don't know?'

'Yeah, I know – I just enjoy wastin' me breath. 'Course I don't bloody know! Now – tell me. For God's sake tell me, where have you been? Just when I need you and you vanish off the face of the earth!'

Need – bet she didn't mean that. Bet she doesn't know the meaning of the word.

'You really don't know? The Yard didn't tell you? OK. I've spent the last . . .' He couldn't remember – it felt like days but it could only be two or three at the most . . . 'I've spent the last few days in jail. Courtesy of Scotland Yard.'

'Wot?'

'They . . . they thought I did it. They thought I killed your father.'

Kitty sat down on the lavatory.

'The bastards. The complete bloody bastards. They knew all along and they didn't tell us. They told Mum they had a suspect, and they wouldn't tell her who. I got on to that old sod Nailer, tried the old pals act on him. Still wouldn't tell me. Just kept saying "a man found at the scene is helping us with our enquiries" – just like he was talking to Joe Public. Like I wasn't a copper too. Fobbed me off with copperspeak. The bastard. The total bloody bastard.'

She sipped at her Scotch. Gulped and gasped. Cal wondered if the tears now forming in the corners of her eyes were grief or misery or the instant effect of neat whisky. He knocked his back in one, felt the delicious cool-burn down his throat, and stuck out the glass for more.

'Why did they let you go? I mean they ain't caught the bloke, have they?'

'No . . . no, they haven't. But somebody vouched for me. Another policeman, someone who'd seen me working with Walter. I got lucky, my own people didn't want to know me.'

Kitty sniffed loudly as though burying a fountain full of tears and took off her jacket – the same formal, plain black two-piece outfit she'd worn when her brothers had died – maybe the only formal clothes she had. Cal sipped at his second glassful and watched in disbelief as the shoes, skirt, stockings and underclothes followed.

'Kitty, what are you doing?'

'Wossit look like, stupid? You don't expect me to get in the bath with me togs on, do you?'

In seconds, it seemed, she was naked. It was, he realised, his abiding image of Kitty – either naked or getting naked, red hair bobbing, eyes flashing.

'Shift up. I don't want a tap stuck up me jacksey, now do I?'

He'd no idea what she meant. That was another

reason he'd miss Walter – who else would translate the English for him?

Shift up or not, the bath was huge – she glided the length of it to settle on his chest, her hair just below his chin, an ear pressed to his heart, fingers lingering on the bruises at his midriff.

'They knock you about, did they?'

'Not much,' he said. 'Nothing I couldn't handle.'

The memory of nausea brought back the taste. He washed it away in whisky. Her hand drifted automatically to play with his cock. At least he assumed it was automatic – he could not see it as a gesture driven by either lust or affection, just the sheer familiarity of it. And he could not respond to it. She played with a limp dick.

'How's your mother taking it?'

The hand didn't stop. There was no magic to be invoked by words.

'Bad,' she said, twirling it like some toy she'd found. 'I don't know that she'll get through it. She rallied after Kev and Trev. All front, mind, but a good one. After this? I dunno. She ain't spoken for more'n a day. I really don't know. Vera's like a tank. Bristling with armour, angry as hell. The girls just cry all the time. And Tel's clueless, hasn't the faintest idea what to do or say. Tries jokes, but nobody laughs. He's shut up about the Navy though. He knows he'll never get away. He's there for ever now. I know how he feels.'

'And how do you feel?'

'How do I feel?'

'I've never lost a father – in fact I've never lost a relative that close. Both my parents are still alive. I have two younger sisters. My grandfather ticks over fairly well at damn near a hundred . . .'

'Grandma?'

'Ah . . . she died before I was born.'

She'd diverted him neatly. He wasn't about to give up.
'So. How do you feel?'

She prised herself up, out of the water, eye to eye, nipple to nipple – the touch of them on his chest brought him up in goosebumps – drew breath and spoke softly.

'There's a hole in my life I'll never be able to fill. All I ask is fill the hole in me.'

He knew it could not possibly be as crude a notion as her phrasing made it seem. All the same, he would never understand it. Sex – that which had been her ravenous hunger had become her consolation, and he could not tell the two apart, could not grasp the shifts of mind that drove her from pillar to post and called both sex.

'Just fuck me.'

He had never heard her use this word before – but then she had never used it, not since first acquiring its meaning on the edge of adolescence twenty years before.

'Just fuck me and I'll kid myself everything's OK.'

§ 71

As ever in the moment of hysteresis he reached for his eyeglasses. Cock down, glasses up, all passion spent, blind as a bat.

He'd not made a good job of it. He'd come too easily, blown his stack like a liquored-up high-school kid. Kitty did not seem to mind. She was smiling at him as she came into focus.

'We'll get through this, won't we, Cal?'

One hand pulled lazily at a strand of his hair. It was more affectionate than any gesture he'd ever seen her make.

'We will?'

'Well – we got to. Ain't we? I mean we'll get through. We'll catch the bastard, won't we?'

It was an odd moment to pick, but perhaps now, for the first time, he could talk seriously to her.

'Now you mention it, there are things I can do – things I have to do.'

'Like what?'

'I have to talk to my people. I can't do a damn thing without I talk to them first.'

'I thought you said they didn't want to know.'

'They didn't. But they're still the bosses. So I tell them what happened and then, if they say so, I can probably tell Nailer.'

'Wot? Tell Nailer wot?'

The smile vanished, the other hand locked into his hair, held him like a wrestler. It hurt, but he didn't move.

'Kitty, I don't know who killed your father. But there've been other people – the enemy – looking for the man he and I were chasing. It all revolves around him. I can't name him without the say-so from my people, but if they do say so then my telling Nailer is the only chance he's got of catching the killer. Without our man he doesn't stand a chance. Without me he doesn't stand a chance.'

She thrust him aside, leapt from the bed, naked and trembling with the force of her own anger.

'Are you out of your bleedin' mind? Tell Nailer! Nailer doesn't want a result. All he cares about is the honour of the Met. And that's not the same thing by a long chalk. You tell Nailer anything, you might just as well piss into the wind. You don't want Nailer, you want a real copper, not one of those plodding berks.'

'You're the only real copper I know.'

'Not me, you fool. I'm just plod, I am. A plonk in a uniform. You want . . . you want someone like . . . like an old boyfriend of mine.'

'An old boyfriend?'

'Chap I used to know on the Murder Squad. Flash as they come, but a first-rate copper.'

'Aha.'

'Yeah. Bloke I used to . . . go out with.'

Her mood had changed utterly. She wasn't angry, it seemed, more cautious, almost coy.

'A bloke?' he echoed.

'Troy,' she said at last. 'You want Frederick Troy.'

'Kitty, come here.'

She sat down on the edge of the bed. He took her hands in his. She was calmer, but red in the face, still reeling from her own outburst.

'Kitty. It was Troy got me out of the slammer. He was the cop the Yard sent when I phoned in the news of your father's murder. He was the first to get there, the first to see Walter. Then Nailer came along and took over. At some point, he must have found out they had me and spoke up. If he hadn't I'd still be in the cells.'

The look on her face told him not that she did not believe him, but that she would rather not believe him.

'Little feller, black hair, black eyes, talks like a total joe ronce?'

Cal got up, searched through the pockets of his stinking, bloody jacket and fished out the bloodier handkerchief with its fancy, embroidered letter F.

'This feller.'

He held out the handkerchief. She rubbed the scarlet letter between finger and thumb, felt the crispness of dried blood.

'His blood? Your blood?'

'Walter's,' he said simply.

'So Troy knew my Dad was dead before I did?'

'Before anyone but me.'

She crumpled the handkerchief, flakes of brown blood wafting onto the sheets, and put it to her cheek. She wept and cried, 'The bastard. I'll kill 'im!'

Troy was flat on his back on the chaise longue. Kolankiewicz leaned over him, reeking of beer and black-pudding and tut-tutting him in three languages. Into Polish, into English and the odd word of Yiddish thrown in just for emphasis. He had cut away his shirt – a Jermyn Street tailor-made now fit only for dusters – cleaned the wound, though it bled still, and was swabbing it in the hope he could get it dry and closed enough for stitching.

'Does it hurt, smartyarse?'

'Of course it hurts.'

'Good. So it should – it is practically through to the rib, and a little pain will make you wary next time.'

Over Kolankiewicz's shoulder Troy saw the door open. Kitty Stilton entered, took her key from the latch and came up behind Kolankiewicz, hands sunk deep in her coat pockets. He did not care for the look on her face. White, tight and red about the eyes. It was too late in the day, he was in pain, he was bleeding. He did not need whatever bee it was that buzzed in Kitty's auburn bonnet.

Kolankiewicz did not even turn.

'If you are staying, angel from hell, then you must make yourself useful. Hold the edges of the wound while I stitch.'

Kitty did not bat an eyelid. She slipped between the two of them and gripped the wound between thumb and forefinger. It hurt all the more.

'Bastard,' she whispered.

'Aaagh,' said Troy, as Kolankiewicz sank in the needle. 'I thought you said you'd localise it?'

'I was lying,' said Kolankiewicz. 'Now, pretty woman, hold tight, because the bugger will squirm.'

Kitty gripped him as though she had pliers in her hands.

'I was hoping for a word,' she hissed.

'Well, I can hardly not listen, can I?' Troy hissed back.

She pinched him harder.

'In fact I was hoping to make you squirm.'

Troy squirmed.

'Why didn't you tell me?'

'Why didn't I tell you what?'

'Why didn't you tell me my dad was dead?'

'I thought the American would tell you.'

'He was in chokey. How the bleedin' 'ell could 'e?'

'I didn't know that. I only found out today.'

'Troy, you should have told me. You should have come round to Jubilee Street and told me and me mum yourself. Can't you see that? I shouldn't have found out from a routine visit by a gobshite like Nailer. You should have told me. After wot we been to each other you should have told me. No excuse. I don't care where you were, what you were doing, you should have told me.'

It seemed to Troy that the two of them had combined their efforts to torture him, that Kolankiewicz was punctuating Kitty's sentences with every puncture of his flesh. When she finished, he finished, knotted the thread and snapped it off.

'OK. We done. You got one more medal on your chest, copper.'

Troy looked down at the wound. It was a mess, a ragged line made to look like a zip fastener with its row of regular, coarse black stitches. With a gesture like a conjurer about to manifest a pigeon, Kitty produced a handkerchief from her pocket – one of his, with his initial in the corner, the one she had helped herself to just the other night – and wiped his blood off her fingers.

'What we've been to each other?' Troy said. 'Good God, Kitty, what do you think we've been to each other?'

'Vodka still under the sink?' Kolankiewicz asked.

Troy ignored him. He disappeared into the kitchen.

'Kitty, why are you here?'

Kitty sat down on the armchair, stuck her hands back in her pockets and stared at him. Troy swung his legs to the floor and realised he'd be foolish in the extreme to try and stand.

'Kitty, I'm very sorry your father's dead. But taking it out on me isn't going to bring him back.'

'I'm here because.'

This construction had always baffled him. Russian had nothing like this. The incomplete ending implying that he should know how the sentence ended – that it was a moral issue to know, and a moral dereliction to have to ask.

'What is it you think I can do for you?'

'You can help Calvin catch the bloke who killed my dad.'

Troy sank back. He should have guessed – it was typical of Kitty to want the moon.

'Jesus Christ.'

'You can do this, Troy. Calvin can't do a thing on his own. The Yard'll run circles round him. He'll wander round London like a dog at a fair.'

'What you mean is that I should go up against Nailer for you.'

'Nailer ain't gonna catch him, now is he?'

'Probably not.'

'And you don't have to go up against Nailer. You just have to sort of go round him.'

Troy said nothing. He hoped that if he said nothing for long enough Kitty might just give up and bugger off.

'There's no on else can do it,' she went on, undeterred. 'You owe me this, Troy. You do this for me. And if that don't mean nothin' to you, then do it for my mum.'

Troy sighed silently, began to work it out. He could not think that he owed Kitty anything, and her mum was not a viable instrument of emotional blackmail; she was simply a pleasant old woman in Stepney who'd invited the two of them to tea a couple of times last year, eyed him up and down as a potential husband and pronounced him 'too posh' as in 'too posh, stick to your own kind Kitty', but – he could backtrack, get Kolankiewicz to sign him off sick, make his apologies to Stan, take ten days while the wound healed, talk to this American, and if – what an if – he had a lead, follow it. He and the American might run circles round Nailer. It had that hint of satisfaction to it.

Kitty appeared over him, put a hand to his forehead.

'You're hot,' she said.

'I feel cold.'

She went upstairs, came back with a blanket and spread it over him.

'Tomorrow,' she said. 'I can send him round tomorrow.'

'You do that,' he said. 'Tonight's not a good idea. Tomorrow. Not too early. Not before noon. Not before four. I'll listen to his story. See what I can do.'

Kitty kissed him on the forehead, thought better of it and kissed him on the lips.

'Oh, and not a word about you-know-what.'

And she did not even ask what had happened to him.

When she'd gone Kolankiewicz emerged from the kitchen, clutching a vodka bottle and a glass.

'Good,' said Troy. 'I could do with a shot.'

'Tough titty. Is for me. The idea that alcohol is good for the sick is a myth. It opens the blood vessels and hence lowers the body temperature, and with the blood you just lost that would not be good idea.'

'But I feel hot.'

'And two minutes ago you felt cold. QED. Now, you want to know what I think?'

'Does it matter? You're going to tell me anyway.'

'I tell you what I tried to tell you this afternoon. If you going to stick nose into old Stinker's death you should hear me out.'

'I think I'm what you'd call a captive audience.'

'You going to help the luscious Kitty, am I right?'

'I don't seem to have a choice.'

'To find her father's killer?'

Troy tried to shrug. It hurt too much so he said nothing.

'Okey dokey. You will appreciate, death is my business. I see death every day.'

'I'm not unfamiliar with the grim reaper myself. So could we get past the egg-sucking stage?'

'When do you think I last saw two such deaths as these?'

'Such deaths as what?'

'The Dutchman, and then old Stinker.'

Troy craned his neck to get a better look at Kolankiewicz. It hurt too, but this was getting complicated. The look on Kolankiewicz's face might just help.

'Go on.'

'Never in my years in the death business have I had two deaths quite so close together which you, in the force, are keen to ascribe to professional murder – let us say assassination.'

'I'm really not following you. It may be blood loss, but you've lost me.'

'Do you really think there are two such men on the loose? Two such assassins, even in wartime?'

'I haven't thought about it at all yet. But since you ask – what makes you think Walter was the victim of a professional hit?'

'You heard Bob Churchill – a professional's weapon, he said.'

'A professional's weapon but not necessarily a professional. As I recall, he made no comment on that possibility.'

'I say again, Troy, do you really think there are two killers?'

'I don't know. But someone got the drop on the Dutchman. Sneaked up behind him and snapped his neck like a twig. Do you agree?'

'Absolutely.'

'No one got the drop on Walter. He was shot from the side. I'd even say he was turning to look at his attacker when the gun was fired. As though he was expecting someone. Whoever it was came up the alley was not the man he was expecting, but by the time he knew that it was too late. The man was within range and fired.'

'You sure? That's an awful lot of deduction.'

'I had five minutes to look at the body before Nailer stormed in. I could draw you a picture.'

'I never got to see old Stinker's body. But if you going to chase this wild dog, I think you should consider the possibilities.'

Troy did not need to hear any more. It had been explicit in everything he'd heard while the American was under arrest, in everything Peter Dixon had told him, that the American and Stilton had been pursuing a man Cormack could not or would not name. Was he still in pursuit, had he abandoned his mysterious man – a German? – to find Walter's killer? Or was he looking for two people now – whoever it was he was chasing and a murderer? Had it dawned on *him* that they might conceivably be one and the same person? Good God, what had Kitty let him in for? What had he let himself in for?

'Did you see the report?'

'No.'

'Totally different MOs, of course. A world of differ-ence between a hands-on killing and a shooting. Neither are for the squeamish, but I've always thought the former required nerves of steel and emotions scraped back to the bone. I could do with a look at Spilsbury's report. Just to be certain I'm not wrong and that the shooting wasn't to finish off a botched attempt. Can you nick me a copy?'

Kolankiewicz shrugged. 'Easy peasy,' he said. 'Now, can I give you a hand up the stairs?'

§ 73

'I've nothing to wear.'

'You sound just like my sisters every time we get ready for a dance up West.'

'No – I mean. My suit's a write-off.'

Cal held up the sad sack that had once been his fifty-shilling suit.

'Should have called laundry the minute you got in.'

'The minute I got in all I wanted was a bath. And then you got in.'

'Awright. Don't get shirty.'

'My shirt's ruined too!'

'Couldn't you go out in your uniform?'

'No, Kitty, that's the last thing I can do.'

Kitty picked up the phone and asked for Stepney 315.

'Vera. It's me. I need you to do something. (pause) No – I'm at Claridge's. (pause) No, I don't see that that matters a toss. I'm not calling for an argy-bargy. I need something and I need it now. (pause) Of course I know you're up to your ... (pause) Yes, I'll be back. (pause) Vera – for Christ's sake, will you just bloody listen! Calvin has to see the police about Dad. He's nothing to wear. (pause) No – don't ask, it'd take too long. Just do it. Get that plain blue suit of Kev's out of his wardrobe and bring it over. (pause) Well he's not going to need it now is he? (pause) A clean white shirt an' all. (pause) Then send Tel! I don't care as long as somebody does it!'

'I'll swing for that silly tart one of these days. I swear I will.'

She turned to him.

'Tel'll be over in about half an hour.'

Tel arrived, a cigarette stuck to his bottom lip, a new swagger in his walk. The assumed posture of instant adulthood. The man of the family. He handed the suit to Cal, leant against the tallboy and flicked ash vaguely in the direction of an ashtray.

'Wotcher sis.'

'Wot do you think you're playing at?'

Cal left them to it. Ducked into the bathroom and slipped on the suit. It was a far, far better cut than his old one. It could have been made for him. It had been made for Kevin Stilton. The label over the inside pocket was that of a Savile Row bespoke tailor. Kev and Trev had, literally, spent like sailors. He sat on the edge of the bath, slipped on his shoes and surveyed himself in the looking glass. The suit was perfection. The shoes were clean and buffed – Kitty had had the foresight to stick them outside the door before they turned in for the night. They'd come back gleaming. Gleaming but regulation US Army brown, and about as fitting for this suit as his last. Blue and brown, it would have to do.

When he emerged Tel was no longer smoking, and his left cheek bore the red imprint of Kitty's hand. The veneer of manhood wiped from his face, a spotty, gawky seventeen-year-old once more.

'You sure you know where you're going?' Kitty asked.

'Sure. Cab to that pub you and I met in, cross the road and down the alley.'

'I could come with you.'

'I'm better on my own.'

She kissed him softly.

'Good luck.'

Did he need luck? The prospect, the necessity of luck had not occurred to him.

The cab dropped him by the Salisbury in St Martin's Lane. There were, he thought, no two things more guaranteed to make you glad to be alive than the proximity of sudden death and the dazzling light of a sunny afternoon. He found his way down Goodwin's Court, an alleyway little wider than a path, to Troy's front door. He hesitated a moment, wondering what his first words to Troy might be, and then reached for the knocker – rat-tat-tat.

§ 74

Troy regretted that he had not accepted Kolankiewicz's offer of a helping hand up to his bedroom on the first floor.

'No thanks,' he had said. 'I think I'll just lie here for a while. Things to think about.'

Hours later he had awoken, stiff and sore, and mounted the stairs. Searing pain had shot through his side, he had sunk to his knees and felt one of Kolankiewicz's carefully sewn sutures burst apart. In the morning he awoke to blood on the sheets again. It looked to be about a cupful. So what, he had thought, he lost that much shaving every week. By late afternoon he had changed his shirt twice, slapped on every inch of Elastoplast he could find and staunched the bleeding. All the same he felt weak, and dearly wished he'd put the American off for another day. He was just fiddling hopelessly with the cufflinks on his third shirt when the rat-tat-tat came at the door.

'I guess it's time we introduced ourselves,' the American said. 'Calvin Cormack, Captain, United States Army.'

He stuck out his hand, a disarming smile upon his face that Troy could not but think was genuine. He did not know why it should surprise him – the openness, the friendliness of most Americans – but it always did.

'Frederick Troy,' said Troy. 'Detective Sergeant, Scotland Yard.'

His cuff flapped as he shook.

'You having a problem with that?'

Troy did not want to have to explain.

'Arm's a bit stiff,' he said simply – and before he could stop him Cormack reached out and deftly threaded the cufflink, like a father teaching a twelve-year-old boy how to wear his first grown-up clothes.

The yard was flooded in May's sunshine. Troy beckoned him inside, propped the door open to let some of the light bounce off the wall and into the sitting room. Cormack looked around with what seemed to Troy to be a mixture of bafflement and curiosity – he looked too big for the room, as though his hair would dust the paint from the ceiling, his feet catch every obstacle and those long, long legs never prove capable of bending themselves to sit in any of the chairs. Along with their openness and friendliness went their inordinate size. Cormack plonked himself down in the chair Kitty had sat in only last night, contracted to a human size, pushed his glasses that bit further up his nose and smiled nervously. Human once more, almost Troy-sized.

'Can I get you a cup of tea?' Troy asked inevitably.

'Sure.'

Troy stuck the kettle on. Its whistling would give him an excuse to get up and move when the talk lulled. He could not say why, but he had the feeling that this man and he would find little in common but their common cause and Kitty. And Kitty was you-know-what.

'Cute,' Cormack said as Troy sat down. 'Always loved these little houses.'

Troy found himself staring at Cormack, seeking the man Kitty had described to him: tall, six foot two or thereabouts, skinny, speccy, already losing his hair at the temples, full in the mouth, wide, fleshy lips – not the handsomest man alive . . . but comforting. An easy man to be with, a shy, gentle man, restrained, good-mannered and not particularly good between the sheets. An inexperienced lover.

'And don't you get so damn cocky. A bit of the other ain't everything, you know.'

Troy had said nothing. She said she felt safe with this man – enveloped, cared for, snuggled – all words she had used.

'But do you love him, Kitty?' he had asked.

'Wot's love got to do with it?'

'So you don't.'

'Did I say that? God, you're nosy when you want to be!'

Troy had said nothing, assumed the conversation was over. Then she said, 'But I could.' Then, 'Stop lookin' at me!' Then she threw something at him.

'Kitty seems to think we have a lot in common.'

Cormack was speaking to him. Troy was miles away. Recollecting in tranquillity.

'Eh?'

'I was saying, Kitty seems to think we have a lot in common.'

Kitty had talked about him? To the American? Told him what? That they shared the you-know-what?

'We do?'

'Fathers,' Cormack said simply, and Troy began to get the message.

'Ah, I see. You're the son of that chap who makes all the fuss about isolationism.'

'And you're the son of the guy who makes all the fuss, period.'

Troy had to smile at this. It was undeniable. His dad had dedicated his life to stirring up trouble.

'Yes, I suppose I am. But then, I am my father's son in so many senses. In fact I get on rather well with my father.'

'I don't,' Cormack said.

'Figures,' said Troy, and it was Cormack's turn to smile. 'Why don't you just tell me what you know?'

As Cormack told his tale, Troy found himself responding to it with a prism of feeling – to the end of the rainbow and all the way back again. He'd never understand the spooks if he lived to be a thousand. It seemed to require a degree of patriotism he could not imagine, a faith in one nation that defied intelligence. At the same time it was the biggest lie of all – all spooks were playing parts, all spooks were liars. Who, Troy wondered, did they see when they looked in the mirror?

Such dedication was a part of his father he did not understand. He would not level a simple charge of patriotism at his father – he would only reply with Johnson's tart words if he did – but throughout his father's long opposition to Stalinism he had seemed to retain an almost mystical faith – was that the word? – in the Russian people. Troy could not share that either. And as Cormack recounted the personal nature of the tragedy – the two Stilton boys blown to smithereens, old Walter himself cruelly murdered – it was impossible for his love of Kitty not to seep through. It popped every stitch and staple the man had put into controlling his feelings. Troy thought an age ago, before Christmas, so much younger then, that he too might have loved Kitty, but she had not given him the chance. Listening to the heartbreak in Cormack's voice was like listening to a version of himself he'd sloughed off like a snake shedding skin.

'What's Stahl like?' Troy asked.

Cormack reached for his wallet. Pulled out a piece of shiny paper, folded in quarters, and passed it to Troy.

'Walter had me do this. I talked, the artist drew. It's not a bad likeness.'

Troy found himself looking at the face of a mythical hero – the Wagnerian features that made up the elusive, nonsensical Aryan ideal.

'I meant as a person.'

Cormack seemed to have to mull this one over. Odd, thought Troy, it can hardly require a deal of thought.

'You know,' he said at last, 'Walter never asked me that. I worked side by side with Walter for more than two weeks, and he never asked me that.'

'He wouldn't, would he? Walter was in the Branch. He dealt in certainties and he dealt in facts. I'm in Murder. Facts don't kill people. People kill people.'

'I met him only a few times – but I read endless letters from him. And I do mean letters, not just reports. You could say it's a rash conclusion, reading too much between the lines, but whatever Wolfgang Stahl really was, he buried long ago. The man I knew was a man he invented. He chose the code name himself. Tin Man. Hollow. He wasn't kidding. I think Wolf was probably a talented, considerate man. The Tin Man lacked heart. It was as though he'd taken a Bowie knife to the inside of his skull and scraped his emotions back to the bone.'

Troy had not expected to hear his own words repeated back to him quite so soon, and quite so precisely, if at all. But this was his cue.

'Let me recap. The Tin Man killed the Dutchman.'

'Yes.'

'You killed the German.'

'Yes.'

'And do you think there's a third man at large? And that the Third Man killed Walter?'

'I know what you're saying. It doesn't make sense. It's . . . well, excessive. To mint a phrase, it's overkill. But who else?'

'Have you considered the possibility that the Tin Man killed Walter?'

Clearly he hadn't. The pain on his face was sharp as etching.

'No. No. I hadn't. Truth to tell, it doesn't bear thinking about. It's the saddest thought I ever had to think. Worlds have collapsed for less.'

'Captain – I'm not telling you the tooth fairy doesn't exist, I'm just reiterating what you told me. Stahl is trained in all this malarkey. As capable of breaking a man's neck as of shooting him at close range and vice versa.'

'I know. Believe me I know. It's just that in this scenario I seem to have taken on the role of the Cowardly Lion. I guess I'm shocked. Stahl and I were on the same side. Walter and I were on the same side. Stahl was my working life. Almost my *raison d'être*. And Walter Stilton was the kindest, sweetest man I ever met. Here . . .'

Cormack dug into his inside pocket and pulled out an envelope.

'See. Always the joker. Always a smile on his lips.'

Troy took in the letter at a single glance. The note that had become Walter's death warrant – and there at the end 'Wot larx'.

'He was always saying that. A grin as wide as the Chesapeake Bay when he said it. And I still don't know what it means.'

Troy did. It was the first thing that looked even remotely like a clue.

They had talked away the day. Supped his week's tea ration. It was still light, but it was close to nine in the evening. Troy was flagging badly. He dearly wanted an early night.

'Forgive me if I don't show you out – arm's playing up a bit – but you'll have no difficulty finding a cab in the Lane.'

'I was thinking of taking the subway. I've never actually been on it.'

'Underground,' said Troy. 'Tube at a pinch, not subway. Turn right at the end of the court and head up to Tottenham Court Road. Perfectly straightforward. Central Line. Two stops to Bond Street and you're home. Be warned, it'll be filling up already.'

'Filling up?'

'Shelterers. They tend to bag their places early. Nobody waits for it to get dark anymore.'

'But there hasn't been a raid in weeks. Not since early May.'

'I doubt that Londoners think a few weeks' respite means it's over.'

§ 75

Cal had always had a little difficulty with right and left. It seemed to go with eyeglasses and a generally poor co-ordination. The only two physical skills he had ever mastered were the bicycle and sexual intercourse, and he wasn't too confident about either of those. Emerging from Goodwin's Court, he turned left, and walked off in the direction of Trafalgar Square. Missing the subway sign he walked on – past Charing Cross railway station and down to within sight of the river. He realised he was lost. Surely Troy would have mentioned crossing the river? But – there was another subway station. Its route map made no sense to him. Something from the Modernist school – a Mondrian or some such. A mass of coloured lines and precisely graded angles and countless interlocks, dozens of them, maybe even hundreds. He asked at the ticket booth.

'Bond Street, guv'nor? You want the Bakerloo. Change at Oxford Circus.'

Bakerloo. That was easy. It was what you got when you married Waterloo to Baker Street. But he could have sworn Troy said Central – and he certainly hadn't mentioned any changes.

The depth was startling. Washington had no subway. New York's ran in trenches just below the surface, bolted to the Manhattan bedrock. This system required two escalators to take you down to an oppressively narrow tunnel, from which the train emerged as closely fitted as a cork in a bottle. He took a northbound train, sat in a completely empty car – he'd never seen a padded cell, but this could well resemble one – and stared at the map above the long row of seats. The train pulled into Trafalgar Square. He'd just about got the hang of it now. He'd found Bond Street on the map, though he still wasn't wholly sure where he had gone wrong. A man got in – black hat, black suit – and sat opposite Cal, clutching a folded newspaper. Cal gave him the merest glance – the English were not inclined to impromptu chats with strangers – and went back to the map – still looking for the proof of his own error – how had he managed to miss a string of words as long as Tottenham, Court and Road?

The man took off his hat, Cal's eyes drawn back to him by the gesture. Bald at the forehead and crown. Black hair turning salt and pepper. A small black moustache, and pale, steely – he thought the cliché insisted – blue eyes. It was Stahl. Stahl with his hair carefully shaved and dyed. He would never have known him but for the intensity of the gaze. Aimed at him like gun barrels. He should have guessed. Of course he would have changed his appearance. The police sketch looked nothing like him – it looked like 'Peter Robinson'.

'Wolf?' he said tentatively.

'Calvin,' said an accented Mitteleuropean voice.

'I . . . I . . . don't know what to say.'

'Then perhaps you should listen instead. There is, after all, so much at stake.'

Cal started forward for no reason he could think of, got up from his seat half standing. Stahl waved him back down with the folded newspaper, like a gunsel sticking a gun out through the fabric of his coat pocket. At once both hammy and effective.

'You're not carrying a gun, are you, Calvin?'

Cal sat back in the seat, felt his bottom bump against it sharply.

'No,' he said. 'No, I'm not. I'm kind of off guns at the moment. Do you really need a gun? You didn't seem to need one when you killed Smulders.'

'Was that his name? No – a gun would have brought heaven and hell down about my ears. However, as you will observe, we are a hundred feet under London and quite alone.'

'You surely don't think you have anything to fear from me?'

'No. Of course not. Just your willingness to panic.'

'Then why didn't you just come in?'

'Who was I to trust? I had been safe in Berlin until someone gave me away. Someone on our side. That's a very limited number of people.'

'You mean you thought it was me?'

'I didn't know who it was, hence I suspected everyone and trusted no one.'

'What changed your mind?'

'Stilton.'

'Walter? You met Walter?'

'Stilton was beyond suspicion. He knew so little, after all. An honest copper, as the English are so fond of deluding themselves. Stilton convinced me you were innocent. *An* innocent, to be precise. "The lad's guileless, could no more fib than George Washington and the cherry tree." Said you couldn't even keep your affair with his daughter a secret. Lies showed in your face like etching in glass.'

Cal felt he must be blushing deeper than bortsch. Was this what Walter really thought of him? Had Walter known everything?

'Walter knew about me and Kitty?'

'Calvin – *I* knew about you and Kitty. I watched her park her motorbike in Brook Street night after night. I should think the whole of Claridge's staff knew about you and Kitty.'

'You were watching me? All this time?'

'Yes.'

'And you met with Stilton?'

'The night before he died. And the morning of the same day.'

'How do you know he's dead?'

'I was there. Stilton wanted you and I to meet. I asked for somewhere outdoors with more than one way in and out. He chose Coburn Place. All three of us would have met there if everything had gone well. I got there first. I stood in the cellar of the pub next door. I was in total darkness, but I could see anyone who passed through the drayman's hatch. I saw Stilton go by. A minute or so later a second set of feet passed by. I was about to step out, when I heard the unmistakable sound of a low-velocity bullet. A fraction louder than a silencer, nothing more than a pop, but enough to know it for what it was.

Then the second man came back down the alley. I waited a couple of minutes, then I left. It was obvious Stilton had been killed. I didn't need to see the body to know that.'

'Couldn't you have stopped it? I mean . . .'

'I didn't have a gun, Calvin. My only defence was to be closest to the exit. I bought this the day after.'

Stahl lifted the newspaper, to show a small revolver pointing down his leg, aimed at Cal's groin.

'But you did see the man who killed Walter?'

The train slithered into a station, the doors slid open. The soft hubbub of a thousand shelterers already preparing for a night's sleep along the platforms. The whistle of a kettle on a primus stove. A smell like boiling collard greens.

'Up to the knees, yes. I didn't see his face.'

'Oh hell.'

'And,' Stahl went on, 'he had better taste than you, but his shoes no more matched the suit than yours do.'

Cal looked down at his shoes. Regulation army brown roundies. With the blue suit Tel Stilton had brought him from his brother's wardrobe. Brown shoes, blue suit. Good God, what was Stahl saying? He looked up.

'What now?'

But Stahl had gone.

Cal leapt through the door, snagged his jacket as the door hissed to on him, jerked it free and tried vainly to run after Stahl. He tripped almost at once over a man sprawled full length across the platform.

''Ere. 'Old yer 'orses!'

He stumbled on. A human quagmire of arms and legs. He felt as though he had fallen into the grip of a giant octopus.

'Wot's a bloke gotta do to get a decent night's kip 'round 'ere?'

''Oo the bleedin' 'ell d'you fink you are?'

Someone reached up to thump Cal on the thigh and nearly brought him down. Someone else stamped hard on his toes. He fought his way to the exit, heard the predictable cry of 'Don't you know there's a war on?' following him, and way ahead saw Stahl striding up the escalator. He'd never catch him now. The blow to his leg had all but numbed the nerves. He was dragging it after him as though it were made of wood.

'Stahl!!!!'

Stahl stopped at the top. The staircase moving up beneath his feet, into an infinity of moire patterns that made Cal's eyes swim.

'Stahl! The shoes! What colour were the shoes?'

Cal heard his voice echo up the shaft, like shouting at God in the vault of some bizarre cathedral. But this wasn't God, this was the Devil tempting Cal to think what he would not think. And instead of placing him on a pillar in the wilderness he had left him in the pit of darkness.

Stahl stood a second or two, looking down at Cal. Cal dragged himself onto the escalator.

'Brown,' Stahl answered, turned on his heel and vanished.

§ 76

He had drifted beyond his station – he was at Baker Street. At least a name he knew, but when he emerged at street level, to a darkening sky, it was not a part of Baker Street he recognised. He flagged a cab. The romance had suddenly gone out of tube travel. Where was Sherlock Holmes when you needed him?

When he got back to Claridge's Kitty was sitting in the dark, curtains open, a summer breeze gently blowing. It seemed to him that she might have sat and waited in that position all day. Silently focused on him. Oblivious to all else. A poker face if ever he saw one.

'Did it go all right?'

Cal did not know what to say to her. It was Troy he needed to talk to, and he did not know how to talk to Troy with Kitty present. He could not calmly discuss her father's murderer with Troy whilst she was sitting there.

'I guess so. I have to call Troy. Do you know his number?'

She picked up the phone, asked for a number and handed the receiver to Cal.

'Troy – it's me, Calvin Cormack.'

'So soon,' said Troy.

'What?'

'Never mind. I'm listening.'

'I've just seen Stahl. He was waiting for me when I left your house. Cornered me on the subway.'

'He was watching?'

'Ever since I got here, it seems. He was . . . in Islington.'

Cal dearly wanted not to have to state the obvious. Let the place-name be enough for Troy and too little for Kitty. Kitty was watching him across the room, expressionless. Cal turned his back on her. Troy let him off the hook.

'You mean he was there when Walter died?'

'Yes.'

'And he says he didn't do it?'

'He says he saw. . . .'

Again Cal searched for a word best chosen not to cause alarm.

'He saw . . .'

'The perpetrator,' said Troy – a bland, unemotive police term – 'He saw the perpetrator?'

'Yes.'

'And he can identify him?'

'No. But he gave us a lead. An American soldier out of uniform.'

'How on earth does he know that?'

'The shoes. Regulation US Army brown roundies. Just like the ones I wear.'

There was a prolonged silence. Cal could hear his own breathing, coming back to him through the earpiece above the crackles and static hiccups of the connection. Kitty walked around him, came back into view still staring at him out of no particular expression, nothing he could read. Then Troy said, 'Let me talk to Kitty.'

Cal was startled. Troy was deducing far too much.

'She's there isn't she?'

'Well . . . yes.'

Cal handed the phone to Kitty.

'He wants to talk to you.'

'Wot?' she said flatly, paring any feeling from her voice.

'Was your father a Dickens reader?' Troy asked.

'Eh?'

'Did he read the novels of Charles Dickens? To be precise, do you know if he'd ever read *Great Expectations*?'

'Only every summer holiday. Two weeks at Walton-on-the-Naze. He'd fish off the end of the pier all morning and sit on the beach all afternoon with Pip and Joe Gargery. When I was a nipper he read it out loud to us at bedtime. Read it to all of us. One after another. Same battered book, reeked of fish. I still think of Pip whenever I smell cod.'

'Wot larx, eh?'

'Yeah. Wot larx.'

'Tell Calvin I'll be round in the morning, first thing.'

Kitty put the receiver back in its cradle, weeping silently – the dam burst – great, bulbous salt-tears coursing across her cheeks. Cal put his arms around her.

Almost happier now that she proffered recognisable feeling to which he could react.

'What's wrong?'

'Wot larx,' she said, and wept the more. Cal still didn't know what it meant.

She wept an age. His shirt was soaked. He lifted her head by the tip of her chin and said, 'I love you, Kitty.'

She said, 'Yeah. Great, init?'

§ 77

Troy was having a very early breakfast when someone knocked on his door. At first he didn't recognise the young woman clutching a large brown paper envelope. She thrust it into his hand, and then he knew. That new girl out at Hendon who worked for the Polish Beast. Anna something or other. She declined his offer of a cup of coffee, told him Kolankiewicz wanted it back and dashed. Troy had never thought of himself as a charmer. If he had, this might have punctured his ego. Pity, she was a looker.

He read the report over his second cup. It told him nothing he did not know and confirmed his rash assertion to Kolankiewicz that there were two distinct *modi operandi* for the deaths of Smulders and Stilton. There was precedent in Kolankiewicz's argument, and logic, but everything about this case told him to look for two killers, not one. There was definitely a third man.

When he got to Claridge's he found Cormack alone. The bed had already been made up. He'd no idea whether Kitty had spent the night there. He didn't much care – what he didn't want was to have to talk to both of them at once. If he was to do this, he never wanted to find himself in the same room as Kitty and Cormack.

Cormack said, 'Do you still have that sketch I gave you?'

Troy took it out of his pocket. Cormack took a pencil and drew on it. Shaded the hair and sketched in a moustache.

'He looks more like this now. Walter and I would never have found him with what we had.'

'Older?' said Troy.

'Yep. Makes him look fortyish. All this time we were chasing a younger man with blond hair.'

'The German you shot?' said Troy.

'Yep.'

'My turn,' Troy said. He took Stilton's letter from his pocket. 'Take a good look.'

Cormack glanced at it. 'I know what it says. I know it by heart.'

'Wot larx,' said Troy.

'I know. You're going to have to explain it to me. You know what Walter meant by it, and so does Kitty. Only I didn't feel I could ask Kitty, the state she was in. I feel like I'm on the outside of an in-joke.'

'Not quite. It's the catch phrase of a minor character in Walter's favourite novel.'

'Oh – I get it, this *Great Expectations* you were asking Kitty about. I never got past *David Copperfield* myself.'

'It's what a simple, good man by the name of Joe Gargery seems to say at every opportunity, to his innocent, ambitious apprentice, Pip.'

'Innocent apprentice. That's me in this equation, eh?'

'If you like. But the clue is in two parts. Walter says "Hope this reaches you one way or another."'

'Walter left me clues?'

'Not in the sense you mean, no. I mean simply that his choice of words reflects the way his mind was working. There's nothing idle or throwaway about the phrasing he used. "One way or another" – it simply means he left you more than one note. He left one here and one at the embassy.'

'How can you be so sure? Or is this where I tell you I think English policemen are wonderful?'

'Deduction. And a little inside knowledge. There is another character in *Great Expectations* called Wemmick. He's a solicitor's clerk, he's the man who knows everything and fixes everything. He moves through the book almost like a secret agent. One of the most curious characters Dickens ever created, and that's saying something. At one point in the book, when Pip is in danger, Wemmick leaves the same note at all four entrances to Barnard's Inn. And when he knows Pip has received one he goes round and collects the rest. I think Walter was having difficulty finding you. I think he left a note at both places you were likely to be.'

'I was in the embassy at five p.m. There was no note.'

'Then he left it later. In the meantime someone, the same someone Stahl saw, was able to read it and realised what it meant.'

'Jesus, Troy. That's a hell of a lot from two lines.'

'If I'm right, the note will still be there. After all, Walter never went back for it.'

'Why? Why wouldn't the killer just destroy it?'

'Because he doesn't know what's in the note you have. You might be expecting to find the copy. And if you didn't it might give you a lead. After all, it's easy enough to read it and put it back unmarked.'

'It is?'

'Calvin – you're a spy. How do you open letters?'

'With a paperknife.'

Cal left Troy sitting in his car in Grosvenor Square while he went into the embassy. Ten minutes later he came back, sat in the passenger seat and handed Troy an envelope addressed to Captain Cormack.

'Where was it?'

'Would you believe I have an in-tray?'

'What did your colleagues have to say to you?'

'Nothing. The place was almost deserted. If I'd run into Major Shaeffer, well, things might have been said. He's the guy who dumped me into the tender care of Chief Inspector Nailer. I'd have a bone worth picking with him.'

Troy held the envelope up to the windscreen.

'Well – it hasn't been steamed.'

He examined the edges, sniffed the paper, then he tore it open and let the letter sit on the palm of his hand. It looked to Cal like a comic-book impression of a private eye. More Hercule Poirot than Nick Charles.

'Observe the way it curls.'

'That mean something?'

'Yes – whoever our man is, he extracted the letter without breaking the seal by inserting two small knitting needles into the top seam and rolling the letter around them until it was small enough to pass through the gap at the top where the gum has failed. When he'd read it he put it back the same way. It's as old a trick as they come. I'm surprised you didn't learn it in spy school. Alas for you spooks, the tension thus exerted remains in the paper rather as it would in a watch spring. Hence it curls. Would you care to read it?'

Cal read it. It was exactly the same as the other one.

'Does this really get us anywhere?' he asked.

'Yes – of course it does. For one thing, it backs up

what Stahl said. We've moved from odds-on that it was someone from the embassy to it being a dead cert, wouldn't you say?'

'I guess I would. But – what now?'

'Now, a short list of probable suspects would help.'

'Why not start with Shaeffer?'

'Why not start without obvious prejudice? How many people work in that section of the embassy?'

'A lot. Twenty, maybe thirty. A lot more than did before the war. I don't even know some of their names.'

They sat an hour or more. Hardly anyone entered the embassy.

Cal said, 'I hate to slow us down, but we'd have better luck if we came back and sat here from six until seven. Catch 'em as they leave.'

§ 79

Cormack had run off so many names. Troy was writing them down and trying to find a mnemonic in two or three words that would fix a face in his mind. It struck him that the United States of America might have a little difficulty entering into a European war. It was too partisan a notion. Cormack had so far pointed out Lieutenant D'Amici – Troy had written down, short and ugly – Lieutenant Corsaro – short and handsome – Major Shaeffer – tall and broad, a bit like Johnny Weissmuller in *Tarzan* – two Sergeants Schulz – both as stout as Eugene Pallette – a Corporal Pulaski and a Captain Pulaski – they could have been twins – a Colonel Reininger – tall and thin, a bit Raymond Massey – a Captain Berg – utterly nondescript, his own mother couldn't pick him out in a line-up, Troy thought – a Sergeant O'Connor and a Corporal Schickelgruber.

'You're kidding?' said Troy.

'Nope. Used to work with me in Zurich up to the new year. Absolutely won't consider changing his name. Born Adolf Schickelgruber, he says, and he'll die Adolf Schickelgruber.'

'Adolf? His parents christened him Adolf?'

'He's in his twenties. Probably born in the last war. The only person who'd heard of the other Corporal Adolf Schickelgruber then was the paymaster in the Austrian infantry.'

'Couldn't you promote him? Anything but a corporal.'

'Sure. If we live through this I'll see to it personally. Hold on, here come another two.'

Troy peered out. A tall soldier and a short soldier were approaching, side by side. The tall one looked up at the sky and said something Troy could not hear or read. He'd bet they'd picked up the English habit of filling silence by talking inanely about the weather.

Cormack said, 'Don't know the tall guy, but I hate to tell you who the little one is.'

'Let me guess, Corporal Mussolini?'

'Close – that's Joe Buonaparté. He accents the "e" and never fails to tell you there's a "u" in his name. You've played this before, haven't you?'

'I'm grateful for the education into the great American melting pot, but I rather think this is getting us nowhere,' said Troy. 'There's simply too many of them.'

'I don't see what else we can do.'

'I can,' said Troy. 'We can set a trap for our chap.'

'Trap? What sort of a trap?'

§ 80

Troy stood outside a large block of working-class flats – the East London Dwelling Company's Cressy Houses in Union Place, E1 – a few yards from Stepney Green, a few more from the Stiltons' house in Jubilee Street, a mile or so from Leman Street police station, where he had served as a uniformed constable before the war, and home to his old station sergeant, the recently widowed George Bonham. Troy climbed to the second floor and rapped at the door. Bonham towered over him, a duster in his hand, a floral pinny on his chest, a look of surprise on his face mingled with the unremitting sorrow which seemed to Troy to have been his lot since the Blitz and the death of his wife Ethel.

'Freddie, long time no wotsit. Come in, come in, what brings you to this neck of the woods?'

Troy followed him to the sitting room, a box no more than ten feet by eight – the warm heart of a tiny flat in which George and Ethel had raised three sons. George had the china cabinet open. His wife's collection of Crown Derby set out on the dining table.

'I was just giving 'em a bit of a going over. Didn't like to see 'em gathering dust.'

Troy was sure they never gathered dust. This room was kept as a shrine to Ethel Bonham. In the six months since her death, George had changed not a thing. Troy would bet money that her clothes still hung in the mahogany-veneer wardrobe in the end bedroom, and that George still slept on one side of the bed only with two pillows side by side upon the bolster.

'It's almost six. Will you stay and eat?'

It was too early to eat – besides, Bonham was a dreadful cook. No man of his generation, and few of Troy's, were in the slightest way capable of looking after themselves. Widowers were uncommon creatures, floundering through the latter life like beached sea monsters.

'I'm afraid I can't, George. It's business. In fact I need your advice.'

Troy knew how flattered George could be by a simple lie, the slightness of exaggeration.

'O' course, Freddie. But I'll put the kettle on all the same.'

Once the magic word 'kettle' had been uttered it was pointless trying to stop him. Tea was the universal salve – birth, marriage, death and all stations in between. Troy wondered how long Bonham's tea ration lasted him. He made tea for two, black and sweet and of the consistency of molasses. You'd need a torch to see through it even before you put the milk in.

'Well then, ask away. It's not often you come to your old boss for a bit of advice.'

'George, this has to be a secret. I'm investigating the death of Walter Stilton.'

'Nuff said,' said Bonham, nodding, tapping the side of his nose. Troy knew now that wild horses, let alone Scotland Yard, would not get him to talk. 'He was a good 'un, was Walter. A prince. And poor old Edna, left alone with all them kiddies. I've known Edna since I was a tot, y'know. Redmans Road Board School, 1894. Anything I can do for Walter, just name it.'

'I need a private place.'

Bonham looked blankly at him.

'Somewhere where we won't be overheard or interrupted. Somewhere quiet.'

Bonham's expression did not change.

'Somewhere I can bend the law a little without old plod lumbering in.'

'I see,' said Bonham.

Troy wondered if he did.

'You used to walk Tallow Dock down on the Isle of Dogs when you was on the beat, didn't you? Well it got blown to buggery by the Luftwaffe just before Christmas. Hardly a house left with a roof on. Most of the warehouses are deserted now. You could set off a bomb down there and no one would hear.'

Bonham paused as the word 'bomb', and the frequency with which they did go off these days, sank in.

'There's only one intact building left. Still got its roof – it was in use till last week. Might suit.'

'Could I see it?'

'Now?'

'Car's outside.'

Bonham stood. Troy tried and found a sharp pain shooting through his chest where Kolankiewicz had stitched him up.

'Wossup?'

Troy prised himself off the chair by its arms, breathless and flushed.

'Been in the wars, have you?'

'Something like that.'

'One day, Freddie, they'll have to bury you in bits.'

Bonham swapped his pinafore for his police blue tunic and took his pointy hat off the sideboard where it sat like a horned tortoise. Driving down to Tallow Dock, he sat with his knees up to his chin, bent double in the little car, the hat clutched on his lap more like the world's biggest cricket box.

Troy found himself staring. All the way across Stepney and down into Limehouse. The devastation was not unimaginable, but it was on a scale he had not bothered to imagine. He looked out at mountains of rubble – the detritus of lives lived and homes abandoned. Bonham looked at him.

'You been up West too long.'

'Eh?'

'If this has come as a shock, then it's 'cos you don't get down here enough. When was you last here? Ethel's funeral?'

That had been over five months ago.

'No – I've seen you since then . . . surely . . . ?'

Bonham wasn't helping.

'I was here in February. I'm sure it was February.' The making of an argument was curtailed as the Bullnose Morris reached the junction of Tallow Dock Lane and Westferry Road.

They turned right towards the river and pulled up about six hundred yards further on, within sight of the Thames and outside a vast warehouse. The company name was stencilled in white down the side of the building in letters ten feet tall – 'BELL AND HARROP. IMPORT EXPORT. EST. 1837. LONDON, SHANGHAI, HONG KONG.'

They stepped out onto shards of broken slate and glass. The only sign of life a roaming, skinny, mongrel dog. Bonham slipped on his helmet and tucked the strap into the dimple of his chin. It was a moment that never failed to strike awe into Troy. A man of five foot six, too short to be a copper except by a waiving of the rules, confronted by a man nearly seven foot tall from his boots to the little silver knob on top of his pointy hat. It was one of the reasons Troy had been so glad to become a detective in plain clothes. Bonham looked like a giant, a Greek warrior, Achilles or Agamemnon; Troy had looked like a gnome who'd lost his fishing rod.

'Are we going in?'

'Sorry, George. I was miles away.'

Bonham led off. Prised a door open with his giant's paw, swung it back on its hinges with a mighty, metallic clang. Troy looked around. Once the echo of the clang had dwindled away, and the dog bolted, nothing stirred – and the only sound he could hear was the occasional hooting of ships on the Thames. George might be right. This could be just what he needed.

Inside, the ground floor was open to the second, a ceiling twenty feet high had mostly collapsed.

'It's the top floor I was thinking of,' said Bonham. 'Used to be old Georgie Bell's office. We finally talked him into leaving a few days back. Or is that not what you want?'

'No, that sounds fine. As long as there's another way out.' Bonham and Troy wound their way up the stone staircase to emerge right under the roof. A suite of low office rooms. A huge glass skylight, its coat of blackout paint peeling off in strips. A battered steel desk with a dip pen and inkwell, looking as though their owner had just stepped out for lunch. A forgotten Burberry on the back of the door.

'I don't want to be surprised,' Troy said.

Bonham looked puzzled.

'Is there another way in and out?'

Bonham yanked off one of the blackout screens, slid up a sash window and pointed down the fire escape.

'Goes all the way down to the first floor. After that you'd have to jump into the alley. But I reckon nobody could get up that way. O' course you'll have to be careful of the light if there's a raid on – but don't worry about wardens, they've given up on Tallow Dock.'

'You mean there's electricity?'

Bonham flicked the light switch on and off to show him. It was a bonus. Troy had been dreading having to catch a murderer by the dim glow of a bull's-eye torch.

'They haven't got round to cutting it off yet. They will though.'

This looked right. In fact it looked ideal. Troy would never have chosen Coburn Place for a stake-out. He would have chosen a place like this. Indoors, with a quick escape route if it all went wrong. And, above all, no witnesses.

'I think this will do the trick, George,' he said.

'What exactly is the trick, then, Fred?'

'It's less of a trick and more of a trap.'

'I see,' said Bonham, not seeing. 'A trap, who for?'

'Wish I knew,' said Troy. 'Wish I knew.'

Troy and Cormack sat facing each other in his sitting room at Goodwin's Court. Cormack had brought a bottle of bourbon – not a drink Troy was accustomed to. Sweet, heady stuff. He knew what his dad would say, that it was a cheek to call it whisky – but Troy was rather taken with it. After three large glasses it eased the pain in his ribs. He began to feel a bit less like a puppet held together by Kolankiewicz's staples.

After three large glasses Cormack managed to utter, 'Kitty, I've been meaning to ask you about Kitty . . .'

And Troy said, 'Later. We've got work to do.'

Cormack rallied, stuck his elbows on his knees and tried to look a bit less as though booze had just dumped him down in the armchair.

'You cracked it?'

'I think so. We're going to set a trap.'

'That's what you told me yesterday. So what's new?'

'We re-run the same plan that Walter did. I'm going to send you a note asking you to meet me at such and such a time and such and such a place, and you're going to let it sit in your in-tray at the embassy till somebody reads it.'

Cormack exhaled, a breathy explosion somewhere between a guffaw and complete incredulity.

'You actually think that'll work?'

'We know whoever it is reads your mail, right?'

'Sure. But the same scam twice – he'll never fall for it.'

'Which is why the trap needs very tasty bait. I'm going to say that I've found Stahl. And that this is the only way Stahl will meet you.'

'You're assuming that Stahl is of interest to our man.'

'If he isn't then we're lost. But equally, I can see no other reason why our man would ever have wanted

Walter Stilton dead. And I'm damn sure Walter died because whoever read his letter deduced that Walter was close to finding Stahl. Much as Walter avoided stating it.'

Cormack thought about this. Just mentioning Walter's name seemed to bring tears to his eyes.

'He had found Stahl. I just didn't know that. He went off on his own and said he'd keep me posted and didn't.'

'We won't make that mistake.'

Troy had tried to make a glib phrase sound as reassuring as he could, but for half a minute he did not know whether Cormack was going to agree to the scheme or not.

'Where is such and such a place and when is such and such a time?'

'I thought tomorrow night. Say around eleven p.m. And I chose a place on the Isle of Dogs –'

'We have to go on a boat?'

'Let me finish – not that kind of island – it's a promontory that sticks out into the Thames opposite Greenwich. It's where most of London's docks are. I've got us a warehouse, or what's left of one, in Tallow Dock. There's only one way in but two ways out. It couldn't be better. You turn up at the agreed time, but meanwhile I've got there half an hour earlier. We'll be ready for him.'

'Just a minute. Why can't I be the one to get there early?'

'Because "our man" knows what you look like. He'd be much more likely to follow you than to follow me. In fact, I'm acting on the assumption that he'll work out for himself that killing Walter is unlikely to have made you give up – but also that he hasn't a clue about me. There'd just have to be somebody like me – logically – some other copper doing what Walter did. I'm playing up to his expectations.'

'So – what you're telling me is that you'll be going in there on your own?'

'Initially, yes.'

'Then you'll need this.'

Cormack reached into his jacket pocket, pulled out a handgun and slid it across the table to him. Troy just looked at it. Did not touch it. It wasn't the same make as Cormack's. It was an automatic, but it was bigger, a .38 at least. Cormack clutched his own gun in his right hand.

'You'll need to know how to speed load. Your life could depend on it. Our man will be armed. Goes without saying. He could have real stopping power. Standard issue is a .45.'

'No,' said Troy. 'He'll have a gun like yours.'

Cormack looked at him with incredulity.

'What? How can you know that?'

'Because Walter was shot with a .35.'

'Why didn't you tell me that?'

'It didn't seem important,' said Troy. 'And I didn't want you to feel your brush with Chief Inspector Nailer had been quite as close as it was.'

'Not many people use these, you know.'

'I do know, and I think the fact is rather in our favour.'

'Whatever. Just watch me.'

Cormack held a spare clip in his left hand. The flick of a switch and the old clip fell out, the new was banged in and he had racked a bullet into the chamber and levelled the gun.

'Less than two seconds. Try it.'

It had seemed to Troy like the handiwork of a magician. One second he was watching Cormack's face, the next he was staring down the barrel of a freshly loaded gun. The hand was truly quicker than the eye. Cormack was looking straight at him now, picking up on his incredulity.

'Or did you think that because I wore glasses and did a desk job I somehow wasn't a real soldier?'

'Not at all,' said Troy. 'I was thinking more about myself. Sorry, I'm not a gunman.'

'Picking up a gun doesn't make you a gunman.'

'Doesn't it? Then what am I, a pretend gunman? I don't live in your world of habitual pretence. I think I'd find pretence a dangerous illusion.'

'Troy, this could be ... no, goddammit, this *is* dangerous.'

'Sorry. Can't do it. Tell me I've been a London bobby too long, any cliché you like, but I can't do it.'

He slid the gun back across the table to Cormack.

'You mean you're going in there with just a cop's nightstick, that truncheon thing?'

'Only detectives of Walter's generation carry truncheons. I'll have a pair of handcuffs and you'll have a gun. That ought to be enough.'

§ 82

It was pissing it down. It had been a cold spring and threatened to be a capricious summer. Troy stood in the doorway at Goodwin's Court, hoping for a lull in the downpour. It didn't ease. It was not quite torrential, but it was still the sort of rain to slice through his overcoat in the time it took to get to the car. He looked at his watch. He was ahead of schedule. He'd give it five more minutes. It was almost possible to see it as romantic – the onset of a short night, dusk scarcely fallen, the beat of rain hammering down in the courtyard and rattling the windows. Where was WPS Stilton in the romance of rain that made the scalp tense, the skin tingle, and wrapped you in its rhythm? He looked at his watch again. It read exactly the same time. The sweep hand was

333

not moving. The damn thing had stopped. He reached for the phone and dialled the speaking clock and the clock-woman told him what he'd guessed. His watch had stopped twenty minutes ago. He wasn't ahead of schedule, he was late.

He dashed to Bedfordbury, yanked open the car door. Kitty was sitting in the driver's seat, buttoned up in her blue mac, hands in tight leather gloves gripping the wheel, her hair wet and flat and rain streaming down her face like tears. As if he had summoned her by thinking of her.

'Kitty . . .'

'Get in, Troy. Just get in.'

He ran to the passenger door, slammed it behind him, suddenly almost deafened by the pounding of rain on the tin roof.

'You're up to something. I know. He won't tell me what, but I know.'

'Kitty. If Calvin won't tell you, then neither can I. Please, get out and let me do what I have to do.'

She turned on him, voice soaring to outshout the rain.

'If you think I'm going to let him get blown away like me dad then think again. You're up to something and I'm in. Like it or lump it, I'm coming, Troy.'

Troy froze. Simply seeing those gorgon-green eyes fixed upon him was enough to make his wits shrivel.

'Well?' she said at last.

Troy said nothing. He lurched across her, grabbed the keys from the ignition, tore his coat from her grasping hands and ran. Down Bedfordbury to Chandos Place, out into Trafalgar Square in search of a cab. He stood in front of St Martin's church waving desperately at every cab in the hope that some dozy cabman had simply forgotten to put his light on. No one had. It was the perfect night to wave forlornly at the cabmen of olde London while getting soaked to the skin.

Then he watched as his own car crawled towards him, stopped at the kerb and Kitty leant over and pushed open the door.

'Get in! Get in, you silly sod!'

He sat next to her as wet as she was, hair plastered to his skull, rain puddling at his feet.

'How?' he said.

'Jesus H. Christ, Troy. Call yerself a copper and you don't know how to hotwire a car.'

He looked at the tangle of wires she'd pulled out behind the steering column. A trick he'd never learnt. But then he'd never learnt to lock his car either. Kitty slammed into first.

'Where we going?'

'Limehouse,' he conceded. 'Tallow Dock Lane.'

She drove a car as furiously as she drove a motorbike. Troy was all caution and cock-up. Not a natural driver. Kitty flung the little Morris around corners and pushed it to its limit on the straight – even so, its limit was less than sixty miles per hour. With every landmark passed Troy ticked off another five minutes on his mental clock. He dared not tell Kitty that they were screwing up in precisely the way Cormack and her father had screwed up, so he said nothing.

Less than a mile from the warehouse, in Westferry Road, the car juddered and jerked and lurched and stopped. Kitty pressed the self-starter. It grunted at her and refused. She pressed again – it grunted, whined and died.

'What's wrong?' said Troy.

'How should I know? There were so many wires back there. I just joined up the ones that looked right.'

'Kitty, we're already late. For God's sake make it go! Make it go!'

She bent down, the bundle of wires fell into her hand like a fat wodge of macaroni.

'Oh, bugger,' she said. 'Half a mo.'

There were no half mo's. Troy got out of the car and ran. He'd no idea how late he was. His 'half hour early' was most certainly blown. Could he possibly get there before Cormack – before the killer? He turned the corner into Tallow Dock Lane and felt his sides begin to burst. It was like those forced school runs he and Charlie had always hated, the onset of stitch, the stab in the side that made running agony. The great white BELL AND HARROP sign loomed up. The steel door was wide open. He leant against it, put his head tentatively inside – all he could hear was the pounding of his heart and the roar of his own breathing. At the foot of the staircase all he could hear was the wind and the rain whistling down the shaft, amplified as though by a tunnel. He set off up the stairs as quietly as he could, flicking his bull's-eye torch on and off as he went. A rat scurried across his path, slithered across the toecap of one shoe, and he felt his heart explode in his chest. Cormack was right. For the first time since he had gone into plain clothes, he missed his truncheon.

At the top he thought he could hear a faint moaning. Nothing else but the elements. The glare of overhead light bursting from the office into the black pit of the stairwell. He looked into the first room. The naked lightbulb swinging gently at the end of its cord like a hanged man twisting on the gibbet – a black-coated man was slumped against the far wall with blood congealing on his head. A revolver on the floor in front of him. One huge hand spread across the cracked linoleum as though performing a five-finger exercise. Troy bent down and lifted the man's head. The wound was just above the left ear. It looked like a gunshot, but it was superficial – the bullet had simply stripped the skin, scraped the bone and glanced off. Troy touched the face, smeared away the blood gathering in the left eyebrow with the ball of his thumb, felt and saw the scar above the eye. He looked like Wolfgang Stahl. The pianist's hands, the duellist's scar. Was he Wolfgang Stahl? He ought to be Wolfgang Stahl. It had better be Wolfgang Stahl – it would be so handy if he were. But what was he doing *here*? And who had shot him? More importantly, who was moaning if Stahl was not? And he heard the door swing to on unoiled hinges and turned to see another man, clutching a bloody wound to his stomach, easing himself off the wall behind the door.

Troy did what he thought any intelligent person should do when confronted by a man pointing a gun at him – he raised his hands. The man was struggling to find words. He'd lost a lot of blood – it ran between his fingers, soaked into his overcoat and dripped to the floor. He could scarcely point the gun steadily. A small .35 automatic wavered between Troy's chest and the wall. He ran through his list of handy mnemonics, watching the face dip in and out of light and shadow as the light bulb swung back and forth, wondering which one was this, which of all those bewildering American faces Cal had pointed out to him was this. Raymond Massey, it was Raymond Massey.

'Put down the gun, Colonel Reininger,' Troy said, putting his faith in the clichés of the job. 'It's all over.'

It was. Reininger coughed blood and collapsed. A bloody, silent mess in the corner. Troy slowly lowered his hands, wondering all the time if the gun were not suddenly going to jerk upwards in his hand and fire off one last shot. He took a few steps forward, kicked the gun from Reininger's hand and breathed again. But he could still hear the moaning. He pushed at the door to the inner office. Cormack sat roped to a metal chair, black canvas gaffer tape across his mouth. And he was not moaning – he was grunting with all the force he could muster until his eyes almost popped.

Troy tore off the gaffer tape, started on the ropes, and Cormack began to gabble.

'Troy – where the fuck have you been?'

And gabble.

'Half an hour? Jesus Christ!'

And gabble.

'Reininger was waiting for me when I got here. Stuck a gun in my ribs and then sapped me with the butt. I must have been out for a minute or two. When I came round he already had me trussed up like a turkey. He stood behind the door and waited, then I saw the door open and expected to see you walk in and get shot. It was Stahl! Jesus Christ it was Stahl! He didn't even have to look. He shot Frank through the door at point-blank range, but when he stepped past it there was more firing – then the draughts caught this door and I couldn't see any more. Tell me, for Chrissake tell me. Stahl's dead, isn't he?'

'No – he's out cold, but it's just a graze. Reininger's in a bad way, though.'

Troy undid the last knot. Cormack leapt to his feet and said again, 'Troy – where the fuck have you been?'

Troy watched his eyes roll up in his skull, his legs buckle and his head hit the floor. He knelt down. The draught caught the door again and banged it shut. Troy let Cormack's head loll against his hand – two bumps now instead of one – reassuringly warm, a pulse beating steadily, solidly in the neck. He'd fainted. The eyelids flickered, his lips opened, the merest of moans. Then the blast of a gun set the door shaking, swinging inward on its creaking hinges. Kitty stood framed in the doorway, head down, arm outstretched, a smoking revolver aimed steadily at the corner.

Troy crossed the room hoping she wasn't completely mad, that she knew who he was and would not simply turn the gun on him. She kept her gaze and her aim fixed. He looked at Reininger, lifeless in the corner, blood pouring down his face from the hole in his head. He looked at Kitty, blank and glassy-eyed.

'Kitty,' Troy said softly. 'Give me the gun.'

Kitty seemed not to hear him.

'Just give me the gun, Kitty.'

It was as though a light had gone on behind her eyes. A flash of attention. Suddenly she was looking at Troy, hearing him, the crazy stare gone from her face. She lowered the gun to her side.

'Nah. I don't think I'd better. You're not wearing gloves.'

In the distance, faint as a whisper, Troy could hear the bells of a police squad car.

'Give me the gun Kitty. We haven't got a lot of time. We'll need it to think up a story.'

'No,' she said. 'You go.'

'Go?'

'There'll be shit for this. You mark my words, Fred. They'll want someone. Heads'll have to roll for a cock-up like this. They'll suspend us, bust us back to constables. Might as well be me. I'll never be more than a sergeant. Never thought I would. You – you're a hot tip to be Met Commissioner one day. There's blokes at Bow Street running a book on you. Don't disappoint 'em. Nip down the alley while you can.'

She bent down. Pressed the gun into Stahl's hand. It all looked so neat, so plausible. The grieving daughter on the trail of her father's killer, arrives a moment too late to see rough justice done.

'Cal's all right, isn't he? I mean he's alive, isn't he?'

'He's in the next room. A nasty lump on his head, but, yes, he'll live.'

'Then you'd better scarper.'

The bells of the police car rang louder now – at the most they could be only two or three streets away. The nearest nick was Millwall – if they came from the south they'd miss his car completely. If he stuck to the alleyways, they'd miss him too. Troy threw open the window to the fire escape, took a last look at Kitty, Kitty smiling faintly at him, Kitty among the carnage of a bloody night, and vanished into the dark and pouring rain.

§ 83

'I'm awfully sorry, but I'm afraid I'm going to have to lock you up.' Cal relished the contrast. The first bobbies on the scene had burst in, truncheons up, yelling 'Nobody move!'

Kitty was binding up the wound on Stahl's head with strips she'd torn from her petticoat, like the solitary female in a John Ford western when the wagons have circled. She'd already licked her handkerchief and washed his face like a mother cat. Cal had never felt his wagons more circled.

'Nobody is moving, you berk,' she'd said. 'Get on yer wireless and call an ambulance.'

Then they'd noticed the bloody heap that had been Reininger.

One dashed back to the squad car. The other stood and said 'Jesus Christ' over and over again, until Kitty said, 'You don't know what to do, do you?'

The ambulance arrived only minutes before a second squad car. They were loading Stahl onto a stretcher when two more cops walked in, a man in his late thirties and a younger one, younger even than Troy, who ran to the stairs and vomited at the sight of Reininger. Over the sound of his retching, the older man said, 'Miss Stilton, isn't it? Inspector Henrey, Murder Squad' – and turning to Cal – 'And you are?'

Cal told him, made the briefest of explanations, then Henrey said, 'I'm awfully sorry, but I'm afraid I'm going to have to lock you up.'

§ 84

Cal told him a version of everything – everything except Troy's part in it all. They sat in an office at Scotland Yard until it was nearly light. When Henrey asked him how 'Miss Stilton', as he insisted on calling Kitty, came to be at 'the scene of the crime', he was able to give his first wholly honest answer, 'I don't know.' Eventually Henrey said 'Is there anyone at the embassy I should contact in connection with this?' Cal said 'I don't know' again, and then Henrey really did lock him up and he crashed like a felled redwood.

It was a different regime. In the morning they brought him a bowl of warm water, a razor and a cup of tea, then they brought him breakfast of toast with butter and that shredded orange jelly the English were so fond of and then, when he asked for coffee, they brought him coffee. Afterwards he lay on the cot all morning reading *The Times* and the *Manchester Guardian* – Scotland Yard could not run to a copy of the *Herald-Tribune*. The Luftwaffe had bombed Dublin last night. The first raid in weeks and they'd missed by miles. He was beginning to think he could spend the rest of his life in jail and let the war go to hell above his head, they could let him out in six or seven years – in the meantime he could finish *Moby Dick* – never had managed that feat as a teenager – when the door opened and another, completely different cop strode in, shook his hand, introduced himself as

341

Major Something-or-other 'of the Branch', and said, 'I contacted your man as soon as I heard.'

'My man?' said Cal. 'Who the heck is my man?'

'I am, old boy!'

And Reggie Ruthven-Greene stuck his head round the door.

§ 85

On the way out Cal caught sight of Kitty. He wanted to stop and talk to her. He wanted to stop and put his arms around her, but she was being escorted – steered – across the courtyard by two policemen.

Out on the Embankment Reggie had his hand up for a cab.

'Where are we going, Reggie?'

A cab pulled up.

'I rather thought after a night in jail that you'd fancy a spot of lunch.' Then he opened the door for Cal, leaned down to the cabman and said 'Dorchester'.

After a sodden night the day had cleared beautifully, the sun shone. It was, Cal realised, the 1st of June and the prospect of summer preoccupied Reggie's chat inanely all the way to Park Lane. There were questions Cal would have put to Reggie, but he knew he'd never answer them in the back of a cab.

'My treat,' Reggie said, as they were seated at the Dorchester. 'Do you know, one can still get Krug '20 here. Amazing, isn't it?'

Cal's heart sank. He'd known as soon as he heard the word Dorchester that Reggie meant to splash out – but champagne? It was dry sherry and smoked salmon among the ruins all over again.

'Are you ready?' Reggie asked over the top of the menu.

'Don't wait for me,' Cal said.

Reggie rattled off his order. 'I think . . . yes . . . the foie gras, the Dover sole, the roast pigeon and a nice garlicky salad . . . and a bottle of Krug '20.'

He looked at Cal. Cal looked at the waiter.

'Do you have any Brown Windsor soup?'

The waiter looked nonplussed. 'Brown Windsor, sir?'

'Yes, Brown Windsor. This is England. We are in a restaurant. We are in a restaurant in England. You must have Brown Windsor.'

'Would you give us a minute,' Reggie said to the waiter. To Cal, he said, 'There's something wrong?'

'There's everything wrong. There's a fucking war on.'

Reggie looked quickly around. 'If we're going to have a swearing contest, could you keep your voice down?'

'Reggie, if you don't stop talking about the weather, and ordering vintage champagne and goose liver and pretending there isn't a fucking war on, I'll run the entire gamut of obscenity. Tell me what the fuck is going on. So far, all you've done since I got to England is string me out with more tall tales and half-truths than Fibber McGee.'

Reggie did not look crestfallen or apologetic. He looked cornered. The waiter chose this moment to return.

'We've changed our minds,' Cal said to him. 'Brown Windsor for two, and we'll save the champagne for another time.' And to Reggie, 'Do I have your attention now?'

'It was meant as a treat for you. An apology, if you like.'

'An apology for dumping me?'

Reggie nodded.

'Jesus Christ, Reggie, you can't apologise enough for that. While you were gone four men died. Reggie, you can't buy me off by spending a week's wages for the average Londoner on an off-the-ration meal that makes me feel I'm cheating the English – that makes me feel any Englishman with money cheats his fellow English. For fuck's sake, Reggie, looking around this room, would you even know there's a war on? Do you think these people know what's in a Woolton pie? Have you ever had to eat Woolton pie?'

'Like humble pie, is it?'

'Yes – that's exactly what it's like. The self-imposed humility of the English as they tighten their belts and pull together. Now – why don't you tighten your conscience and tell me the truth? And the truth is that you dumped me on Walter Stilton when you got a crack at Hess. It was Hess, wasn't it? Don't answer. I know. Hess was a bigger fish than Stahl. Hess knows almost as much as Hitler. So you grilled Hess and got what you wanted and now you don't need Stahl. So here I am, four dead men later, being kissed off in a classy restaurant with a bottle of Krug '20. Reggie – fuck you.'

'No,' said Reggie.

'No? No what?'

'No, I didn't get what I wanted out of Hess. In fact, as you might put it, I got fuck all. That's why I'm back. We need Stahl. We really do need Stahl.'

The waiter brought two bowls of Brown Windsor. Cal was not partial to it, but he was damn certain Reggie hated it, and if the only way to ensure Reggie ate it was to eat it himself – and if they were going to work together again, destroying his taste buds was about the least penance Reggie could do – then so be it. He picked up his napkin and said, 'Tuck in, you sonovabitch.'

Reggie pulled a face as though he were sucking on a ripe lemon. When they'd both finished the course in silence, Cal summoned the waiter and told him his friend would have seconds. Cal let him get halfway through it and said, 'Stahl.'

'Quite,' said Reggie. 'Stahl.'

'Where've you got him?'

'"Got him" isn't quite the phrase. He's not a POW. He's in a private room at the Queen Alexandra Military Hospital on Millbank. In fact, he's got rather a nice view of the river.'

'A fine bullshit, Reggie. You mean you don't have half a dozen of your guys guarding the door?'

'Well, of course he's guarded – a couple of London bobbies, as a matter of fact.'

'And how is Stahl?'

'Came round late last night. He was in the London Hospital in the East End then. I had him moved this morning, just before I came to see you. I haven't seen him, but I gather he's going to be fine. Nothing more than mild concussion. A couple of stitches to the scalp and an aspirin.'

'Asking for me?'

Reggie sucked on the lemon.

'Yes,' he said. 'Will you come, or do I have to suffer three helpings of this Cherry Blossom boot polish gruel?'

§ 86

Stahl rubbed the side of his head. He could feel the ridge of torn, stitched flesh beneath the dressing. It was his own fault. Whoever the man behind the door was, he should have kept firing bullets into him till he heard the body fall. He must have been tall – Stahl had been aiming for his heart, and his last memory was of seeing a blurred figure clutching his belly with one hand and a gun with the other. Then the night went green, and green became black. The black became light and light was day and nurses with incomprehensible London

345

accents were chattering at him. And a young British bobby, so cleanly shaven his skin shone pink as a washed baby, called him sir and asked if he felt 'OK'. An hour or so later a doctor had examined him – speaking to him all the time in fluent if accented German – and had pronounced him fit to travel. Then they'd bundled him into an ambulance, driven him, he thought, three or four miles across London and put him here – in his own room, in a hospital that must be the preserve of some sort of ruling class. It reminded him of those he had had access to in Berlin, where party members could be pampered back to good health.

A new doctor examined his wound, then said, 'I never thought I'd see the day I'd be treating a German here.'

'Austrian,' said Stahl, the first word he had spoken.

'Difference is there?'

'What do you think the Anschluss was? A day trip?'

This had shut the man up – and Stahl had not privileged him with the truth, that he had been in the Führer's entourage as they swept into Austria and that his people – Stahl's as well as Hitler's – had lined the streets and cheered and cheered at their own conquest. Days later, in Vienna, when the new regime had begun to make its mark, he found Storm Troopers standing over a group of Jews in the street. They were scrubbing the paving stones with brushes. Other Austrians stood around and watched. Stahl had looked for faces he knew among the crowd and found none. Then one of the Jews had looked up from the gutter and he and Stahl had recognised one another.

Now, Stahl looked up and recognised Captain Cormack.

'I must be slipping. I didn't hear you come in.'

'You're among friends, for the first time in years. Maybe you can afford to relax,' Cormack said.

Stahl eased himself up on the pillows to be more level

with Cormack, who had propped himself against the mattress at the foot of the bed.

'Who was he?' he asked.

'One of ours, I'm afraid. You were right about that. Frank Reininger, a colonel in US Intelligence at our embassy here. I'm as surprised as you are. He was pretty close to being the last person I suspected. Known the man since I was a teenager.'

'We're both speaking of him in the past tense. Is he dead?'

'Yes. I know it might have been useful to get him alive. But I can see why you didn't take chances. That last shot to the head killed him outright. If it hadn't, who knows – it could be both of us stretched out in the morgue.'

Stahl said nothing. He hadn't fired to the head. He hadn't had the chance. Cormack said, 'The British are waiting. You know that, don't you?'

'Of course. Let me wash and eat something and then I'm theirs. After all, I'm their prisoner.'

'They're calling you their guest.'

'And Hitler called the Anschluss a "reunification". We're in a war of words. Meaning was the first casualty.'

'A couple of hours?' said Cormack.

'Yes. I'll be ready.'

§ 87

Stahl acknowledged Reggie's introduction of 'Brigade-führer, I'm Reggie,' with a terse 'Colonel'.

'Oh . . . so you know me?'

'Born Edinburgh, February 1900. Expelled from your private school over an incident with marijuana. Sandhurst 1919. Commissioned in the Royal Welch Fusiliers 1921. Recruited to Military Intelligence 1926. Married twice, a daughter by each marriage. Despite a playboy

347

image your grasp of German language and history is said to be excellent. Christened Alistair, always known as Reggie.'

'Ah,' said Reggie. 'And what do I call you?'

'Stahl, Wolfgang, anything but Brigadeführer. The Brigadeführer died in Berlin on April 17th.'

'I see,' said Reggie, looking ticked off. 'Stahl it is.'

Stahl lay on the bed in slippers, pyjamas and a dressing gown. With his receding hairline, his salt and pepper colouring and the clipped, dark, moustache, he could easily have been the British officer recuperating from wounds who might ordinarily have occupied a room such as this. There was only one chair. Reggie took it. Cal stood, wondering if there was anything symbolic in Reggie's brusque assumption of command.

'It's . . . er . . . not too soon for you?' Reggie asked.

'No. Now is as good a time as any. Ask me whatever you want.'

'Well,' said Reggie. 'There was one thing in particular.'

'Russia,' Stahl said.

Reggie glanced quickly at Cal, and said, 'Oh, you know?'

'What else could be quite so urgent? You had Hess. Hess told you nothing, so you come to me. Fine. I know more than Hess.'

'You do?'

'Hess is "the heart of the Party" – not the brains. It's been a while since he had that level of confidence placed in him. Russia is very much Heydrich's dream, and what he knows I know.'

'Oh. Jolly good. Where shall we start?'

'Why don't we start with you getting me a blackboard?'

'A blackboard?'

'They're bound to have one somewhere or do your

hospitals teach nothing? And while you're at it, some chalk. Four different colours of chalk.'

'I see,' said Reggie, not seeing. 'Chalk.'

'I have a visual memory – let me visualise the battle plan for you, and everything else will fall into place.'

'He's right, Reggie,' said Cal. 'This is the way we've always done things. Wolf thinks in images. He remembers text as images.'

Ten minutes later two hospital orderlies staggered in with an easel and a blackboard and set it up. Stahl swung his legs off the bed and picked up a stick of white chalk.

Cal had seen the results of so much of the work of Stahl's photographic memory. Lists and charts that he had reconstructed from the eidetic snapshots of the mind and forwarded to him. Once, in a rare face-to-face meeting he had roughed out a scheme for some troop manoeuvre on a single sheet of foolscap. Before he began to draw, he said, he could not have described it. Once drawn, he had burnt the sketch in an ashtray and recited the battle plan to him. It was, Cal thought, an odd relationship between image and language, a mental short-circuit, a conative loophole – but it worked. Undeniably it worked.

He watched as Stahl roughed in the boundaries – the Bug River, the current front line between the Axis and the USSR – the Baltic coastline – a jagged set of inverted Vs to mark the Urals – a scoop of the Black Sea at the bottom of the board. All of which amounted to a steel wall of armament around Eastern Poland, Byelorussia, the Ukraine and the Baltic states of Estonia, Lithuania and Latvia – now earmarked as a new circle in hell.

Stahl switched to green chalk.

'Let us start with Army Group North.'

He drew a box up near the Baltic Sea and wrote in the name von Leeb. Reggie finally seemed to have caught on. He took a tiny notebook from his inside pocket, unscrewed the top of his fountain pen and started to jot down notes. Under von Leeb's name Stahl began to chalk in the formation of battle – the 18th and 16th German Armies under von Küchler and Busch, the 4th Panzer Army under Hoepner – 11 divisions of Infantry, supporting 10 Tank divisions ... Reinhardt ... von Manstein ... the Panzer Army Reserve SS Totenkopf. Cal saw Reggie reach for his glasses as the chalk names got smaller and smaller with each sub-division Stahl made.

Stahl switched to the red chalk – von Bock's Army Group Centre ... his hands began to fly across the board, sometimes writing in the horizontal, sometimes the vertical as though he thought or saw in two planes at once ... 32 Infantry divisions ... Guderian's Panzers. Often gaps would appear as he skipped over some name or number, only to double back seconds later, scrawling furiously, chalk snapping off and flying across the room with the speed of bullets. To blue chalk. Army Group South under von Runstedt ... another 24 Infantry divisions, 15 divisions of Panzers and the Axis partners – troops from Hungary, Italy and Rumania. Reggie could scarcely keep up. His head bobbed like a doll's on a coiled spring, up and down from the paper, weaving right and left as he peered around Stahl to the multicoloured jigsaw now assembling itself in front of his eyes.

Then Stahl began shooting arrows across the board. Green arrows aiming at Leningrad, red arrows forking across central Poland to reunite at Smolensk in a push for Moscow, and blue arrows driving across Kiev to the Volga and Stalingrad.

It took more than quarter of an hour.

'What're those last two at the bottom there?' The first words Reggie had spoken in what seemed to Cal to be an age. He'd never known the man to shut up for so long.

'More Waffen SS regiments,' Stahl said. 'The Adolf

Hitler and the Viking.' Stahl no longer looked at the board – he turned his back on it. Cal was staring at it, overawed, chilled by the magnitude of it, the sheer power of what it stood for. Reggie was smiling. Not pleasure, not smugness, he thought, more like a schoolboy thrilled to have finally got what he wanted.

Cal moved closer to the board while Reggie scribbled and said, 'Will it work? Will anything so colossal hold up once you get it off the drawing board?'

'It's perfect country,' said Stahl. 'The flat plains that stretch from Prussia to Moscow. Perfect Panzer country. The tanks will simply throttle up and roll – and when they've cleared a way through, there are more than three million men in uniform to follow on. Hitler thinks it will be over before winter sets in – although it might be more accurate to say that he prays it will be over by then. These men have not been issued with winter uniforms. There aren't even orders placed with the factories for any winter uniforms.'

'Air power?'

'The Luftwaffe will pound the Russians first. Rather like what was meant to happen here last year.'

'How many men was that?' Reggie chipped in, head bent over his notebook.

'Three million. But that is a conservative figure.'

'Could I ask you to run through it again?'

Cal looked at Stahl. He didn't seem to resent the question – more as though he had expected it. He didn't even glance at the blackboard.

'Pick a column,' he said simply.

'Okey doh,' said Reggie. 'How about von Kleist's Panzers?'

Stahl rattled it off like liturgy.

'3rd Panzer Korps, von Manteuffel, comprising the 14th Panzers, the 44th and 298th Infantry. 14th Panzer Korps, von Wietersheim, 13th Panzers. 48th Panzer

Korps, Kempl, comprising the 11th Panzers, the 54th and 75th Infantry.'

'Astonishing,' said Reggie. 'I don't suppose you could recite that backwards?'

Stahl closed his eyes as though projecting an image onto the back of his eyelids and recited the entire list from bottom to top, Reggie checking every item against his notes.

'Jolly good. Do you know, I think I've got enough to be going on with. I think we might take a bit of a break now, eh?'

He smiled at Cal. Cal knew he was bursting, simply bursting to tell somebody.

'There is just one thing,' Stahl said. 'The date? You haven't asked me the date.'

'Oh,' said Reggie, as if surprised that he might have forgotten anything. 'Oh bugger.'

'June 22nd. The anniversary of the 1812 invasion by Napoleon. At dawn, needless to say.'

'Right,' said Reggie. 'If you chaps will excuse me for an hour or so . . .'

He scuttled out.

Stahl looked at Cal.

'Is that it?' he said. 'So soon?'

'I doubt he means to be rude, but I guess you told him what he wanted to know.'

'There's more,' said Stahl. 'Much more than dates and division numbers. There are ideas in this. And an idea of Russia so big that it would shock Mr Ruthven-Greene.'

'Try shocking me instead.'

Reggie would not take no for an answer. He brushed McKendrick's secretary aside and took the inner office by storm. McKendrick looked at him across the top of his glasses and said, 'What's so bloody important you have to barge in here like a gatecrasher? As if I couldn't guess.'

He waved his secretary away and told Reggie to close the door.

'Let's hear it, Reggie.'

Reggie was almost breathless with glee.

'Stahl is everything the Americans cracked him up to be. Memory like a Pathé newsreel. Marvellous stuff, sir, simply marvellous.'

'Give me the edited version, Reggie.'

'June 22nd, dawn. Luftwaffe attack precedes Panzer invasion and Infantry. He reckons three million men under arms, possibly more.'

McKendrick thought this important enough to merit taking off his glasses.

'As many as that?' he said flatly. 'Oh well, it's pretty much what I thought. Just the scale is a wee bit bigger. No matter ...'

'When do we tell the Russians?' Reggie asked.

McKendrick thought this important enough to merit putting his glasses back on.

'We don't,' he said.

'What?!?'

'We don't tell them. But, to be exact ... we have already told them.'

'I do hope I'm not being dim, sir, but I don't get it.'

'Remember Reggie, I said all along that you were "confirming sources"?'

Reggie vaguely remembered.

'Our ambassador in Moscow saw Vice-Commissar Vyshinsky at the Soviet Foreign Office on the twenty-third of April. He'd asked for a meeting with Stalin in person. A Vice-Commissar was all the audience he got. Nonetheless, he delivered our warning. We gave Stalin the date and the time of the German invasion six weeks ago, and as far as our sources can tell, Stalin's only reaction was to dismiss the ambassador as some sort of *agent provocateur*.'

'Six weeks ago? How did we know six weeks ago? Six weeks ago Stahl was still on the run.'

McKendrick said 'Reggie, shut up. Don't ask. Don't tell' . . . and looked enigmatic.

§ 89

'Imagine,' Stahl began, 'a German settlement as a series of concentric circles, like the rings on a target – but each ring is a layer in a racial hierarchy. At the centre, the pure Nordic stock – not just Germans, but Dutch and Danes and Norwegians. English too – the maddest of plans has planned for the eventual surrender of the English. As the circles fan out, ripples around a stone in water, the lesser races. Perhaps a circle of Estonians or Byelorussians, until you get to the perimeter, and beyond the perimeter are the races condemned to barbarism. The Slavs.'

'And the Jews?' Cal asked.

'No. Not the Jews.'

'Then where are they?'

'Nowhere. The Jews are no more. Imagine a series of such settlements strung out from the Bug River to the Urals, from the Baltic to the Caspian, linked by new roads, roads made straight for soldiers and Panzers, or made high along every ridge to keep them clear of snow. And what you have is a map of the moon or Mars in some scientific romance. The Soviet Union has ceased to exist. It is occupied by the higher races as though in some atmosphere unbreathable by man; the colony is a bubble – the bubble civilisation. Enough barbarians have been left this side of the Urals to labour for us all – they sow and reap the Ukrainian wheat fields, they drill and pump the Caucasian oil – they are taught to sign their names but expressly forbidden literacy, and if they prove too fecund they are sterilised. But, being inferior they are happy in their inferiority. Does any of this sound familiar? Because this is what those madmen are going to do.'

'It's part *Brave New World* – "gee, I'm so glad I'm not an alpha" – but it's Roman in its model,' said Cal. 'It reminds me of all those Roman forts scattered across Britain, linked by military roads. But the Romans at least absorbed the local populace eventually – they made Romans of some of them.'

'The Germans won't. Russia will know a new slavery beyond the bounds of the serfdom they shook off less than a hundred years ago. Beyond the fort, a new dark age. Within a new civilisation.'

' "They make a wilderness and call it peace." That's what Tacitus wrote of the Romans' first century in Britain.'

'Exactly,' said Stahl. 'The Pax Germanica – a bubble of civilisation in a vast wilderness of their own making.'

'And the Jews. They're going to exterminate the Jews?'

'Eventually. They have no scheme I know of as yet other than sticking them up against a wall and shooting them. Thousands of Polish Jews have died that way. But Heydrich will think of something. The Jewish Question long ago became the Jewish Problem. A problem requires a solution. Heydrich's good at that sort of thing. And east of the current front line, the entire territory is already regarded as an SS fiefdom. The only law will be death's-head's law. Himmler sees himself as an Emperor for the East – but Heydrich is the smarter man. If they succeed, it will be Heydrich who rules this wilderness.'

§ 90

Crossing the lobby of Claridge's, Cal heard a woman's voice say 'There he is now', and turned to see the receptionist talking to an RAF officer.

'Captain Cormack,' she called out to him. 'A gentleman to see you.'

A gentleman he might be – but he was the oddest-looking RAF officer Cal had ever seen. RAF blouse, with green corduroy trousers, an open-necked shirt and gumboots.

'I'm Orlando Thesiger,' the scarecrow said, in a voice as posh as Reggie's.

This meant nothing to Cal. It was hardly a name to be forgotten once heard.

'Walter worked for me,' he added. 'It was me seconded him to your operation.'

'I'm so sorry, Walter never did tell me your name. Always called you the Squadron Leader. Told me odd bits about all the fun he had out in Sussex.'

'Essex, actually. Wot larx, eh?'

'Yeah, that was pretty much how he saw things.'

'Look, you must excuse the clobber – we're a bit off the beaten track in Essex, and the walk to the station's a trifle muddy . . . all the same, I was wondering if you'd care for a spot of lunch. A spot of lunch and a bit of a chat.'

Cal wouldn't. He couldn't face the off-the-ration

356

champagne and foie gras diet of the English upper classes again. It seemed somehow to run against his current feelings. It seemed like pissing on the graves of dead men. He knew the time – there was a huge clock on the wall just above Thesiger's head – but feigned looking at his wristwatch.

'Won't take long,' Thesiger said. 'I brought sandwiches.'

He tapped the side of his gas mask case.

'I thought we could just sit in the park for quarter of an hour.'

'Sandwiches?' Cal said, warming.

'Yes. In the park. Brought enough for two.'

Grosvenor Square was sunny. Thesiger slipped off his blouse and sat in his shirt and braces. With the last vestige of rank and service stripped from him he looked more like a pig farmer having a day in the city than a spycatcher. But, then, what did spycatchers look like? Cal carefully hung Kevin Stilton's blue jacket on the end of the bench. One day he might have to give it back.

Thesiger flipped the lid on his sandwich tin.

'Help yourself, old chap.'

Cal bit into an indeterminate paste. He knew he was pulling a face, but it tasted like nothing on earth.

'Sardine and Bovril,' said Thesiger. 'My favourite. Ever since Nanny used to make them when I was a boy. Many's the time Walter and I ate sardine and Bovril butties together.'

Cal forced down a lump. Very salty, very fishy, with a curious undertaste of beef. 'That's why you're here, isn't it? Walter.'

'Quite. No point in beating about the bush, is there? My line isn't the front line. I've never lost a man before. If you can see what I mean. Walter's death was shocking, simply shocking. I'm sorry I couldn't do more for you, but by the time those thick buggers in Scotland Yard

357

bothered to tell me what had happened, someone else had already got you out. If I'd known, I'd have cleared you right away. I gather you had rather an awful couple of days. And after that, well, it was Reggie's show, so I kept out of it until now. But you're right, it is Walter that brings me here. I want to know exactly how he died.'

Cal told him.

For several minutes Thesiger sat in silence, slowly finishing his sandwiches.

Then he said, 'You say he felt nothing?'

'I think he died instantly.'

Thesiger thought for a while.

'This is tricky. Please don't take this the wrong way, but could Walter's death have been avoided?'

'If I'd got there on time.'

'No, no. I don't mean in terms of such detail. And please don't start blaming yourself. I mean, as simply as I can put it, did my colleagues throw Walter away?'

'Squadron Leader, right now I'm not the greatest fan of your colleagues. The Special Branch treated me like a criminal. If this were the USA I could cite you the clauses in the Bill of Rights they violated. But as you don't have a bill of rights, let's say they treated me like shit and leave it at that. But your more secret colleagues have given me the runaround from the moment I got here. Reggie's a decent guy, I'm sure, but he feels no obligation to share anything with me and certainly not to tell me the truth. Since I got here I've been expecting to see a nation locked into total war – what have I seen? Playboys who know where the Krug '20 is always to be found. Society women playing at being interim cops while they wait for the next London Season – or serving sherry and smoked salmon in East End shelters . . . old generals lost to the present in re-living old battles . . . I could go on, but we'll take it as read. England shocks me. They talk the war, they live the war, but they don't seem to know it's happening. The worst things happen – the *Hood* going down, dammit even the sinking of the *Bismarck* – and still something in England is unmoved by this. Some eternal core is unchanged. The crassest, the stupidest things happen ... but throwing away Walter wasn't one of them. I can't blame your people for that. I'd love to, but it was my people killed Walter. There are moments I wish they'd killed me instead.'

Thesiger thought about this too. Where Reggie would have an answer on the tip of his tongue, Thesiger seemed to have to ruminate.

'You're right. Of course. The worst things happen. I don't know whether the English were unmoved by the death of all those German sailors. You might say they were already numbed by the loss of the *Hood*. Perhaps you could say we accepted the necessity. What I saw was not celebration, it was acceptance. Personally, I was moved. You may have noticed, I've a German surname.'

Cal hadn't noticed, but if he thought about it he supposed Thesiger might be as German as Reininger or Shaeffer or von Schell – his grandmother's maiden name.

'I had second and third cousins fighting on the other side in the last war,' Thesiger went on. 'And doubtless their children fight me in this. But don't underestimate us. It is, as you so rightly say, total war. Deep down the English know this. Deep down, that's why we'll win.'

Cal forced down a whole triangle of surf and turf, just to be polite.

'You say your nanny taught you how to make these?'

'Yes – doubtless another English indulgence, another denial of reality – this fondness for nursery food.'

'Walter had a thing about spotted dick.'

'Ah, my dear chap – the hymns I could sing you in praise of spotted dick ...'

Cal let him. It was their wake for Walter Stilton.

§ 91

Stahl was shaving. The dye in his hair would take weeks to grow out. The shaved patches at the forehead just as long. The moustache could come off now. He shaved blind, eyes closed, feeling for the bristles with his fingertips, braille-tracing. He had managed not to look in a mirror since they brought him in. Now, the moustache gone, he opened his eyes, saw a face in the mirror he could not recognise, and the presence or absence of a moustache seemed to have nothing to do with it. He did not know this man. He reminded him of someone he once knew years ago before ... before all this nonsense began. A talented Viennese youth, a bit gawky, with blowaway, fine blond hair and bright blue eyes, who had played piano with an occasional quintet at school, made up of the school's usual string quartet and him. Schubert. Always the Schubert. The school's principal insisted on hearing it every year. He tried to think when he had last played the Schubert Trout Quintet in A. 1927 or '28 perhaps – and when had he last seen any of the quartet? That required no thought, he knew that. It had been in the March of 1938 – he had seen Turli Cantor, second violin, scrubbing flagstones with a brush in the gutters of Vienna. Vienna – her greatest son Franz Schubert. Dead at thirty-one. Stahl was thirty-one.

§ 92

When Cal got back to the hospital Stahl was dressed. Someone had brought him his suit, cleaned and pressed. He sat, jacketless, in a starched white shirt upon the window-sill looking out at the Thames, his image all but bleached out to Cal's eyes by the searing glare of June light through the open window.

Stahl said, 'I can read it in your face. You are not happy.'

'I thought it would be crucial,' Cal said. 'I thought this was vital – everything they've been chasing these last few weeks.'

'And?' said Stahl.

'And they're in huddles. They're cutting me out again. They're not jumping for joy, they're not even openly analysing what you said. They're . . . goddammit, they're playing cloak and dagger.'

'Don't be stupid, Calvin.'

'I'm not. I know what my eyes tell me.'

'I meant – what else could you expect? They're English, secrecy is their nature. And if it were not, it is, is it not, our trade? To expect anything else from them is stupid.'

'You've just handed them a gem – Jeez, that's understatement. You've given them information that could save thousands of lives, hundreds of thousands of lives.'

Stahl seemed so calm, so unruffled by all this. 'No it won't,' he said.

'What do you mean?'

Stahl shrugged.

'Is there such a thing as a secret? Ruthven-Greene may have feigned surprise at what I knew about him, but he knows just as much about me. I have told the English what they already knew. I doubt it was more than that. The detail, yes, the fine print of battle formation, yes . . . the fundamental truth, no . . . I think you have a saying in English, "the world and his wife"? . . . Let us update it for our time, the world and his ragtag army of camp-following, light-fingered, cut-purse, throat-slitting whores know that Russia is going to be invaded. What, then, have I given the English?'

'The time, the place, the battle order. Enough for the Red Army to prepare.'

'And you think that will save a single life? You think you and I can save a single life? Could you save Walter Stilton?'

'No . . . but . . .'

'No buts – you were not there to save Walter. Calvin, believe me, I have been *there* and I still could not save a life.'

Cal waited. He did not know what to say to this. He hoped Stahl would go on.

'It was three years ago – and I tell you not because it is the only time I have seen life slip through my fingers – but because it was the most vivid, the closest. After the Anschluss I went into Austria with Hitler. I was favoured. A fellow Austrian, he wanted me to feel the thrill of the joining together of the two Germanys. It was a privilege. Heydrich told me so himself, the Führer had asked for me personally. I was in a good position. I was alone with him half a dozen times. I could have shot him like a mad dog on any one of a dozen occasions. I did not. It was not my role. My role was to learn all I could and feed it back to you or someone like you. A few days later – March 19th to be precise, I cannot forget the date – I decided to walk in the old neighbourhood. The SS had Jews on their hands and knees scrubbing the pavements. At first I looked in the crowd to see if I knew any of those onlookers, the passively guilty. I did not. Then one of the Jews looked up. He knew me at once and I him. A schoolfriend from the twenties. At first I thought the moment would pass like a secret between us, but then he rose up and cried "Wolf". Took a step towards me. And an SS trooper shot him dead. Then the man holstered his gun, turned the body over with the toe of his boot and saluted me. I returned the salute and walked away. I have never been able to walk away from Turli Cantor since. His "Wolf" meant "save me". I didn't have the chance, and if I had I would no more have done it than I would have shot Hitler. Now, Calvin, do you understand what I'm saying? Could I save Turli Cantor? Could we either of us save Walter Stilton? Do you really think you will spare the life of a single Russian soldier?'

Cal felt swamped, buried alive in the torrent Stahl had unleashed upon him.

'I . . . I . . .'

'Would I have been the better man if I had dropped the pretence and stepped in to save the life of Turli Cantor? If I had been for once the man I thought I was, not the man I pretended to be? Are we any of us who we think we are? Or do we become who we pretend to be? Pretence is the dangerous game.'

'Jeezus . . . I . . .'

Cal turned to look into the room. The light from the window was too bright. He took off his glasses and rubbed his nose where they pinched. He pulled his feelings together and looked to Stahl again.

'Wolf?'

Stahl had vanished. Cal rushed to the window. Stahl was falling without a murmur, eyes wide, looking back at Cal, arms outspread like Christ crucified, falling to earth.

§ 93

They – whoever they were – Cal was no longer sure whether he was at the beck and call of his own people or the British – *they* kept him waiting. He passed the time scanning the *Herald*, *The Times* and the *Manchester Guardian*. How did the British manage to keep things so secret? A man jumps to his death from a window smack dab in the middle of London – and no one records the fact, no newspaper so much as hints at it. Whatever else it was – class-bound, dank, obsessive – Britain was, above all, a secret society – Stahl had been right about that – and that, he thought, had little to do with the war. That was simply the way they were.

He placed a bet with himself that when someone finally shoved the door open it would be Ruthven-Greene, with a bullshitting yarn to spin him. It wasn't. It was Gelbroaster.

'Son,' he said simply. 'Mind if I pull up a chair?'

They were both on foreign territory.

'Be their guest,' said Cal.

The general smiled at this. Lowered himself into the only other chair in the room with an old man's sigh, rested his hands a moment on his knees, then sat back. Rolled an unlit cigar between his fingers. Thought better of it. Stuck it back in his top pocket.

'You've done a man's job, my boy. They found pages and pages of notes in Stahl's room – he'd filled a legal pad. The British are well pleased.'

'You know, sir,' said Cal, 'I can hear the "but" coming.'

'But . . . there are one or two chiggers in the shoo-fly pie.'

It was a Stilton moment without Walter. Cal had always half felt that Walter made up some of his English turns of phrase. He was damn sure Gelbroaster had just made up an American one.

'Such as?'

'The information you unearthed about the Soviet Union is . . . prickly.'

'Prickly?'

'Spiky as a saguaro in the Arizona desert. How we, how they, use it is going to be a delicate matter. Kind of thing you only pull out with tweezers.'

Gelbroaster was labouring the point. Cal already had the message.

'You mean they're not going to tell the Russians.'

Gelbroaster looked faintly surprised at this.

'Perceptive of you. But yes, that's exactly what I mean. The decision's been taken. What you and Reggie found out will be kept a secret. Wasn't my decision, you understand. But I'm going to go along with it.'

'Who's decision was it?'

'Churchill's.'

'Are we bound by what the British do? The Germans have three million men poised to rip all hell out of Russia – and we're not going to tell them?'

'If it were up to me I would, but we're in the army, we take orders. Churchill has spoken to the President. He's the commander-in-chief, and his orders are we don't tell 'em. I've never questioned a presidential order. I don't intend to start now.'

'And I don't mean to question your orders either, sir. But they're going to massacre the Russians and those they don't massacre they'll turn into slaves.'

'I don't doubt it. But Churchill wants Russia in the war on his side. He wants no loophole that would let Stalin pull off one more deal with Hitler. It may sound heartless, but this way the Russian entry into the war is guaranteed.'

Cal got out of his seat. Ready to leave.

'Heartless? It's murder!'

Gelbroaster waved him back down.

'Sit down and hold your fire, son. There's more to come.'

Cal stood.

'Such as? I don't see what more they can do. Walter Stilton died getting us that information. Stahl died for it, in his own mad way. I damn near got killed myself. And they're just going to throw it away?'

'Sit down.'

Cal sat.

'It's this. With Stahl dead, your mission in Zurich is over. So we're flying you back to Washington.'

'You mean they're flying me out of here because I know too much?'

'Churchill insisted on it. He wants nothing to get out. Believe me, son, there's no disgrace. There's even a promotion. You'll go home a major and there'll be a good job for you at the War Department.'

Gelbroaster paused.

'And?'

'This is the hard bit. You know who I mean by Fritz Kuhn?'

'Sure, everybody's heard of him. He led the German-American Bund. He got nailed for embezzlement about two years ago.'

'His successor in the Bund was a guy named Wilhelm Kunze. Kunze fled to Mexico earlier this year and the Bund has kind of fallen apart. It's no real threat to anyone any more. But – and this is a huge but – there's no denying that a fifth column back home was a dangerous thing for a while. Mostly assholes who liked fancy uniforms and parading up and down doing idiotic salutes. Get 'em in every town, particularly when there's nothing worth hunting and nothing much else to do. What mattered was who they'd got in power. Nobody much cared if a potato farmer from Idaho dressed up like a Nazi at the weekend – what mattered was who mattered. If you catch my drift. Feds have been trying to crack the Bund for a while. Pick up the messy trail Kuhn and Kunze left. Well, they finally got their hands on the Bund's files. A lot of it's coded, in a crude kind of way – fake names, that sort of thing, box numbers rather than real addresses, nothing a high school kid couldn't crack overnight. Mostly it is potato farmers in Idaho – but it

366

also seems fairly certain that they've identified Frank Reininger as a member.'

'Jesus!' Cal said softly. Then, 'How long have you known?'

'Not long.'

'How long? Long enough to get me here and flush him out for you?'

Gelbroaster drew a deep breath, his pace and his manner altering not one jot.

'I know this has been a hard time for you. You've lost something very precious to you. I don't doubt that after two years there was some sort of bond between you and Stahl, and it seems from all I've heard that you and the English cop were good friends, but the biggest loss is the loss of innocence. I think that's what you've been through. The loss of innocence. But son, the biggest loss of innocence has got to be a refusal ever to believe in coincidence again. I didn't get you here to flush out Frank. If I'd known or even suspected Frank was working for the Germans I'd've busted him myself. Believe me, you did a great job in catching up with him, but neither I nor Deke Shaeffer had any idea that it was Frank you were after.'

Cal felt almost chastened – but not quite.

'But I'm still being sent home?'

'Fraid so, and there's more. We're fairly certain that your father had links with the Bund too.'

Cal whispered 'What?', his voice buried somewhere in the back of his throat.

'Maybe I shouldn't mince words, dammit. Son, he was a paid-up member, he donated funds, he fed them information. Now that's about as plain as I can tell it.'

Cal found it hard to be outraged, but disbelief came readily.

'My father supports America First, plenty of people do, patriotic people do – and even then he does it low key – he's never spoken on their platform as far as I know. He writes speeches for Lindbergh. He gives the idiot the facts and the arguments he needs to address an audience and be taken seriously. General, that's one hell of a way from joining the Bund.'

'And he thinks there's a conspiracy between Churchill and Roosevelt to bring America into this war by any reasonable pretext.'

'By any reasonable pretext.' The phrasing was too close, too accurate. It had stuck in Cal's mind too.

'You've been intercepting my mail?'

''Fraid so. Necessity. But there you are.'

'Sir, that's just my father being cranky. He sees conspiracies everywhere. Given his opposition to the war, he's bound to see one between the Prime Minister and the President.'

'I agree,' said Gelbroaster. 'And he's absolutely right. There is.'

'What?'

'I doubt they call it a conspiracy. Personally . . . if the cap fits wear it . . . in effect . . . what your father perceives is exactly what is happening. Right now we're looking out for that reasonable pretext.'

'You mean you want another *Lusitania*?'

Gelbroaster shrugged. 'Something quicker, I'd hope. Took two years to get us into the war after the *Lusitania*. Something less drastic would do. We may not get that lucky of course.'

'You know,' said Cal, 'I was getting ready to write to my father and tell him he's nuts.'

'You'll be able to tell him in person. We can't use this information publicly, you understand – but privately . . . well, your father's career is over. If he so much as mutters that he's thinking of running for any other office but the one he's got, then someone will show him an FBI file and he'll be quietly told to stand down. He's an ambitious man, but any dreams he might have had of running for president in five or ten years . . .'

Gelbroaster didn't bother to end the sentence. They both knew how it ended.

'Why not?' said Cal. 'Why not reveal the names, just publish and be damned?'

'Son, I was with Joe Kennedy when he picked up a paper knife and broke the lock on the *Red Book* – now do you know what that is?'

'No – I don't.'

'It's the membership list of the British Right Club. Bunch of Jew-baiting Anglo-Nazis. We got hold of it last year. The Right Club gave it to Tyler Kent, thinking diplomatic immunity was eternal. When MI5 blew the whistle on Kent we busted him and Joe busted the book. It read like a *Who's Who* – members of parliament, dukes and earls – would you believe the Marquis of Graham, Lord Redesdale, the Duke of goddam Wellington? Publish and be damned is just about right. The effects would have been crushing on British morale if we'd let any of that out. Even Kennedy could see that. He threw Kent to the wolves and high-tailed it out of here before the next bomb could fall. The same's true back home. We have our own morale to sustain. We're going to war – it might last another two years or another ten. The press would be deadly – better by far to know who's rotten in the barrel and let 'em know you know.'

'And the British still want me to go back to Washington? To the same city my father lives in? And they still expect me to tell no one?'

'*I* expect you to tell no one. And I didn't say it was logical. That's too much to ask of the British at the best of times, and this is one of the worst. Besides, we have our secrets too. The British will never know how far the Bund penetrated into the Army or the Capitol.'

'It's still crazy. I'm a safer bet right here. In London.'

'But you're going home, all the same. First flight we can get you on.'

Cal knew he had lost. They lapsed into silence. Gelbroaster retrieved his cigar and lit up. For a minute or more all Cal could hear was the puffing and lip-smacking of the smoker's ritual.

'How long do I have? I mean, there are one or two things I have to do. Things I have to sort out.'

'Three or four days. There's a log jam of people trying to get out to Lisbon, but we'll bump you up the list.'

Gelbroaster got up to leave. Dirty work done.

'I want you to know that I personally could not be more grateful to you.'

He was heading for the door now, the last remark all but thrown over his shoulder. Too casual to be literal. 'If there's anything you need, anything at all ...'

'There is one thing,' said Cal, being as literal as he could.

Gelbroaster turned back to him. Clearly he'd not expected Cal to want anything quite so soon.

§ 94

Troy was having a lazy day. There was a brilliant June sun in the sky, after yesterday's unseasonal cold. He had been up to the urban 'farm' at Seven Dials, where a bloke he knew kept goats and hens not spitting distance from Shaftesbury Avenue's theatres, and had haggled for half a dozen eggs. He offered to tip the nod to the local beat bobby to keep a close eye on the 'farm' at night and came away with four hen and two goose. Enough to let him indulge in a three-egg scramble for late breakfast, or was it early lunch? It was corruption, of course, but after what he'd been through lately it troubled that near-dormant organ, his conscience, not one whit. Besides, he'd paid more than twice the pre-war price.

The first egg fell into the pan and rose up proud as an orange jelly, a thick mass of albumen orbiting it as precisely as the rings of Saturn. He'd not seen an egg this fresh for the best part of a year. It seemed almost a shame to scramble it but scramble it he did – on toast with the meagre scraping of his butter ration.

Then he put a dining chair out in the courtyard, aimed it at the sun, and read in the western light of a London summer's afternoon.

The Times ran an obituary for the late Kaiser. Troy glanced at it with a 'so what?' running through his mind. He was not, he realised, much in the mood for news, even the last word on a man not much heard of these twenty years. He was in the mood for fiction. He tried *Ulysses* by James Joyce, loved the opening bit about the fat bloke shaving – he always did – but then he sort of got lost – he always did. Then he picked up *The Edwardians* by Vita Sackville-West and had read twenty pages before he realised he had read it before. At last he settled upon *The Professor* by Rex Warner – a book Rod had given him about the time of the Munich crisis. Dirty deeds in one of those Continental republics cobbled together at the Treaty of Versailles. Rod was forever giving him books. Rod read new books. Rod read topical books. Rod loved the idea of authors – he was forever saying he'd met 'so and so' at a 'do'. This appeared to be the tale of one Professor A. Oh no, thought Troy, not initials, not like that bugger Kafka with his K bloke? He wasn't sure about this, but he read on and was still happily engrossed an hour later when he heard Onions, police boots sparking on the cobbles, lumbering down the yard from St Martin's Lane.

'Starting a library, are we?' Stan said, eyeing the pile of

half a dozen books next to the chair. Stan read little, if at all. Half a dozen probably was a library to him.

'Just passing the time,' Troy replied.

'Wound giving you gyp?'

'A bit,' said Troy.

'You've not been out much then?'

Troy saw the trap for what it was and decided not to answer. He got up, stuck *The Professor* on his chair and said 'I'll stick the kettle on.'

Stan followed him inside.

'Don't bother for me. I don't want to use up your ration.'

'Well – perhaps a belt of something a bit stronger then?'

The sofa groaned as Onions lowered his bulk onto it. He was sweating. Suit, tie, as well as the regulation-issue boots.

'Not for me. Still on duty.'

Troy sat opposite Stan and said nothing, waiting for Stan to speak his piece. What could bring Stan round in duty hours in the middle of the week? As if he couldn't guess.

'You'll have heard by now, I suppose. We caught the bloke as killed old Stinker Stilton.'

'Yes,' said Troy.

'Someone been round, have they?'

'Kolankiewicz. He mentioned that you'd caught someone. Didn't seem to know much more.'

'I see. I thought 'appen it was George Bonham. All took place on his patch, ye see. I wonder about you and that mad Pole sometimes. I suppose it's summat to do with coming from abroad.'

Troy ignored this.

'On George's patch, you said?'

'Oh, aye. Down by Tallow Dock. It turned out to be

an American from their embassy. Would you believe, young Kitty and Captain Cormack cornered the bugger and some German old Walter had been chasing, and the German shot him dead. Quite a mess by all accounts. Like something out of Dodge City. Enough guns to kit out the Seventh Cavalry.'

'Well,' said Troy. 'Tallow Dock's a quiet place for a shoot-out.'

'Not quiet enough. Someone heard the shots and dialled 999. A squad car answered the call. When they saw the mess they called Murder, and Tom took the case.'

Tom Henrey was Troy's immediate superior, an inspector, between him and Stan in the pecking order. A hard-working, unimaginative copper.

'Of course as soon as word got round, the Branch steamed in and took over.'

'Not Nailer again?' said Troy.

'No – Dennis Crawley took this one in person. But once Tom had set the routine wheels in motion, they sort of trundled on without him, and twenty-four hours later the reports from the local beat bobbies on the night's activities landed on his desk. I took a gander.'

Troy looked at Stan, knowing what was coming, with as much indifference as he could muster. Stan took two sheets of stapled paper from his inside pocket. This was untypical. Troy had hardly ever seen Stan flip open a notebook or refer to paper in his life. It was all in his head, every last damn detail. This was a theatrical prop.

'PC Arthur Pettigrew, aged sixty-six, constable 872 . . .'

'He should be retired,' said Troy.

'He was. In fact he retired from your old nick at Leman Street two years before you got there. They brought him out in '40 when the young coppers started enlisting. Anyway, that night he was pounding your old beat on Westferry Road, and he says –' Stan consulted his pieces of paper '– that at 11.57 p.m. he was approaching the junction of Tallow Dock Lane and Westferry Road when he saw a car in trouble. Says the bonnet was up and a man appeared to be fiddling with the engine. Then the car came to life, and the man leapt in and drove off as fast as he could. Arthur got a look, reckons it was a Bullnose Morris. Thinks the number plate was either NEB or NED, 50 or 80.'

'Hmm,' said Troy. 'Does he describe the man?'

'No – he couldn't rise to that it seems. Just the car. A Bullnose Morris. You drive a Bullnose Morris. NED 50 as I recall.'

'What's your point, Stan?'

'I was coming to that. Captain Cormack's been hauled off by the spooks. I reckon his own people will have summat to say to him. Stands to reason they wanted that bloke alive. Kitty's been suspended. She'll face disciplinary action. She'll be up in front of the Commissioner later today, as a matter of fact.'

'Busted back to constable?'

'There was talk of that for a while – but it'd be very unpopular. She's Walter's daughter, she caught Walter's murderer. As far as the Branch are concerned – guns or no guns – she's a hero. And then there's the loss of face. She's the only woman Station Sergeant in the entire Metropolitan Police Force. The Commissioner wouldn't be happy about busting her. Promoting a woman in wartime was a pet scheme of his. Freed up a bloke for summat more important. He'd've taken it away from her on the first day after an armistice, but ... to bust her now'd be like admitting he was wrong. No, he's going to stand by her. A formal reprimand you understand, but no more suspension and no loss of rank.'

'But?'

'But – there's one thing bothers me. Kitty's just an ordinary copper – a good one mind, but that's about as far as it goes. Cormack – I reckon he's lost in London. Like a fish out o' water. Pulling a stunt like this took brains and it took local knowledge. Between the two of 'em they had neither the nous nor the brains to think this one up.'

Troy said nothing.

'But you've been off sick . . .'

Troy said nothing.

'And if I were to ask you'd like as not tell me that Bullnose Morris o' yours has been stuck round the corner every night for weeks.'

Troy said nothing. Stan said, 'I think I'm ready for that cup o' char now.'

Troy got up. Stan held out the pages of PC Pettigrew's report.

'Bin these while you're at it.'

Troy boiled a kettle and tore Pettigrew's words to shreds. When he came back from the kitchen, Stan had his jacket off and was loosening his tie to pop a collar stud. Typical Stan – he'd still be popping studs on loose collars in 1970, when every other man in London had switched to sewn collars and buttons. He'd still be wearing boots, too.

'Ahh,' he said. 'Just what I needed.'

He took a pocket watch from his jacket and looked at it.

'Do you know – I've been off duty for three minutes?'

He slurped at his tea and aahed again.

'Off and duty. Put 'em together you get one of the sweetest words in the language. Off duty. Now – now we're both off duty, why don't you tell me what really happened?'

375

Later, Onions, standing in the doorway, pulling on his jacket, muttering 'Jesus wept', looking over his shoulder at Troy said, 'How long? How long d'ye reckon you'll be off?'

Reluctant as he'd been to be signed off sick, Troy was in no hurry to get back. A bit of space between him and Stan would do no harm.

'Two or three days,' he said.

'Do you recall badgering me about needing more back-up last Christmas? Well. I've got you a new jack. Can't be more than twenty-three or thereabouts. Fresh out of uniform. Niagara behind the ears. One of those graduated coppers you'll have heard about. Recruited from Oxbridge, rushed through Hendon, a year on the beat and straight into CID. I was wondering, have you anything he could be getting on with?'

'Just tell him not to touch anything,' said Troy.

§ 95

Late in the evening Troy sat up in bed and read. He had finished *The Professor*. It had not been a cheery read. He had picked up another of Rod's books at bedtime – *No Bed for Bacon*, by Caryl Brahms and S.J. Simon. Troy had no idea how two people could ever write a book together, but Rod had insisted it was a hoot. He was right, it was.

'Wot's so bleedin' funny?'

He looked up from the book. He had not heard Kitty come in. She seemed always to steal in, to turn the key without noise and to tiptoe upstairs. She was framed in the doorway, hands deep in her pockets, looking tired and miserable. She didn't wait for an answer.

'I hope you had a better day than I did. I've had a

rotten day. The Commissioner had me in, hauled me over the coals.'

'And?'

Kitty kicked off her shoes, started tugging at hooks and eyes and press studs.

'Suspended till Monday at least.'

She ducked out of the door. Troy heard the bath begin to fill, then she reappeared, stripped down to her underwear.

'And on Monday he'll deliver his verdict. That's what he called it. Pompous old arse. If I'm booted off the force, why can't he just tell me?'

Troy said nothing. Watched Kitty strip to naked for the umpteenth time that summer, stretch her cat stretch, arms up, long legs longer as she stood on her toes.

'I'm going to have a bath. When I get back you're going to put that book down and lick me dry. Capiche?'

He read on – the adventure of a 'born leader of men' and a performing bear. Then Kitty flopped onto the bed next to him, damp and scented.

'Start on me backbone, work north and don't stop till I tell yer.'

Around the back of her neck, Troy lifted her hair clear, ran his tongue around the rim of one ear and whispered, 'Stan came to see me today.'

Her face, half-buried in the pillow. 'That's a passion-killer if ever I heard one.'

'He told me the verdict.'

Kitty shot up, grabbed the pillow and whacked him with it.

'You bugger, you bugger. You could have told me that quarter of an hour ago!'

She pinned him flat, straddled him, and grabbed him by both ears.

'Tell me, tell me!'

'A reprimand.'

Kitty let go. 'Wot? Is that all? A bloody reprimand? After what we did?'

'They don't know the half of it. They don't know you shot Reininger.'

'I'd rather not have known his name.'

'They don't know, and Stan doesn't know.'

'You're sure?'

'Of course.'

'And Calvin?'

'I haven't told him. Have you?'

'He wouldn't understand.'

She fell off him, lay on her side.

'We've got away with it haven't we?' she said.

'Looks like it. But then I find if you keep your mouth shut and stick to your story, you usually do.'

She was softening, almost smiling, the day left behind.

'So no more suspension, and I keep me rank and me station?'

'Kitty, how much reassurance do you need?'

'Lots.'

She pointed at her sternum, a silky sheen of skin between her small breasts.

'Start again. Reassure me some more.'

Troy woke around dawn to find Kitty awake too. He got up, slipped on his dressing gown and made tea. Her mood had swung back. She was miles away, sad and dreamy.

'Kitty?'

'Wot?'

'Penny for them.'

'If you must know – I was thinking about my other lover.'

'What about him?'

'Will I ever see him again? Do I want to see him again?'

'I'd say it was up to you.'

378

'But it isn't, is it? He got hauled off!'

'The Americans won't be hard on him. He did a good job for them – it just didn't work out perfectly.'

'Wasn't the Americans hauled him off. It was our lot. Some spook from MI something or other. I saw the two of them outside the Yard. I could hear the bloke blathering on. Posh voice. Bit like yours.'

She sipped at her tea. Troy thought at first she was choking, then she ran to the lavatory and threw up. He followed after a decent interval, found her pale of face, one arm resting on the pan, breathing heavily.

'You make awful tea,' she said.

'Don't be daft. It wasn't the tea.'

'Nah. I ate fish last night. Must have been off.'

Back in bed, Troy thought they might both sleep now. He was tired, Kitty must be exhausted. But she wanted to fuck, and in the morning the only thing that woke him was the sound of someone hammering on his door. Kitty slept through it. He looked at the alarm clock. It was gone ten. He threw on his dressing gown. It couldn't be the Yard, could it? They'd phone, wouldn't they? Descending the stairs he remembered there was a new boy at the Yard. He hoped he hadn't chosen this moment to introduce himself.

He hadn't. It was Cormack. Somehow Troy had got it into his head that he'd seen the last of Cormack.

'Do you have the time? I need to talk.'

'Of course,' said Troy.

He glanced around the sitting room looking for evidence of Kitty's presence and while Cormack had his back turned to close the door, he quietly booted her crash-helmet under the sofa and hoped she'd stay in bed.

Cormack slumped on the sofa. Troy could see the helmet framed between his ankles as menacing as a land-mine. He looked unhappy. He looked troubled.

'I'm being sent home,' he said. 'I'm the man who knew too much.'

'Is that really a hardship?'

'I guess not. It's not as though I were being deported. But . . . I had unfinished business here.'

'Stahl?'

'No – Stahl is finished business. Stahl is dead.'

Troy was shocked. He'd examined the man's wound himself. It wasn't serious.

'Stahl killed himself. Jumped from a hospital window. I reckon your people have had the most hellish time covering up. But if you haven't heard, then I guess they succeeded. Before he died he told me everything.'

Cormack ground to a halt, a tearful sadness in his eyes, his head shaking gently from side to side as though denying what he knew.

'Which part of it was too much?' Troy prompted.

'All of it, I guess. Tell me . . . would you feel compromised if I told you? I have to tell somebody. I'd feel better telling you than Kitty. I don't think she'd understand somehow.'

'Fire away,' said Troy, and he did.

Afterwards, Cormack seemed sadder than ever, as though a burden shared was a burden doubled. Little of it surprised Troy. Of course the Germans were going to invade. His dad had been telling him that for years. The bit about the slave state was new to him – but if you thought about it, it was merely an extension, the putting into practice, of everything they'd ever preached about the 'inferior peoples', the logical explosion of what they'd begun in Poland. The Jews and the Slavs were always going to catch it sooner or later. It was not surprising. It was shocking.

'It leaves a bad taste in the mouth,' Cormack said at last. 'It leaves me wondering, guessing. Suppose it wasn't Russia? I mean, supposing it was my country that was going to be attacked? Supposing Churchill and Roosevelt knew of an imminent attack on the States? Would they not tell us? Would they find it expedient to let it happen?'

Troy tried reassurance, the flat plains of uninspired logic. 'I don't think there's a German bomber made that can reach America.'

'You know what I mean. It's the principle. I find it hard to have faith in a benign conspiracy.'

'When will you be off?'

'Two or three days, maybe four at the most. They're sending me back on the clipper from Lisbon. In the meantime I'm hardly a prisoner. They've set no restrictions on my movements . . . and that kind of brings me to the other reason I called on you. I've been trying to find Kitty. I know the police let her go. And I phoned her sister Vera, but Vera doesn't know where she is or else she won't tell me. Never did figure out how to read Vera. I wondered – Kitty has a room in Covent Garden, near the police station, she said. But I never went there. I never knew the address. I wondered if you knew.'

''Fraid not. I never went there either. I think it's Kitty's little secret. But if I see her I'll tell her.'

'Could you tell her it's urgent? I know everything is in a country that's at war, but I mean it. It's about as urgent as things can get.'

'A matter of life and death, eh?' said Troy.

'Well . . . life, for sure.'

Troy watched him go down the yard towards St Martin's Lane. Then he listened. He'd not heard a sound from Kitty while Cormack had told his tale, but he could hear her now.

Upstairs Kitty was in the bog, throwing up again. When she'd stopped, washed-out and drooling, Troy said, 'Whose baby is it?'

381

'What do you think, clever dick? Cal's a good soldier. Uncle Sam gives him a gross of frenchies to see he don't catch the clap, and he uses them. Wellie on, glasses off. Always in that order. And every single one stamped "Made in the USA". You, you can never be arsed, can you?'

§ 96

It was going to be a red day. His red woolly dressing gown with the black piping. The last, late crimson wallflowers nestling in the cracks between the paving stones just beyond his window. A ruby red broom by the flint wall at the back of the terrace. Delicate, beautiful crimson bergamot like burst pincushions in the herb bed. A streak of pink in the sky, and a startling magenta legal pad to replace the blue one he had used up in the effort to finish his Russian leader.

Alex was searching for a red poem in an anthology of First War poets – Owen, Graves, Sassoon – weren't half the poems of 1914–18 called Flanders Poppies? – when he noticed his younger son leaning in the doorway of his study.

'Still on Russia?'

'Need you ask?'

'Wells still helping?'

'Bert and I no longer see eye to eye on the matter. I shall write my piece, and Bert will surely write his.'

'I thought I might give you a hand.'

'Freddie – if your contribution is to be as helpful as your last, I may do better without it.'

Troy pulled out a chair and sat opposite his father.

'I have news of the invasion.'

Alex scarcely looked at him, flicked through the index of first lines, still looking for a red poem.

'Unless you have a date for it I doubt it will help. The world and his wife know it will come. When is what matters.'

'June 22nd. About dawn.'

He had his father's attention now. Alex let the book fall closed and reached for a pencil.

About an hour later Alex had scribbled furiously over half a dozen of the magenta sheets. Troy said, 'Are we ready for this?'

'No,' said his father. 'We are not ready. Stalin has had most of the cream of the Red Army shot. We were better equipped in 1935 than we are now. But it will be the Germans' greatest folly nonetheless . . .'

Realising he had unleashed a lecture where he had wanted merely an answer, Troy ducked out when the telephone rang. His father picked up the receiver and waved to him.

'Alex?'

Beaverbrook. Again.

'I thought I'd plan ahead a little this time. Winston wants to see the editors.'

This was wishful. Most of the newspapers would send deputies and flunkies to any briefing.

'I was wondering – let me add your name to the list.'

'When?' said Alex.

'Tomorrow at ten. In the bunker.'

'The bunker?'

'Cabinet War Rooms under Storey's Gate – you know, round the back by Horse Guards Parade. Now – can I add your name to the list?'

'What is it the Prime Minister has to say to us?'

'You won't know that unless you turn up. What do you say?'

'I'll be there. But Max – a favour. Just put "representative of Troy papers". Don't put my name.'

'Of course – it's Winston's show – he'd hate to be upstaged.'

Beaverbrook laughed at his own joke and hung up.

Alex leafed through the pages of notes he had taken as his son talked. June 22nd. He reached for his diary, wondering what day of the week that was. A Sunday – or, as Hitler most certainly saw it, very late Saturday night. Hitler pulled all his strokes on Saturdays. He had butchered Roehm and the SA on a Saturday, he had reintroduced conscription on a Saturday, he had retaken the Rhineland on a Saturday. Perhaps he thought to catch Russia napping or 'gone fishin'?

§ 97

In the morning Alex shaved and dressed in a black suit with waistcoat. It must be his age. At seventy-nine, even in summer a trip out seemed to require more layers than it had a year ago. He rang for Polly the housemaid. She came, still wearing her firewatcher's outfit from the night before.

'I 'ope this is nothing urgent. A night on the roof is about as knackering as a night on the tiles.'

'No matter, child. It is my wife I seek. Would you find her and ask her to have the Crossley brought round to the front. I am going into town. And do not say "blimey", "stroll on" or any other of your cockneyisms. I am not housebound.'

'Can't do that. Your wife drove down to Hertfordshire two hours ago. In the Crossley.'

Alex thought about it.

'The Morris, then.'

'You gave the Morris to young Fred in 1939.'

'The Lagonda?'

'Up on blocks in the garage in Hertfordshire.'

'The Rolls?'

'Well – the Rolls is actually here. It's in the mews, but no one's driven it since last autumn.'

'Fine,' said Alex. 'Tell the chauffeur to have it out front in fifteen minutes.'

'No, boss. Not fine. The chauffeur joined up just after Dunkirk. And I doubt the Rolls'll start. Battery's gonna be flat as pancake Tuesday.'

'Battery?'

'Battery – as in electricity, you know?'

'Nonsense. I may not be able to drive a motor-car, but I know for a fact that they run on a petroleum derivative. My brother runs his Armstrong-Siddeley on kerosene. They're not electrical.'

Polly led him outside, round to the mews, pushed back the garage doors to show him. Rats had eaten the tyres. There was no point in even demonstrating the silent frustration of a flat battery.

'I could get you a cab.'

The two of them walked back to the end of Church Row and stood ten minutes without a single black taxi passing. Alex looked at his pocket watch.

'Urgent, is it?' Polly asked.

'A meeting with the Prime Minister.'

'Why didn't you say so? Come on, we'll get the tube.'

She slung her tin hat over one arm, extended the other to the old man and lugged him across the road in the direction of the Northern line.

'We?' said Alex.

'You think you can make it on your own, do you?'

He capitulated quietly. He had not been on the tube in donkey's years. It might even be an adventure.

It was a little after ten when they arrived at Storey's Gate. A naval lieutenant with a list of names did not ask Alex for his. He simply turned to a colleague and said, 'It's Alex Troy!'

Alex insisted on Polly accompanying him inside, described her as his 'amanuensis' – a word he doubted meant much to any of these young sailors who waited on Churchill, foot as well as hand. In the press room, the reaction was the same. A rising whisper that ran round the room and turned every head as they took their seats – 'Good God, it's Alex Troy.'

He recognised hardly any of these men. Most of them had risen in Fleet Street as he had retreated to his study and his garden. But he knew their papers. *The Times*, which had wilfully ignored the reports coming from their own man in Berlin throughout the early thirties, the *Observer*, which had applauded Hitler's invasion of the demilitarised Rhineland in 1936, the *Daily Mail*, which had been stupidly pro-Nazi, and Beaverbrook's own *Daily Express*, which had repeatedly furthered the shaky cause of peace by urging 'no intervention' as Hitler tore up treaties, broke rules and extended his territorial imperative. Since 1930 Alex had opposed, criticised and, as he saw it, used his papers to alert the world to the menace of both Hitler and Stalin. When, in 1939, he had reacted to the Nazi-Soviet pact with a leader urging Britain not to judge Russia on this act, every single one of these newspapers had sent him to Coventry – a metaphor, but also a city that might not now be in ruins had such people not so espoused the little corporal at a time when he was still vulnerable.

Now, they were staring. Alex Troy had not been seen in public for two years. He stared back. Only the gruff harrumph made by Churchill as he entered the room swung their attention to the front. Alex had hoped that Winston would wear one of his siren suits. He had a passion for dressing up. Peaked caps, pea jackets, Royal Navy battledresses, now romper suits for the grown up – a touch of silliness that Alex found an endearing characteristic. Churchill was not in mufti of any kind –

black jacket, stripy trousers, waistcoat-with-watchchain, spotty bow tie. Alex waited. If he mentions Russia, if he tells these assembled hacks the truth, all well and good – if he does not . . . .

Churchill looked straight at him. Not a trace of double-take. All the same, Alex knew he had not expected him. This was Beaverbrook's game with the two of them.

'Gentlemen,' Churchill began. 'Crete . . .'

§ 98

The wound in his side was giving gyp. God alone knew why. Who would have thought a potato peeler could inflict such damage? He lay on the chaise longue and ached.

Once on the mind, Russia was hard to shake off. It was not something Troy could take or leave – it was, after all, an ancestral homeland he had never seen, and given his father's role in international affairs, one he never was likely to see. He suspended feeling about the country in much the same way many intellectuals willingly suspended their disbelief. Many a fellow-traveller had fellow-travelled to the old country in the years between the wars, and come back singing the praises of good order, collectivisation and the latest Five Year Plan. Wells had come close to falling for this himself. But to Troy – to any Troy sibling – over-exposure to their father's abiding interest carried with it the danger of the arousal of a sense of longing – of what Troy could only render as 'rodina', a word for which he had found no precise English equivalent. He sated his longing by winding up the gramophone. He had recently acquired, on no fewer than six twelve-inch 78 r.p.m. records, Shostakovich's 'A Soviet Artist's Practical Creative Reply to Just Criticism', otherwise known as his Fifth Symphony. After ten minutes Troy could only conclude that the challenge of pleasing the Party had brought out the best in Shostakovich. It blew him away. This was an achievement that outstripped any of the man's other symphonies. This put into the abstraction of harmony what Troy had felt when Cormack had described the Nazi plan for the enslavement of the Slavs, what he was certain he had passed on to his father when he in turn had told him – heartbreak. It was music to tear you to pieces.

During the *Largo* he heard a key turn in the lock on his front door, saw Kitty steal in. Instead of putting the key in her coat pocket and sinking her hands in after it – her habitual gesture – she laid it on the small table next to him, in the pale arc of light thrown by his reading lamp. She wasn't wearing a coat, she was in a pretty summer dress. White, with pink flowers and green leaves, and a halter top. This wasn't the old Kitty – but then, the return of his latch key had told him that at once.

'Calvin's asked me to marry him,' she said.

Troy could not see her face. The voice fell on him from darkness. She sat on the armchair and one side of her face came into view. She displayed no given or visible emotion. Her face was as plain as her statement.

'And?' said Troy.

'I said yes.'

'How do his people feel about this?'

'They'll let him do anything that means he gets on that plane to Lisbon. The marriage is being rushed through.'

'When?'

'Tomorrow. Finsbury Town Hall. Mum's lodger Miss Greenlees arranged it all. Special licence. Then I'm Mrs Cormack. Then I'm off to America. I'll be a sort of GI bride.'

'How do you feel about that?'

Kitty shrugged, but it didn't work. Everything about her told him she felt anything but casual.

'I feel . . . I feel like I'm caught in a riptide. You know, like the song says . . . caught between two loves . . . the old and the new.'

'But you don't love him. You told me so.'

'I know . . . but . . .'

'And if you loved me you never told me.'

'I know . . . but . . . .'

'But what, Kitty?'

'But . . . it gets me out of London, doesn't it? Just like joining the force got me out of Stepney. You can't imagine what it's like to be me, can you? You grew up with a mansion out in the sticks, a town house in Hampstead. The only time you've ever lacked room to swing a cat is at that posh school you used to moan about. You never had to share anything. You never competed with your brothers and sisters for a damn thing. And you're a youngest. Spoilt rotten they are. I'm the eldest, Troy. My childhood stopped when I was ten. I been sharing a room with Rose and Reen since I was three 'cos me mum and dad always needed lodgers to keep up the rent. You ever wonder why I never asked you round to my place? You know what I got in Covent Garden? One room, that's all. A bed at one end, a gas ring at the other and a tin bath trundled out in front of the gas fire on bath night. It's a hole. But it's a damn sight better than sharing a bedroom in my mum's house in Stepney.'

'A house in mourning,' Troy said, tacking away.

'Wot?'

'You're leaving your mother in the lurch. She's lost two children and her husband. Has it occurred to you she might just need you?'

'Need me? Mum don't need me. If I stay it'll be like

being a kid again. It'll be like being the eldest kid in a family of seven. I was minding Kev and Trev by the time I was five, I brought up Vera and Tel. My mum don't need me. My mum's got Vera now. You think Vera's ever gonna give up her place in front of the Aga? That's better than sitting at God's right hand that is. You think Vera's ever gonna get herself a man? She's there for life, is Vera.'

'I say again, your mother needs you.'

Kitty was crying now. Silent tears upon her cheeks. She moved off the chair, on to her knees, next to the chaise longue where Troy lay stretched out like an invalid, her hands touching Troy, one on his chest, the other wrapped in his hair above his ear. She looked up at him.

'My mum needs me, does she? Troy – *you* don't need me. That's about what it comes down to, isn't it?'

Troy said nothing. Kitty kissed him once on the lips. Got to her feet. Walked to the door and looked back at him.

'I'm going now. I'm going to America. Do you hear me Troy? I'm marrying Calvin in the morning. I'm going to follow the yeller brick road and I'm going to live in America.'

'And?'

'And you could mind. Just a bit, you could mind. You could care just a bit more.'

No he couldn't.

Shostakovich's *Largo* spun on to its end. Troy heard it out, heard it spin to infinity in its final groove. He let it spin, over and over again. He did not bother with the *Allegro non troppo*. There would be another time.

Reggie was sitting up in bed. A glass of brandy, a good book – *The American* by Henry James, the tale of a young, rich American – well, obviously – marooned among the importunate toffs of Europe. Pride and no-old-money versus innocence and oodles of new-money. Wasn't that the plot of every Henry James? How can a chap get away with telling the same story over and over again? Anyway, it seemed appropriate. It put Reggie vaguely in mind of . . . and dammit, what was it Maisie knew? He'd forgotten.

The telephone rang. It was 2 a.m. Another night owl.

'You weren't sleeping, were you Reggie?'

'You know me, Gordon. Up till the birdie tweets.'

'Are you dressed?'

'A matter of seconds, old chap.'

'Good. Get over here right away will you. The PM wants a word.'

'With me?'

'Yes.'

Reggie could hear a wee tinge of exasperation creeping into McKendrick's voice.

'Where exactly is "here"?' he asked tentatively.

'Down Street. He's decided to sleep in Down Street tonight. Don't ask me why.'

Reggie could not remember quite when the London Passenger Transport Board had abandoned Down Street Station on the Piccadilly line – it had stood opposite Green Park, pretty well halfway between his old house in Chester Street and his tailor in Jermyn Street, quite the handiest of stations – but in its new guise it made an absolutely bomb-proof private shelter for Churchill. He understood McKendrick's 'don't ask me why' – keeping track of precisely where the PM laid his head each night was a nightmare. Both Downing Street and the bunker of rooms clustered around the Cabinet War Rooms had been strengthened, and he had beds in each, he also had Chequers, the country home of every Prime Minister since . . . since someone Reggie couldn't quite remember had given it to the nation in the reign of . . . God knows . . . Etheldogg the Scoundrel? – and on nights when the moon was full he had Dytchley Park, and, of course, he had his own home at Chartwell. Being Winston Churchill, Reggie thought, was a bit like being England's most well-heeled gypsy.

Well-heeled and well-guarded. When Reggie got out of the cab a couple of young Naval lieutenants were waiting for him, and behind them in the shadows, two armed guards in plain clothes.

'A twopenny one to Earl's Court,' said Reggie.

From the darkness of the station entrance McKendrick's voice growled, 'Stop arseing about!'

Reggie followed McKendrick down the spiral staircase, deeper and deeper, wondering if Churchill might actually have a hammock strung between the tracks. Not far above platform level, McKendrick opened a steel door in the wall, led Reggie through an ante-room into a small dining room, with a central table, six chairs and a standard lamp with a big floral shade. It looked like a dream. A complete confusion of categories. The dining-room furniture, in that immovable Georgian taste that characterised every upper-class dining room in the land, a lamp from a suburban sitting room in South London, and instead of the stripy Regency wallpaper – also immovably upper class – London Transport's black and white tiles, delicately interspersed with electrical junction boxes, cables as thick as sausages and a polite notice urging the reader to 'Now wash your hands!'

Reggie plonked himself on a chair, McKendrick picked up a newspaper off the table and looked grim.

Churchill shuffled in. Carpet slippers and a siren suit in a tasteful shade of brown. Reggie found himself wondering what he'd look like in a yellow siren suit and the image of Winnie the Pooh sprang into mind. Winston and Winnie, simply swap Hunny for Havanas.

'Good evening, Reggie, or rather I should say good morning.'

He flipped open a flat cigar box on the table and went through the smoking man's ritual of clipping and pricking, saying as he did so, 'Sorry about the ungodly hour, but Gordon has something we'd like you to read.'

McKendrick handed Reggie the newspaper. It was tomorrow's, or rather today's, *Sunday Post*.

'We received this at midnight. If you'd just read the editorial . . .'

Newspapers were so thin these days. Four pages on the ration. And editorials so short. Reggie flipped to the centre pages. It wasn't short. It was inordinately long. The papers might be rationed for newsprint, old Troy was not rationed for words. The first waft of best Cuban drifted across the table.

THE SUNDAY POST

When I first came to these islands in the winter of 1910, I did not doubt that I would make my home here. As I have most certainly told my readers on too many occasions, having seen the prospect of England opened up to me when I stood upon the French coast and watched M. Blériot take flight, I entered into an exchange of letters with Mr H. G. Wells on the subject, fascinating to us both, of powered flight. When Mr Wells invited me to visit him in England I came. I stayed. My wife, our son, our two daughters and I ended our years a-wandering. I knew, had known throughout that time, that I would be unlikely in the extreme to see my native Russia again. Perhaps the luxury I have allowed myself of speculating in this column upon the nature and the fate of that unhappy land has been the nostalgic indulgence of an exile – or, on the other hand, perhaps it has been a necessity. In their fate lie all our fates. When, two years ago, I warned my readers that the Nazi-Soviet pact was not the act on which to judge and condemn a country making itself anew, I was all but deluged in mail. Little of it complimentary. Indeed I had not felt so scolded since my denunciation of the Zinoviev letter as a forgery in 1924. Well, I will say to my critics, read no further or take a stiff drink now, I am about to hector you again upon that same matter. Russia . . .

Russia is a land of extremes. To those of you who think it a land locked in permafrost, I would say that I have childhood memories of sunshine quite as glorious as any summer that tinges your memories of the playing fields of Eton or Wakes Week in a Lancashire mill town. But it is the extremes of mind that matter. In the last century the evolution of extreme doctrine produced the antithesis of religion – Nihilism – and the antithesis of politics – Anarchism. The indivisibility of church and state made extremes inevitable, made them the natural outcome for Russia. Her revolution, too, was natural in that it was inevitable. It should have surprised no one. It surprised many. And many of us in the West have reeled from that act in shock ever since. We should not. Russia has ever been a troubled land and I doubt that I, or my children, shall live to see the day when it is untroubled.

Russia has an inordinate capacity for suffering – to have pain inflicted, to absorb it and to transmute it. Where else lies the origin of the inextinguishable myth of the great Russian mission to the West? It is in Tolstoy, born in the blood and snow of the long march he depicted in *War and Peace*, it is in the suffering of those lamentable brothers, the Karamazovs, there is more than a hint of it in the work of my fellow exile Berdyaev, and it informed every jot and missive of my father's work in those interminable letters he wrote to newspapers other than my own – we were not, alas, the paper of record in his eyes – and it is, ironically, at the heart of the late Mr Trotsky's opposition to Socialism In One Country. Russia suffers and in her suffering lie all our fates. Russia is the soul of Europe.

Some of the trouble of my native land I have seen at first hand – or, to be exact, heard and felt. When I was twenty-two I was a street away and heard the blast when Alexander II was assassinated. According to my father I was closer still when an earlier attempt was made upon the Tsar's life in the 1860s, but being six years old at the time I have little memory of it. And, when I was forty-one a second cousin on my mother's side shot and killed Nicholas II's Secretary of the Interior. In each case, and emphatically if metaphorically in the last, I was, it would seem, too close for comfort. So are we all. Whatever happens now in Russia will affect us all. We are but a street away from the explosion. To go on telling ourselves, as we did in the thirties, that the Soviet Union is godless and Marxist and as such the natural enemy of both mankind and democracy would be nothing short of folly. Like it or not we have a new ally. And I am here to tell you all that it is time to stand by our new ally.

Alexei Troy

'Bloody hell,' said Reggie. 'I mean to say it's a bit steep. New ally? Talk about jumping the gun!'

Churchill took out his cigar, trailing spittle. 'He knows,' he said.

'Surely, Prime Minister, he's just guessing. He's

picked up on the speculation – he's a pretty poor excuse for a press baron if he didn't – and he's heard what everybody's heard about troop movements in Poland . . .'

'He knows,' Churchill said again. 'Look closely at the final paragraph. Lift out the figures he gives, the odd ages he says he was at such and such an atrocity.'

Reggie scanned the paper, wondering what he'd missed. As he found them, eyes down, scarcely daring to look up, he could hear Churchill growling out each number in turn.

'Twenty-two, six, forty-one. June 22nd 1941. The only thing he's missed out is the time, but since we all know that Hitler calls at the same time as the Metropolitan Police making a raid, he need hardly spell out the word "dawn".'

The truth dawned on Reggie. 'Oh bugger,' he said softly.

'Oh bugger,' said Churchill back to him. 'I looked him up in *Who's Who*. Alex Troy's propensity for being coy with the truth about himself notwithstanding, he gives his birth date as 1862 – which would make him nineteen when the old Tsar was assassinated, not twenty-two. He knows, and he's letting me know that he knows. I've known him for thirty years or more. In all that time he has only ever signed about half a dozen editorials. When he signs one it's a mark of the importance he attaches to the issue and it inevitably means he's talking to just one person – the editorial becomes an open letter. All that's missing is "Dear Winston". He came to the briefing I gave only yesterday. A rare enough appearance in itself. He heard what I had to say, and then he went home and wrote his "Dear Winston" letter.'

Churchill uttered the words 'Dear Winston' with a dash of sarcasm, much as Americans used the phrase 'Dear John'.

'Prime Minister. I'm most frightfully sorry. But I've no idea how he found out.'

'The American?' McKendrick asked.

'He's been sent home, as requested. And he was as green about England as it's possible to be. I shouldn't think he'd even heard of Alex Troy. He'd be as likely to write to *The Times* as anything. The obvious but naive gesture. He was nothing if not naive.'

Churchill waved the argument away with his cigar hand, a trail of pungent smoke filling the air.

'We're not here to dissect the corpse, Reggie. We're here to decide what needs to be done.'

Reggie was silent in the face of this. McKendrick's look told him to stay that way.

Churchill inhaled deeply, blew a smoke ring or two at the ceiling.

'And I think there is only one thing to be done.'

He blew another smoke ring, head well back puffing out a perfect O. Reggie watched it float up to the ceiling, feeling as though he was on the carpet in front of the world's most eccentric headmaster.

'We shall take Alex at his word. We shall tell Stalin just one more time. He won't believe us, but we shall tell him just the same.'

§ 100

When Troy got back to his office in Scotland Yard, a tall, impossibly young, young man with the palest blue eyes he'd ever seen was snogging a uniformed WPC in front of his desk.

The woman blushed red, smoothed down her skirt and dashed past him. The man straightened his old Etonian tie, stuck out his hand, a smile on his lips, as though nothing had happened and said, 'Jack Wildeve. You must be Sergeant Troy.'

Troy did not take the hand so proffered. Silently he cursed Onions that his revenge should be to stick him with an English public school, totty-chasing twerp. He was going to hate this bloke. He knew it in his bones.

§ 101

Over breakfast in the Avis Hotel, Lisbon, waiting for the Pan Am Transatlantic Clipper, Cal whispered to Mrs Cormack, as he did every morning, 'I love you. Did I tell you that today?' Kitty said nothing.

§ 102

In the month or more that Cal had been gone Corporal Tosca systematically went through the entire contents of his Zurich office a few pages at a time, noting anything that she thought important, whether she understood it or not. When it was clear that Cal would not be returning, she sent a coded message to Moscow, on June 9th: 'Stahl is US agent. Not dead. Probably escaped to GB. US and GB very anxious to find him. Can only conclude vital information at stake. No idea what. Cormack posted to Washington. What am I supposed to do now? Any ideas?'

On the afternoon of the same day Reggie's number two, Charlie Leigh-Hunt, used a dead letter box in London to send a message to his controller at the Soviet Embassy: 'Hess mission authorised. H not mad. GB were expecting him. GB pressed him to confirm invasion of USSR. H did not. Talked incessantly of "common cause against the Bolshevik menace". Conclude GB now thinks invasion imminent.'

Churchill issued his last warning on June 10th.

When this news reached Joseph Vissarionovich Stalin, he did not wish to know. He had just dispatched the Artillery Corps tractors eastward, away from the front line, to help with the grain harvest – besides, he'd been warned already. Not only by the British Ambassador Sir Stafford Cripps, but also by Count Werner von Schulenberg, the Reich ambassador to Moscow, who had risked treason to warn the Soviet Union – nor would his treason be the last.

On June 18th, a Wednesday, Private Gunther Bruhns, recently demoted and posted to the Waffen SS on the Eastern Front by Heydrich for one cheeky remark too far, fearing that there was yet worse to come, chose a rash means of escape. He crossed the German lines into the Soviet Union, offering to trade information for sanctuary – his father had been a good communist and he'd always had some sympathy for the cause himself.

'You'll be invaded at dawn on the 22nd,' he said. 'If you don't believe me, and the tanks don't come, you can shoot me.'

Stalin did not wait for the tanks and had him shot at once.

On June 22nd, the shortest night of the year, 2,700 planes, 3,600 tanks and three and a half million Axis troops poured into Russia.

Barbarossa.

Historical Note

What have I made up? Most of it – that's what fiction's for. But there is a brick foundation to this. Umpteen people tried to warn Stalin, and Churchill issued warnings on April 23rd and June 10th 1941. I found out about the first from an English translation of A. Rossi's *Deux Ans d'Alliance Germano-Sovietique*, published in 1949, the source for which was the collected papers of the Nuremberg trials. I've forgotten where I found the second noted, but it was at that point that I started to think of a story that would end with and 'explain' that second warning. Until fairly recently it had, I think, been assumed that the source of the British information on Barbarossa had been Rudolf Hess, but as Hess did not land until May 10th the warning given to Mr Vyshinsky by Sir Stafford Cripps on April 23rd must have been perplexing if not actually fatal to the theory. However, the role of Enigma has since become if not clear then somewhat clearer. It is the most likely source.

The battle plan of Barbarossa is taken from Alan Clark's (1966) book of the same title (Penguin), the German scheme for the subjugation of the USSR from the essay 'What If Nazi Germany Had Defeated The Soviet Union?' by Michael Burleigh in *Counterfactuals* (ed. Niall Ferguson, Picador 1997).

The principal written sources for life in London at this time are *The London Observer: The Wartime Diaries of General Raymond E. Lee*, the London head of US Intelligence (Hutchinson 1971), and the *Diaries of Sir*

John Colville, Churchill's private secretary (Hodder & Stoughton 1985). Also fairly useful were *Berlin Diary* by William L. Shirer (Knopf 1941) and *Hess* by Peter Padfield (Weidenfeld & Nicolson 1991). *Backs to the Wall* by Leonard Mosley (Weidenfeld & Nicolson 1971) was indispensable.

I've bent a few bits of history. Clothes rationing was not introduced until June 2nd, after the sinking of the *Bismarck* – Churchill thought a major victory might soften the blow of clothes rationing and held it off until he'd got one. Food rationing was more severe than I've suggested – I doubt any restaurant would have served Reggie with the meal he orders at the Dorchester as late as June 1st 1941. And to the best of my knowledge the US Embassy never supplied coffee beans for the exclusive use of its officers billeted in London hotels. I made that up too. Al Bowlly did die in a German air raid in the small hours of April 17th 1941, but the reciprocal raid on Berlin did not begin until after midnight and lasted nearly three hours (which wasn't quite as useful for this fiction) and I've no idea whether the raid, targeted on the Alexanderplatz, hit any building in Kopernikusstraβe, a mile or so to the east – I just liked the name.

Lastly, Robert Churchill really existed and his life and work were recorded by MacDonald Hastings in *The Other Mr Churchill* (Harrap 1963). I'm grateful to my brother Frank, who knows more about guns and bullets and things that go whizz or bang than most people alive, for reminding me of Robert Churchill's shop in Orange Street, and for a wealth of knowledge on the Smith and Wesson .35.

All Orion/Phoenix titles are available at your local bookshop or from the following address:

Mail Order Department
Littlehampton Book Services
FREEPOST BR535
Worthing, West Sussex, BN13 3BR
telephone 01903 828503, *facsimile* 01903 828802
e-mail MailOrders@lbsltd.co.uk
(Please ensure that you include full postal address details)

Payment can be made either by credit/debit card (Visa, Mastercard, Access and Switch accepted) or by sending a £ Sterling cheque or postal order made payable to *Littlehampton Book Services*.
DO NOT SEND CASH OR CURRENCY.

Please add the following to cover postage and packing

UK and BFPO:
£1.50 for the first book, and 50p for each additional book to a maximum of £3.50

Overseas and Eire:
£2.50 for the first book plus £1.00 for the second book and 50p for each additional book ordered

---

BLOCK CAPITALS PLEASE

name of cardholder _____   *delivery address*
                     _____   *(if different from cardholder)*
address of cardholder _____   _____
_____   _____
_____   _____
_____   _____
      postcode _____   *postcode* _____

[ ] I enclose my remittance for £_____

[ ] please debit my Mastercard/Visa/Access/Switch (delete as appropriate)

card number [ ][ ][ ][ ][ ][ ][ ][ ][ ][ ][ ][ ][ ][ ][ ][ ]

expiry date [ ][ ][ ][ ]   Switch issue no.   [ ][ ]

signature _____

prices and availability are subject to change without notice